China Star

Also by Bartle Bull

Safari: A Chronicle of Adventure
The White Rhino Hotel
A Café on the Nile
The Devil's Oasis
Shanghai Station

China Star

Bartle Bull

Carroll & Graf Publishers
New York

CHINA STAR

Carroll & Graf Publishers
An Imprint of Avalon Publishing Group Inc.
245 West 17th Street
11th Floor
New York, NY 10011

First Carroll & Graf edition 2006

Library of Congress Cataloging-in-Publication Data is available.

ISBN-10: 0-7867-1677-0
ISBN-13: 978-0-78671-677-7

9 8 7 6 5 4 3 2 1

Printed in the United States of America
Distributed by Publishers Group West

For My Father and Mother

Bartle and Rosemary Bull

On Honeymoon 1931–1932

New York, Gibraltar, Genoa, Suez Canal, Ceylon, India, Burma, Singapore, Indonesia, Malaya, Thailand, Cambodia, Hong Kong, Philippines, Shanghai, China, Korea, Japan, Canada

On board S.S. Conte Grande, *S.S.* Empress of Russia, *etc.*

—*The Characters*—

Olivio Fonseca Alavedo *A rich Goan dwarf, the owner of the Cataract Café in Cairo.*

Oskar and Todor Androv *Brothers working for the Cheka, the Soviet secret police.*

Dr. Hervé du Moulin *A French surgeon on the China Coast.*

Jason Hammond *The stepson of Mrs. Derrick Hammond (Laila).*

Laila Hammond *A woman from Ceylon, the wife of Derrick Hammond, an English tea planter.*

Count Alexander "Sasha" Karlov *A twenty-two-year-old White Russian living in Shanghai.*

Katerina "Katia" Karlov *The twin sister of Alexander Karlov.*

Inspector-General Arkady Katkoff *An old White Russian officer resident in Paris.*

Violetta Katkoff *The granddaughter of General Katkoff.*

Robert Knox *An English tea planter in Ceylon.*

Marina Kulikovski *A Polish woman who assists White Russian refugees in Paris.*

Hak Lee *Known as "Big Ear," or "the Master of the Mountain," the leader of Shanghai's biggest tong or secret society.*

Lily *A sing-song girl from Madame Wong's brothel in Frenchtown, Shanghai.*

Percival Palliser *An English tea planter in Ceylon.*

Viktor Polyak *A Russian commissar, a member of the Cheka and an agent of the Comintern (the Communist International).*

Richard Richards *A successful English cotton broker.*

Ivan Semyonov *A Cossack hetman (chief) who fled to Shanghai after the Whites lost in Russia.*

Hideo Tanaka *The son of the Japanese Consul-General in Shanghai.*

Mei-lan Wong *The madam of an exclusive Shanghai bordello.*

- 1 -

Paris, 1922

"Do you find Paris too quiet after Shanghai, Count Karlov?" Several grains of black caviar sparkled in General Vashkov's wide white mustache as he spoke. The Order of St. George hung from the high collar of the old cavalryman's tunic.

"A bit quiet, General," said Alexander, clicking the heels of his black boots. "But at least this evening the French are waiting on us, sir. In Shanghai, we serve them."

Not to mention how our young Russian girls are earning their way in China, Alexander thought. He felt surprisingly fresh after a sleepless night battering the clubs with an old schoolmate from the *Corps des*

Pages, a friend he had long assumed was dead, murdered by the Bolsheviks. Now a taxi driver, Gregori Radinsky knew every haunt from Pigalle to Montparnasse and St. Germain.

"Remember, young man," replied General Vashkov, "that for us Paris is not as gracious as it seems. We must all be careful. Now that the Reds have won the war at home, Lenin's assassins are hunting their enemies abroad."

The general glanced around the noisy smoky room at the other refugee officers, each man trained at Imperial Russia's finest military academy. The small ballroom of the Hotel Vendôme was lit by candles. These were not slender elegant white tapers, but, in the Russian style, substantial columns of dense amber tallow with thick linen wicks that evoked long winter nights and bitter winds from the steppe.

"And where else would the Bolsheviks find a collection of enemies such as this?" added the general. "We are everything they hate."

"I understand, sir," nodded Alexander Karlov. His own father had been murdered in Shanghai by the Commissar. The old Hussar had been buried in his uniform, with his dress sword at his side and his well-polished boots at the bottom of his coffin, but with both legs and one arm missing.

"Forgive me, young Karlov," said General Vashkov more gently. "Of course you do." He accepted a glass of iced vodka from a harried waiter and continued.

"How we dreamed of Paris when I was in the Corps with your father! The girls, the cafés, the dance halls, the food. We would lie awake in our dormitory whispering of absinthe and the Moulin Rouge. This city was our paradise, the romance we craved." The general emptied his glass. "Now we have Paris, but we have lost Russia." He shrugged and raised both bushy white eyebrows. "And now we are too old for the girls. And too poor." He smiled and gripped Alexander's arm. "Have you ever seen a young girl with a poor old man?"

The general turned to greet two Dragoon officers arriving late. Their czar's-green uniforms were brushed and pressed, but the gold braid was threadbare and the cuffs were worn. Alexander guessed the two had come directly from work as doormen at one of the lesser Paris hotels that welcomed such traces of distinction on their staffs.

Shifting his weight to his black cane, Alexander excused himself and limped to the least crowded bar. There two officers were disputing the proper manufacture of an Imperial Cossack Crusta as they gave inconsistent instructions to the harried bartender. The Frenchman ignored them, splitting a lime lengthwise and rubbing its oils and juices over the insides of two glasses and down the outside edge of each rim. Fine powdered sugar was spread thickly on a nearby plate. He lowered the lip of one glass upside-down into the sugar as one Page nodded.

"Nonsense!" cried the other officer, himself filling the second glass with sugar before pouring out all the sugar that did not cling to it. "There!" he said, staring at Alexander for approval while his companion pulled two pink petals off a rose taken from a nearby vase.

The barman mixed orange bitters, cognac and kümmel in a large bar glass with cracked ice as other Pages gathered around assisting with their opinions. He poured the drink into the two glasses and topped up each with champagne. *"Messieurs,"* the bartender nodded as he pushed forward the drinks and the first Page dropped a rose petal into the center of each glass.

The two officers tossed back the drinks while their fellow Pages lifted roses from the vase and roared for twenty more Imperial Cossack Crustas.

Tonight they would all be drinking like Russians. Alexander Karlov took a glass of champagne, raised it in memory, and then glanced up at the Maltese Cross in the center of the green banner that hung on the wall behind the bar. "1802–1922" was written in bold numbers below the cross that the czar's military school had borrowed from the Knights of Malta, the ancient order of the crusaders.

A portrait of Czar Alexander I, the academy's founding benefactor, hung behind the *zakuski* table from a braided silk cord secured above the ornate molding of the high-ceilinged ballroom. The Emperor's dark eyes gazed down on the old Pages who crowded about the hors d'oeuvres. Platters of pelmeny and piroshki, smoked trout and sour cream, salmon and caviar and blinis were spread before the guests.

Karlov was aware that some of the men had not eaten properly for days. Destitute, now habituated to hunger as once they had been to luxury, most were too proud to appear desperate or greedy. "After you, please, Captain," said one officer known to pass his nights sleeping under a stone bridge on the Seine. "Be sure and try the golubtsy."

All deferred to the senior Page present, Inspector-General of Artillery Arkady Katkoff. Blinded in one eye as a young lieutenant at the siege of Sevastopol in 1855, Katkoff had killed two French Chasseurs with a cannon spike as they forced a breach at the Malakoff strong point. Tonight the Inspector-General sat in a tall black wheelchair pressed against the side of the zakuski table. Thin and long-limbed as a spider, his single eye shining red above his scarred cheek, he gulped down the caviar like so much porridge. A monocle hung from a black silk cord around his neck.

"The Turks swarmed around us like flies on the fresh droppings of a mule," said the old cannoneer to several younger officers as he reviewed the Caucasus campaign of 1887.

Alexander's schoolmate stood beside Katkoff. With unusual care, Gregori was preparing generous servings of roe, blinis and sour cream for the Inspector-General. Radinsky had not changed since school, still moving with the angular awkwardness of a shore bird picking its way among the rocks. He turned aside and whispered to Alexander.

"The old man's granddaughter, Violetta, is working as a seamstress, raising hems for a bourgeois family in the Marais." When Alexander did not comment, Radinsky hurried on. "At court Vita was famous for her ankles and lavish *poitrine.* Those Empire ball gowns presented her like a bowl of *crème fraîche.* Whenever she stopped waltzing, men gathered to watch her pale breasts pumping as she caught her breath." Sensing Alexander's interest, Gregori added, "She has skin like a baby's bottom."

Alexander nodded to his friend, then bowed to the Inspector-General, offering the girl's father a side plate of lemons. "Allow me, sir," he said with respect. "Alexander Karlov, *à vos ordres.*"

Katkoff raised an eyebrow and pressed his monocle into place. He stared up through the lens before speaking. His gaze reminded Alexander of the protruding eye of an agitated stallion, each raised vein alarmingly prominent.

"Ah, young Count Karlov." Ignoring the lemons, the old soldier wrinkled his face as if smiling at Alexander. "I hear you are doing well in Shanghai, very well. So few of our young men are managing today." He drew a leather case from one pocket and offered his only cigar to Alexander. "You must come by one evening soon and call on my granddaughter. Violetta is so lonely in Paris."

"As you wish, sir." Alexander bowed again but declined the tobacco. He carried his father's dented silver cigar case in one pocket.

"You will find us across the Seine, living quietly at sixteen rue Bonaparte."

"I will look forward to it, General." Perhaps tomorrow, Alexander thought. He had not seen Violetta since they were children. He recalled the Katkoff house on the English Embankment in St. Petersburg, its large stone courtyard crowded with coaches or motorcars or sleighs. That life had perished.

Annoyed, Gregori Radinsky tightened his lips and walked away.

The charge for dinner was a modest few francs, so that many might come. A few Pages, Alexander amongst them, had quietly contributed more. He remembered what it had been like to be almost penniless in China. The sight of starving Russian officers selling their boots and medals in the street, and others pulling rickshaws, had induced his father to begin a business two days after they disembarked from the icebreaker in Shanghai. Dimitri Karlov's only previous labor, apart from amassing debts, had been soldiering and breeding black horses for the Guards on his estate at Voskrenoye.

Alexander and his classmate were the only guests not wearing either medals or some part of a uniform. Still young cadets when the Corps des Pages had closed in 1917, they had missed the opportunity to serve their czar, both at court and in the field. The men around them tonight had fought the Turks and the French and the English in the nineteenth century and the Japanese and Germans and Austrians in the twentieth. Finally, these old soldiers had battled their own countrymen, the Reds, from Archangel to Vladivostok.

After four years of brutal civil war, the last of them had escaped to Constantinople on the British fleet a few months earlier. The most fortunate had wives and families waiting in Paris. Their ladies had traded pearls for passage, dispensing the lustrous gems one by one from the linings of their cloaks as they escaped St. Petersburg and Moscow by steamer and rail and lorry. When others had celebrated the end of the Great War and gone home, the White refugees had lamented a world lost and were struggling now to start again. Leaving Russia meant the wrenching of the body from the soul.

"One day we will all go home," Gregori had told Alexander as they drove across Paris the previous evening. "That is why I keep a valise always packed on top of my wardrobe."

It was a dream that Alexander no longer believed. Though he despised it, he understood why revolution had caught hold in Russia. Four years of civil war must be enough.

"Gentlemen! Messieurs!" called General Vashkov in a commanding voice. *"À table, s'il vous plaît."*

The men, noisy with drink and cheer, old wounds forgotten, for this evening young and on honorable service once again, went slowly to their places. The single table was set in a T like their great table at the Vorontsov Palace in St. Petersburg. A gift to the Corps from Alexander I, the palace was originally the home of the Knights of Malta. Tonight was the second anniversary dinner of their new émigré organization, the Union of Pages. All had served the czar either as soldiers or as diplomats. They were Orthodox and Catholic, Buddhist and Muslim, from every province of the empire, from the North Sea to the Pacific, from the Crimea to Turkestan and Siberia.

Four glasses, and rows of silver, sparkled at each place in the candlelight. Every Page stood behind his chair, waiting for the Imperial toast. In the tradition of their school, all but a few were seated randomly, rather than by age or rank or title. Menus and five carving sets of a large knife, a fork and a sharpening steel were spaced evenly along the center of the table. Carving the main dish, *Porc Entier à la Façon Polonaise,* would be the duty of the most junior nearby Page.

Gregori Radinsky wheeled the Inspector-General to his place beside General Vashkov at the head of the table. Alexander saw his friend turn the wheelchair to face the portrait of Nicholas II that was mounted on the wall beneath a large flag bearing the double eagle of the Romanovs. A black silk band crossed each corner of the picture, a reminder of how the emperor had died. Their *Batiushka,* the "Little Father" of all Russians, had been butchered with his wife and five children in a cellar in the Urals, despite the gallant effort of several Pages to rescue them. None would say so tonight, but many blamed the inept weakness of Nicholas and the hysterical foolishness of his domineering czarina for the tragedy of their nation.

"The Czar!" called General Vashkov, lifting a glass with his right arm fully extended towards the portrait.

"The Czar!" roared eighty voices. Every man emptied his glass. White-gloved waiters appeared with bottles of wine while the Pages took seats. Alexander hung his black cane on the back of a chair and seated himself beside a colonel of the Horse Guards. Karlov's young companion sat directly across the table. Gregori was already flushed and excited with the celebration.

"You look just like your father, that handsome rascal, Dimitri Karlov," said the colonel with affection, tapping his empty white-wine glass for a waiter's attention. "Same big nose. I trust, boy, that you also have his fine strong hand with horses and women?"

"I hope so, sir, but I doubt it." Alexander smiled. "Though I do my best with the horses. My father and I started a riding and fencing academy in China." He thought wistfully of his inconclusive romantic struggle with Jessica James in Shanghai. Sometimes he missed the American girl, especially her brief moments of uncontrolled excitement, but never quite enough to make him heartsick.

"Your father rode like a Cossack," continued the colonel, "and he was a damned devil with the ladies." He tapped his glass again. "Stole one of mine once in Monte. One evening with him, and she never spoke to me again."

About to serve Karlov, the waiter was obliged instead to refill the old officer's glass. Alexander did not mind, preferring to wait for the red wine that he and another Page had provided, though his own glass of white was soon filled. Alexander noticed that the attendant's left hand, almost tight as a fist, seemed to be artificial, though of course it was gloved like his right and was obscured by the napkin that the big bald man used to catch any drops that fell from the bottle. Uncertain in the dim light, unable to see the waiter's face, Alexander tried not to notice the infirmity.

General Vashkov called for a prayer. The entire company bowed their heads and sang grace as the waiters held back from the table. The candlelight and the dark Slavic rumbling of the singing reminded Alexander of the service for his father at the Orthodox cathedral in Shanghai. He had not been to church since that afternoon two years earlier.

His head still lowered, Alexander raised his eyes enough to glance at his friend. He guessed that he, too, was drawn back by this old custom of the Corps, remembering the days when they had worn red cords with green tassels instead of belts as a reminder of the monastic origin of their academy. Gregori Radinsky was not singing. He was staring back at Alexander with shining eyes and trembling lips. Gregori's two brothers, also Pages, had been executed in Moscow by the Reds.

The Meursault and baked oysters were followed by *Vol-au-Vent à*

L'Impératrice and Alexander's Beychevelle. Then, before the suckling Polish pig, there would be a *Coup Normand,* a lemon sherbet to break the meal, accompanied by a small iced vodka. Knowing the carving would be his task, Alexander lifted the steel and the big knife from the table. The knife-throwing competitions at the Salle d'Armes had made him an expert. Sparks flew like fireflies as he sharpened the long blade with swift strokes.

"I see you are not drinking your white, young Karlov, and our waiter seems to have disappeared," said the colonel. "Would you mind exchanging yours for my red? Bordeaux no longer agrees with me."

"Of course, sir." Alexander exchanged the glasses as he confirmed the waiter's absence. "With pleasure."

"What brings you to Paris?" asked the colonel after he lifted his glass and drank. "They say you are very active on the China Coast."

"I am trying to learn what has happened to my twin sister, Katerina," said Alexander. "I have not seen her in four years." Her loss haunted him every day. Even as he made his way in Shanghai, he felt he could not build a life for himself until he had done his best to recover Katia.

"Kidnapped on the Trans-Siberian, was she not? When the Bolsheviks killed your dear mother, Alisa, if I recall."

"Yes, sir," said Alexander. Among this crowd his losses were not uncommon. But he could still hear Katia's screams as she was dragged from the train by the Chekist Commissar in Siberia, the very man who later hunted down and killed his father. "Tomorrow, Colonel, I am meeting with Boris Androvich at the office of the Refugee Society. I am told they are the best at tracing lost relatives and friends."

"Quite right." The colonel nodded and pressed one hand against his stomach as he coughed repeatedly with a grating rattle that seemed to start in his belly. "The Society has located many of our missing friends and helped a few to escape, usually through Warsaw or Helsinki. Money would help, of course." The officer paused and pinched his lips together as if in some pain or discomfort. "But be cautious. Some think the Reds have infiltrated our network, and possibly even the office here. Today our battle is in Paris."

And it is coming to Shanghai, thought Alexander. With Soviet agents active in China, Mao Tse-tung was already following Lenin's example, recruiting and arming cells of intellectuals and workers, while the government was distracted by the warlords, the Japanese and its own corruptions. Soon China would be a pit of conflict. But at least in Shanghai he was at home, and had a business and a new life. As his dangerous partner, Mr. Hak Lee, sometimes told him, instability is opportunity. "Do not be like your countrymen, always looking back," the Chinese gangster had scolded him. "Regret must not be your life. Make change your servant, not your master."

For a long moment the colonel held a napkin to his mouth. Alexander waited, certain that the old officer wished to tell him more.

"No one understands, boy, that all this is nothing new. Paris has long been a Russian battleground," he said at last, speaking more quietly. "Fifty years ago, when the czar's Imperial Police, the Okhrana, suppressed the revolutionaries at home, thousands of radicals and anarchists fled here to Paris. The Okhrana hired retired French detectives from the Sûreté to watch them." The colonel shrugged and finished his wine. "Once we hunted them in Paris. Now they are hunting us."

Though he had drunk only two or three glasses of Meursault, including Alexander's, the old officer's face seemed flushed and mottled as he leaned close to Karlov and added in a different voice, "Whatever happens, boy, do not let them lure you back to Russia, even to find your sister." The officer drained the final drops from his glass. "No one ever escapes twice." Then the colonel coughed deeply and turned to address the neighbor on his other side.

"Where shall we go after dinner, Sasha?" Cheerful again, Gregori Radinsky leaned forward across the table as he spoke to Alexander. "We can use my taxi." Gregori would not be the first White Russian to drive a Paris taxi in a dinner jacket.

It would be Gregori's automobile, and Alexander's money, a reasonable arrangement. Karlov could imagine how the evening might end. It would be wild enough, but after his education in Shanghai he was not so taken by the girls of Montmartre as was his friend.

He thought of Lily and all she had taught him at Mei-lan's bordello: the arts of patience, the Devil's Knot, and so much more. Most important of all, how to please a woman. Now, of course, she was a *vedette,* a film star in the new cinema of Shanghai. He wished he could go to sleep, exhausted, with his face against Lily's smooth copper skin.

Distracted by the memory, Alexander recalled Mei-lan's words about the skin of a young lover. "Young men smell better, too," she had said, stroking his hand. "It's the skin. Nothing smells and feels like a baby's skin. When a woman ages, if she cares for herself, her skin still has a softness, without being dry or deeply lined. But it is a different softness, slack and yielding to the touch, no longer with the smooth firmness of a hard-boiled egg without the shell."

Before Karlov could answer Gregori, the colonel coughed violently and rose roughly to his feet. His chair slammed to the floor behind him. His face had turned scarlet. His temples throbbed. He braced both hands flat on the tablecloth as he rocked forward. His mouth opened and closed like a hungry bird's.

"Messieurs!" the colonel screamed in a strangled voice, as if another man's hands were at his throat. *"Mes braves! Je suis empoisonné!"* His rigid fingers drove forward across the table like a rake, sweeping plates and silver before them, knocking over two candlesticks.

"They have poisoned me!"

Then the colonel lifted his empty wine glass and crushed it in his fist as he crashed face down onto the table.

"Close the doors!" yelled Alexander, instantly pale with the chill of recognition as he recalled the powerfully built waiter who had served them.

Could it be the Commissar who had killed his father? Polyak, Viktor

Polyak. Was he still alive? Karlov glanced around the dimly lit room and recognized the heavy-shouldered figure standing by the service door. He remembered the man's brutal strength when he had broken Alexander's leg on the train four years before. Only the bald head and the gloves were different.

Their eyes met. In that instant Alexander recalled the severed left hand that had been found between the railroad tracks after his fight with the Commissar on the night train for Nanking.

Alexander grabbed the carving knife by the end of the blade as Polyak pressed his right hand against the swinging door to the kitchen. Turning sideways, seeing only his target, Alexander raised the long knife above his shoulder and held it there trembling for a fraction of a second. Then his shoulder plunged forward and he hurled it with all his force as his hand opened and his fingers pointed towards his enemy. An old Page flinched and screamed as the blade flashed past his head in the candlelight.

The knife turned end-over-end once and struck Viktor Polyak like a spear. It lodged deep in the back of his right shoulder just as he barged through the doorway to the kitchen. At the same instant Alexander reached behind him and lifted his cane from the back of his chair. He drew the short sword from the cane with a silver flash of steel.

Blade in hand, Alexander forced his way between the tables and rushed towards the service door. "Don't let him escape!" he cried. Several Pages hurried after Karlov. Others opened the colonel's collar and stretched him on his back upon the table.

The narrow hallway to the kitchen was crowded with jostling waiters and a line of wheeled service tables carrying the five suckling pigs. Platters of baked pears were waiting on a warming table beside brown jugs of steaming melted chocolate. A waiter lay injured on his back. Two of the service tables had been knocked over by the fleeing man. The glistening slippery pigs rolled about on the floor. The crisp golden skin of one carcass was smeared red with the fresh blood that had fallen onto it.

A portly chef stood leaning against a butcher-block counter at the entrance to the kitchen. His toque was still in place above his sweating round red face, but he gasped and grunted like an animal mired in mud. The heavy man held both hands pressed against his left side. His apron and one leg were soaked from the blood that seeped between his fingers from a deep wound at his waist. A shiny wet cleaver lay on the floor in front of him.

Alexander stumbled on the slippery wide blade and pushed his way into the kitchen. There all the lights were out and he did not know which way to turn. He pressed on, determined to finish the hunt and kill the Commissar. Finally Alexander forced open a rear door of the hotel and stepped out onto the pavement. He squinted into the gentle drizzle through the dim orange glow of a street lamp. A taxicab was pulling away up the empty street.

-2-

With the knife wound deep in the shoulder of his good arm, Viktor Polyak knew he could not look after it himself.

Hurtling along the crowded service passage towards the kitchen, slamming down a waiter as he passed, the Commissar had paused for an instant and tried to reach the knife himself by bending his right arm back over his shoulder. But even ignoring the fierce pain that the effort produced, he was unable to reach far enough back to grip the handle. Instead, in his groping desperation, his hand seized the base of the blade itself. The sharp edge cut deeply into the flesh and muscle between the base of his thumb and forefinger. He could not believe that the fancy White bastard had driven the long blade so far into his shoulder.

At the entrance to the kitchen, a deep-bellied man in white sought to block his way. As others screamed, Polyak lifted a heavy cleaver from a butcher-block. With all his force, as if axing down a tree, he drove the thick blade into the man's waist with a single horizontal blow. Then he released the cleaver and left the butcher's tool lodged in the chef's side as he ran through the kitchen, smashing the lights on his way out. Bursting onto the dark wet street from the service entrance of the hotel, Polyak climbed into the front seat of a parked taxicab, crouching forward so as not to press against the knife. The silver-haired driver was asleep beside him.

The big Russian struck the old man across the face with his gloved wooden hand, then screamed at him to pull out the knife. His nose bleeding from the blow, the stunned driver seemed strangely unconcerned as he complied. Probably a veteran of the trenches, Polyak judged.

"Drive for your life," he yelled in Russian, lifting the bloody blade from the floor and holding it to the man's chest. Though the Commissar's rough French had improved during his time in the French Concession of Shanghai, he still found the language awkward. The driver stared back at him, confused, then fumbled with the ignition button.

"Clignancourt!" Polyak jabbed the old man through his jacket. "Clignancourt! Rue du Poteau."

The black Renault surged forward as two men came rushing out the back door of the Hotel Vendôme. One held a short sword in his hand. Karlov. It was the second time the young dandy had injured him instead of being killed himself.

By the time they passed the Gare du Nord, blood was soaking down Polyak's back until it covered the seat itself. Finally the driver pulled over the taxi on the first corner of the rue du Poteau. Polyak gestured to the right with the knife, flicking it several times until the driver did as he was instructed. The car slowly turned the corner and drew up beside a closed kiosk on the rue Ruisseau.

Although Viktor was reluctant to aggravate the wound of his shoulder and the deep cut, he was proud that he was able to strangle most men with one hand. He had accomplished his first strangling in St. Petersburg when he was sixteen. That night at the docks he had driven his thumbs so deeply into his friend's neck that the skin was punctured as if by the incisors of a wild animal. Since then he had found many ways to kill a man, including the one he would use tonight.

Polyak swung his wooden hand against the driver's throat, forcing back the man's head. With one powerful motion, he drew the knife across the driver's thin neck, slicing through his hard bulbous Adam's apple and almost to the neck bone. The man gargled once as blood sheeted down his chest. Then he died quietly. Only his legs convulsed against the edge of the dashboard.

The smell of fresh blood filled the taxi like the bitter odor of rusted iron. The Russian wiped the blade on the dead man's trousers. Ripping open a bulging pocket, he took the driver's money and identity papers before stepping onto the empty street. He walked swiftly back to the rue du Poteau and turned the corner. He dropped the knife and the man's wallet down a street drain. A block later he came to the Clinique Syndicale. All the lights were out on the first floor of the clinic maintained by the city's most radical Marxist unions, the railroad workers, street sweepers and trash haulers. From time to time the facility also served as a meeting place for the syndicalists and their political supporters. Polyak glanced up and down the deserted street, then banged on the door with heavy blows of his wooden hand.

After a moment it opened. A stout middle-aged woman in a coarse blue-and-white uniform held a lamp to his face, then stared at his blood-soaked waiter's jacket. Her thin white hair was drawn back in a tight bun.

"Camarade," said Polyak, pushing one foot inside and almost leaning against her. *"Je suis un ami Soviet."*

"Entrez." The woman stepped back and gestured for him to pass before bolting the door and leading the wounded man up the stairs to

the surgery. Unframed photographs of Lenin, Trotsky and Jaurès were taped to the wall beside an open shelf of medical supplies.

The nurse removed Viktor Polyak's jacket and cut off his shirt. The powerful thick muscle of his shoulder was torn and inflamed. It was welling blood like the lanced shoulder of a fighting bull.

The woman flushed both wounds with alcohol and directed him to lie face down on a chipped enamel table. A shallow trough bordered its edges.

Not daring to risk unconsciousness, Polyak refused a breath of ether. He gripped a soiled towel between his teeth as the nurse prepared a curved stitching needle.

The Commissar had learned to isolate pain by using anger as an anesthetic, concentrating instead on what he must do next in his struggles with his enemies. But even thoughts of the Karlov twins could not insulate him from sharp flashes of pain as the woman pierced his flesh again and again stitching near his damaged nerves. He ground his teeth through the smelly towel and stared up into the unsympathetic eyes of his own son's namesake, the People's Commissar for War, Leon Trotsky.

When the nurse was finished with his shoulder, Polyak spat out the towel. He sat up and controlled his trembling. The woman rinsed her hands in a basin and wiped her brow with a fresh cloth. A smear of blood remained on her forehead.

"Do not make this all for nothing," she said over her shoulder. "Be careful not to stretch your shoulder and reopen that wound. It's a bleeder."

Then she seized his right wrist and examined the injured hand.

Polyak clenched his teeth. As the nurse stitched and bandaged his hand, the Commissar thought with hatred of Alexander Karlov and his family. The young bastard had already cost him his left hand in their fight on the train in China.

In two weeks Katia Karlov would be joining Viktor in Paris. As a young Red agent, she would have important work to do, using her family's background to help her spy on the White Russian refugees. But Viktor must see that her brother was dead before she arrived. Katia's child, which of course was his own as well, would remain in Moscow as a hostage for her conduct, if that were necessary. Polyak believed that Katia's commitment to the Revolution was now sincere, but with these old White families, one could never be certain. Her twin brother, he reckoned, still might be able to overturn his own powerful influence and reverse four years of the girl's re-education at the most rigorous Party training schools.

Polyak was confident he himself was the only man with whom Katia had ever had sexual relations. What had begun for her as violent rape in the forest near the railway had developed into resignation, then habit, and finally, he believed, into acceptance after the birth of their son, Leon. How ironic that his own boy was the first grandchild of that old Count Karlov he himself had butchered on a boat near Shanghai. What a triumph that he controlled the fate of a White family of such pretension.

"Voilà," said the nurse, fatigue and satisfaction in her voice. She lifted Viktor's right arm into a soiled canvas sling. *"C'est fait."* She turned her back to wash her hands and rinse her apron as Polyak got to his feet. Suddenly he felt dizzy and immensely tired.

He must have lost more blood than he realized. Bizarre, he thought, that after all he had endured, a brutal childhood and years of revolution and civil war, battles and murders, only this precious young aristocrat had ever been able to wound him severely. Even the boy's father had died without causing Viktor Polyak any injury. Tough and experienced soldier as he was, hardy as an old grey wolf, Major Karlov had died uncomplaining at his feet, the count's eyes still alive with hatred as the blood drained from him onto the deck.

"That's done," said Polyak as he steadied himself against the operating table. He rested his wooden hand heavily on the back of the nurse's shoulder as she hung the wet apron on a hook. "Now I must lie down for a few hours. You will never say anything about this." He pressed his hand down on her shoulder as she turned and listened to his words without expression. *"Ne dites rien. Pas un mot."*

The nurse led the Commissar up two flights of stairs and left him in a windowless back room with four narrow empty cots. She handed him a soiled army blanket and closed the door before entering her own small room across the dark corridor.

Three hours later she awoke as a great weight pressed down against her chest. The nurse opened her eyes wide and struggled to breathe. The first pale light was brightening her narrow window at the back of the building.

She saw only a glimpse of it before she became alive to her peril. The big Russian was pinning her down. The lower half of his left leg pressed across her upper body with his full weight. As she thrashed beneath the bedclothes and sought to move his leg with her hands, she felt the pressure of his wooden hand pulling against her left jaw. She was unable to speak with the strain on her neck as he forced her head sideways against her right shoulder. The woman stared up at him out of the corner of her eye. He jammed her head further to the side with a sharp movement, then once again. She heard a crack like a snapping branch as her neck broke.

Polyak rose from the still body and opened the vertical window by its metal handle. She stared up at him, breathing in long whistling gasps as he slipped his right arm from its sling and lifted her like a child. There was no feeling in her body. Her head flopped back as he carried her to the window. Her long white hair fell loose from its bun.

The nurse's heavy unclothed body jammed briefly in the window frame. Polyak grunted with pain as he struggled to force her head through first. Blood leaked through the bandage of his hand and slicked her face. Her last sight was of the filthy courtyard as she plunged down towards its chipped bricks.

Chambre à Louer

- 3 -

Alexander paused under a street lamp in the gloom of the late afternoon. He raised the collar of his long leather coat against the drizzle and gazed along the slick shiny cobblestones of the rue St. Benoît. His father had told him a worldly gentleman must learn to relish the *grisaille* of Paris, the melancholy greyness that shrouds the city during the wet winter months, enhancing every smoky warm café and any afternoon of lovemaking. So far, alas, Alexander had not found the opportunity to enjoy either one.

He heard a shuffling and tapping behind him. He quickly turned to look, wary of any unexpected approach. But he spied merely a one-legged man swinging along on crutches, a common sight in Paris since the end of the Great War a few years earlier. Perhaps noticing Alexander's cane, sensing an affinity, the man came closer and hung on his sticks close to the lamp. Two medals were pinned to the left lapel of his faded blue greatcoat, the rough cloth of the *"horizon bleu,"* the long wave of sky-blue uniforms that had risen from the muddy trenches for each new attack across the desolate land of wire and artillery craters.

"Salut!" said the man in a husky voice. *"Une cigarette, camarade, pour un ancien grognard?"*

Alexander nodded and handed him a tin of du Mauriers.

"Prenez-en quelques-unes," Karlov said, glancing over the veteran's shoulder and stiffening as another, taller person came towards them along the pavement. But the approaching passerby was hunched and elderly. The crippled soldier whistled and folded back the silver paper. He took four cigarettes and shielded them carefully from the rain. *"Merci, camarade."*

Scolding himself for his nervousness, regretting he had not given the entire tin, Alexander resumed walking to the old Hotel Gitan. His left leg was stiff and painful in the damp. He resolved to take some exercise, perhaps an early morning ride in the Bois. The better horses, an old Hussar had told him, were available at Duchon on the rue Lhomond. But perhaps, with what lay ahead, he would do better to refresh his taste for fighting with an afternoon of fencing at Lambert's, even though a sword would never be the Commissar's choice of weapon. In Shanghai, to compensate for the weakness of his leg, Alexander had strengthened his arms and confidence by swinging hand over hand along the splintery beams high above the floor of the Salle d'Armes. Even his father, famously oblivious to risk, had forbidden more of that foolishness.

As Karlov approached the hotel he found knots of refugees gathered on the sidewalk by the entrance, clustered tightly against the wall under the shelter of the narrow overhanging balconies of the three upper floors. He shook the rain from his coat and stepped inside and looked about the small crowded entrance as he removed his hat.

Belted suitcases and bulging cartons tied with heavy rope were piled in what had been the lobby. A woman with her back to him stood behind the tall concierge desk, stuffing letters and messages into the former room-key boxes that were now labelled alphabetically rather than by number. Beneath the boxes, he saw an old hotel safe that no doubt today held the treasures of the refugees: pearls and brooches, medals and pendants, all the currency of flight.

The woman turned to face him while Alexander removed his coat and straightened the high rounded collar of his Russian shirt. Older than Alexander, perhaps thirty, she wore a once-elegant beige dress that seemed too large for her slender figure. The woman assessed Alexander with careful tired eyes.

"Welcome to the Refugee Society," she said in the educated Russian of St. Petersburg. "How may I be of service, sir?"

"Good afternoon, madame," he replied with a smile. "I have come to see Monsieur Androvich, if you please."

"I am Boris Androvich," said a man who emerged from the narrow door beside the letter-boxes with a cigar in one hand. Thick angular white eyebrows dominated his broad face like the steep snow-covered roof of a dacha in a mountain forest. He glanced at Alexander's cane before lifting the panel of the reception counter and extending a welcoming gesture. "Count Karlov?"

Alexander bowed and passed through the counter into a small office with a coal grate, a cork board covered with notes and lists of names, and a map of Poland and European Russia.

"I brought something against the damp." Karlov handed a parcel to Androvich.

"Aha! Well done, young man. A little Armagnac will do us good." Androvich opened the bottle and passed the brandy beneath his nose. Then he groaned as he stooped, holding a small fire shovel. He took coals from the edge of the grate and slipped them into the heating chamber of a samovar that rested on a side table. "General Vashkov told me to expect you. With all that disturbance, I was not able to speak to you at dinner. But I understand you are searching for your sister?"

"Thank you, sir," said Alexander, accepting a cigar and a glass of tea. "Yes, it has been four years since I last saw Katerina, when they kidnapped her on our way to Vladivostok. But I believe I am familiar with one man who knows where Katia might be found."

"One man?" Androvich rose and closed the door.

"Yes, sir. Viktor Polyak, the Commissar who killed my parents, and who poisoned the colonel at our dinner."

"Your friend Polyak stole the guest list before he fled," said Boris Androvich, sipping his tea through a large lump of light-brown sugar held in his teeth. "Now he has your address, and mine, and all the other Pages. They say it was you he was trying to kill. If I were you, I would change my residence today."

Alexander was certain what his Chinese partner, Mr. Hak Lee, would counsel in such a situation: hunt the hunter. Even in a city where brutality and crime were common as rice cakes, Hak Lee had forged a reputation distinguished for its savagery.

"Perhaps we should find him first," said Karlov, thinking of the Commissar's wounded shoulder. Had it been a competition target, he knew his knife would have entered to the hilt. Throw with your body, not your hand, Alexander had been taught, and he had done so. "We might check the hospitals and clinics, perhaps any Russian doctors."

The older man shrugged at the idea. "The Reds are always after us," he said. "They know they have no more determined enemies than the Corps des Pages. When they speak of 'Revanchists,' they speak of us. We are the only group the Cheka can never penetrate, where they cannot plant their agents or enlist traitors. No matter their deceptions, we know our schoolmates. For us, they have not changed since we were twelve."

Alexander knew all of this. "I need your help, sir . . ."

"What you wish is what we do." Androvich sat back and drew on his cigar. "But the game is dangerous, and expensive. And the more important the hunt, the more dangerous and the more costly."

"If money and risk are the price," said Alexander Karlov, "I will pay them."

Androvich shook his head. "Young man, I owe it to you and to your family to tell you more." The older man poured brandy into two glasses and passed one to Alexander.

"In Moscow, when I was young, long before the war, my uncle found me a position with the Third Section, as we used to call the secret political police. That is how I learned to understand this game. For twenty years I served the czars. Not hounding common criminals. That was child's work for the constabulary, but hunting the rising dangers that threatened Russia herself. The Nihilists, the Anarchists, the bomb-throwers, the assassins. From time to time they would succeed at something that gave us new energy and more latitude, murdering a general or wounding some grand duke. One year after I started, in 1881, on their seventh attempt, Anarchists assassinated Czar Alexander the Second with a hand grenade. Nitroglycerine. The first grenade missed, and the Czar stepped down from his carriage to comfort the wounded. But a vengeful Pole, you know how they are, threw a second grenade. It exploded between the feet of the Emperor and blew off both his legs."

Androvich emptied his brandy glass into his tea and finished the drink. "As a result, the Third Section was replaced by the Okhrana, which opened a Paris bureau two years later on the rue de Grenelle. During the Great War, nineteen fourteen and so on, we operated here under the cover of a private detective agency." He paused and threw his cigar into the coals.

"The Okhrana did what we had to, of course, and we thought we were good at it. We used prison, floggings, isolation and fear. Exile and labor in Siberia, a bit of torture, whatever we could think of, anything to protect the throne. At first, when I was your age, the brutality disturbed me, but after a time one had no shame about the little things. As long as you don't have to watch, what does it matter? The screams, you get used to.

Everyone dies, somewhere, sometime. Please don't look so shocked, Count Karlov." Androvich refilled both brandy glasses.

"What do you think the world is like, young man? When Nicholas the First appointed my uncle's friend, Count Benckendorff, head of the Third Section, the Czar gave him a silk handkerchief and said to him, 'This is your entire directive. The more tears you wipe away, the more faithfully you will serve my aims.'"

Alexander drank and smoked as he listened. He was not surprised. There was much he was not proud of in the Russia they had lost. He recalled stories of his grandfather selecting pairs of serfs like horses and forcing them to marry against their will. Other serfs had been rented to factory owners or used like currency to pay off gambling debts. His own mother's family, eminent as it was, had been exiled to Siberia in 1826. Decembrist revolutionaries, they had advocated constitutional monarchy in place of Romanov autocracy.

"Cruel as the Okhrana was, we were but children," continued Androvich. "We knew nothing of terror and torture. The Okhrana were amateurs. Today, these Bolsheviks have learned how to use our prisons, and how to use Siberia. We wasted both. We were like blind cripples trying to dance in a grand ballroom with no music. Now these Chekists are the Ballets Russes dancing to Tchaikovsky." He leaned forward and gripped Alexander's arm before continuing.

"They make a ballet, a symphony, of pain and fear and hunger. Until the Bolsheviks, I used to dread the guilt that would haunt me in my old age. I feared I would wake up at night and feel my hands slick with blood. But the Cheka has freed me from my own crimes, made me feel clean and innocent. Thanks to those devils, I sleep better."

Androvich sat back and raised his eyebrows. "We used to consider hunger a menace to the throne. We feared famine like an assassin. But Lenin and Stalin manufacture hunger and use it as a weapon. We tortured hundreds. We exiled thousands. They torture tens of thousands and starve and exile millions."

For a moment neither man spoke. Alexander's leg felt better near the fire. He remembered learning in Shanghai that Lenin and the Cheka were importing torturers from China to elevate the skills of their own men in Russia.

"I must find my sister," he said finally. "What do you suggest I do?"

"Nothing." Boris Androvich tossed his cigar into the grate. "Pay someone to do it for you."

"Who?"

"If you have money, there are always people to help. I would suggest the Pole, and her husband, but you cannot meet them here. She prefers to use the stranger's Paris, places only a few foreigners might visit, where you would never expect to see the same person more than once."

General Katkoff had said 16 rue Bonaparte, Alexander recalled as he walked along St. Germain a short time later, concerned that at such an hour he must already be smelling of brandy and tobacco. Glancing back, he stopped at a café and bought a *tilleul* at the zinc bar. He took a big mouthful of the lime tea and stepped into the lavatory. There he gargled with it and spat and rinsed his face. He pressed down his wavy dark hair with both hands, careful to smooth his center part. Despite his leg, he was growing more confident in his attractiveness to women.

At number sixteen he pushed open the heavy street door and presented himself at the concierge window inside. As his father had taught him, he looked the old woman directly in the eye, as if she were the only girl in the world. But this time he had the sense that nothing would work.

"I am calling on General Katkoff, if you please, madame."

The concierge stared at his wet footprints and dripping overcoat. She shook her head and clucked with Gallic disapproval. A broom and mop leaned in the corner behind her. She squinted up at him and fastened the top button of her frayed sweater as if he had been staring at her uneven lumpy chest with some indecent ambition.

Alexander passed his card to the concierge and waited while she descended from her stool. She pressed a button on the wall. Dim lights flickered on to illuminate the stairway. Groaning with complaint, coarse brown stockings rolled down to swollen ankles, one hand on her hip, the woman climbed the steps behind her post. Alexander tried not to notice the dark hairs on her legs. He heard her voice echo in the stairwell as she called from partway up. He noticed a sign pasted to the window of her cabinet: CHAMBRE À LOUER.

The concierge descended and reclaimed her stool. "The General will see you," she announced after a moment, as if surprised at this visitor's reception.

"Welcome to you, young Karlov!" said the Inspector-General of Artillery, leaning forward in his wheelchair in the doorway of the second-floor apartment as the stair lights blinked off.

"You are just in time for an aperitif," said the old cannoneer cheerfully. Not the first for either of us, thought Alexander as he glanced around the small sitting room. Traces of frugality mingled with a few old treasures. Karlov recalled the gossip. The general, it was rumored, was selling his medals, even his Maltese Cross, to buy his daughter a gown for a ball at the Ritz.

"I took the liberty of bringing a small present for your household, sir." Alexander set down a bottle of champagne and a large round box from Rumpelmayer's on a table cluttered with enamel boxes, small oval portraits and a framed menu of the Coronation Dinner of May 8, 1896.

"Quite unnecessary, but thank you." Katkoff set his monocle in place and examined the labels before nodding in appreciation. "Vita will be along in a few moments," the general added. "You know how young ladies are."

Not really, thought Alexander, recalling his difficulties both with young ladies and with his one professional sing-song girl in Shanghai. He looked up at two watercolors hanging in inexpensive frames. One was the Katkoff house on the English Embankment, the other an Italianate residence on one of the family's Crimean estates. Men bent over wicker baskets between rows of vines that grew on steep slopes in the background.

"My mother painted those," remarked Katkoff. "When we fled, I rolled them up in the lining of the sleeves of my overcoat. There were two more, one of the villa at Cannes, the other of our boat, but I was obliged to give my fur coat to a border guard near Riga. I hope he enjoys looking at our yacht."

Leaning to one side, the general sighed and poured Dubonnet into two glasses. "*À votre santé!*"

"*Et à la votre, mon général!*" Both men drank.

"May I ask what you have found to keep you so busy in China?"

"My father and I started a Salle d'Armes a few years ago," replied Alexander. "Shortly after we arrived in Shanghai in 1919. We began with fencing and riding lessons, because that was all we knew. After a time we took on every sort of show and competition. Horse fairs and boxing, knife throwing and gymnastics, Cossack riders and dancers, whatever people want in Shanghai." He smiled. "And in Shanghai they want everything, sir, usually to gamble on."

Alexander sensed a fresh presence behind him, the aroma of just enough French perfume. In his nervousness he rose quickly and turned around, spilling his drink high on his trousers. He groaned to himself.

"Count Karlov, permit me to present my granddaughter, Violetta," said General Katkoff, ignoring the accident. His granddaughter did not. She covered her mouth and giggled. Though short, the girl was even more lovely than her reputation. She had the opulent freshness of a dish of strawberries and cream.

"*Enchanté,*" bowed Alexander, trying not to look at the breasts that pressed wide the pleats of her high-collared blouse. "But I believe we have met before, *mademoiselle,*" he said awkwardly, "many years ago in St. Petersburg." She showed no sign of recognition. His face felt hot as he asked, "Did we not play find-the-bear-cubs once as children?"

"I do not recall, Count Karlov," Violetta answered demurely. "But do step into the kitchen with me for a moment and let me help you. You don't want to have a stain."

"Please call me Alexander," he said, following her without his cane. "Excuse me a moment, sir," he called to the general, pausing at the entrance to the short hallway.

"Plenty of cold water is best," Violetta said in the narrow kitchen, setting down the book she was carrying. The slim volume seemed to be a play, Alexander noticed, *The Gamblers.* Perhaps Gogol, he struggled to remember.

Violetta lifted a dishtowel, not hesitating as she gripped the top of Alexander's trousers with one hand. She dipped the towel into a pan of water and repeatedly rubbed the damp cloth up and down the front of his trousers. Trying not to react, astonished at the suggestion of her touch, Alexander leaned back and gripped the edge of the sink. He breathed in her perfume and admired the clear pale pink skin of her neck and shoulders.

"Mon Dieu." Vita blushed and stopped her work abruptly. She glanced at his eyes before looking away. "There, that should be fine when it dries." Her thick blond hair brushed Alexander's chin as she straightened. He tried to think what to say.

"Violetta!" called the general's voice. *"Des biscuits, s'il te plaît, chérie."*

Alexander went to rejoin his host, leaving Vita, her oval face flushed, preparing a plate of crackers in the kitchen. "I see they have a room for rent here, sir," he said, crossing his legs as he sat down.

"I believe it's rather pleasant," said the general encouragingly, refilling both glasses. "A small apartment on the *rez-de-chaussée,* in the back, with a modest garden and a handsome bath. Up here the plumbing never works. But you would have to enquire of Madame Lafarge downstairs. She manages everything."

Alexander wondered how a man habituated to commanding regiments in battle, and to being responsible for seven thousand souls on his estates, could find it tolerable to obey the petty injunctions of this dragon of a janitor.

"That sounds very sensible, sir," said Karlov, thinking where this might lead with Violetta. "I have been looking for something quiet."

- 4 -

As Katerina Karlov crossed Poland, she saw the signs of war everywhere. Not of the Great War that had consumed Europe and brought down the czar, but the Russian-Polish war that followed. The bitter two-year campaign that ended outside Warsaw with the Miracle on the Vistula in 1920, when the long plumed lances of the Polish Uhlans defeated the numberless sabres of the *Konarmiya,* the Soviet cavalry army. Katerina understood that many considered that battle to be not merely a victory for Poland over Russia, but a triumph for Christian Europe over Bolshevik atheism.

She glanced with little interest at the small, seemingly-empty villages that passed slowly by the filthy window of the train, each hamlet separated from its neighbors by gloomy marshes and dark forests. Katerina was used to the different stages of hunger, and she felt the first one now, the empty grumbling of her belly. A dizzy light-headedness would be next, followed by the long bitter sense of weakness and the effort of holding herself together. Even a bowl of *shchi* would seem a blessing, the peasant cabbage soup perhaps thickened with a little lard or even a potato, if she were more fortunate than most people in her own land.

For the Poles, she knew, her country's civil war provided an opportunity to regain their independence after more than a century of Russian domination. The Soviets, however, despised the czar but coveted his empire, and even more than that. They wanted the world. For them, said Lenin, the Revolution in Russia must be followed by revolution in Germany, and the path to Germany could only be through Poland.

Katerina hunched her shoulders and fiddled with the unmatching buttons of her old wool overcoat. She wished she did not recognize the shadowy outline of her own face in the window. She touched her thin cheeks with the fingers of both hands. The skin of her face was oily and spotted. The skin of her hands felt dry and cracked. Even in Moscow, a small cake of greasy home-made soap was a shared luxury, bartered for a few lumps of coal or handfuls of tea dust.

Ambitious Chekists like Viktor sought to emulate the hardships personified in the sacrificial life of their leader, Feliks Dzerzhinsky. Katerina had learned to accept this example and even to respect it. The lean founder of the Cheka was said to sleep on a mat on the floor of his office in the Lubyanka prison, eating only beets, potatoes and dark bread, rising in the night whenever his telegraph machine began to chatter, coughing up blood each morning like his prisoners.

Katia herself had learned to divide her life rather than to pretend that only half of it was real. An old aristocratic life of memories and privilege opposed to a new Soviet life of purpose and duty. The two shared one thing: the pain of separation. The first life held only the ghosts of her parents and her twin, Alexander. The second was alive with her year-old son, and enhanced by her participation in the transformation of her country. Yet now she was obliged to leave behind her baby, her country and her distant sense of family.

In France she would at last be truly useful to the Bolsheviks. Her perfect French, and her understanding of the White refugees and their bitter sense of loss and grievance, would give her an access that few Red agents could possess. She would have to fortify herself against the weakness of nostalgia, of concern for the vanished life she once had shared with the refugees. Instead she would be obliged to remind herself of the future of her country, and of her child. Russia could never recover or lead the international revolution if men were fighting to restore the old life.

Though she was lonely, Katerina had uncertain feelings about meeting Viktor in Paris. Part of her wished never to see him again, but he was the father of her child and the only man she really knew, if know him she did. Some of his goals were admirable, and she had come to share them. But she loathed his violence and feared his brutality. Even the baby had not changed him. He never touched Leon and rarely spoke to him, and when he did, Viktor seemed only to be searching for signs of himself. The baby, strangely, seemed already to possess his father's angry unforgiving temper. Less than two years old, the boy was slow to smile and quick to rage.

At the same time, Leon had the varied eyes she shared with her brother, Alexander: one green, the other a darkish blue, rather than her own father's seducing slate-blue eyes. Katerina thought for a moment of how much her father would despise her new socialist politics, how he would feel shamed by her activities. With a fretful shake of her head she forced aside the thought, and any hesitation about her purpose. She reminded herself that Leon was still in Moscow, a hostage for her conduct, though cared for well enough at a hostel for the children of important dead or absent Bolsheviks. Her mother, she knew, though unconcerned with politics, would have harbored some sympathy for at least the ideal of revolution. Her mother's own grandparents had been

Decembrists, aristocratic revolutionaries who were exiled to Siberia one hundred years ago.

Katia recalled stories of how her great-grandmother, one of the celebrated beauties of St. Petersburg society, had never complained about her new life, even when she woke up in Siberia with her curls frozen to the mattress. In their cabin on the frigid shore of Lake Baikal, the elegant couple had combined reform and civilization. In the evenings her great-grandmother played Mozart on her harpsichord to a room crowded with unschooled Buryats and woodsmen, while in the other room her husband taught history and botany to village schoolchildren and a few of their elders seated on the floor.

Instead of sepia photographs of her grandparents, however, Katerina's son would be surrounded now by bearded busts of Marx and grim photographs of Lenin at the tractor factory. Even his nursery songs were the lilting slogans of revolution and the ballads of class war. She put aside thoughts of her own days of play with Sasha in the summer room at Voskrenoye, surrounded by costumed French dolls, German model trains and English lead soldiers.

Siberia and Viktor Polyak had changed her. The Party school in Moscow and the Revolution had changed her. Having her child had confirmed these changes and hardened her determination to survive in her new life. What she must do now, she would do for her son.

Like the few czarist officers who had changed sides and were now battling for the Bolsheviks, Katerina had something to prove both to the Reds and to herself. On the way to Paris she would complete one distasteful mission in the Borders, as the Poles called the disputed territories that were home to the cities of Vilno, Minsk and Lvov.

Katerina rested her head against the corner by the dirty window and let her eyes close. The clicking of the wheels reminded her of the nightmare journey on the Trans-Siberian four years before, when she and her mother and Alexander had sought to flee six thousand miles across Russia to join her father, then stationed with his regiment near

Vladivostok. The railroad itself had been a battle front in the long civil war. The trains were like warships, armor-plated and crowded with soldiers, bristling with machine guns and flags and light artillery. Their own train had been ambushed by the Bolsheviks. As she was dragged from the embattled car, the last thing Katerina had seen was Alexander fighting some Reds in the chaos of the aisle. In the years since then she had taught herself not to think of him, lest Sasha's absence become a ghostly shadow that consumed her.

With a lurch Katia sat forward and opened her eyes, drawing herself back to the present. She raised the collar of her coat and glanced out the train window at the countryside. Some fields were bare and plowed over. Others showed the scraggly wreckage of a partial harvest or aisles of trampled wheat and maize where the Cossack cavalry had passed through. In the Border territories of Lithuania, Byelorussia and the Ukraine, even the fields suffered from the conflicts, Poles against Russians, Lithuanians against Poles, Reds against Whites, Ukrainians divided. The train compartments themselves still bore the marks of the campaigns. The woodwork was chipped. Horsehair prickled through torn cushions. Lice waited in the cracks of the seats for their next warm hosts.

Katerina lifted her thick wool cap and scratched her scalp through her tangled hair. She could not remember when she last had an opportunity to bathe. She knew of enough injustice under the old regime not to demand such luxuries herself. Lenin and Trotsky were not alone in despising the capital system that in Europe was reinforcing the inequalities of class with the inequalities of money. She herself had heard her father's landed friends complain about the ugliness of bourgeois materialism and the ambitious new money that came with it. The old aristocrats and the young Marxists shared this one revulsion.

The new factory owners, however, had oppressed the workers just as the rural aristocracy had oppressed the peasants. Instead of slaving all day in fields and peat bogs, twelve-year-olds toiled for ten hours or more in the factories, their nimble fingers adept at oiling the moving gears of the dangerous machinery. Instead of living in smoke-filled huts, the workers slept or drank themselves to sleep in tight stinking rows on plank platforms in the factory barracks.

But now, at last, the Revolution was liberating both peasants and proletariat.

By participating in building a new society she would also be preparing a future for her son, ensuring that Leon would have a place as honorable and significant as any that her own family had once held. Even now his namesake was forging the largest and most politically enlightened army in the world. In many regiments, the officers wore no insignia of rank. In each unit commissars and political agents like herself were educating and inspiring the soldiers around them. Whatever she was asked to do, she must do for Leon, no matter how brutal or distasteful. Viktor had made it clear that her failures would be charged to their son. To participate in her son's upbringing, to be a devoted mother, she must be a devoted Bolshevik.

The train braked with short jarring motions, like a man staggering under a shifting burden. The old man beside her cried out when a basket fell from the overhead rack onto the threadbare seat of the once-handsome carriage.

Soon the train stopped at a crossing where a muddy road led up to the tracks. In the near distance, broken-down carts and the swollen body of a horse lay at the edge of the road. A collapsed sign lay in the dirt near her window. The names of several Polish towns were written in Germanic characters and spellings, a lingering mark of occupation by the Huns during the Great War. Knots of peasants in shabby boots, blankets wrapped about their shoulders, waited to climb aboard. Two Jewish families stood to one side in heavy black overcoats. Piles of tightly packed bundles and parcels lay beside them. A small thin boy dressed like an old man twisted his long black ear curls.

The carriage filled as more and more people crowded inside. The narrow aisle that ran beside the compartments became impassable.

Men and women forced their way into the cabins and leaned over the seated passengers. Katia stood and gave her seat to a young girl carrying a crying baby. Unthanked, Katerina forced her way into the crowded corridor and cleared a round spot in the steamy window with the cuff of her sleeve. Despite her beliefs, she could not help being ashamed of her cracked and filthy nails. Instead of twenty-two, she must look ten years older than her age.

They were waiting for Katerina at the station. A man and a woman stood together at the north end of the platform, each wearing a worn leather jacket and carrying a thick bundle of leaflets bound with string. The woman immediately handed her bundle to her companion as Katia walked towards them with her heavy satchel in one hand and a large dark envelope in the other.

"Welcome to Baranowicze, comrade," said the woman sternly, accepting the envelope without ceremony. "You are just in time for the meeting."

An hour later the three entered the noisy smoky back room of a café on Stanislavski Street at the edge of the Polish town. A crowd of thirty people waited for them. All but two were men.

"We must begin," said a lean white-haired man in thick spectacles as he banged a mug on a table. "The police or the agents of the landowners could be here soon." Behind him, one of the women slid a heavy wooden bolt into a metal clasp on the door frame. The couple from the station distributed the leaflets.

Katerina glanced at the sheet and turned it over. Large letters repeated the same promising message in Polish, Russian and German: "Over the corpse of White Poland lies the road to world conflagration." She nodded and passed the leaflet to a neighbor.

"The Soviets are our brothers, whatever their country," declared the elderly man. "Dzerzhinsky himself, the father of the Cheka, came from

Vilno. Lenin told us to destroy the landlords and the kulaks so that the peasants of Poland could seize the seigneurial lands and forests."

Katerina stood against the wall beside the speaker so that she could search the crowd and identify the correct man among the upturned faces. If she was to do what she had been ordered, she must make no mistake. Most of the faces were middle-aged or older. Tired and hard and lined as if carved from dry wood. A few more years like the last two and she would look the same.

The man would be short and heavy, she had been told, with a trim square beard and the dent of a deep scar across the bridge of his nose. But five or six of the men had something like such beards. Several of them, their height not evident, were seated on long narrow benches against the wall beneath the single paper-covered window.

"Pilsudski uses the Uhlans like Cossacks to hold down the workers and return our villages to the landlords," added another speaker as he banged out his pipe against the wall. "Paderewski and Dmowski are no better."

At the back of the room a man stood and raised his voice in strong protest. Short and portly, dressed better than most, he held a cigarette while he spoke.

"We are Poles first," the man said loudly. "What do we need with Soviet propaganda?" He crumpled a leaflet in one hand and threw it on the floor before continuing. "To us, to Poland, Lenin is just another czar. Two years ago, remember, when the Soviets occupied the Borders, the Cheka killed two thousand Poles in Vilno alone."

Some grumbled, but the rest of the crowd grew silent as the heavy-bellied man spoke, faster and faster. Many began to nod and mutter in agreement. He stamped out his cigarette.

"Though we may be workers and socialists, we are Poles and Christians. First we must secure our country. The Germans are finally leaving, and we must not let the Russians return, socialists though they now may be." The speaker ignored cries of protest and raised his voice as he continued.

"Later, once we have Poland, we can fight the estate owners and the money lenders. But today we must follow Pilsudski, not Trotsky and Lenin."

A shrill voice interrupted him, hollering through the crack between the entrance door and its frame: *"Polizei! Polizei!"*

In a single motion two men lifted a bench and drove it through the small high window at the back of the room. Others knocked out fragments of paper and glass and began to scramble through.

Katerina pressed forward with the others towards the window as heavy blows pounded the door. Her eyes were trained solely on her target. She reached into the right pocket of her greatcoat and primed the two levers on her small double-barrelled American pistol.

The interrupted speaker was waiting his turn to escape out the window. She noticed the inflamed indentation on his nose. The portly man hesitated and gestured urgently for her to climb through first. He clasped his own hands together as a step to lift her up. His fingertips were stained brown.

She placed her right foot in his hands and clambered through as the heavy door splintered at the far end of the room. Outside, others were running towards the nearby forest at the edge of town. Leaflets and the broken bench lay scattered near the wall. Katia turned back to the window as the short heavy man gripped the frame with both hands. He puffed and struggled as he forced his head and shoulders forward.

Katerina gritted her teeth together and lifted the pistol from her pocket. Her hand was steady. As the man clambered through, the buckle of his belt caught on the edge of the sill.

"Help me!" he cried.

Instead, as he stared at her with huge disbelieving eyes, she held the pistol to his right temple and fired both barrels.

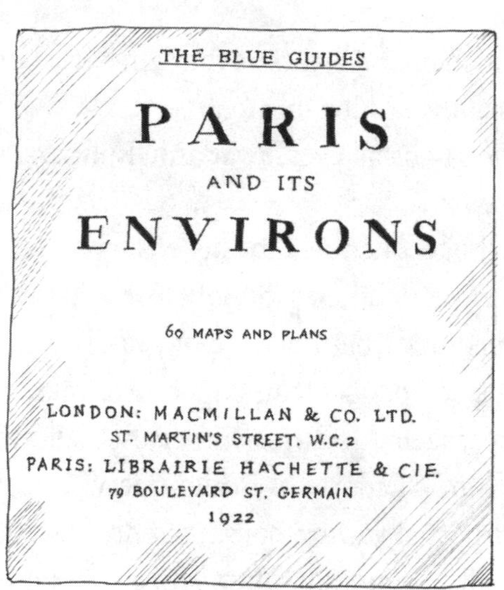

- 5 -

"Today, Count Karlov, we will begin our tour of the more unusual sights of Paris," said the petite Pole as she and her husband waited for Alexander to settle the bill at the Ancienne Maison René Rumpelmayer.

Olga Kulikovski had a soft voice and the warm smile of an unusually contented woman accepting late middle age. She had made no effort to conceal the white that mixed with her shortish brown hair. A dusting of pink face powder made a modest attempt to cover the lines around her eyes and mouth. But in her eyes was the hard blue chill of a clear winter's morning on the Polish plain.

Karlov had the sense that she was studying him with care, the way a new lover might, or a detective. Her husband, facing the door, seemed to cast all his attention on the clients as they entered and fussed about their choice of tables at the fashionable teahouse.

"You have such unusual eyes," Madame Kulikovski said. "One green, the other so blue."

"They are just like Katerina's, my sister's."

"We will help you find her, probably through your Chekist with one hand." She smiled and continued calmly, as if discussing plans for a pleasant evening at Fouquet's or Lapérouse, rather than anticipating violence, kidnapping and torture. "Either this Commissar will find you or we will find him. Of course, we might do well to draw him to us by helping him learn what you are doing, but never where you live."

"Whatever will help us catch him quickly," said Alexander. "I must find Katia, and then I have to hurry back to China." For the most part, he trusted his Chinese partner, but there was too much at risk in Shanghai. Not just everything he and his father had built, but his own plans for the future.

"Patience is the hunter's greatest weapon," Madame Kulikovski replied. "We Poles take a longer view. For you Russians, your civil war was a conflict of the moment. But we have waited for more than one hundred years, mostly under your czars, and the sabres and knouts of his Cossacks. Then under the Huns. Now, at last, Poland is free."

Karlov stiffened as she spoke. To a Russian like him, Poland and Finland, the Ukraine and the Baltics, were provinces, not nations. Named after the emperor who had founded the Corps des Pages, whose officers were chosen to bind the empire together, Alexander had no patience for such rebellions. Yet he recalled his own mother deploring that, at times under the czars, the children of Poland had not been permitted to learn their own language in school, or to speak it in public.

He finished his second madeleine and his café au lait and put down a handsome tip. As he had been instructed, his street map and the 1922 *Guide Bleu* lay open on the table. Two red bookmarks protruded from the bottom of the guidebook. He had not looked at that day's

Matin, with its listings of steamship sailings from Le Havre, Boulogne and Marseilles.

Alexander respected the deception: his own identity and purpose did not require concealment. Those of the Pole and her trim Lithuanian husband did. They would be responsible for more missions than this one.

As a licensed tour guide, Madame Kulikovski had reason to make enquiries at hotels and restaurants, to hang about at railway stations and travel agencies, to leave and collect messages at post offices, and to revisit in varied company all the travellers' haunts of Paris both by day and night. Fluent in six languages, and occasionally useful as a driver or male escort, Adam Kulikovski also had his role, and his small black revolver.

"Our first stop will be the Catacombs," said the Pole as they stepped out onto the rue de Rivoli and Gregori Radinsky opened the door of the waiting taxicab. "Over one hundred miles of abandoned limestone quarries, many dating from the Romans. Now they're a charnel house for bones relocated from the Cimetière des Innocents and other abandoned graveyards, five or six million skeletons. The remains of Madame de Pompadour and many other victims of the old Terror are buried there." She paused. "A perfect place to meet and talk with discretion, and perhaps to hunt."

"Where to, Madame?" said Radinsky as Alexander took the forward seat beside his friend.

"Dans le quatorzième, jeune homme," she said gently. *"Place Denfert-Rochereau."*

They paused in the cool damp air of the Catacombs. They had descended a spiral stone stairway and were perhaps eighty feet below the surface of the city. A party of American travellers on their way out blocked the passage just ahead.

One side of the long tunnel was an orderly wall of bones. Femurs and tibias were stacked five or more feet high, interspersed with neat rows of skulls laid out like shelves. The teeth and lower jaws were usually missing. Alexander rose on his toes and cane. He peered over the top. Water dripped onto his shoulder from the ceiling. The pile of bones extended at least ten yards deep into the walls.

"Here is one of the chambers where they sorted and packed in the bones from the old local cemeteries before Baron Haussmann laid out the boulevards in the seventies. The children are in those narrow piles," said another guide in stiff schoolmaster's English while his American clients chattered among themselves in the dimly lit corridor. Their accent reminded Alexander of his lady friend in Shanghai, the fiercely well-meaning daughter of missionaries from California. A red-haired girl in the group stared at Alexander before whispering to a companion.

"*Pardon*," said Madame Kulikovski as she led Karlov through the party.

"Excuse me, please," said Alexander in British English as he walked carefully across wet patches of the floor.

Monsieur Kulikovski paused frequently to look around with darting eyes. Other tours were gathering further back down the passage as more visitors arrived. Occasionally the chains of mounted lights flickered, then brightened.

From time to time the Pole stopped to point out small plaques set into the walls as she led the two men down a series of narrower passages that spread fork-like from one another.

"After the Revolution, the victims of the Terror were moved to several chambers at the end of this corridor. Of course," she added, smiling, "by that time the skulls of the beheaded rarely matched the bodies."

The Pole picked her way forward in her practical shoes as the hewn floor roughened and the passage became a tunnel. The modest light fixtures were set further and further apart. As in the cheaper hotels, in the remote corridors she had to press a button every few minutes to keep each passage lit. Stalactites had formed where water dripped from the limestone ceiling. Piles of bones had been cemented together by the action of the water, embalming thousands of skeletons in a shiny limestone glaze. A few tunnels were closed off where the erosion of the ceilings had caused the ground above to collapse into the chambers of the quarry. "Several houses have been lost, collapsing into the Catacombs," Olga Kulikovski remarked. "Now building above the quarries is restricted."

At last they came to a brass plaque on which the fleur-de-lis of the Bourbons was embossed in each corner.

"Here reside the remains of the grander aristocrats, or so they say. Madame de Pompadour herself rests somewhere in this wall. In richer days, at Versailles, she had four rooms for her wigs, each panelled in cedar and lined with looking glass."

Alexander thought of his mother's dressing room, with its embroidered screen, prints of Fontainebleau and the Trianon, and dressing table with the pleated silk skirt and china pots filled with pins, clips and cotton wool. One stormy morning he had wandered in, surprising the lady's maid as she dabbed one of his mother's French perfumes behind her own ears.

The lights brightened for an instant, then went dark. Only a small glow came from the corridor far behind. Then that, too, expired. The anxious cries of American voices echoed towards them like the uneven clamor of approaching thunder.

Karlov stood still, clenching his cane in both hands. He wondered if this darkness came by accident. Alexander's eyes adjusted. He saw the far flicker of a torch in the corridor behind them. He heard a scream, sharp and closer than the sounds of panic in the distance. His body tightened. He was in the hunt again.

"Get down," said Madame Kulikovski in a steady voice . She gripped Alexander's arm and lowered herself with her back to the wall.

Unable to crouch with his stiff leg, obliged either to stand or sit, Alexander pressed himself against the rough wall. The surface felt damp and scummy.

The flitting glare of the torch grew closer. Touching Alexander's shoulder, alert and quick as a cat, Adam Kulikovski knelt beside him and drew his pistol. Then he hurried past, crouching low as he made his way towards the wandering torch, taking advantage of each jagged depression in the wall.

Down the passage, the lamp holder stumbled and the cone of light flashed against ceiling and floor with jerky movements. Steady again, it fell full on Madame Kulikovski.

Alexander drew his sword as two weapons fired. Both bullets whined and ricocheted against the walls. Shards of stone cut Karlov's face. He heard shoes scrape against the floor a few steps away. With nowhere to go, he prepared to receive an attack, gathering himself like a fencer trapped at the end of the piste. A gun fired again. Adam screamed. A shadow lengthened along the wall, then collapsed like a falling curtain.

Alexander saw another shadow hunched over the Lithuanian down the corridor. The torch brightened Adam's face. For an instant its uplight revealed the visage of his assailant. Viktor Polyak cursed in Russian and fired into Kulikovski twice more. The lamp went dark and Karlov groped his way towards the fallen man as running steps echoed distantly.

The Commissar waited on the long platform between two tracks at the Gare de l'Est. He was unshaven, with a porter's numbered brass badge on his worn blue cap and a heavy leather luggage strap over his good shoulder. Dark gloves covered both his hands.

Viktor Polyak had been fortunate in Paris, where these details seemed always easy to arrange. Paris, after all, was the cradle of revolution, the first home of the Terror and of the *communards.* Nowhere else in Europe had workers supported Russia's October Revolution as they had here. Every syndicate and trade union seemed to have some leader or some cadre that was sympathetic to Moscow, and willing to help its agents when they required assistance. One day he must pass by the house where Lenin himself had once lived in poverty, somewhere near the Parc Montsouris.

Polyak was still in no condition to carry anything heavy, but there was no better costume for today, and he knew that Katia Karlov would arrive with little baggage.

The platform grew more crowded as a massive black locomotive appeared at the end of Track 3. Brakes screeched as steel scraped on steel. The train slid forward in a cloud of smoke and steam until the bow of the locomotive was nestled near the heavy wooden bumpers. Side doors opened all along the train. Friends and porters, and several men dressed in the caps and trim dark uniforms of chauffeurs, stood waiting and alert as the first passengers descended.

A tall young woman appeared in the door of a second-class carriage. She had a long strong nose and high cheekbones over full lips that bore no makeup. Wearing a dusty coarse overcoat and tall boots, she carried only a thick brown satchel. The woman hesitated on the bottom step and adjusted her cap while she gazed along the platform. Though she appeared drawn and tired, her eyes were clear and bright.

Polyak walked forward and touched his cap and took the passenger's case from her hand.

As the taxi drove across Paris, Viktor silent beside her, Katia could not help but remember all she had heard of this city as a child. To her family, and those like them, Paris was the city of dreams, truly *la ville lumière.* Tutored in French since childhood, brought up as if Verlaine and Hugo were members of her family sharing conversation at the dinner table, she had passed winter afternoons opening her mother's closets and examining her Parisian gowns and hats and shoes. On some days Katerina had been allowed to costume herself in the garments that might one day fit her. Then everything was brushed with care and hung again on padded hangers, each sleeve repacked with tissue paper.

Viktor turned his head towards her and lifted his good hand. His dark hair, always thick and wild, had been replaced by stubble. But his breath still smelled of old tobacco and bad teeth. For an instant she recoiled, thinking he might take her hand. Instead, he reached across and snatched the satchel from her lap.

"Were you successful in Baranowicze?" he asked as he unbuckled the two straps.

"Litovsky is dead," she said, still trying to suppress the guilt for what she had done. The act itself had passed so quickly as to seem unreal. But she would never forget the face of the Polish man as she pulled the trigger. It was not so much horror or even fear that she saw in his eyes. It was disappointment and betrayal.

"The police broke up our meeting," Katerina said. She had not yet found the opportunity to wash the blood from the right sleeve of her overcoat.

Polyak removed a folder and flipped through some papers. Finding a roll of French francs and her false German passport, he placed both between his legs. He rifled through her soiled shirts and underclothes before removing the small pistol from its wrapping of two socks.

"An old derringer," he said, breaking open the compact weapon and looking through both barrels against the light of the side window. The driver hunched forward but said nothing. Viktor sniffed the barrels.

"You fired it, today or yesterday." He placed the pistol and the francs and passport into the pockets of his jacket. "Why did you not clean and reload it?" He forced his cap and strap into the satchel. Pinning it closed with his hook, he buckled the satchel with his hand before dropping the case on her lap.

She had not expected Viktor to change, and he had not.

Resigned, she sat forward and stared at the boulevards and bridges as they drove. She felt that she knew each one already. She regarded the women and the men, and thought that she had not seen anyone so well dressed, so clean and stylish, since certain quarters of St. Petersburg when she was a girl. Did they all enjoy what her mother once told her Paris always had in the years before the Great War: *la vie douce?* Was no one truly poor here? She glanced nervously at her dour companion, but of course he did not read her thoughts, or care to.

Soon they entered a more modest neighborhood. But even here she saw no one wearing garments made of sacks, or with feet bound in rags. She thought of the serf-like old peasants of the villages at home on Voskrenoye, stuffing straw into their felt boots in winter and sleeping pressed together on the tiles of their stoves. On brutal nights, a young colt might join the lambs and piglets sheltering with most families in the smoky single-room cottages. Even in daytime, the excrement was indistinguishable by the little light that filtered in through the barely-translucent windows made from leaves of mica or from the stretched bladders of other farm animals. And even today, in Bolshevik Moscow, the drunken lay frozen in the snow.

The taxi drew up on the shiny damp cobblestones in front of a small hotel. Viktor counted out some change and stepped down without holding the door or looking back at her.

"Merci, monsieur," said Katerina to the driver as she left the taxi and watched Viktor glance left and right along the sidewalk before entering the Hotel Montana.

Viktor nodded at the concierge and pressed a button at the bottom of the stair. A dim light brightened the narrow staircase. She followed him up the worn wooden steps. The light went out just as they came to the fourth floor and Viktor turned a key to room 16. He opened the door and held up one hand. As she hesitated in the doorway, Viktor urinated into the sink, then turned on the single tap. Only a few drops fell from the faucet. She turned away, disgusted. Sometimes he seemed to relish how much he could revolt her.

Katerina entered the small room and threw her coat on the foot of the bed. Stepping to the window, she held aside the shabby curtain and gazed out over the steep green copper roofs and smoking chimney pots. She turned the handle and opened the tall glass door that was the window. Exhausted but excited, she breathed deeply and took in the damp smoky air. If only she were alone. Better still, what magic it would be to be here with someone she loved, and who loved her.

So this is Paris, she thought as Viktor walked heavily towards the window. He pressed himself against her from behind. Then he put his right arm around her and forced his hand between the buttons of her shirt. She determined to swallow her revulsion. One button tore free and fell to the floor as he seized her left breast. His high smell reminded her of previous moments like this, and signaled what this one would be like. She smelled another odor, too. Blood, dried blood? She clenched her fists and closed her eyes, losing Paris, but knowing better than to fight.

"Take off your boots." He released her and sat on the edge of the soft sagging bed to remove his own. A powerful stink rose from his feet.

"I said, take off your boots."

Katia sat and bent forward to do so while Polyak placed his revolver on the narrow bedside table and loosened his belt.

"Let me go down the hall and wash, Viktor," she said. Who would even want a woman as filthy as she was? "Please." Of course, she knew that this was not about romance, or even sex. For Viktor, dominance and the reassurance of his power were the drive.

He did not reply. He stripped himself naked save for his open shirt, the dirty bandages visible above the black blood crusted to the hair of his belly. Polyak knocked her back on the bed with a swipe of his wooden hand. His good hand tore at her clothes.

"No, Viktor," she cried. "Not like this!"

He seized the short curls at the back of her head and forced apart her legs with his.

- 6 -

"I trust this will provide you pleasure, Madame Lafarge," said Alexander without hope as he set the small flowering plant onto the counter before the concierge. Behind him, the taxi driver dropped Karlov's leather cases inside the doorway and departed with a touch to his cap. Not wishing to annoy his friend, Alexander had thought it best not to employ Gregori Radinsky for his move to the rue Bonaparte.

"And who is to water this every day?" The concierge shook her head and pushed the white geraniums to one side. "They think I have nothing else to do," she said as if to herself.

"Perhaps you will be kind enough to pass this letter to General Katkoff," he replied.

I'm becoming like my father, Alexander Karlov thought: not responding to what I do not wish to hear. No doubt a few francs would have pleased the old crone more, though most likely, being French, she would relish ill will more than benevolence, no matter what the gift. He trusted, however, that Katkoff himself would be pleased by Alexander's courtesy in advising the general that he was moving in downstairs, and also with the offer for the officer and his granddaughter to make free use of Alexander's splendid working bath whenever that might suit them. With its generous four-footed tub, the bathroom had one door opening into his own small apartment, and the other, normally bolted, onto the narrow downstairs hallway. Confined to his wheelchair, the old general himself would find it awkward to make frequent use of this facility.

Alexander opened his case and a handsomely-wrapped parcel from 15 rue de la Paix. He hung his clothes in the armoire and sorted a few things about the room. He noticed the stump of a candle standing in a pewter holder. With Madame Lafarge in charge, no doubt the candle was for electrical emergencies rather than romance. He placed his two bottles of Beycheville beside it. Karlov laid his shoes and boots near the tall dresser, then removed a brush and long cloth from inside one boot and brushed each one with a few swift strokes. He took the package to the bathroom and set out with care the soaps and bottles it contained. He trusted they would suit Violetta.

Despite the killing of Adam Kulikovski the day before, Alexander felt no guilt in attending to such indulgent niceties. His father had taught him to make hardship and pleasure comfortable companions. "If you permit one to exclude the other," the old Hussar had told him, brushing regret aside with the gesture of one hand, "your life will be diminished twice."

When everything was arranged about his room, he slipped his suitcase beneath the sagging bed and placed two photographs on the shaky bedside table. One, in faded sepia, showed him as a boy with his mother, father and sister picnicking on the estate at Voskrenoye. It had been one of those unending mid-summer northern evenings, one of the precious "white nights" of pale sunlight that were a reward for the long bitter darkness of the Russian winter. The picture seemed from a different, impossible world.

The other photograph was Shanghai. Alexander, his cane held behind his back, stood between his father and Ivan Semyonov in the great hall of the Salle d'Armes. Torn regimental flags and the sword rack were mounted on the high wall behind them where the shelves of opium once had risen. The burly Cossack's worn wide boots, his crossed but empty bandoliers and the large knife in his belt contrasted with Major Karlov's lean hardy elegance. Dimitri Karlov's tall boots shone as they always did. The long scar on his cheek only added to his sense of energy and readiness, whether for a ballroom or a battlefield.

The photograph gave Alexander a flicker of excitement, and a sense of business not yet finished.

Alexander thought of yesterday's experience at the Catacombs. The Commissar had escaped again. When the lights in the passage had come back on, Madame Kulikovski, astonishingly calm, sat on the floor beside her husband holding his two hands in hers. After a moment she unpinned the campaign ribbons from his jacket and put his pistol in her pocketbook. Then she kissed Adam's cheeks, closed his eyes and crossed herself.

Alexander shut the door to the bathroom before leaving, then set out for the Hotel de Crillon to collect his mail from Shanghai. "Always have your mail sent to a fine hotel, even if you never stay there," he had been advised as a boy. "Unlike the post office, they are never closed and there are no lines."

From whom might he hear? Jessica or Mei-lan, Mr. Hak Lee or Hideo Tanaka? Hopefully affection from Jessica, and advice from Shanghai's most celebrated madam. Perhaps business news from his ruthless partner, the Master of the Mountain, or politics and social intrigue from his only friend from Imperial Japan. He knew better than to expect anything from Lily.

Violetta was comforted to find the bathroom door unlatched. Wrapped tightly in her old dressing gown, she carried their best towel over one shoulder and her book in her left hand. She slipped into the room and closed the door, relieved that Madame Lafarge had not seen her pass down the hall.

She had been careful to take advantage of the bath at a time when she knew Alexander Karlov would not be home, and she had made her grandfather aware of this propriety. Next time that should not be necessary. Violetta pulled the beaded cord on the single wall lamp that was mounted next to the mirror above the sink. How typical of French economy, she thought, as the dim light cast its frugal glow. It would be difficult to read, but she was determined to memorize her favorite lines.

The bathtub was clean, the water blessedly warm. What luxury, Violetta thought as she bent and felt it become too hot for her small hand to touch. Her fingertips were already reddened and sensitive from too much work with needle and thread. She did not mind her trips to the Marais by crowded *autobus*, but her employers kept her ceaselessly at work, in bad light and with only their old scraps for lunch.

While she worked she recited lines to herself as if playing two parts on stage, using the transforming fantasy of the theatre as an escape from her own life. Often she sensed that Madame Reisel, herself once a refugee, enjoyed humbling a Russian girl raised in privilege. Some mornings Madame Reisel stood in the doorway behind Violetta. Smoking, she watched her employee raise hems and pick lint from the cuffs of old trousers, not knowing that her seamstress was far away, on stage with Gogol and Chekhov, that the curtain had already risen.

Violetta Katkoff knew that she must find an escape from this limited dreary life. She was certain, too, that her grandfather thought this young

Count Karlov could be the man to save her. At twenty-three, she would no longer be a young bride, by the traditional standards of society. Today, of course, there were modern women who no longer felt so hurried. They were free to work. But from her own experience, that emancipation had not much charm. She would rather be free to shop, to find her pleasures, and to attend the École de Théâtre Classique near the Sorbonne, or one day even the Comédie-Française itself.

Violetta dropped her robe and began to sing to herself while steam rose from the tub. She picked up one of two boxes of soap from the chipped shelf above the sink. *"Savon Pois de Senteur,"* read the exquisite flowered label, "Sweet Pea, Roger & Gallet, Paris." Rejecting that choice, she took a bar from the second box, *"Guerlain-Tubéreuse."* The soap was wrapped in fine pleated tissue paper and secured by a band of pink ribbon. She closed her eyes as she inhaled. Tuberose. Not a soap for men, she thought. Could Count Karlov, so handsome and rich, have purchased it for her? Had Alexander moved to rue Bonaparte because of her? He must have liked the way she cleaned his pants.

She examined the four bottles that lined the edge of the tub against the wall: bath salts, bubble beads, a flagon marked *L'Huile Ambre Gris,* and one small square bottle, *Essence de Violette.*

"Merci, Alexander," Violetta said quietly with a smile at the name. *"Quelle gentillesse exquise."* She drew the cork of the salts and dropped some into the steaming water, then added a splash of the amber oil. She would save her namesake for a more personal occasion.

As the perfumed water rose, Vita considered opening the door to the adjoining room and peeking inside. No light came from under the door. She turned the white porcelain knob and stepped barefoot into the count's room. She opened the armoire and felt each of the hanging jackets and trousers between her fingers, appreciating their texture and finish. English materials, she was certain. Even the stitching and the horn buttons were admirable. But the labels, Tong Yik and Edward Lee, both of Bubbling Well Road, Shanghai, meant nothing to her. She stepped to the bedside table and bent to study two photographs, not lifting them lest she replace them incorrectly. It was too dark to see them clearly and she dared not turn on the room light in case the old concierge might notice it beneath the door. Another time, she thought.

A folded newspaper lay on the bed, circles inked on it in a bold hand. She squatted down and squinted to see what they concerned: steamship schedules for the East on the Messageries Maritimes and the Peninsular & Oriental line. The schedule for the steamer *China Star* was circled twice, for sailings from Marseilles to Shanghai, with calls at Port Saïd, Suez, Bombay, Goa, Colombo, Hong Kong and Singapore. A voyage to dream of, she thought, a honeymoon.

Vita closed the bedroom door and dipped the toes of one foot into the tub. The heat made her squeal. She waited a moment for the bath to cool, anticipating the indulgence. At home, she had never drawn her own bath. She knotted her hair above her head, pleased that Madame Lafarge would be infuriated by such an extravagance of heated water.

Turning, Violetta regarded herself in the mirror. Too short, she judged, but more than enough for most men to desire. She placed her hands against her rounded hips and stroked them slowly up her narrow waist and across her stomach while she studied her best feature. Was it possible that already her breasts were not quite as high as when she had been younger? She raised one heavy breast in each hand, squeezing them more and more tightly. Then she made a circle of her mouth and pinched her pink nipples until they stung and stiffened. Violetta liked the way that felt when the water was hot. She decided to be a good girl and not do more than that.

In the bath Violetta closed her eyes as the bubbles reached her chin and soaked the fine hair just above her neck. She dried her hands and lifted her slim book from the floor. *Marriage,* read the play's title page, "A Quite Incredible Incident in Two Acts," by Nikolai Vasilevich Gogol. The allure of marriage and the tensions of relationship unfolded as she reread the first act and imagined herself on stage. She recited a few lines out loud with dramatic expression.

Violetta bit her lip while she considered the cruel disappointments of the later scenes. Hearts lost, a marriage complicated. After a few moments, though, she relaxed again. As she grew languid, her imagination turned to herself.

Floating in a damp field of lilies and lilacs, she dreamed of what life might be like as a rich countess in Shanghai. Servants, she had heard, were plentiful and inexpensive, and so wonderfully quiet and obedient.

Alexander set down his mail and pulled off his boots. He had passed much of the day walking about Paris, first along St. Germain to the Quay, then across the Pont Alexandre III to the Champs-Elysées, stopping occasionally at a café to rest his throbbing leg.

It reminded him of his early days in Shanghai, trying to strengthen his left leg by walking home from school each afternoon while the other boys were playing rugby and football. Each day he had sought a different route, alternating the grand boulevards and residential avenues of the French Concession with the alleyways and warrens of Chinese Shanghai. After a time he could close his eyes and know where he was by the odors of spice vendors, fish-mongers and tobacconists, sawdust and garlic and coal dust.

As he paused at the Brasserie Posset, hoping to enjoy the moment and admire the passing girls, he thought instead of his obligation to finish with Viktor Polyak. The man had killed his parents, abducted his sister and broken his leg. Alexander had almost dealt with him that evening on the night train to Nanking, but Polyak had survived, leaving one hand behind in China, partially preserved in the often-bloody water of Mr. Hak Lee's fish tank after being nibbled clean by the snakeheads.

Alexander had walked to the Place de la Concorde to collect his mail from the concierge at the Crillon. As he passed the old site of the guillotine, he thought of what it must have been like for the noble families in the tumbrils waiting to lose their heads while the crowds screamed abuse and pelted them with rubbish. The Great Terror, they had called those days, the heart of the revolution that still divided France. That was the beginning of it all, he thought, when the unthinkable became reality.

Back in his room at last, Alexander sat up against both pillows and the round bolster, hard and heavy as a frozen body. He unfolded his penknife and slit open all the mail, happy to find five copies of *The North-China Daily News* forwarded by Semyonov from the Salle d'Armes.

Mindful of the expenses of his Paris visit, he read first the message from Mr. Hak Lee. Never taught to write, and bound by a lifetime of secrecy, his Chinese partner must have dictated these few lines to the French lady who served him when she was not teaching at the Lycée. Their horses had not been running well at the races, the old gangster reported, though the wagers had gone well enough. Their greyhounds had been no more successful at the Canidrome. The Salle, however, was flourishing. An important new venture that could not be mentioned in a letter required Alexander's participation. Some old enemies, long dormant, were stirring once again. There was no mention of the Casino profits. But a transfer record was enclosed for a substantial draft forwarded to Count Karlov's account at the Banque d'Indochine et de Suez on the boulevard Haussmann. Few problems, the tong chieftain reminded Alexander, cannot be eased by money.

Also in French was a message from Madame Mei-lan Wong, once the lover of Hak Lee. A large German client had damaged one of her most promising virgins, a twelve-year-old from Soochow, the home of China's most beautiful women, where the Ming emperors had procured their concubines. Mei-lan had not guessed that the man possessed such energy. The misadventure would be costly for all three interested parties, particularly for the Hamburg shipowner. But with a little chicken blood, the child would be a virgin once again, for all but the most attentive companions. And there was another new girl who would be perfect for Alexander, if he were finally ready to venture with his second sing-song girl. Caramel was not young, seventeen, French-speaking, and one half Annamese, with sugary skin smooth and tan as honey.

As once she might have done with sexual favors for an elderly client, Meilan teased her protégé by mentioning Lily only in a lengthy postscript.

"I believe Lily misses you," Madame Wong wrote. "But she is too busy just now to write herself. She is filming, as the heroine in *Farm Girl*, the tale of a young woman who comes to Shanghai from Shansi to earn money to care for her sick parents. The girl works first in a silk factory, then in a dance hall where an elderly gangster falls in love with her, taking her as his mistress before making her a courtesan. Lily says you will love it."

He turned to the second page. "Lily has just now arrived to take tea with me and asks that I send you her love, and one of your favorite kisses. (She declines to tell me which that is.) Below is a reminder." At the foot of the page was the vivid scarlet imprint of a kiss, broken by the fine vertical lines of Lily's puffy lips.

Too busy was she? thought Alexander, both aroused and angry. It was Lily whom he missed when he was alone in bed. And Jesse when he sat in a café and wished to talk and laugh or walk about the town. If only he could combine their best elements into one perfect girl.

He turned to Hideo's thick consular writing paper and short English sentences. The rising sun was embossed at the top of the page.

"You must come home, my friend. We need to fence. My father is ill. I hold diplomatic conversations and draft cables on his behalf. All Japanese here are worried. The stronger Japan becomes, the more the Chinese hate us," said his old schoolmate, never impressed by other Eastern nations. "Now that Versailles has taken Shantung from the Germans and given it to us, the Chinese have begun a boycott of all Japanese goods and business. Conflict is waiting like a promise. Two Japanese warships are anchored in Shanghai harbor to protect thousands of my countrymen who live on the other side of Soochow Creek."

He opened a long letter from Jessica James, the alarmingly

compassionate daughter of missionaries from California. Much about the sufferings of China, especially its women, but nothing about Alexander or her feelings. Just then he thought he heard the sound of water splashing in the bathroom. He forced himself to continue reading the tragic catalogue. Mission schools, child labor, foot binding and prostitution still concerned Jesse. The Chinese mistreatment of animals had risen near the top of her portfolio of anguish. "I miss you," he read at last as he heard singing in the bathroom. "When you return home we will go back to Turtle Beach in the moonlight, unless I am working at the Mission in Nanking."

He had hoped for more, though rarely had he been more declarative himself. Cross and disappointed with both girls, Alexander glanced at the bathroom door and strained to listen to the quiet singing. It reminded him of his twin sister, but stimulated different thoughts. When he was a child and shared a copper tub with Katerina, she would often sing while he sailed their wooden swans. Then he would join in, to annoy her. "Stop that, Sasha! You know you can't sing," Katia would complain, splashing his face with soapy water.

The voice rose, and Alexander caught the tune of an old Russian song. He smiled, then joined in, his voice at least loud and clear. The bathroom singing ceased and was followed by a giggle.

Suddenly he felt at home. How wonderful, he thought, to be sharing the songs of childhood through a closed door, to be in Paris but to be singing in Russian. Perhaps he had grown too used to speaking French and English in China.

Alexander rose and knocked on the bathroom door. "May I bring you a new sponge, Violetta?"

"Oh! Is that you? Just one moment, please."

He gave her that, then entered with a Guerlain bath sponge, intending not to stare.

But how could he not? Violetta's pink shoulders rose from the steamy bubbles. Her left hand held a washcloth demurely across the tops of her breasts. But the invitation of what he saw and sensed was irresistible.

"I did not know you had come home," she said innocently, as if a child speaking to her father. "I was reading a play." Her right hand lowered a small book onto the floor. "Don't you love Gogol?"

"Love Gogol?" said Alexander. "Of course."

He stretched out his leg and sat behind her at the back of the tub. He loosened his cufflinks and rolled up his sleeves. "May I?" he asked as he dipped the sponge into the bath. She nodded with the same understanding smile she had shown in the kitchen. He smelled lilacs as he lifted out the sponge, squeezed it a bit and stroked it across the smooth damp skin of Vita's upper back and shoulders.

The girl bent her head forward and arched her shoulders and closed her eyes as he dipped the sponge again.

Alexander cupped her forehead in his left hand, taking the strain from her muscles as he pressed and squeezed the warm sponge firmly against the back of her neck. She sighed quietly and surrendered her head against his hand as he worked. His shirt grew wet. Realizing the book's peril, he kicked Gogol under the tub where the floor was dry.

"Excuse me one moment," he whispered, rising and entering his room. He opened the brass tube of his father's military corkscrew, set the screw into the side of the tube and drew the long cork of a Beychevelle before pausing to light the candle. As he did so, he thought of Mei-lan's advice: women make the first sexual decisions, so a man of experience does not try to seduce them. He induces in them a desire to seduce him. As usual, Mei-lan's advice was easier to recall than to implement, though he had been doing his best.

He returned to the bathroom with candle and bottle. He set the short candle on the shelf above the sink. He opened the bottle of Essence de Violette and pulled the lamp cord.

Violetta, sitting higher in the bathtub, smiled up at him with one plump breast almost entirely exposed. At the sight, Alexander wanted to climb into the tub, trousers and all.

He rinsed the single glass and poured in a bit of his father's favorite

Bordeaux. It is not being wasted, the old horseman would have thought. Alexander tasted the smooth full wine, poured more and handed the glass to Vita.

"Merci." She reached up and accepted the glass as the washcloth slipped into the water from her soapy breasts. He lifted out the cloth and wrung it, then poured onto it thick sweet drops of her namesake perfume. He placed the washcloth across her chest, pressing each breast gently as he spread it.

Alexander took his seat again beside the tub with his bad leg extended on the floor. He smelled the soft aromas of the soap, the girl and the perfume.

They shared the wine and whispered in the candlelight. When the glass was finished he stood to refill it.

Violetta, her eyes wide and innocent, her lips parted, reached up and pressed her hand between his legs as she had once before, and with the same result. Alexander sat gingerly and picked up a bar of soap. He took her left breast in one hand and soaped it smoothly with the other. He lifted the warm sponge from the water and pressed it against her breast while he squeezed it. He brushed it gently against the tip of her rosy nipple. Vita closed her eyes and sipped the wine, spilling a bit and sighing as her nipple stiffened. The wine splashed onto the soap bubbles like drops of blood.

Alexander gripped her other breast and took the slick soapy nipple into his mouth. When her own mouth opened, he kissed her on the lips and tasted her. The candle guttered and went out. Alexander released Violetta and climbed into the bathtub behind her, forgetting that he carried his father's gold watch in one trouser pocket. With one leg tight on either side of her, his body pressed against her back, he squeezed her slippery breasts with both hands, pinching the nipples with thumb and forefinger as he ran his teeth along one shoulder until he bit the corner of her neck.

"Monsieur le Comte!" cried a woman's harsh voice from the corridor. "Count Karlov!" Alexander heard loud knocking on the door to his room. *"Une dame veut vous voir et vous attend!"*

- 7 -

Katerina Karlov, her overcoat buttoned to the neck, waited in the dark hall for the bathroom to be free. Her filthy clothes were bundled in a shirt under one arm. The dirty coarse coat scratched and prickled her bare skin where the material came through the torn lining. Finally she heard the water drain from the tub, the only one on the top floor of the Hotel Montana. She prayed that someone had left behind a scrap of soap.

The narrow door opened. A small man stood before her in old cloth slippers and a faded bathrobe. He had long white hair and the wide staring eyes of a man without his spectacles. A brown towel was wrapped around his thin wrinkled neck and tucked into his robe.

"Pardonnez-moi, madame." He reached back into the room to switch

on the dim light, then turned sideways to let her enter. He glanced down at the bathtub, as if ashamed that he had not cleaned it. He bent and turned on a tap, splashing a thin stream of water against the scummy sides of the tub. *"Laissez-moi le faire, madame."*

Katia stood near the doorway watching, not caring which of the dark rings and old hairs were his. In Moscow her only baths had been at the public steam rooms, always crowded and stinking and unsanitary. In Viktor's flat, shared with two families, she had used an old sponge or a wet shirt to wash herself by the sink with cold rusty water. Better than a peasant hut or a factory barrack, she had often told herself.

"Merci, monsieur," she said. "Have you perhaps a bit of soap?"

The man shook his head and held up two empty hands. Katia watched him shuffle down the hall to Number 15 before she closed the bathroom door. She wondered how much the old man had heard through the thin wall that separated his room from theirs. She slid home the flat metal bolt, draped her coat over the doorknob and took off her crusty socks.

Katerina turned on both taps, testing them. One gave lukewarm water. She turned that off, saving it, and half filled the tub with cold water. She knelt on the chilly tiled floor and soaked and squeezed her laundry as best she could. When the water was dark she drained it out before rinsing the clothes in running water. She wiped the sides of the tub with her hands, then filled it with the lukewarm water until the tap ran cold. She stepped into the bath and stretched out with her eyes closed. She held her nose and lowered her head under the water. She rubbed her hair and scalp, then lay there until the water chilled her through and she began to shiver. She examined her hands and thought of the tobacco-stained fingers of the man she had killed.

Katia climbed out and scraped the water from her body with the sides of both hands. There was no mirror, but she was aware that her body, always boyish, had grown too thin. Even after childbirth, her breasts were flat as blintzes. Now her face was drawn and the hair on her legs and underarms too evident. For the first time, she felt plain and not attractive. "You will always have your grandmother's beautiful face and legs," her mother used to say as comfort. Where was that comforting voice now?

She squeezed out her laundry and rinsed the tub while her body dried. Not wanting to put on her dirty overcoat, she opened the door and glanced down the hall to see if anyone was about. Then she closed the door and rinsed the right sleeve of the coat until the draining water was no longer pink with Polish blood. Katerina hurried naked to her room.

Relieved that Viktor had gone out, she opened the window and hung the clothes over the low ironwork railing. She climbed into bed, wishing the rough sheets were clean. Still trembling, Katia lay there with her eyes open as the sky darkened over Paris. She thought of Leon, and her mother, and her brother. Then she thought of what she had done to that man in Poland, and what she had become. For the first time in months, she cried, sobbing like a little girl.

"Open the door!" the voice demanded as the knob rattled and the door shook with violent knocks.

"What's the matter with you?" Polyak asked when he saw her naked. "We have work to do." He was wearing a worn leather jacket and the soiled blue beret of a Parisian workman.

"I'm hungry, Viktor." Katia brusquely turned to the window and lifted some damp clothes from the railing. The clothes were lined with black grit from the ironwork. If Viktor tried to touch her, she would kill him if she could.

"We will eat soon." He was already busying himself with a cablegram and his codebook. "And tomorrow we will prepare you to do what you have been trained for."

On the way to a bistro, they passed a corner kiosk. Katerina was drawn to the stacks of newspapers in French and English, and to the fashion magazines hanging from cords by wooden clothes-pins, but Viktor would neither let her dally nor give her money. He bought copies of *L'Humanité* and *L'Eclair* while she stared hungrily at *Le Miroir des Modes* and a glossy picture magazine named *Vogue.*

They ate nearby at a modest restaurant called Le Cochon de Lait. Katerina thought that she had never eaten better. For a few francs they devoured fresh bread, green salad, steak and crisp fried potatoes. Viktor refused to pay for butter.

At first they both ate urgently without speaking. Katia knew better than to offer to help him cut his meat. He pinned the steak to the plate with the edge of his wooden hand, then ripped it into a few rough pieces with fierce movements of his knife. A hyena could do no better. Since their first meal in Siberia, Viktor had always eaten like a bear gorging itself before its winter sleep.

If only she could be sharing the carafe of red with another man than Viktor. She listened to him eat with his heavy forearms resting on the table and his head hanging low above his plate. He scraped the food towards him with the edge of his fork. His head dipped down like a ground-feeding bird as he took in each mouthful.

As Viktor spoke of political conflicts in France and Russia, she thought of her mother promising her a gay young life of balls and suitors, house parties and troika rides with ringing bells.

"There is one dangerous Romanov left. He calls himself the Grand Duke Nikolai Nikolaevich, and he is somewhere here in Paris. He thinks he is a general," said Viktor, getting her attention. "The Grand Duke Mikhail Alexandrovich, the czar's brother, we have killed already."

Katerina tried not to react as she thought of the czar's five children slaughtered with their parents in the basement at Ekaterinburg, and of the empress's sister, murdered together with five Romanov princes the following day.

Was that much worse than her own crime? Now she had made herself part of all this.

"Four trunks have arrived here from Harbin," continued Polyak, "brought by sea from Shanghai to Marseilles on a French battle cruiser. They are full of relics of the Romanovs, bones and jewelry, stolen by the White army after they reoccupied Ekaterinburg."

He paused to empty the carafe into his glass. His lips were crusted black after another day of drinking.

"In twelve days you will be attending a grand reception at the Polish embassy. It may even be a ball. This pretender, Nikolai Nikolaevich, may be there, or at least those close to him. There will be diplomats and politicians, a few members of the gross bourgeoisie, and what remains of the leading White criminals who have washed up in Paris like a plague of rats hunting for bodies after a flood."

Katerina's lips tightened.

"In a single room," Polyak said, "you will find a swarm of conspirators and revanchists. You will meet Poles and Germans, French and English, all with the wish to destroy our Revolution. Their League of Nations does not even recognize our government. In the middle of our war with Poland, they let our enemy Paderewski, that piano-playing politician, address the founding assembly of the League."

She shook her head slowly as he continued. She felt anger surging deep within her, even though she reminded herself to behave like a dedicated Bolshevik.

"That party will be your opportunity to penetrate this nest of vipers, to become part of them and learn which we must kill." His fork scraped against his teeth. "And if you can learn who has these stolen chests, and exactly what is in them, Moscow will remember us, and Leon will be safe."

The muscles of Katerina's jaw tightened at this threat to her son.

"Your job will be to identify each prominent Russian who is there and to find out where he lives." He paused and reached deep inside his shirt to scratch at the thick scab that covered the inflamed center of his shoulder wound. "We cannot kill them all, you know. We have to choose.

You must learn which ones are friendly with the foreign minister and the generals, who has the influence. Those are the names I need."

"Look at me, Viktor." She pulled at the collar of her own filthy ragged shirt. She placed her hands flat on the table and looked down at her dirty broken nails. "Do I look ready for a ball?"

"In twelve days you will be ready to dance." He shrugged and drained his glass. "You must look so well that they will come to you, not you to them."

"Ridiculous," she said contemptuously. "You do not understand what you are saying. That would all be very costly. More than someone like you can imagine."

He did not answer at first. In the lull of silence she wiped her plate with a bit of bread and began to recall the names of her mother's *fournisseurs,* each one discussed repeatedly at Voskrenoye as if it were a shop around the corner: shoes from Biset and A la Gavotte on the avenue de l'Opéra, dresses from Poiret on the avenue Victor Emmanuel III, ball gowns from Les Soeurs Callot on the avenue Matignon and Premet on the Place Vendôme, silk stockings from Au Carnaval de Venise, and, if Katia remembered correctly, lingerie from A la Cour de Batave. Each season her mother brought to Paris her own new furs from Siberia, the finest snow lynx and sable in the world, and had them cut and fashioned at Grunwaldt or Revillon on the rue des Petits-Champs. The fox and marten could be done at home, the fashions copied after those of Paris.

What about she herself? Her skin? Her hair? Her face? Her body? In St. Petersburg, the best at these things had been the Rumanians. But in Paris, Katerina was not certain.

Was it possible that Viktor Polyak and the Cheka would countenance all this?

Viktor answered for her.

"Tomorrow I will be selling a case of jewels sent here from Moscow to finance our missions. One stone I will not sell. A big emerald that you will wear to the party. They told me it is greater than thirty carats. It is more precious than your child. You will carry that small pistol in your purse and guard the green stone with your life."

Before continuing, he rested his wooden prosthesis across her hands. She had never felt a more repellant touch.

"Money there will be for whatever you must do, but you must be certain not to disappoint us. Two lives will depend on it."

Katerina knew Viktor Polyak was not speaking of his own.

- 8 -

Before anything, she must get clean. She could not enter Helena Rubenstein's or Lecomte or Pontet as she was. It was not her lack of clothes. It was that she had the deeply unclean body of a coal miner or a cannery worker. The pores of her face were blocked and oily. Her hands, red and dry as a washerwoman's, embarrassed her. Like a soldier too long at the front, Katerina carried faithful lice. She could still smell herself. Her mother would be ashamed.

"MARINA DE BUCAREST," read the stencilled window. "SPA DE ROUMANIE." Below that, in smaller letters: "Bains de Luxe" and "Nettoyages Profonds de la Peau."

Katerina entered the establishment. There was a suggestion of steam in the air and a faint aroma of some astringent scent. She set down her bag of new clothes, modest but acceptable, and studied the available treatments that were listed on the wall behind the reception counter. Skin bleaches and pumice pedicures, steam baths and Rumanian massages, deep cleansing and facial peeling, clay masks and chilled seaweed wraps, pore tightening and *épilation,* all the personal luxuries available to the *haute bourgeoisie* and beyond. For an extra charge, a personal review and treatment plan could be scheduled with Madame Marina herself. What woman could resist?

Sitting stiffly in a starched white clinical uniform, the receptionist eyed Katerina, then marked notes on several file cards on her desk. Beside the cards stood a tall pale sculpted bottle of Guerlain's *Blanc de Perles. "POUR BLANCHIR LA PEAU,"* read the label.

"Alors, mademoiselle?" the receptionist said at last. *"Je peux vous aider?"*

She thinks I have come here for employment, thought Katerina. For the first time in three years she allowed herself an instant of social indignation. She reminded herself that Rumanians, like White Russians, had a close tie to the language of France.

"Madame Marina, s'il vous plaît," Katerina said just as a short trim woman with a face like glowing porcelain appeared beside the desk. A crisp white bandana was bound tightly over her head and knotted neatly above one ear.

"Marina Carescu," said the woman. *"A votre service, madame."*

"Je suis Katerina Karlov." Katia extended her hand. *"Je désire le traitement complet, s'il vous plaît."*

Madame Marina held, then quickly released her hand, staring down at it as if she had touched a lizard.

"Suivez moi, s'il vous plaît, madame," she said, and Katerina followed her into a small private salon. As instructed, Katia undressed and put on a light white cotton dressing gown. Madame Marina held her hands under a lamp by their fingertips and examined her face and neck and

feet. She gently pinched Katerina's nose with a white towel, then studied the cloth. "You have come to us just in time to save your youthfulness," said the Rumanian woman, not unkindly.

"When Dr. Payot met your greatest ballerina, Anna Pavlova, she enjoyed a brilliant epiphany that has helped all of us in this profession. Nadia Payot was astonished by the contrast of the extreme youthfulness of the dancer's body and the early aging of Pavlova's facial skin. In the middle of the night, Dr. Payot rose from her bed and wrote down the lesson that had come to her: 'We must exercise the muscles of the face as we exercise the muscles of the body.'"

Madame Marina paused and handed Katia a copy of a magazine called *Votre Beauté*. "Now please excuse me while I instruct your attendant."

In the early afternoon a different woman stepped onto the rue Daunou. A well-dressed gentleman stared at her and touched his hat as he passed. Katerina noticed the first blossoms on the chestnut trees that lined the street. She felt a little like that herself.

It had been raining gently. The air and cobblestones smelled fresh. Her dark hair was pinned in a bun, not yet cut or set, but it was clean and wavy and becoming. She was comfortable in her checked skirt and white pleated blouse. Her brown Belgian shoes were low-heeled, practical but presentable.

"Étonnant! Ravissante! Quelle métamorphose!" Madame Marina had exclaimed, and she appeared to mean it. "Kindly accept these three small jars, Mademoiselle, with my compliments. Never forget the hands. The neck and the hands tell everything. These creams will help your skin to live and keep your beauty fresh."

Katerina had tipped the staff and abandoned her old clothes gladly. Now she could go to Antoine's or Pontet and have her hair done properly, like a lady. She wondered if she could find the hairdresser who used to serve her mother. She struggled to recall his name.

Once she was fully presentable, she could stop by Lanvin and start working on her evening dress. Katia felt excited. Among a swirl of memories she could hear her mother saying how romantic Jeanne's clothes were, and how the brilliant Breton couturier often designed for mothers and daughters together, frequently in *"Lanvin bleu."*

At six Katerina would be meeting Viktor at Le Cochon de Lait for dinner. She was hungry again. Tonight she would insist on butter. After dinner, he'd informed her, he was to have a meeting at which she was not welcome. She had not replied, although pleased at the exclusion.

What she dreaded was sharing the night. Not just the threat of further physical intimacy, though that was hideous enough, but the usual stink and lice and fierce control that were part of Viktor's presence. Katerina feared that no matter what she did, how much she bathed and changed, he would drag her back down to an unclean rough world of violence and degradation.

Walking back to the hotel near midnight, pausing as usual to look behind him, Polyak considered carefully the arrangements he had been making. Soon, he had learned, the Polish woman and Karlov would be taking the tour of the Paris sewers. What better place for him to finish the job, before that dilettante could meet his sister and infect her with his revanchist poison? Like his father in Shanghai, young Count Karlov would die on a small boat, in pain, knowing who had finished him.

Polyak stopped under a lamp and relit his pipe. He had downed some drinks, his first vodkas in Paris, taken with two men who understood their work and shared his tastes. But, clever and ruthless as they were, the Androv brothers had failed in their assignment to organize the fabric workers in Lyons, and for that effort had been beaten by the strike breakers. But Todor Androv, the small lean one with a head narrow as a sturgeon, had a connection to Olga Kulikovski's tour business, and was keeping him advised.

The Androvs were recognizable as brothers only by the extreme closeness of their eyes, set tight against their noses like two knuckles of a fist. Todor's large brother, Oskar, was celebrated as one of the Cheka's early amateur torturers. Everyone answered his questions. Although not intelligent in the ordinary way, Oskar had a peculiar aptitude for such work, for learning what men feared. In time he had been replaced by the more sophisticated experts imported by Dzerzinsk from China. Due to their ease with languages, the two brothers had been assigned to foreign operations in support of the Comintern.

Polyak's mind turned to Katerina. He knew she would be waiting for him in the dark in the hotel room, fearful of his touch, feigning sleep with her knees raised and her face to the wall, hoping to avoid him. Who did she think she was? The czarina? Princess Anastasia? He thought of the costly skin creams she had brought back from her day of waste. He had sunk his thumb into one and smelled it, dropping the lid on the floor and kicking it under the bed. A peasant family could buy enough dark bread for a month with what those jars must have cost the Cheka.

"You look like a painted puppet doll," he had told her at dinner, detecting the new pleasure she was taking in her appearance. "Your face is unrecognizable, ridiculous. Give me those bills and the money that you have not yet wasted."

She had handed him both, remaining silent as he counted the currency and coins and matched the result against the bills.

"Where is the rest?" he had demanded. "That money was not yours."

"It's gone. I spent it." She shrugged. "For tips, of course. That is money paid for service, Viktor. I thought you cared about the workers."

Polyak sucked old tobacco juice from the curved stem and spat onto the edge of the sidewalk as he recalled that moment. He had raised his hand and nearly struck her from across the table. Instead he had controlled himself and gripped the two sides of her face in his fingers. She made no sound as he squeezed. After a moment he had released her. Dark red marks appeared on her cheeks like bruises on an apple.

Ever since Katia had carried out that assignment of her own in

Poland, she seemed more assertive, almost defiant. Was it the sense of power, the mortal confidence, that came from one's first murder? Worse still, could it be that violent secret strength, now further fortified by the restored arrogance of her old class?

"Service money! 'Tips!' Why tip unless you are planning to go back?" he had said angrily "Tips exist to confirm the superiority of the tipper, and to compel slavish service."

"How would you understand?" she had replied with insulting dismissal. "How could you?"

He had taken back every *sou* she still possessed, denying her the coin she needed to secure clean sheets from the hotel. Then he had reached across with the tip of his knife and lifted the rest of her steak from her plate.

He could sense her changing. It was in her voice, her carriage, her new and different self-possession. Not just in the superficial ways of acquiring a changed look as the decadent parasites of Paris worked on her hair, her skin, her nails, even her face. It was more than that. Still worse. She was changing inside herself, down to the bone and blood. She now looked at him differently.

Her new clothes, he was certain, especially the shoes, would do the rest. Even at home, whether in squalor or luxury, it was the feet that made the difference. To a peasant or a worker, or even an officer, the boots came first. Without them, a man could not work or march or ride. When a man's feet were wrapped in rags, as so many were in Russia, he was on the edge of life.

Polyak was certain that these new luxuries, and their associations with her youth, would separate Katerina from him and draw her closer to a different world. As he walked, Viktor reflected that he had worked for four years, from the forests of Siberia to the cobbles of Paris, to transform Katia from a spoiled useless child of the rich into a responsible Soviet citizen, a woman fit to be with him, and able on her own to execute missions for the Cheka. But today, like a butterfly in its final stage, she was changing once again. She was being corrupted by becoming who she once had been.

Instead of seeing herself now as an artificial creature in a temporary costume to be used as a soldier would a uniform, she seemed to think that at last she had become again who she was meant to be.

Both as a Bolshevik and as a man, Viktor Polyak could not accept this, and he would not. At the same time, as he circled the block of the hotel, he recognized that one exciting possibility remained.

If he could find a way still to make her truly useful, then this new butterfly could serve the Cheka, and him, even better than before. He must find a way to control her without inhibiting the usefulness of her transformation, a way to make her retreat impossible.

He stopped near the door of the hotel when the answer came to him. It was a brief thought of Leon that gave him the idea. It was Leon Polyak who controlled her now, not him. That was why he had arranged for the child to be moved to a less elitist facility without her knowledge.

It was little Leon who had made his mother kill in Poland, and who would force her to obey. Trotsky would be proud of his young namesake.

Viktor Polyak hurried upstairs, knowing what he must do, thrilled by his flash of insight: he must encumber her with another child.

Perhaps a little Josef, to bind her hopelessly to him, and to Moscow. That would be more important to her than all the old associations, more important even than her brother. Another child, who also must be a Polyak, not a Karlov.

He undressed quickly without concern for noise. Searching for the water carafe, his groping hand found Katia's jars of ointments. He picked up the three in his hand, cursing as he strode to the open window. He hurled the jars into the night, listening to the sharp crack as each hit the street like a bomb.

Then he lifted the carafe from the bedside table. He rinsed his mouth and gargled as he walked back to the window. He spat across the railing into the night, closed the window, then climbed into bed. He unstrapped his wooden hand and set it on the table before he scratched the stump. Polyak wondered if his aching wound was still infected.

Already aroused, he gripped the woman's shoulder and turned her to him.

"No, Viktor!" Katia protested as she fought to push him off. "Not tonight!"

She raised her knees against him and pressed her legs together. He slapped her hard across the face, first one side, then the other. Her head swung left and right with the blows.

"Suka!" he snarled. "Bitch!"

He took her cheeks in his hand and pinched them fiercely until he forced her lips to pucker. He kissed her on the mouth until at last her lips parted like the resisting halves of some unripe fruit still clinging to the pit.

Her body thrashed like the first night in the forest as she tried to kick off the covers and rise from the bed. He gripped her hair close to her scalp between his fingers and forced her head back against the bed while he drove one knee between her legs and pressed his heavy body down on top of her as she began to sob and pound him with her fists.

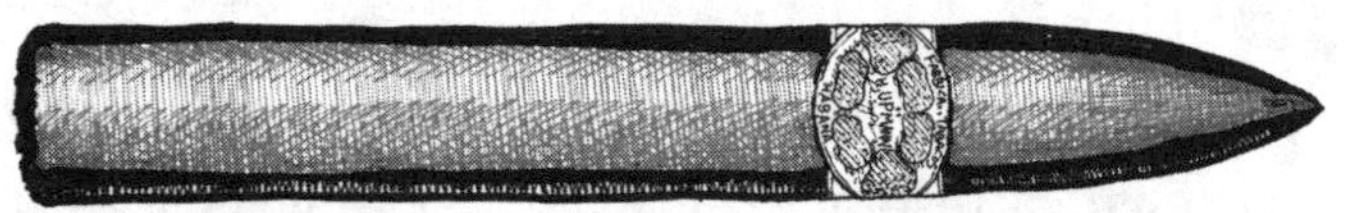

- 9 -

The British colonel waited in line, several places ahead of Viktor Polyak. A tall woman stood close to him, sheltering under the black umbrella that the officer held above them with his good arm. The colonel wore a fitted khaki uniform and four medals. Crisp as a martinet in the English way, the slight man had a long face, a narrow mustache and shiny dark hair. The leather of his belt, shoulder strap and shoes shone like the bright silver metal of his artificial hand. Raindrops rested like crystal beads on the burnished leather of his toecaps.

Like most in line, Polyak carried no umbrella. He stood close against the wall of the Théâtre Gaumont on the boulevard Poissonière with his collar raised and his cap pulled low as he studied the double hook of the colonel's left hand. It was exactly what he required, though made for this smaller man. The upper hook, the larger one, had a smooth rounded end, suitable for pulling or pushing, or holding something down, or bracing oneself on a handrail or overhead railing. The smaller lower hook was less complete in its arc. Its outer edge was narrow, almost knife-like. The hook itself ended in a sharp point. The two hooks were separated by several inches at their extremities and met in a tight narrowing cleft that would be useful for gripping or for wedging things together.

The sophisticated instrument reminded the Commissar of all the advantages that the British and their allies had enjoyed during the years they interfered with the Russian Revolution, from Archangel to the Crimea and Siberia. Modern artillery and machine guns, tanks and ships and aircraft, blankets and winter coats and boots, all the product of their own working masses exploited without success against the Soviet proletariat.

With a new hand like this English one, properly made for his size and needs, he himself would outmatch any man.

Finally the double doors of the cinematograph opened. The line pressed forward into the theatre, divided as usual by class, by the cost of the tickets. The British couple moved to comfortable seats in the center stalls. Viktor Polyak took his place in the second balcony.

The newsreel passed quickly, jerky flickering images visible through the cigarette smoke that clouded up from the orchestra. Scenes from Canada of giant new tractor combines harvesting in line. The launching of the first new English ocean liner since the end of the war. A parade of women in swimming costumes somewhere in the United States. Was this our new world? questioned Viktor Polyak with bitterness. An American adventure comedy followed, with automobile chases, rich lovers kissing and two men fighting with toy racquets across a low net. An old man provided noisy musical accompaniment on a piano in one forward corner of the theatre. Polyak rose and left before the moving picture was finished. He wanted to be waiting outside when the others left.

It was raining harder. The evening had cooled and darkened early. The crowd emerged in a rush, babbling about the film and complaining about the rain. The colonel and his friend were almost the last to leave the theatre. The woman stood against the wall under their umbrella while the Englishman folded his eyeglasses and waited his turn for a taxi at the curb. Polyak cursed when the man succeeded in securing a vehicle. But the officer only held open the door as his companion entered. Then he kissed her pathetically on the cheek and waved as the automobile pulled away.

Polyak followed the colonel as the man crossed the road and walked slowly up the rue Rougemont to the rue Bergère, favoring one leg as he proceeded towards the Folies. The officer stopped at the corner of a small side street and pulled a map from his tunic pocket, managing both umbrella and map with the help of his clever hook. Polyak seized the moment and drew closer. As the colonel held the map to his face under the dim light of a street lamp, the agent struck him from behind with a hard blow of his wooden hand to the man's temple.

The colonel gasped and stumbled. Polyak gripped the shorter man around the throat with his good arm and dragged him into the dark alley.

The Commissar knelt on the man's chest. Strangling him with one hand, he banged the officer's head against the wet pavement until the body was limp.

Still kneeling, Polyak pulled a knife from his pocket and sawed open the colonel's left sleeve from wrist to shoulder, slicing along the flesh in the near darkness as if splitting a sausage. He severed two leather straps with the knife, breaking a third strap when he wrenched the artificial hand from the man's thin forearm.

It suited his requirements. Satisfied, Polyak rinsed the implement in the running rain water of the gutter. Then he stood and placed the still-bloody metal hand inside his leather jacket. As he departed, he snatched up the fallen man's umbrella and hurried back to the rue Bergère.

• • •

"I hope you enjoy Upmanns, sir?" said Alexander as he presented the Inspector-General with a box of his own favorites.

"Splendid, Karlov. I thank you." Arkady Katkoff lifted the cigar box close to his face. He sniffed and ran a thumb along the seal. "How did you know I like torpedoes best of all? Always hold together better. May I offer you an early aperitif?"

"That would be most kind, General." Alexander followed the officer's wheelchair into the small sitting room. He accepted a port and took a chair near the old artilleryman. "I wanted to stop by, sir, and ask your permission to invite your granddaughter to a reception."

That seemed to surprise the old man. "What sort of thing is it?" The general set his monocle and peered at the younger man with a large eye. "I do not recall that we have been invited to anything just recently. We so rarely go out now, you know."

Alexander thought of what he had been contemplating doing with Violetta. "It's a musical evening at the new Polish embassy, sir, on the avenue Kléber." Karlov's invitation had been arranged by Madame Kulikovski.

As Karlov spoke, the general drew a small penknife from his waistcoat. He sliced through the seal and opened the box with slow stiff fingers.

Alexander wondered if his host understood more than he was letting on. "A reception for Marshal Pilsudski, sir, to celebrate the anniversary of the Treaty of Riga, ending the Soviet war with the Poles." Alexander accepted a cigar and the knife when his host extended the box. "Thank you."

"A bit confusing, this Polish question, wouldn't you say, Karlov? Not what I would call a clean campaign. Never is with the Poles, of course." The general did not suspect anything, Alexander reckoned with relief. Instead the older man rolled his torpedo between his fingers and shook his head as Karlov cut off the narrowing tip of his own cigar.

"Never cut off the tip of a torpedo," said the general, taking back his knife before continuing. "It spoils the purpose." He made two long horizontal cuts into his own cigar, one on either side of the tip, each one slanting slightly towards the center. "The tip traps the nasty tobacco juices and stops those little flakes from sticking to one's tongue. The slits breathe for you like the gills of a fish." The old man folded his knife before continuing.

"On the one hand, the Poles defeated the Bolsheviks and stopped that Red plague from spreading this way." He rotated one wheel of his chair and pivoted to face a large map of central Europe pinned to the back of the kitchen door. Like an old soldier's face, the map bore the creases and cracks of a hard life in the field. Notes and arrows were marked in varied inks.

"On the other hand, this treaty cuts us off from Lithuania and moves that Polish frontier east into Russia. Mark you, boy, it's been a long time since the Poles captured Moscow. Sixteen eleven it was, but one never knows." The general leaned forward and moved his forefinger from Warsaw to Borodino before resuming.

"When Napoleon took Moscow two hundred years later, one fifth of his men were Poles. The Polish *Chevaux-Légers* beat back our Cossacks and covered the Corsican's retreat. Oh, they were formidable soldiers. At night, the French sentries wore Polish caps and jackets to frighten off the Cossacks. Even after Napoleon abandoned the army and fled in a sleigh wrapped in his furs like a French tart, the Poles never lost a single regimental flag or field gun during the entire retreat from Moscow. They are always trouble, and damned good in the saddle. Bit mad, of course, too romantic to survive. Used to dye their horses red and white like the Polish flag."

General Katkoff tapped the map with the box of cedar matches that his guest had brought with the long pointed cigars. "Just means we'll need another war to push them back again. No one ever thinks ahead anymore." His long match flared as the general puffed in and out and turned the cigar between his teeth. "Best thing about that Polish victory was that it proved that cavalry still counts, of course, no matter the tanks and trenches. A useful lesson for the next war."

"No doubt, sir." Alexander paused and lit his own torpedo. He returned the subject to his invitation. "This party is really a piano recital. They expect Paderewski, their former prime minister, to play. It will be his first time performing in Paris since he refused to play until Poland was free."

"Free? Poland? Most of it belongs to us. To Russia. Is that man a politician or a piano player?" The general grew agitated. "Chopin, of course. It will be nothing but Chopin. That's all they ever play. Chopin, Chopin, Chopin. The Poles don't know anything else."

"Yes, sir. I . . ."

"I'm afraid Violetta won't be able to manage this reception, Count Karlov." Katkoff hesitated before continuing, gazing down at his leg. "It's a bit awkward, actually."

Alexander believed he understood what was troubling Vita's grandfather. So many of the old Russians, whether in Paris or Shanghai, would rather stay at home than appear shabby or improperly dressed in public. "It is expensive to be a gentleman," Alexander's father used to say, "and sometimes even more costly to be a lady."

"I trust you would not find it presumptuous of me, sir," Alexander offered smoothly, "if I arranged to assist Mademoiselle Violetta with her preparations for the evening. Perhaps a dress and so forth. You would both be doing me an honor if she could accompany me."

"Impossible," muttered the general, puffing vigorously. "No, no. We couldn't hear of it." Smoke clouded his map like a battlefield in the days of black powder.

Alexander had anticipated initial opposition. "I believe my mother always maintained credit accounts with her Paris fournisseurs, sir. She complained that otherwise my father took so long to settle their accounts that they would never serve her as she liked." He paused until the old man smiled. He guessed the general would be sympathetic to his father's reputation for wild extravagance and perpetual debt.

"At Poiret, for example," Alexander lied casually. "I could just draw on some of those old credits, sir. They're no use to me. A dress wouldn't really cost anything at all." Poiret was the only name he could remember. He trusted it was still in fashion.

The general brightened at this news. "Poiret, did you say? Believe I attended one of his parties before the war. Nineteen eleven or so. Persian costumes. The Fête of the One Thousandth and Second Night, I believe Paul Poiret called it. I attended as a sultan. Splendid costume, if I may say so." The officer looked up at last, pleased with young Karlov. "Well, perhaps if you insist . . ."

"No one would ever hear a word about it, sir. And I believe Mademoiselle Violetta has a birthday shortly, so possibly you could permit her to receive a small present in that spirit, General, if that would be agreeable."

Two more fittings, thought Katerina, and the blue silk dress would be perfect for the evening. The pleated skirt suited her slender figure and moved naturally with her body. *Mouvementé*, her mother would have remarked. Paul Poiret's sumptuous work might be more exotic, often inspired by Moscow and the East, Countess Karlov used to say, but for youthful design, for young mothers and their daughters, there was nothing like the Maison Lanvin.

Jeanne Lanvin herself had recalled Countess Karlov with affection.

"Quelle femme charmante, votre mère, Madame la comtesse!" the couturier had said on greeting Katerina, taking both of Katia's hands in her long cool fingers as she studied the younger woman for a resemblance.

"La même taille," Madame Lanvin said approvingly. *"La même ligne."*

From a cedar storage closet her assistant uncovered an unfinished dress that had been partially fitted for Katerina's mother several years earlier. There would be no time to start and finish something new.

"Your mother had wanted one of my new *robes de style,*" Jeanne Lanvin told Katerina, "based on an eighteenth-century design, with this full skirt and small waist. I saved it, for good luck, trusting that one season the countess might return. It will become you! You have such a delicate waist."

Madame Lanvin waved her fingers. The assistant turned the hanger front and back, making the silk swirl, displaying the dress as if it were alive. The couturier inserted a cigarette into a long ivory holder as she continued. "The world is changing, and fashion with it. Today's dresses are less ornamental. The body is made more slender, with *'la ligne haricot vert.'* This gown will suit you."

Katerina stepped behind a curtain, excited to be putting on something of her mother's. Her modest undergarments contrasted with the richness of the dress. When she emerged, Madame Lanvin looked at her through the smoke.

"Now kindly stand still, if you don't mind. We must open the seams and rebuild the dress."

The assistant knelt with pins in her teeth and opened the basting of the hem. Jeanne Lanvin stood at a distance, her narrow chin raised, and murmured instructions and approval. Then the couturier sat against the wall on a small gold chair normally reserved for clients. She watched the Russian girl turn slowly in the full-length mirrors, observing her as she might a professional displaying the latest styles of the house. "You could be a mannequin, my dear, *un modèle*. We have several Russians now."

Katia inspected herself. She was relieved that her long slender legs were freshly waxed. Altogether, *Maman's* dress did indeed become her. She was as excited as a young girl. So many things that she had missed seemed brought together now by her preparations for this one occasion. She was pleased by the figure she saw in the glass, proud of herself, but saddened that the skills and transitions of becoming a young woman had been so accelerated, and that she had been so alone. She had compressed into a few mornings what her old schoolmates would have fussed over for months, with their friends and mothers and sisters and servants sharing in the joyful process.

Katerina Karlov lamented that first she had missed her own youth, and that now she was losing the opportunity to raise her own child. Sometimes she found peculiar comfort in the thought that she herself, a bit like Leon, had been brought up largely by others, though in her case by nannies, servants and a governess.

Though Katia had tried not to think of him, her mind turned to Viktor Polyak. While other girls had flirted and dreamed of romance, she had been habituated to cruelty and rape. In the forest, on the floors of freight cars, in Party hostels and training camps, and in crowded Moscow apartments while others shared the room divided by a curtain hanging from a wire. No one was foolish enough to interfere with the pleasures of the Commissar.

Now Katerina felt that the possibility of her own freedom was opening before her. In Russia, life was a controlled struggle, but elsewhere most of the world was bursting free. She thought of what she had read in *Vogue* as her treatments ripened at the Rumanian spa. The end of the Great War had changed the world, liberating more than fashion.

Everything was quicker, freer, more alive. Airplanes, jazz, the cinema, convertible automobiles, communications, even the League. And most of all, a sense of the emancipation of women. For some women, liberty meant becoming a bit mannish, with short hair, suits with shoulder pads and *"la silhouette androgyne."* Another magazine, *Votre Beauté,* had contained the review of a scandalous new novel said to express it all: *La Garçonne.* Victor Margueritte's heroine smoked in public, cut her hair short and rejected male deceit and control as she lived by her own adventurous morality.

As Katerina stood before the mirror, her body still but her mind racing, a door opened and a young man entered with a large pad and took a seat beside a screen. "Monsieur Iribe," announced Madame Lanvin. "To make a sketch."

The gown was dressy enough for dancing, but sufficiently versatile for less formal occasions, if Katia understood what the magazines were saying about the season's styles. The appropriate shoes, of course, would dress it either up or down, and would make the most of her ankles.

"There are three more things, my dear, required to prepare yourself," said the couturier as the man raised both eyebrows and sketched with confident bold strokes, an unlit cigarette tight in his lips. "*La coiffure, le maquillage* and jewelry. I will write you a note to Antoine and he will give you *une coupe garçonne.* And with those astonishing eyes, you must have *le maquillage perlé.* Today the eyes are everything."

"Perlé?" asked Katerina.

"A slavic touch." Jeanne Lanvin stepped closer to her and took Katerina's chin in her fingertips. "A tiny drop of liquid wax on the tip of each eyelash to make them like a string of pearls. Then a bit of silvery kohl on the lids and a shaded outline around each eye. Yours will be magic." The couturier stepped back, clasped her hands and smiled.

"Have you suitable jewelry, Mademoiselle Karlov?"

"I believe I have," Katerina replied quietly, not saying more. She thought of the emerald she was going to wear. "Diamonds are to help old ladies sparkle, and to make other women envious. They are cold and hard. Pearls are for all ages," her mother used to say while she fastened on her own. "But if you are still young and beautiful, *golubka,* little dove, you need no jewels."

Viktor had shown her the treasure: a single very large stone, a rectangular-cut emerald, in the center of a collar of diamonds set in platinum. Such chokers were more rare than necklaces, and Katerina thought she might have heard of this one once before. Emeralds, Countess Karlov used to say, were evening stones, lush and softer, more passionate and glamorous than sapphires or diamonds. Each emerald carried forever a story inside it, sad or happy, from one woman to the next.

But Katia would have preferred to be wearing her own mother's pearls. She recalled how her mother had been wearing them, hidden beneath the high collar of her travelling dress, when their train had been attacked in Siberia and Viktor had abducted her.

Katerina shuddered at the recollection, and Madame Lanvin glanced at her in concern. Katia smiled weakly to show that it was nothing. Yet the tormenting memory of her family persisted.

Polyak had refused to tell her how her father had been killed, sometime during the end of the Russian civil war. Apparently her mother had died during the fighting on the train. Her brother Alexander, he had told her, lived in China. She guessed it was Shanghai, where she knew Viktor had spent the most time, but it could be Singapore, or perhaps Harbin or Hong Kong.

Since leaving Russia, Katia had found herself thinking more and more of her twin. Within her new surroundings, sometimes she felt that she could merely turn her head, or enter a room, and she would see her brother once again, or hear his voice or laughter. Was Alexander still the same, she wondered, the proud young soldier son of a czarist officer, thinking only of glory and girls, horses and fencing? Or had Sasha, too, adapted to their changed world? Did he understand that Russia had required its Revolution, and that now they must share its future?

For Katerina, this diplomatic party would have a double purpose. It would be the first social event since the flight of her family on the Trans-Siberian in 1918, her first taste of the life she might have had if there had been no Revolution, and no Viktor Polyak. But she knew that behind this elegant facade she would also be exercising a different life, as an instrument of the Cheka, doing for them what Viktor himself could not. That part of it did not disturb Katerina, only that she and her son were not together.

She thought again of her own prospects, and about how to liberate herself from Polyak. She must recover her son, but she suspected that Viktor might have moved Leon without her knowledge, making it impossible for her to find the boy without his assistance.

As long as Viktor was alive, she knew, he would never let her go. Politics, paternity and pride would compel him to fight to keep her. It would not be from love of her or Leon, but from his fear of being defeated, and from a lifetime of resentment for what her family represented, a sentiment that she herself had learned to understand.

For her part, accumulated rage and her hatred for Viktor burned inside her like orange coals in the heart of a furnace. Despite her training by the Bolsheviks, Katerina knew she was still her father's daughter. Gracious and elegant as the old soldier had been, he was known for his ferocity when fighting.

Fortunately Polyak and the Cheka had taught Katerina things that she could now use. Not merely political goals, which she had come to share in part, and not so much clandestine skills, though they had taught her those, but new attitudes: ruthlessness and concentration. They had taught her how to kill without attaching too much to the act, as if distantly, outside oneself. She had thought about that lesson, and how it might now serve her instead of the Bolsheviks. At the same time, Viktor was her child's father, and she did not want Leon to hate her later. One day she would tell her son the truth, and he would understand. In the meantime, she must use her training to free herself of this man.

- 10 -

"Laid end to end," said Madame Kulikovski, raising her voice to reclaim the attention of her clients, "*les égouts*, the sewers of Paris, would reach from here to Istanbul." Her voice echoed off the arching tiled walls. She had not mentioned her husband's death, only closing her eyes and nodding with appreciation when Alexander spoke of him with grateful regard.

"Istanbul?" whispered Violetta Katkoff to Alexander, squeezing his hand. Vita had stolen a day from her employment in the Marais to accompany Karlov on this tour. "What is she talking about?"

Like a gondolier, a sewer guide stood at the back of the flat-bottomed *bateau-vanne*, gripping a pole with long dark gloves, guiding the boat forward with steady swinging strokes and pushes. Alexander found the stench surprisingly mild, but the air was thick with humidity. He was astonished by the broad vaulted ceiling of the tunnel and the paved walkway that ran along the side several feet above them.

A perfect day for this, he thought. A misty rain was settling across Paris, washing the streets and flushing into the drains. "Sometimes after heavy rains," Olga Kulikovski had warned them before they descended the iron stairway, "the sewers rage and flood below the streets, drowning any *égoutier*, any sewerman, who stays below too long."

From time to time they passed an égoutier, patrolling by himself, staring into the black water. Each sewerman was armed with a *rabot*, a heavy seven-foot pole. A large shovel-like blade was attached at the bottom end. Each man wore gloves and hip boots. Alexander recalled the Pole advising him that the sewermen had organized Paris's first union of municipal employees and that most were Communists.

"The sewers were built in the Second Empire," continued Madame Kulikovski. "All planned by the Prefect of the Seine, Baron Haussmann. Until then Paris had cesspools instead of sewers. Pigs ate the garbage in the streets. Rats devoured it below ground. Farmers would sell their produce at Les Halles, then load their carts with *poudrette*, dried human guano, to fertilize their fields. Even today the finest Paris restaurants buy their carrots and cabbages from nearby farms fertilized with the city's sewage."

"What's that?" cried Violetta when something living fell onto her lap from the ceiling. Long as a cigar, swift with its many legs, the nimble creature began to wiggle and dance across her skirt as the girl screamed.

"Ah, a centipede," said Madame Kulikovski as Karlov brushed the active arthropod into the water with a sweeping stroke. "Their fangs are poisonous, of course, but their bites are not as bad as the big spiders, which down here grow larger than your hand." Violetta trembled and peered up at the ceiling.

"In Shanghai, we sauté our centipedes in old pork fat," said Alexander as Olga resumed her lecture. Vita tightened her grip on Karlov's hand.

"Haussmann wanted the sewers to function like the waste system of a healthy human body. Until the Napoleons, most of the sewage was dumped into the streets before being washed into the Seine to mix with the drinking water. '*Tout-à-la-rue*,' the Parisians used to say. That brew gave Paris cholera and the Black Death. Now it's *tout-à-l'égout*."

The boatman leaned against his pole and the vessel turned down a narrower passage to the right, moving swiftly with the current as rainwater poured down through the street grates and cascaded from the feeder tunnels. "Boulevard Raspail" read a blue-and-white enamel sign mounted on a post at the corner of the turn, mirroring the street that ran above the sewer, Alexander guessed.

"All the égoutiers wear those leather hip boots," said Olga Kulikovski as they passed another worker. "Because of the acids and fats in the sewers, the uppers become wonderfully hard and durable. Once the bottoms wear out, the egoutiers sell the uppers to the finest shoemakers, who use them to make stiff arches for the most fashionable ladies ankle boots." She seemed engrossed in her normal tour patter, proud of each repeated detail. "Of course, in cities like Marseilles and Toulon, the sewers are so low and narrow that men cannot do the work. So they train small dogs to drag scrub brushes through the mains."

"Look!" exclaimed Violetta, pressing herself closer against Alexander on the front bench of the vessel. "A rat!"

The powerful rodent swam vigorously along one edge of the sewer, repeatedly turning its head towards the wall with swift alert movements, as if searching for a step up to the walkway. Its long whiskers were spread on the thick dark water like the legs of a large aquatic insect. The creature reminded Alexander of Shanghai. There the rat catchers attracted business by carrying long bamboo poles over their shoulders with the rodents, dead and alive, swinging by their tails from one end and cage traps hanging from the other.

"He's huge," said Violetta. "He looks more like a beaver."

"There are two million of those *gaspards*, one for every citizen of

Paris," said Olga Kulikovski with geniality, as if detailing a gallery at the Louvre. "And they serve the city better than most. The rats consume one half of all the solid waste of Paris. Each sewerman kills one or so a day in his *chasse aux rats*." She adjusted the black ribbon that circled her left arm. "Just like they used to do in the trenches, one told me."

On the walkway just ahead, a big égoutier gripped his rabot in one hand. With the other he awkwardly checked the casing of the *pneumatique*, the great cylindrical tube that was mounted high against the wall below the fresh-water pipes and that carried messages hurtling across the city in short metal capsules.

The man's clumsy effort caught Alexander's attention. He observed that this sewerman wore a glove only on one hand, his left, and that it was not the long dark cuffed glove worn by the other sewer workers and the boatman. The heavy-shouldered man wore no boots.

Karlov yelled a warning to the Pole, knowing she was armed.

As the bateau-vanne approached him, Viktor Polyak turned to face it. He raised the long pole in both hands and swung it violently like a club.

Violetta screamed as Alexander stood to protect her from the blow. Madame Kulikovski fired twice, missing and striking the ceiling as the boat rocked.

The heavy blade knocked aside Alexander's arm and struck him at the base of the neck. Stunned, he fell to the side, collapsing against Violetta as they both fell into the moving water. At the moment he lost consciousness Alexander was aware of the rabot smashing the line of lights as the attacker completed his swing. The tunnel went black as the boat passed on.

Alexander awoke a moment later. He was on his back in the powerful current. The sewer was running even faster than he had thought. Blinded and choking on the filth, he felt an arm hooked around his shoulder, keeping his head above the fluid. He heard two distant gunshots echoing down an adjoining tunnel, then one more. He could not tell if the shots came from one weapon or two.

"It's all right," said Violetta near his ear, pausing to spit as she paddled. "Can you swim?"

"Of course," gasped Alexander, though his neck ached and he felt heavy in his boots and clothes. He could just discern Vita's head as she swam near him in the gloom. He kicked with his good leg and touched the wall of the sewer and stretched up with one arm. He was not able to reach high enough to grasp the edge of the walkway. The shape of the sewer channel, the *chunette*, worked against him, for the lower sides and floor were egg-shaped, to inhibit clogging and speed passage of the sewage, Olga Kulikovski had explained.

"No use to fight the current," he said hoarsely. "We must float along until we find some steps or can reach the parapet."

"As long as we don't get carried into the dredging tunnel where she said that machine sucks up the silt and heavy garbage," Violetta said calmly, spitting again.

Vita seemed to be a strong swimmer, having an easier time of it than Alexander, staying a few yards ahead of him and always near the edge. Karlov collected himself and swam with slow breast strokes, enough for him to keep her pace.

"Here!" she said, pulling herself into a recess of the slimy wall. "A ladder!"

He followed her. The current swirled in the cavity. Several rats swam in circles in each corner of the indentation. Noses raised, their eyes shone brightly above the sheen of the water as they peered about, perhaps resting or waiting for some special food to pass nearby.

Iron rungs were mounted in the center of the recess, rising to form a metal ladder set against the edge of the walkway.

Violetta started to climb, but lost her grip on the first slick rungs and fell back into the water against Alexander. For a moment he held Vita around the waist. Once again, he was in the water with her, fully dressed. But this bath did not smell of violets.

"Let me go first," he said. He climbed slowly, using his arms and dragging his bad leg. Once at the top, he lay on his belly and reached down with both hands. He seized her wrists and pulled Violetta up until her feet were clear of the slippery wet rungs. She collapsed on her knees beside him. Her blond hair was dark with filth. Her chest was pumping for air. Alexander noticed her wet blouse was molded tight to her body.

"You're so strong," she said after a moment. "Are you all right?"

He felt a swollen lump on his neck but could not tell if he was bleeding.

"And you're such a good swimmer," he said, thinking about the gunshots and hoping Madame Kulikovski had not been wounded. "Thank you for holding me up."

"I always swam in the sea at Sochi," said Vita, sitting back against the arching tunnel wall.

"Why did that man attack us back there?"

"I'm not sure," said Alexander, though he knew too well. The Commissar had already killed two men in Paris while hunting him. Alexander felt the guilt of his responsibility. He must be more on his guard and find a way to end this.

- 11 -

The black piano bench was empty. The magnificent Pleyel grand waited nearby, its ivory keys still protected by their folding cover.

The Polish embassy's reception rooms at 11 avenue Kléber were already crowded with thirsty friends of Poland, hundreds of them, a few old, most new. Framed by the high ceilings and deep gilt moldings and rich red curtains, all were at their best display. The dress uniforms and evening clothes, jewels and decorations, and the elegant fashions of the rue de la Paix and the rue St. Honoré suited the spacious legation. Guests drank and gossiped. Heavy ladies in concealing garments disparaged younger beauties.

"Where were all these friends when Poland needed their help? When we alone defended Europe against the Soviets like the Spartans at Thermopylae?" asked a colonel of Uhlans. The silver braid and rigid collar of his blue tunic reached almost to his single ear. "When our carbines were empty, my wounded were lying on farm carts and potatoes were being sold like pearls on the streets of Warsaw?" He took a fresh glass from a passing waiter. "First we gave these people our blood," he observed. "Now we give them our champagne."

"Lloyd George always prevaricated," said the officer's companion, a white-haired bishop. "One day this, one day that, but these French were still worse."

"Each day they promised us more, weapons and supplies, diplomacy and medicines." The colonel did not bother to lower his voice. "My regiment waited with empty rifles and no boots at the station in Lvov for the supply trains that never arrived from Paris and Strasbourg. Scarcely a bandage or a bullet came from France until we sent the Bolsheviks galloping home."

"Of course," nodded the cleric. "Now the French want us to help them face Lenin and the Huns, to be the outpost of Christian Europe."

The colonel did not reply. He was staring at a young beauty who had appeared across the room.

Violetta Katkoff, her shoulders bare, stood near the doorway, as inviting as a freshly peeled peach. One hand rested on Alexander's arm. The other held a glass of champagne. Her face had the clear rosy freshness of a girl with no makeup, though that was not the case. Men pretended not to stare at her figure as they passed. Ever since he called for her, Alexander's eye had been drawn to the fine blue veins of her chest. Her dress was just what he had hoped.

"She will not look like that in twenty years," said one French lady to another. "That sort never ages well."

"All the same," said her companion, "she must have a generous admirer. That dress comes from Vionnet or Poiret."

"Poiret, of course. No wonder he's out of date. Tight skirt and almost no top. His parents were cloth merchants near Les Halles. What would you expect?"

"You know what that man said: 'I have freed the breasts and shackled the legs.' Just look at her."

Only Marshal Pilsudski seemed to gather more attention.

Lean, sharp-faced, the father of the new Poland accepted the recognition in the drawing room that he had earned on the battlefield. He wore a trim simple uniform with no medals. His pale skin and long drooping mustache reminded Alexander of a mandarin. But his steely, clipped and razored hair was of the Prussian school. His deep-set blue eyes were fierce and unblinking like those of a high-soaring bird of prey. Alexander admired the confident hard resolution that must have sustained Jozef Pilsudski through five years of Siberian exile and long campaigns on the Eastern Front during the Great War. His commanding look reminded Alexander of his own father, but without the same spark of *joie de vivre*.

"*Messieurs, mesdames,*" called a major domo, clapping his hands like gunshots. "Monsieur Paderewski will play."

Two hundred guests squeezed into the principal reception room. Most of the small gold chairs, arrayed in tight rows, were already taken. The eager guests gazed up at a long mural mounted on the wall to the right of the piano.

As Madame Kulikovski had recounted, the painting depicted the Hussaria, Poland's seventeenth-century "winged cavalry," who had cut down Swedish and Russian invaders and butchered German and Scottish mercenaries. Each horseman carried an eighteen-foot lance, a six-foot rapier, two pistols, a carbine, a small bow and a *czeken*, a long steel hammer designed to crush helmets. Attached to the back of each rider were two lines of black eagle feathers mounted on tall wooden frames.

Alexander found Violetta a seat at the end of a row. He stood beside her, leaning against the wall and facing the entrance door across the large room. Several women sought to catch his eye, but when Vita raised up one hand, he took her fingers and they smiled at each other. Perhaps this evening, he thought. At last. In Shanghai, it had seemed easier to conclude this sort of thing. But Lily, after all, was a working girl who had no choice, though he believed she truly had liked him for himself. Alexander abandoned his effort not to look down the front of Vita's dress. He understood that for her, this was not a party, but a stage.

He studied the faces and uniforms of the guests as they collected around the walls and clustered in the doorways. He recognized several from the dinner of the Corps des Pages, men who thought of Poland as a Russian province. Most of these wore in their buttonholes the Corps' small rosette of a Maltese Cross. The White Russians were drinking to the Miracle on the Vistula not as a victory for the Poles, but as a defeat for the Bolsheviks.

At the end of the room, Ignace Paderewski flipped the ends of his tailcoat over the piano bench and sat down. The rack before him held no music. He stared briefly at Poland's winged cavalry as he stretched his fingers. The long grey hair that swept back from the maestro's high forehead contrasted with his thick dark mustache and the bushy patch of hair beneath the center of his lips. Paderewski nodded towards the guests. He flexed his long fingers above the keyboard like the wings of a bird in flight.

It was the moment for which Europe's greatest pianist and his nation had waited.

Alexander Karlov had never known so many people to be so silent.

He took advantage of the quiet to take a telegram from his pocket. Madame Lafarge had handed it to him as he and Violetta left the rue Bonaparte that evening. He was certain the old concierge had read it herself, then resealed it as carefully as she would count each morsel of goose in her *cassoulet*. He unfolded the horizontal grey paper and read the message for the third time:

> MAUVAISES NOUVELLES STOP YOUR
> ESTEEMED PARTNER MR HAK LEE IS IN
> AMERICAN HOSPITAL STOP COLLAPSED AT

YOUR CASINO STOP HE SUSPECTS OLD
ENEMIES STOP HE SAYS YOU ARE HIS SON
AND YOU MUST RETURN AT ONCE TO
SHANGHAI STOP HE AND YOUR BUSINESS
NEED YOU URGENTLY STOP MILLES AMITIES
MEI-LAN WONG

Karlov folded the message and slipped it into his pocket as Paderewski played the opening notes. He recalled Mr. Hak Lee assisting with his father's debts, with the Salle d'Armes, with the races and, most of all, in the hunt for his father's killer. "My friends are your friends," Hak Lee once had told Alexander. There had been no need to state the corollary. Alexander reflected that any enemy of Mr. Hak Lee must be formidable indeed to have survived in Shanghai.

Frederick Chopin soon filled the room as if he himself were playing for Poland. A concerto, a mazurka and a nocturne. Paderewski played alone, but it did not seem so.

Alexander was absorbed, astonished by the romantic power of the music that seized the senses. He thought of his mother, her head gracefully swaying from side to side as she played Mozart during long winter evenings at Voskrenoye, while his father and friends from neighboring estates smoked like steam engines and drank pear brandy over whist and backgammon.

The audience applauded after each piece, then became instantly silent as the maestro began "La Polonaise."

Passion flooded from the piano like a charge of the Hussaria, long lances lowered, red silken pennants flying as the winged horsemen of Poland cut through a century of enemies. A few more minutes, thought Alexander, and we will all be Polish. He glanced around the room at the faces of a score of nations, all captured by a single instrument. He saw a colonel with one ear, standing like a guardsman as tears slipped down his cheeks. The officer was not crying alone.

Alexander noticed two men in white tie step back from a doorway to permit a striking young woman to pass between them.

The music seemed to rise as she entered. She was very slender. Not beautiful, but tall and gracefully erect in a blue silk dress. Her short dark hair, sculpted tight to her head like a film star's, almost touched her straight eyebrows and ended in two love curls at the line of her lips. Her long straight nose and darkened lids enlarged and dramatized her eyes. Her only jewelry was one magnificent green stone worn high on her neck. She reminded Alexander of a portrait of his own mother, though her nose was far more prominent. The young lady turned her head and glanced around the room until her varied eyes caught his.

Alexander felt his heart stop. He was unable to think or move or speak. It was Katia, his twin, his sister, his other self.

The piano rose in a crescendo, then quietened and finally soared again until it seemed to crash all around them. The audience rose. All the company roared and cried out as Paderewski stood and twice bowed stiffly from the waist. The room shook as if the walls themselves were cheering. The maestro's face and eyes were wet.

In the meantime Alexander pushed his way to a nearby door. He circled around through two anterooms until he came to the doorway where his sister had stood. At first he feared he had lost her again.

Then Katerina appeared before him, as if presenting herself, trembling, her lips tight, tears flooding, but her chin high.

"Katia," he said, his own eyes moist.

He put his arms around his twin and clasped her as the crowd hailed Paderewski.

"Sasha!" she whispered into his ear, her body shaking. "Oh Sasha, can it be you at last?"

Katerina leaned back, holding both his arms, regarding him bit by bit, as she might a fine painting she had just discovered. "What has happened to your leg? Isn't that grandfather's cane?"

"Katia," he said quietly, taking her in his arms again. After a moment he took his sister by one hand and led her to the furthest reception room. They sat together on a small sofa as the piano resumed, a gentler Chopin. "*Une Étude*," she said, staring hungrily at the extravagant buffet.

They accepted champagne, and talked and whispered until the music stopped. The Trans-Siberian, the loss of their mother and father, Moscow and Shanghai, bad and good. She told him briefly of a hard life struggling to survive in a Russia of misery and conflict. It reminded him that while he had shared a year or more with his father in Vladivostok and Shanghai, Katia had been alone.

"How did Maman die?" she asked. "Tell me, Sasha."

"She was killed on the train," he said gently, taking her hand. "By the same Red who kidnapped you. He broke her neck and stole her pearls."

Katerina's hand went cold in his. Her other went to her throat, covering the emerald. She thought of Viktor's instructions for this party: identify the Russians we must kill. She glanced around the room, searching for some escape, needing to speak and think of something else. She found it in the opulence.

"How can they waste so much food?" said Katerina after a moment, sharpness in her voice as she stared at the unfinished plates.

He shrugged, wanting to tell her more about Shanghai and what her father and brother had built there.

As she spoke, a guest left a plate of barely-touched asparagus and cold tenderloin on the low table before them.

"How disgusting," Katerina said harshly. "Don't they know how many hungry people there are outside in the streets?"

"I'm sure they do," said Alexander, not certain why Katia was so disturbed by this when they were speaking of their mother. He had known hunger in Siberia and on the icebreaker. But in Shanghai the food had seemed inexhaustible and the poverty of most Chinese had made one feel rich again.

"That is why the world needs revolution, Sasha." She regarded her brother, wanting to see if he had learned anything in the four years since their world had disappeared. "It's our fault. People like us. Don't you see? All of Russia is hungry."

This sounded like Bolshevik cant. He finished his glass and put it down without replying. He did not wish to speak his mind if it meant losing the sister he had just found. He put off asking her how she had obtained such a dress and such a necklace.

"In the Ukraine and on the Don, children are still starving." Her voice rose. "They gather in packs like dogs in the villages begging from strangers and passing trains."

Alexander forced himself to speak calmly. She was blaming their family for the suffering of their country.

"That is the work of the Bolsheviks."

He saw Katia's face harden as she, too, suppressed an answer. Even when she was young she usually made the right point in the wrong way, often confusing compassion with judgment. She had not changed, except to extend her convictions to extremes. Could she be one of them? he wondered.

"Until the Reds came," he added quietly, "our Russia was known as the breadbasket of Europe."

"Yes, because while the peasants starved, grain speculators used to buy the rye from landowners like us and ship it all to Königsberg."

Her brother did not reply. He recalled the whispered tales of hungry peasants being driven off by Cossacks as they threw stones at trains loaded with grain vanishing towards Germany.

"Why do you think they were eating 'famine bread?' " she continued fiercely. "*Golodnyi khleh*, flour mixed with goosefoot weeds. It gave them all diarrhea and made the children vomit. In one year, four hundred thousand died in a single famine."

Alexander rose abruptly to get them each a drink. While he was gone, he hoped she would steady down and become his sister once again.

When he returned, Katerina said nothing of Leon, or of Viktor Polyak, or of her commitment to the Cheka, and Alexander did not recount the cruel details of their father's death by the Bolshevik Commissar, nor of the murderous hunt now under way in Paris. Both knew there was so much more to say. Even as they spoke of less disturbing things, there seemed a shade of distance in her, a sense that he could not identify.

Dressed in modest black, still grieving for her spouse, Olga Kulikovski came up to them.

"Madame Kulikovski," said Alexander, rising, disturbed that her husband had died trying to find his twin, "may I present my sister, Katerina."

"I knew it was you, child," said the older lady, her pleasure evident. "By your eyes, and your strong high nose. No one has eyes like the Karlov twins. You cannot know how your brother has yearned for you. He has crossed the earth to find you."

Alexander was grateful to have someone else say it for him.

As Olga Kulikovski introduced his sister and him to a passing Polish world of priests and diplomats, colorfully dressed officers and widows in black, Alexander noticed a gaunt elderly woman standing by herself, watching them with sharp concentrated eyes.

When the three were alone for a moment, the old woman approached with slow careful steps, leaning on a lacquered cane as black as Alexander's, but with a rubber tip. Her white hair was sparse, her thin shoulders hunched. Her black lace dress was of a timeless prewar elegance. She stopped before them, resting from the effort of her approach and attempting to straighten her arched back. The lady planted her cane before her and leaned on it with both hands. She drew breath before speaking.

"Mademoiselle," she said to Katerina in a quiet firm voice. "I am Lyuba Malakov. *Où avez vous trouvé ce bijou?* You are wearing the necklace of my sister, the Countess Leptinskaya."

At that moment General Vashkov joined them, first with a smile, then in silence as he understood that there was some difficulty. Alexander had not seen his father's old friend since the dinner of the Corps des Pages.

"What do you believe you are wearing, mademoiselle? Some gypsy bauble from the open mining pits of Egypt?" The old woman's cane tapped the floor. Her powdered cheeks hollowed. She began to shake. General Vashkov touched Madame Malakov's elbow with concern as she continued.

"This stone is an Inca treasure from the secret mine of Muzo in Colombia. Spanish conquistadores brought it to Madrid before the year sixteen hundred. Finally it came to St. Petersburg."

Instinctively, Katerina covered the green stone with the palm of her hand, protecting the treasure as she felt its power. She was aware of Sasha eying her intently. Her color heightened as she opened her mouth but could not speak.

"Madame," intervened Alexander. "Permit me to introduce myself. I am Alexander Karlov, and this is my . . ."

"I knew your mother and your father," said the woman without taking her eyes from Katerina's throat. "If you doubt what I say, have the emerald weighed. It is thirty-three and one half carats."

Two elderly officers, champagne in hand, joined them and stood beside General Vashkov. Both wore the Order of St. George. Violetta appeared nearby, her face flushed and her lips tight as she stared at Alexander and Katerina before walking to him and taking his arm. Vita started to whisper to him, then was silent as she became aware of the drama she had joined.

"That necklace is not yours to wear," the old woman said, loud enough for all to hear. "It can never become you. That emerald was stolen by the Cheka when they murdered Count Leptinskaya and arrested my sister." Her voice grew unbearably tight. "The life of my family is in that stone."

General Vashkov nodded as she spoke. "Madame Malakov, I knew your sister well," he said, bowing. He looked at Alexander and raised his eyebrows with expectation. Both men knew that everywhere in Paris the treasures of their countrymen were for sale, some by emigrées, others by the Reds.

Alexander watched Katerina's face pass from red to white. She offered no words of explanation. He thought his sister would collapse from the mortification. She must be part of some Bolshevik scheme and she had been unmasked. Who had provided this treasure and sent her to this reception?

Still without speaking, Katerina stepped close to her brother, then turned her back to him and lowered her chin to her chest.

Certain of her wish, relieved by her swift decision, Alexander raised his hands to the back of Katia's neck. He unfastened the clasp that held the emerald and diamond collar, then unhooked the tiny gold chain that secured it on the inside. The emerald fell into his sister's hand.

Katerina Karlov raised her chin high, then turned and handed the necklace to the elderly woman.

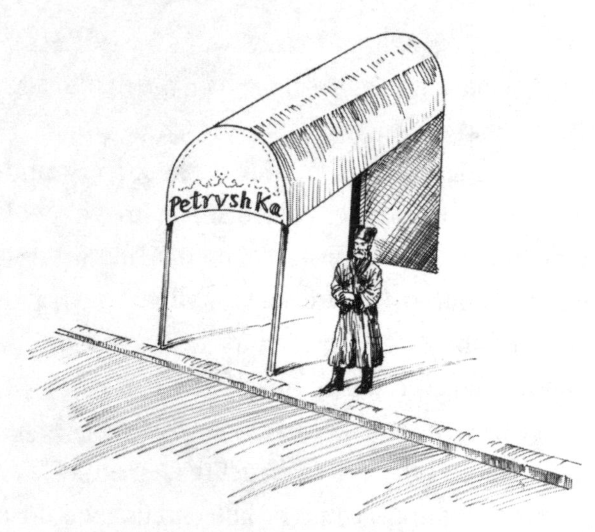

- 12 -

"Excuse me, Vita," said Alexander urgently, turning aside and following his sister into the hall.

"I must talk to you, Katerina," he said, taking her elbow firmly.

"Let me go, Alexander." She freed herself with a sharp movement. Her jaw was tight but she did not permit herself to cry.

"How did all this happen, Katia?" He struggled to lower his voice. "You disgraced us. Where did you get that emerald, this dress?"

Katerina seemed to harden as he spoke, her composure restored, the humiliation suppressed. "How do you think I have managed all this time, Sasha?" she hissed. "How can you know what my life has been? Didn't you and Father do terrible things to survive?"

"We did not steal from other families." Alexander spoke slowly, each word firm and clear. "We did not betray who we were." He ignored the glances of other guests passing down the hall, the first to leave. "I asked you where you got that stone."

"I have a child in Moscow, Sasha, your nephew. The grandson of our parents." She looked in her brother's astonished eyes without blinking. "I am doing everything I must to protect him. It is all part of that." Katerina shrugged. "And anyway, the wreckage of all that old privilege means nothing. Who cares about the estates and the houses and the jewelry? Who do you know who ever earned any of it?"

"Father and I earned every sou I have today." He paused and spoke to her in a low slow voice. "Where did you get that emerald?"

"You don't know anything. I could be killed tonight because I lost that stone. Now I have nowhere to go."

Alexander paused, relenting. He must not lose her again. This was more than an argument. His sister needed sanctuary from whoever had made her wear that necklace.

"We will go somewhere and talk," he said more calmly. "And I have a safe place where you can stay."

Madame Kulikovski stood nearby, explaining to Violetta that this was Alexander's sister, not a rival or a film star. "I understand," said the girl, her resentment softening. She accepted the smile of an elegant Polish officer but waited for Alexander. He stepped to Violetta and took her hand. He whispered to her until she appeared to accept what he wished to do. Her hair brushed his cheek while they spoke and she hunched her bare shoulders forward to hold his attention.

"Madame Kulikovski," he said, "would you be so kind as to assist Mademoiselle Katkoff to the rue Bonaparte, so that I may take my sister for a drink?" The general would whip me, he thought, if I permitted his daughter to journey home alone. The old soldier might disregard mischief, but never discourtesy. He did not even know about the violent misadventure in the sewer. "I will tell Papa that our rowboat overturned in the Bois," Vita had said after that experience.

"I will escort Mademoiselle Katkoff home with pleasure," replied the Pole, before adding more quietly: "Be careful tonight, young Count. Tomorrow morning I will find a man to guard your sister." She touched her fingers to her neck, indicating the mysterious emerald. "He will come to you at your café."

In half an hour, Katerina and Alexander stepped down from a taxi and were received by two doormen at the canopied entrance to the nightclub Petrushka. Both men were red-bearded and wore the high soft boots, crossed bandoliers and braided caps of Don Cossacks in service to the czar. The pair reminded Karlov of Shanghai. There many such horsemen found employment as guards and doormen at restaurants and casinos, hotels and bordellos. Loyalty and ferocity were their strengths, alcohol and idleness their ruin.

Alexander requested a quiet table at the back. He ordered a bottle of Charles Heidsieck, resolved still to celebrate the reunion with his sister. For a long moment he sat at the table and looked at his twin without speaking, searching her face for something that he had not yet found.

"To Mother and Father." He lifted his champagne.

"And to Voskrenoye," she replied. They touched glasses, both knowing how happy their parents would have been that at last they were together. "Papa's champagne," she observed.

Katia matched him glass for glass as they talked. She seemed to have the family gift for drink. Or was it a Russian inclination? Perhaps the only one shared by both Whites and Bolsheviks.

"Please tell me everything, Katia," he asked, touching her hand. She began to do so, but spared him what she had done in Poland, and the full extent of her new political beliefs. Alexander drank and refilled their glasses as he listened, trying to understand what her life had been. He thought of her words at the embassy party and told himself not to make things worse. He suspected the drinks would add to both the candor and the intensity of their differences.

Finally Katerina spoke to him of Leon, and of Polyak, though not completely. How could she tell him that this brutal commissar was the father of her child? She explained that the emerald was to be sold, like so many other things, for the benefit of Russia. She had no notion whose it once had been, nor did she care. "I would do more than that for either my son or my country," she said, as if testing him.

Katia could soon tell that her brother's own convictions had changed little. His attachment to their family was inseparable from his hatred for the Soviets and his scorn for their system. Like their father, he would never have been a Decembrist, let alone a Red.

A Gypsy violinist roamed the room. The music was light but quick and powerful as the small man in boots, an embroidered vest and a bandana played for tips. The violinist settled near the table beside theirs. There a party of five men were drinking short glasses of vodka from two bottles set in an ice bucket. One nodded at Alexander as he raised his glass and smiled through the thick smoke.

"We could be in Shanghai," said Alexander as the man called for another song of longing and lost love. He remembered evenings at the Salle d'Armes when his father shared everything they possessed with fellow refugees and his Hussars sang and drank until there was no more night or drink.

"These old soldiers want to hear the songs of their camp fires," said Alexander with affectionate understanding. He knew the legend. When the songs began, the shadows of lost friends would join them at the fires one by one. "Every regiment loved it when the Gypsy musicians came to camp." Not to mention the Gypsy girls, he thought, famously sultry, thieving and obliging.

Katia did not share the fondness. "These are the sort of men who bled Russia for four years, Sasha, fighting the Revolution instead of building a new country. Can't you understand?"

So she did believe all that Leninist propaganda. He felt anger and alcohol mixing in his blood. If she were a man or not his sister, he would either fight or rise and leave the table.

"Like these men," he said severely, reminding her, "Papa was fighting for Russia, Katerina, and for our family."

"Poor Papa never understood," she replied, dismissing the idea. "All he cared about was horses and the czar."

Alexander sat back and stared at his sister without speaking. She had not told him everything. Whose child was it? Had she participated in the scheme to steal the emerald? His suspicion worsened as he thought about it. Why had she gone to the party?

The music changed. Four Cossacks in long jackets with bullet loops across their chests set their sabres in a square in the center of the dance floor.

"Who do you think we are, Katerina Karlov? Who do you think killed our parents?"

She had already answered this question for herself.

"Injustice made the Revolution, Sasha, and the Revolution killed our parents."

"You make it so remote." He stared at her and rubbed his eyes. "Both Mother and Father were murdered. And the same Red butcher may now want to kill us both, unless I kill him first."

"You are right about Viktor Polyak, Sasha, but you understand nothing about Russia and the Revolution."

The dancers slapped their gleaming boots as they leaped and roared. The audience began to stamp and clap, overwhelming any conversation.

Alexander tapped his good foot, after a time aware that the music had spared him words that would have changed nothing and spoiled everything. His father would have fought any man who insulted the czar. But he would have told Alexander to ignore Katia's foolishness, to remember only who she was and that she was a girl, his own rule whenever his wife began such nonsense.

"Katerina," said Alexander later. "In eight days the *China Star* sails from Marseilles for Shanghai. She is a British Royal Mail steamer, a passenger freighter, well-appointed, and calls at Egypt, Bombay, Goa and Ceylon on her way to Shanghai."

The music changed. The dance songs of America replaced the wild music of the steppes.

"I must sail back on her, and I cannot leave you here to be murdered, too. You must come with me, Katia, and see why Papa and I stayed in Shanghai, and what we have done there." He touched her hand. "We will have time to talk on the boat. Please."

Instead of answering, she asked, "Do you dance, Sasha?" Katerina took her small evening purse in one hand and began to rise. She thought she would be the only lady carrying a pistol to the dance floor.

They stood and people looked at them as they danced. Despite her evident affection, Alexander could feel the stiffness in his sister's body.

"Send a bottle of your finest vodka to the next table with my compliments, if you please," he said to the sommelier before they left Petrushka.

The next morning, as he smelled the fresh warm croissants and sipped the frothy coffee, Alexander realized how much he would miss Paris. By now he understood why all the old Russians had loved this city so. His corner brasserie had become a refuge and a club. There he never felt lonely, yet always private.

"*Voilà, mon petit.*" The proprietress set down his butter curls and apricot jam without being asked. Today he had taken not his corner table, but a seat where he could watch the doorway to his residence. Whoever had sent Katerina to the party might have followed them home last night.

He thought of Katia, still asleep in his downstairs flat. In many ways she seemed the same. In his heart, however, he knew that his twin had changed too much. Politics had replaced family. He was not certain how much they still shared, how much they remained truly twins. He had gone off to the Corps des Pages at thirteen. There loyalty to czarist Russia was the first and final lesson. It was in their evening hymns and in the portraits on the walls above their cots. But Katia had been tutored in the library at home, curled up with *Emile* and *Du Contrat Social*, in the evenings reading aloud in French from their great-grandmother's diaries written during her Decembrist exile in Siberia. Following that gracious introduction to revolution, his sister had experienced nothing but four years of brutality and Bolshevism.

Was it more than just those years of hardship, and missing her child, or was there something deeper, some change in her heart or character that made Katia seem truly different? Was it possible that she could be attached to this man who was their enemy? Even when speaking of young Leon, Katia did not seem to miss the boy as another mother might, though Alexander could imagine why. Could Viktor Polyak be the father? He himself had some difficulty in regarding such a child as his nephew. Katerina seemed now to have some of their father's battlefield hardness, but without his sentimentality, and certainly without his devotion to the past.

He thought of the old count's demeanor when he had returned home in 1915, wounded for the second time in the German war. For several days he had barely spoken. Then one evening, after sending Alexander back to the cellar for another bottle of his favorite claret, Major Karlov had asked his son to join him by the fire and had spoken to him about the war.

"We used up our men, our farm boys, the way the Germans used up steel," he said finally, offering Alexander the last of the Beycheville. "One day they will not stand for it."

Alexander's coffee grew cold as he thought of how correct his father was.

"Good morning, sir," interrupted a thick-set man in a frayed dark suit with the overly short wide-shouldered jacket favored by the French of all classes. "Count Karlov?"

Alexander nodded and folded his newspaper as the man snapped a quick salute. "Igor Norodsky at your service, sir. Formerly training sergeant of the Grand Duke Boris's Hussars."

"Coffee?" said Alexander, noticing Norodsky was staring at the croissants and rolls stacked on a tray at the zinc bar. A pyramid of hard-boiled eggs rested on a nearby platter. "Perhaps a *brioche*, or an egg, Sergeant?"

"If you don't mind, sir." The man sat down on the front edge of the wicker chair, his back still straight. "Madame Kulikovsky tells me your sister requires a bodyguard."

"Quite right,"said Karlov, setting down his copy of *Matin*. "You must watch for one man, an assassin of the Cheka." Alexander glanced about the restaurant. "My family, and many others, will not have peace until this man is dead. His left hand is wooden. His head is shaved. His name changes, though often it is Viktor Polyak. He is tall and powerfully built and dangerous. Are you armed?"

The sergeant nodded and held up both his hands, showing them front and back. He patted the right side of his jacket near his hip. "As long as it is not too public, sir, these French police seem content to leave it to us to kill the Soviet agents. *Ratissage Russe*, they call it. Russian laundry."

Norodsky poured salt on a small plate and cracked two eggs on the edge of the table. "Your Chekist will not be my first."

"I would prefer to do this myself," said Alexander, "and I will attempt to do that. But if you have the opportunity, Sergeant, you must do it." He passed the man an envelope. "If you kill him quietly, the French police will not trouble you, and an unknown friend will reward you well."

- 13 -

"Is the new hand ready?" asked Viktor Polyak without taking off his cap. Even to him, his voice sounded loud and angry in Dr. Grillard's small windowless anteroom. After rinsing the metal hand again in the washroom of a bistro, he had brought it here to have it copied for a larger man, paying extra for immediate work.

The tired-eyed receptionist scratched the hedge of pale hairs above her upper lip and shuffled a file of papers as if not wishing to respond at his direction. While he awaited her reply, the Commissar considered all that he must do.

He was still enraged by the failure of Katerina Karlov to return to the hotel after the party. He had barely eaten the next day, though he had drunk enough. However it must be done, he would recover the precious stone she had stolen. More than that, he must kill Karlov and return Katia to Moscow, or to one of the new camps for more rigorous re-education. The difficulty would be to recover the emerald before the two escaped from Paris.

The Androv brothers might be useful. They were unknown to Alexander Karlov and his sister, and better trained than Polyak himself at disguise, surveillance and other refinements of the Cheka.

While Polyak had been working in China fomenting revolution for the Comintern, the brothers had been students of the political secret police in Moscow. After his years in prison, first in hard labor for the czar, later as an interrogator for the Bolsheviks, Oskar Androv, the bigger younger one, had a grave-like demeanor that even Polyak found dispiriting. The conditions in Oskar's work camp had been one of the few stable factors during the long confusion of the civil war. During the first year under the Soviets, before his brother, Todor, had arranged for his freedom, Oskar Androv had survived by serving as a "presser." These favored prisoners were dedicated to reforming uncooperative anti-socials by punishing them in pressing huts where the resisters were raped and beaten until they were forever broken.

For several days the Androv brothers had taken turns following Karlov around Paris. Oskar was obliged to do so at a distance, due to his striking prison tattoos. It was Todor Androv who had spotted the Karlovs leaving the Polish party together.

The Commissar had realized that the embassy party might revive Katia's sense of privilege and superiority. He had sat waiting on the window sill of their hotel room for hours with his back against the frame. Painted and powdered like a Chinese whore, everything paid for by the Cheka, she must be dancing with some precious peacock. Polyak waited with increasing anger, staring out over the yellow foggy glow of nighttime Paris. He drank from the bottle as he contemplated how he would tear the costly dress from her back and remind her who and whose she now was. As the first morning light brightened the sooty copper ribs of the rooftops, Polyak had realized that Katia was not coming back, that she had re-entered her old world. Abandoned and betrayed, he had pitched the empty bottle across the street and flung himself on the bed with his wooden hand still attached.

"You have been so urgent, Monsieur Marinsky, but your instrument is ready," replied the physician's receptionist finally. "First we must wait for Dr. Grillard. He will decide if adjustments are required. At the moment, he is fitting a difficult prosthesis. The war still keeps us busy." Her left eye appeared to wander away from the right one while she regarded Polyak, as if the eye itself did not wish to look at him.

"If you are rushed, you may settle the account while you wait." She pushed a folded sheet of paper towards him, perhaps seeking to avoid the contact of handing it to him directly.

Polyak stared at her without replying. In the new Russia, medical attention would cost nothing. In a different situation, he would respond by reaching across this woman's desk and seizing her throat in his right hand, strangling her as he hauled the witch towards him across the narrow desk, then cracking her neck and dropping the body on the floor. For several years the rough justice of revolution had permitted him to work freely at his best.

But in Paris the Commissar knew better than to complicate his situation. He already feared that his connection with the Androvs could be the link that would endanger him. One more incident might be all the police required. "It is time we left Paris. We have all been too busy here," the small smart Androv brother had said the previous day after finishing his turn following Karlov. "But first we should leave your spoiled young friend floating in the Seine," said Todor. "He lives as if nothing has changed, as if we have made no revolution, as if he is still a count and we still are nothing. Parties, restaurants, an apartment of his own, presents for women, the best clothes." Just like his damned father, thought Polyak.

To make trouble over payment at the doctor's office would attract police attention. It would be best to kill Karlov outside Paris.

The Russian unfolded the paper and looked at the outrage: a fortune for a monstrosity of wood and metal and leather. All of this caused by the brother of the woman who had now abandoned him. At least the money was not his own. Polyak took satisfaction that it came from selling jewels liberated from women who fancied themselves of a superior class. It was they who were the thieves. And this French receptionist with the mustache was little better.

"I will pay when everything is finished," he replied at last, wondering what other deformities had received the attention of this hen.

A door opened at the end of a short corridor. At first no one appeared. Then a tall thin-shouldered man advanced into the waiting room with sideways jerking steps, like an awkward child playing some game of balance. He leaned on a cane as his body pivoted from side to side. Several medals were pinned to his faded blue jacket. His right leg appeared to be his own. His left was stiff until he swung his weight above it. Then the leg moved as if misdirected, somehow hinged in the wrong place and wanting to go off uncertainly on its own.

What will this Dr. Grillard have done for me? thought Polyak. The capitalist war had created a bonanza of horrific medical specialities. Lungs and limbs, mind and skin, all were ravaged, yet had become financial opportunities for certain bourgeois vultures. Referred here by the sewermen's union, promised that the service would be speedy and economic and discreet, the Commissar was not overly concerned for himself. This substitute hand, after all, would be something that he could accept or decline or replace.

He was tired of the rough wooden hand that had been fashioned for him at the busy hospital manufactory in Moscow where carpenters collected from the villages were replacing the human works of nature. The hand was clumsy as a weapon and of little use for anything else. Now he was waiting like a rich child eager for his birthday gift: a double metal hook mounted on a wood-and-leather cup that would strap onto the stump of his wrist in a harness secured above the elbow. Viktor Polyak had never in his life been so eager for anything material.

The Russian watched the limping veteran, his face white, collect an envelope from the receptionist, then slowly make his way to the door. No one made any effort to assist the old soldier as he leaned against the wall and opened the door with his free hand. The man swung through the door and left it open behind him.

"Monsieur Marinsky," said Dr. Grillard in a high voice as the uneven dragging footsteps echoed from the outside hallway. "You will come in now." A short man, the doctor wore a butterfly bow tie, round metal spectacles and a crisp white jacket buttoned tight as a bandage over his heavy round belly.

The prosthesis waited on the doctor's table. Other devices rested on a nearby shelf. Where was the original, the one he himself had killed for? Had this Frenchman already sold it?

Polyak lifted the new device in his right hand and turned it slowly as he examined it with care. He was not displeased, though the artifact did not have the smooth polished finish of the British hand. The details were more crude, this French metal inferior, but the blunt hook was blunt, and the sharper pointed one even more sharp and pointed. The dull metal surface would not attract as much attention. With this he would be able to grip and stab, to pull and push and even squeeze. He appreciated the way the leather cup was designed to extend high over much of the forearm. Two small straps or belts would wrap around the upper arm. The single heavier strap would be secured above the elbow, taking the strain whenever the arm was bent at the joint and a forceful effort was required with the hook.

"Roll up your sleeve and discard that clumsy hand," the doctor ordered, removing his eyeglasses and wiping them against his immaculate white cuff.

The Commissar took off his wooden hand and set it heavily on the edge of the table. The familiar flakes of dry skin speckled its butt.

Dr. Grillard examined the condition of his stump. He lifted Polyak's heavy forearm as if preparing to shoe the hoof of a farm horse. He pinched and squeezed the end of the stump until it grew red beneath the heavy calluses.

"Fine circulation. Skin still alive. These dry flakes show that, like that dandruff on your scalp." The physician bent and blew at the particles of old skin on the end of the wooden hand. "But I doubt our fabricators have allowed for these thick muscles of your forearm." He nodded and released the stump, wiping his fingers on a cloth as if he had touched some filth. He opened a container of blue powder and covered the inside of the leather cup with the colored dust.

"Hold your arm out straight and pointed slightly up. So."

Dr. Grillard slipped the cup over the stump, forcing the two together and wiggling the cup from side to side. Then he pulled away the cup and examined the stump, now evenly colored blue.

"Perfect fit," he said, blowing at the powder. He pulled the cup as high up the stump and forearm as it would go. But he was unable to secure the buckles of the smaller straps as the holes to receive the prongs were not positioned far enough along the narrow leather belts to accommodate the Commissar's muscled forearm.

"Just as I thought. Too much meat." The doctor rose and took the device to a side table. There he selected a small auger from a rack of tools. He placed a wooden board beneath the two straps and punched additional holes in the small belts. He replaced the prosthesis on Polyak's arm and belted the straps.

"Perfect." He secured the heavy elbow strap. "Stand up."

The doctor gripped the blunt hook.

"Tell me when I hurt you."

Grillard pulled on the hook, then twisted it when his patient did not react. First clockwise, then counterclockwise. Polyak looked at the man without blinking and made no sound as his arm was turned this way and that. He could tell the physician enjoyed this aspect of his trade.

The doctor released the hook and held up one hand. "Now push against me."

There was a knocking at the door.

"Almost finished," called Dr. Grillard, his voice shrill.

Polyak pressed the longer rounded hook against the doctor's upraised hand.

"Not enough." The man rocked slightly backward. "Press hard against the wall beside me."

Polyak did so. "Where is my other hook?" he asked as he pushed against the wall. "The one I brought you."

"Ah." The physician hesitated, then spoke quickly. "It is being used now by the president of an important municipal union, *un grand mutilé de la guerre*." The doctor dropped his eyes from Polyak's.

"It was a more valuable piece than this one," said the Commissar. "You must pay me for it."

"One final test," said Dr. Grillard, ignoring the comment and speaking with the imperious tone of a physician. "I will grip one hook in each hand. Then you must bend your elbow and pull hard and tell me when it gives you pain." Carefully he took one hook in three fingers of each hand. "*Tirez!* Pull!"

Polyak snapped back his arm as if nothing were attached to it.

"*Ah! Mon dieu!*" the doctor shrieked, falling forward against Polyak's chest. "You have stabbed me! *Je suis mutilé!*"

The sharper hook had pierced the palm of Grillard's left hand like the nail of a crucifixion. Polyak made two quick movements as if flinging aside a sack of rubbish.

The pointed hook came free as the doctor screamed. The two center fingers of his left hand were torn apart to the middle of his palm, separated like the tail fins of a fish. Blood flooded down the physician's sleeve to his elbow and splashed the front of his crisp white jacket as he waved his arm.

The receptionist opened the door. Striding out, Polyak thought he detected a look of satisfaction on her face when the woman rushed to the doctor's side.

As he hurried down the stairway, Polyak paused, then stopped and cursed. He should not have left the two alive. His eyes brightened. The Commissar turned to go back up. He could use one of the augers on them both, though it would be a pleasure to strangle either one.

But he was too late.

Two young men were climbing slowly onto the landing just below him. They appeared to be assisting each other. One, with a small striped ribbon pinned to his shabby jacket, seemed to be blind. The other man was missing his right leg. Groaning as he moved, one arm around the blind man's shoulder, the cripple clenched a burned-out cigarette between his teeth. More grist for Dr. Grillard, thought the Russian, more wreckage of the imperialist war.

Polyak pulled his cap lower and turned, coughing, to face the wall while the two edged slowly past him.

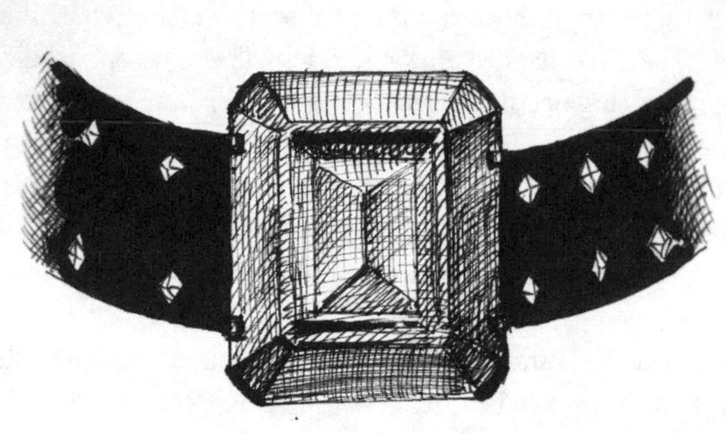

- 14 -

"Here you are, Count Karlov. Tickets for two adjoining first-class cabins on the *China Star*, together with stickers for your luggage and tags for the cabin baggage."

The English clerk passed a large envelope across the desk. The blue, white, red and yellow house flag of the Peninsular & Oriental Steam Navigation Company filled the upper left corner of the envelope. The clerk ignored another customer who, instead of waiting his turn in line, was crowding forward close to Alexander in the French way. "*Un plan de Paris*?" repeated the small sharp-faced man as his close-set eyes tightened. He was again ignored. He seemed to be rolling something in one hand, perhaps dice or worry beads.

"Both cabins are nicely forward on the port side, sir, so they should be cool." The clerk handed Alexander a smaller envelope while the waiting man drummed his fingers on the counter. "And these are your places on Friday's boat train to Marseilles. The Cook's car will call for you both at seven thirty in the morning. Will there be anything else, sir?"

"One additional ticket on the Marseilles train, if you please. Name of Norodsky, Igor Norodsky, and accommodations ashore for the two long stops."

"That would be Cairo and Colombo. In Cairo, sir, would you prefer in town or near the pyramids?"

"The pyramids."

"Then it would be the Mena House and the Galle Face, I should think."

"And would you be kind enough to send this telegram for me to Shanghai?" Alexander read over the message before handing it across.

> MADAME MEI-LAN WONG-
> ARRIVING CHINA STAR 26 JUNE WITH MY
> SISTER STOP KINDLY ADVISE MR HAK LEE
> AND IVAN SEMYONOV STOP TRUST YOU ARE
> BOTH WELL STOP JE T'EMBRASSE STOP
> ALEXANDER

He began to think of all his obligations in Shanghai and of the opportunities and excitement that awaited him. Even for a carefree traveller staying at a grand hotel on the Bund, the throbbing city had an intense complex vitality that existed nowhere else. He wondered how Katerina would take to it. At least she should be safer.

I must be careful not to neglect my friends, thought Karlov. What should I bring from Paris for Mei-Lan, for Mr. Hak Lee, and for Jessica and Lily? He had already found the perfect thing for his Cossack friend at a print seller's on a quay on the Left Bank. Ivan Semyonov was not a student of the fine arts but he would appreciate the two colored engravings of the Cossacks camped along the Champs-Elysées after the capture of Paris in the spring of 1814, particularly the eager French girls soliciting at the Russian camp fires and the drunken horsemen dancing above their crossed sabres.

The other presents would be more troublesome. For women, Madame Wong had advised him, the enhancement of vanity can be the key. Something flattering to wear, he thought, but what? A French dress would not become Mei-Lan. A fashionable hat, still worse. The latest elegant shoes could be best, but with her feet just under four inches long, only the silken pearl-decorated miniatures suitable for bound feet were possible. Even Pinet or A la Gavotte could not create such things. A pin or bracelet would serve, something unusual, at once decorative yet practical, like her girls. Hak Lee required a gift that demonstrated that his young partner understood who this man was, and what was the source of his distinction.

Madame Malakov could manage it only once a day. The climb back upstairs was too much for her heart, and for her back and feet, and even for her nose. She could identify each landing by the odor of its floor.

She had learned to make the most of each descent from her tiny room. If the weather were agreeable, and occasionally even when it was not, she would emerge at the door of her inexpensive hotel and rest for a moment, leaning on her cane with both hands. Then the Russian lady would walk slowly along the rue Vavin before sitting on a green iron bench at the entrance to the Luxembourg Gardens. There she would glance about frequently, sitting forward, as if waiting for a friend, never feeding the pigeons or speaking to a dog or admiring a baby or watching the chess players, always careful to avoid the lonely appearance of a bench *habitué*, of someone who knew no other home.

Today Lyuba Malakov carried back with her a wedge of cheese and a cheerful bunch of leafy bright radishes wrapped in yesterday's newspaper. The radishes replaced the vivid fresh colors of the flowers she could not afford. She wished she had a bit of butter to go with them. The rebluchon would have to do. A baguette, also yesterday's, stuck out from both ends of the little parcel. Each morning she first enjoyed the luxuriant smell of the warm fresh bread in the bakery, before buying yesterday's at a fraction of the cost. She believed that the baker found this arrangement reasonable, rather than charitable, though the sale of day-old bread was against the law of France. Contrary to her taste, she ate only the center of each long loaf, dipped in her glass of red wine to soften it. The crusty hard ends chafed her gums and hurt her teeth.

Madame Malakov also carried something else this morning: her elder sister's necklace, the emerald that had belonged to their mother, and before that to their grandmother, who, at seventeen, had received it from her besotted lover, a cousin of Nicholas I. Never before had Lyuba Malakov worn this treasure, for until yesterday it had not been hers. She wore it now under the high collar of her old grey dress. A green scarf was wrapped about her wrinkled neck above it.

The elderly Russian entered the dark lobby of the hotel. She ignored the snoring concierge and the set of upper teeth that rested in an ashtray near his head. Madame Malakov paused at the bottom of the worn wooden steps before hooking her black cane over one arm. She tried not to smell the garlic and the greasy odor of old lamb or goat coming from the rooms of the numberless Moroccan family on the floor above.

She collected herself and placed a foot on the first tread, then pressed the light button and immediately began her climb. She gripped the rail firmly and set both feet on each step. The bulb blinked out just before she reached the first landing. The light buttons on the upper floors never worked. The concierge complained that the tenants always stole or exchanged the bulbs. But Madame Malakov knew the hollowed-down shape of each step and continued up to the first narrow platform, pleased that she could still manage on her own.

For some time she had worried how she would survive when she could no longer climb the stairs to the less costly rooms of Paris, when her legs and eyes no longer served her. To date, this fear, and her pride, had fortified her with the discipline required to hold herself together. But now, at last, she could be carefree again, as she had been as a young girl. Her sister's emerald would provide her with the greatest luxuries of aged infirmity: security, respectful company and supportive care. She would enjoy the privileges of generosity, the manifold powers of being a rich old lady. Even in the best families, only money gave old people the dignity that comes with power.

She walked the few steps to the next flight and paused once more. With distaste, she gripped the filthy stair rail with her left hand. Madame Malakov possessed no gloves, but she was still proud of her hands, indulging herself occasionally by recalling the reassuring compliments of an earlier time. Though the backs of her hands were mottled like tortoise shell with the liver spots of age, her fingers remained slender and elegant, the nails presentably long and sharp. Her climbs and descents had kept her hands strong as she used the left one for each ascent and the right on her way down.

Half way up, she recognized the powerful odor of the second floor, the sour stink of urine from the unworking bathroom at the end of the hall.

She turned around at the beginning of the third flight and sat down carefully on the second step, sweeping it first with the edge of her bundled newspaper. From here up, everyone would be out for the day, and she need not fear embarrassment. She removed her painful shoes and tucked them under her right arm above the cane.

Madame Malakov thought of the emerald while she rested. She could feel its warmth against her neck. Despite the coldness of diamonds, she had always preferred their severe beauty to the candy-like qualities of the colored stones. But wearing this piece had changed her mind. The finest emeralds, such as this one, were like green honey, her mother had said. Instead of offering the coldness of crystal, such stones were sensual and voluptuous in the suggestive richness of their depths.

By itself, shabby as she was, this necklace made her feel well loved and magnificent, as if she were a different person, living in another world. She felt that a lover's hands and kisses were at her throat. She had once been young, but never beautiful. This stone made her feel both.

She understood now what this jewel had meant to each of the women in her family.

Lyuba Malakov touched the scarf at her neck and felt the rectangular cut of the stone beneath it. She recalled the evening before a ball when she and her sister had stood beside their mother's dressing table and watched the elderly lady's maid prepare her hair.

Their mother loved to dramatize every storytelling. She had opened the velvet box on the table and slowly lifted out the emerald and diamond collar with both hands. As the girls watched, she sat more erect and grew almost beautiful while she held the piece to her neck. "Think of the mountain tribes enslaved by the Incas to toil deep in the darkness of their secret mines," she had said. "Later the Inquisition tortured the Inca priests until they revealed where their great stones were mined. Until that day, in 1558, all emeralds had come from Egypt and the East. But the Cairene emeralds never possessed the clarity and color of the Colombian gems."

Madame Malakov resolved to keep the jewel for two weeks, until her eighty-fifth birthday. Then she would wear it exposed on her own neck, at dinner with three friends from the old days in St. Petersburg. That would remind them who she was, and what her family had been. Like the stone itself, her three friends would then speak for her. Too many of her fellow White refugees sought to enhance their Parisian misery with pretensions of position and wealth that they had never truly possessed at home. Even in old Russia, many nobles and fine families were poor, clinging to rank and privilege by their fingertips. For a single evening, this emerald collar would distinguish her from this rabble of pretenders.

The following morning she would present the jewel at 13 rue de la Paix and learn what it might fetch. She might also enjoy a visit to Boucheron on the Place Vendôme. Why not, while she had this opportunity? Other émigrés claimed to have secured higher prices by offering their jewelry and Fabergé *objets* to small specialized jewelers like the eminent Lebanese dealer Kettaneh et fils, upstairs on the rue Cambon. But that meant more risk, Madame Malakov felt, and she would miss the satisfaction of being invited to a small private salon at Cartier on the great boulevard, perhaps offered a cup of tea while she took the collar from her neck and laid it upon a black velvet mat in the center of an inlaid Empire table.

The treasure should yield more than enough to buy this wretched hotel and the structures adjoining it, and perhaps to acquire a distinguished elderly admirer, she thought with a girlish smile, possibly even an officer of the Corps des Pages. A gentleman who was needy but not quite desperate, who would appreciate the gift of a new suit of evening clothes, and who would know how to wear it when he escorted her about town. Someone a few years younger than herself, who still possessed a twinkle and a touch of dash, to hold doors, pull out chairs and stir the bitter envy of other ladies. A man with enough infirmities to make him sympathetic to hers, and to shorten his leash, but not enough to weaken his enthusiasms. She would provide him in advance with money sufficient for each evening, to enhance their common dignity before friends and waiters, while still keeping her suitor mindful each day of his source of luxury. He would indulge her whenever she felt a bit *coquette*.

By now her eyes had adjusted to the darkness as much as they ever would these days, and she continued to the fourth floor. Here she was careful to raise her feet neatly as she walked, as if at dancing class again, for the rooftop leaks had rotted the old planks of the hallway and made it a forest of long splinters.

Lyuba Malakov paused outside her door in order to prepare and enjoy her own entrance. What did it matter that there would be no one to receive her? She hung the cane over the doorknob and removed her scarf with her free hand before opening the top button of her dress.

She exposed the emerald and adjusted the diamond collar so that the piece was perfectly centered on her thin loose-skinned neck. The stone itself gave her a feeling of luxuriant comfort. She raised her chin and straightened her back as best she could, as if about to enter a drawing room after the announcement of her name. Always pause, her mother had said, and she did so now.

As her fingers pressed against the wood to find the keyhole in the darkness, the door swung open swiftly of its own accord and banged against the wall.

A beam of light from the small garret window dazzled her eyes.

A hand clamped around her neck and pulled her violently into the room. Her parcel scattered on the floor. The radishes fell between her feet. Something cold and sharp punctured her neck as it forced its way inside the diamond and emerald collar at her throat.

Madame Malakov tasted her own blood, then cried out once before she began to cough and gargle.

She clawed fiercely at her assailant's face with both hands as life left her and her blood covered the green stone.

- 15 -

"You can smell it all!" Katia gripped her brother's arm as they walked through the crowds along the Quai des Belges. Eels and octopus squirmed in buckets set between scales and cutting blocks. Sturdy men with wet leather aprons knotted in the front and sleeves rolled high on their arms worked with knives and small hatchets as they bargained in rapid clipped French. "The fish, the sea, the tar and oil and coal. It makes me feel free. Is Shanghai like this, Sasha?"

"On a very quiet day." Alexander smiled. No other city could have the teeming turmoil and ceaseless clamor of Asia's biggest port. But Marseilles seemed the spirited city it was meant to be, a seafaring town like St. Petersburg or Shanghai, open to the water, with the promise of far horizons. And he was pleased that he had accomplished what he had come to France to do: finding Katerina. Soon she would be safely on board. But his duty was not complete. He had failed to avenge his father.

They left the Vieux Port and climbed up the narrow brick and stone step-streets of the old Thieves' Quarter. The curves of the lanes and buildings echoed the ancient lines of the city's walls. Sometimes Igor Norodsky followed them. At other moments he walked on ahead, pausing to look back along the busy streets, taking little interest in the narrow shops that drew Katerina's attention.

One store carried antique tools and weapons: huge rusty fish-hooks with blades like scythes; double-handled saws and long drills with broad bits from the days of sea carpenters and ocean sail; edged weapons from North Africa and Spain, Malta and the Turkish coast. Rows of iron shackles of varied gauge hung like jewelry from hooks along one wall. A few were sized for children.

An old man in wide trousers, sabots and a matelot's striped jersey sat on a stack of binnacles. He gripped a short-stemmed clay pipe in his teeth while he watched the three visitors examine his treasures. The handle of a boarding axe rested on the floor between his feet while he sharpened its edge with long strokes of a grey stone. Marseilles's occupiers and their periods were listed on a wooden board behind him: Ligurians and Phoenicians, Greeks and Romans, Saracens and Crusaders. Perhaps to spare the shopkeeper the questions of travellers, guessed Alexander. Only the pirates survived every period.

Norodsky swung a shackle by its long chain.

"For the ankles of the galley slaves," said the proprietor before he was asked. "There used to be ten thousand kept ready in the walled docks. When they were not at the oars, they were made to twist rope in the hemp factories."

Katia lifted a small band of heavy ridged brass with four holes set in an arch. "What is this?" she asked, handing it to Norodsky.

"Ça, madame, c'est un coup de poing américain," said the owner, showing his fist.

"Brass knuckles," said Alexander as Norodsky slipped them on his right hand. "The French like to name nasty things after foreigners." Igor flexed his fingers and smiled for the first time that day.

"How much?" said Alexander as something more appealing caught his attention.

He hung his cane on the edge of a shelf and picked up the weapon. He pulled a double-edged dagger with a long narrow blade from a leather sheath attached to two straps. The edge of the blade cut his thumbnail when he tested it. He balanced the knife on two fingers at the middle of the blade. Heavy enough to throw. Light enough to conceal. With a weapon like this, he would have killed Polyak at the dinner of the Corps des Pages.

"Toledo," nodded the shopkeeper. "*Pour 'poignarder à l'écossais,'* for stabbing someone in the back stairs." He squinted at Alexander's cane and extended a hand towards it. "*Permettez?*"

Karlov nodded.

The man stood and drew the sword from the cane. His eyes brightened. His wooden shoes tapped the floor as he tried a swift stroke left and right.

Each man studied the other's weapon with evident appreciation.

"Isn't that knife to be worn hidden on one's forearm?" said Katerina, surprising her brother. Then he remembered her training in Moscow.

"It's the perfect present for the Master of the Mountain, a Chinese friend with long baggy sleeves." Alexander paid for the dagger and the knuckle-duster. "Mr. Hak Lee will find a use for it. And it makes a lovely throwing knife." He handed the brass knuckles to Norodsky. "With my compliments, Sergeant."

Alexander was pleased that Katia took his arm as they left the store and walked back to the harbor, crowded now with the masts of fishing vessels as men rinsed decks and worked on nets and rigging.

"We just have time for a visit to the Château d'If," said Alexander. "We should be able to see the *China Star* from her walls."

They took a ferry for the island. A party of English visitors, dressed practically for Continental tourism, crowded the benches of the boat. An elderly lady in a straw hat read underlined passages from the *The Count of Monte Cristo* to her companions in a steady dominant voice.

" 'So many loathsome animals had made their noises in his cell at the Château d'If that little by little Edmond Dantès had grown accustomed to them and did not let them disturb his sleep.' "

The Englishwoman read steadily as the boat crossed the choppy water, as they walked along the dock of the small island and as they climbed the steep rocky hillside to the looming castle walls. Dumas' imprisoned count was with them in the fortress.

" 'His eyes, having been accustomed to twilight and darkness, had acquired the peculiar faculty of distinguishing objects in the dark, like those of the hyena and the wolf.' "

Nearby a goat nibbled patches of thin grass between the dark rocks. Karlov leaned against the wall. His knee and hip ached from the climb.

"She must have been a school teacher," whispered Katerina as the woman read aloud. Alexander smiled. Could Katia not remember that this book had been a favorite of his, one he used to read at night by candlelight? He recalled the fourteen years of unjust imprisonment of Edmond Dantès as if they were his own. Dantès had taught Alexander early lessons in injustice, lost love and patient vengeance.

Tourists clustered about the reader as they moved, attentive to Dumas rather than to their young French guide.

"*Mieux que les Boches, au moins*," Alexander heard the young man mutter to himself. "Better than the Krauts, at least." The guide stood by the arch of the gate and counted his clients as they entered the courtyard, doubtless assuming that these Britishers spoke no French. Alexander followed, cursing himself for not having his leg attended to while he was in Europe.

"Montecristo is an island near Elba. There was no treasure. There was no count," said the guide in loud slow English when he had the travellers trapped in one corner of the thick stone walls. He accepted a cigarette from a client and tucked it over his right ear before continuing.

"The Château d'If was built in the fifteen twenties as the first defense for the southern coast of France. Soon the castle became a political prison, mostly for the losers of our religious wars." The young Frenchman paused and looked at the ruddy faces of his clients as if he could imagine all of them in the dungeons. "For our Protestants, the Huguenots. And of course the man in the iron mask was imprisoned here."

The elderly woman resumed reading as they walked along the top of the wall that faced the sea. From somewhere near here, thought Alexander, Edmond Dantès had been hurled into the water wrapped in a dead man's burial sack, a cannonball tied to his feet. Escape, riches and vengeance had followed. Never had an ugly death been so transformed into a brilliant life.

" 'Now Dantès must return into the world,' " the woman read, " 'and take the rank, influence, and power in society bestowed by riches only, the first and greatest force at man's disposal.' " The Master of the Mountain would agree.

Clover and small yellow flowers filled the cracks between the massive stones underfoot.

"I think that's her." Alexander pointed at a broad-beamed vessel with a black hull, light yellow deck housing, and black funnel and masts moored at the mouth of the harbor. "Those are the P and O colors. About sixteen thousand tons." Booms reached out from the steamship and lifted nets of cargo from the crowded decks of two nearby lighters that were low in the water. "All the docks are busy and she's loading some mixed cargo now, most likely wine and olive oil. She'll tie up later to take on passengers."

"We have two more things to buy," said his sister. "Books and your binoculars. It's a long voyage. About four weeks to Shanghai."

"What is *The Count of Monte Cristo* really about? These French tales are so confused," whispered an English woman who had been less attentive to the reading than the other travellers. "Patience, fortitude?"

"No, ma'am." Alexander shook his head. "It is about the strongest human emotion," he said quietly as his eyes searched the sea. "The only one that lasts for generations."

"Love?" asked the woman, smiling like a girl. "Love?"

"Sadly not," said the young Russian. "Revenge."

Alexander set off for the marine supply quarter of the Vieux Port while Katia and the sergeant hurried to find a bookstore. In case either of them were delayed, he had given his sister her boarding tickets and luggage receipts. He had started to hand the papers to Norodsky, but Katia, moody and irritated, had insisted on taking charge herself. "I can manage, thank you, Sasha." Although he had paid her bills cheerfully and without comment, he was surprised by the amount of her baggage.

Alexander was certain she was upset and thinking about her son. Before leaving Paris, the twins had visited the Refugee Society and promised a very handsome reward for finding Leon in Moscow, and more for assisting in his deliverance from Russia. They had explained the situation to Boris Androvich and Madame Kulikovski. Both had pledged to do everything possible through their friends in Moscow. They would wire Alexander in Shanghai as soon as they had news. For now, there was nothing more that either Karlov could do.

Boris Androvich had told them that Lyuba Malakov had been murdered in her garret and her emerald stolen. Both Karlovs were certain who had killed her.

Although it was still the afternoon, friendly women in tight bright clothing stood smoking near the doorways of modest hotels as Alexander passed.

"*Une petite séance, mon chou*?" called one, younger and more attractive than the others, though clothed as briefly.

Alexander Karlov was not above temptation. It would be a long voyage and in Paris he had failed to achieve fulfillment. Despite a tender goodbye he did not expect to see Violetta again. Fortunately his sister was not with him. He slowed his step and returned the girl's smile. Why not?

"*Du feu, trésor*?" The girl raised dark eyebrows and placed an unlit cigarette in the center of her red lips. She took her young client by the hand and led him through the bead curtain that hung across the doorway.

In less than an hour Alexander stepped quickly from the hotel, embarrassed but relaxed. He reminded himself that he must wash again after he boarded the *Star*. As he walked on, he smiled when he recalled what Madame Wong had told him one afternoon over a cup of tea and pastries on his way home from school. "It is not the men who give me all this business," Mei-lan said, referring to the activity in her bordello next door. "It is their women and their wives, especially the English. Some women get men to marry them by withholding sex. Others get men to marry them by providing exactly the sex wished for, and then denying it later. Those are the ladies who make me rich."

In the chandlery Alexander was more extravagant than he might have been. Telescopes, anemometers and binoculars, new and old, were displayed on shelves near rows of compasses and sextants. He bent to examine a set of binoculars housed in a cabinet that contained the more precious instruments. This pair, black and longer than most, bore an eagle embossed on the center bridge. "U-21" was engraved just below the German symbol and above the words "Karl Leitz."

"How much are these, if you please?" asked Karlov, thinking of the unfashionable heavy Leitz glasses his father used to carry at the races in Shanghai, captured from a German officer near Osterode.

Alexander surprised the proprietor by paying the first price asked. The shopkeeper held the banknotes to the light and grunted as he pulled at the kerchief rolled tightly around his neck. He nodded and tucked the money into the broad waistband he wore instead of a belt or braces. Not wanting both his hands encumbered, Karlov hung the binoculars from his neck, as the submarine captain must once have done while he braced himself against the tiny pitching conning tower and searched the endless rolling seas for his mother ship.

Katerina found exactly what she wanted: a morocco-bound edition of *Le Comte de Monte Cristo*. It will be good for Sasha's French, their mother would have said, and Katia knew he loved the story.

For herself, she bought *Les Misérables, Le Rouge et Noir*, a French edition of *Das Kapital* and more.

"Please, Mademoiselle Karlov, we must go," implored Sergeant Norodsky, fiddling with his new brass knuckles. "We cannot be late."

"*Un instant*," she said. "Just one more thing." She took a copy of the new French novel of woman's liberation and set it on the pile.

Katerina removed the bold cover of *Das Kapital* and carefully folded it inside the book before the clerk tied up the third parcel. The sage bearded face of Karl Marx would infuriate her brother. Sasha would say he had not worked to pay for that. Since that first evening, both twins had avoided politics. To her, the German philosopher represented the intellectual morality at the core of Bolshevism, before it was corrupted by the personal abuses that came with power.

Still wearing his brass knuckles, Norodsky waited by the door with a parcel in each hand. "We must hurry down to the harbor," he said as she passed him. "Through that alley just across the way."

Katerina hastened into the narrow winding street. "Chemin du Port" was painted in black on one whitewashed wall.

As the sergeant followed her, a big man in a cap emerged swiftly from a doorway where he was loitering with two others dressed in the work clothes of the shipyard. He seemed to have been nibbling at a bunch of radishes. He dropped the vegetables. Suddenly a pistol appeared in his hand. He pressed it to Norodsky's side and pulled the trigger twice. His French companions threw down their cigarettes and stepped towards Katerina.

"Run!" screamed the sergeant as he staggered and dropped the packages. Gathering his strength, he seized his attacker's belt and pulled the big man with him to the ground.

Katia saw the two collapse. The assailant had lost his cap and weapon in the struggle. She recognized him as he fell. One of the other men hurried over and kicked Norodsky in the back with his heavy boot.

"Viktor!" Katerina yelled. She backed against the rough wall, swung violently and hit the third man in the face with the large net bag that held her purse and a package of books.

"*Putain*!" screamed the man. "*Sale putain*!" The Frenchman belted her across the face as she struggled to free her pistol from her purse, but the net bag was entangled on her arm.

"Run!" cried Norodsky. With less than his full strength, he slammed Polyak in the ear with his brass knuckles. Blood was staining the cobblestones by the sergeant's side, but still he gripped Polyak's belt with one hand as he flailed at his second adversary with the other.

The Commissar's face was cut and bleeding. Dazed, he rose to his knees and swung wildly at Norodsky with his new metal hand.

Katerina's attacker bent to recover the pistol dropped by Polyak.

"Katia!" yelled Alexander as he rushed towards her from the entrance to the alley. His sword flashed from his cane as the Frenchman raised the pistol.

Slipping on the cobbles, Karlov dragged his bad leg behind him as he lunged. The blade passed through the man's upper arm and lodged between two ribs.

The man screamed and grabbed the blade with his left hand. As if fighting two-handed in the old Italian style with sword and dagger, Alexander pressed close against the Frenchman and clubbed him on the side of the head with the cane as he twisted and freed the short blade with his other hand.

The Frenchman collapsed on his knees. The pistol clattered on the stones before him. He raised both bloody hands before his face like a saint posed in prayerful martyrdom. Behind him his two companions fought to finish Norodsky.

Alexander hesitated for an instant, uncertain whether to fight all three or save his sister. He saw the blood pooled beside Norodsky. Taking both cane and sword in his right hand, he grabbed Katia's arm with the other and rushed with her down the alley. The binoculars banged against his chest.

Katerina glanced back. Sickened, she saw Viktor's hook puncture Igor Norodsky's throat. The sergeant's head jerked sideways. Blood gushed from Igor's mouth and neck as Polyak grunted and twisted his artificial hand.

The Karlovs hurried down the passage towards the port as passersby gathered screaming at the entrance to the alley.

The twins finally paused where the Chemin du Port opened onto the broad stone embankment that led to the docks. The *China Star* was berthed alongside the next pier. Alexander wiped his blade on his handkerchief and sheathed it. His limp had never been more painful. He looked down and saw that Katerina held a pistol in one hand.

"That was Polyak," he gasped. "Why didn't you shoot him?"

"I couldn't." Katia shook her head. "He is still Leon's father."

Alexander groaned, certain his sister was still entangled with her Bolshevism. "You go on down and board the *Star*." He took the weapon from her hand. "I am going back for him."

- 16 -

Unsuccessful, furious with himself for not having killed the Commissar, Alexander Karlov hurried back down the Chemin du Port for the second time. At the edge of the gathering crowd, an excited woman had told him that two dead men were lying on the stones near the top of the alley. Norodsky and one of the Frenchmen, Alexander realized. Polyak and the other assailant had escaped.

He braced himself by recalling the patient admonition of Edmond Dantès, the master of revenge: "All human wisdom is contained in the words 'wait and hope.'"

Alexander dropped his handkerchief and Katia's pistol into a barrel of rubbish at the end of the pier and hurried to the *China Star*. He wanted no trouble with the French police before she sailed.

"My baggage is already on board," said Karlov to a purser as he tapped his papers on the bottom post of the First Class companionway. Stepping back to allow several other late passengers to ascend, he glanced along the long black side of the steamer towards the stern. The Second Class gangway was already being raised and secured against the side of the ship. He looked up and noticed ten white lifeboats suspended above the upper deck. Katerina waved down at him.

To one side the ship's bursar was in contention with three aspiring passengers who appeared not to have paid for their passages. The uniformed ship's officer spoke with a thick Scottish accent. His cap was tucked high under one arm. He made arrangements for two of the three, an elderly couple, to pay a reduced fare in Second Class.

The final disputant, a woman with her back to Alexander, protested quietly to the bursar in a clear firm voice. Her cabin was reserved, she said. Her family had sailed with the P & O for forty years. Her passage had been arranged by their London bankers. With Ceylon tea at record prices, there could be no question of a shortage of funds. There was dignity in her tone rather than complaint.

Alexander could not see the woman's face. She was wearing a wide-brimmed tan straw hat, a cream linen suit and rather elegant French shoes. More important, the lady had exceptional ankles. He judged her accent to be well-educated English, but with some foreign or colonial complication. He had learned the difference in Shanghai, and how much it mattered to the British.

"Mrs. Hammond," said the bursar, shaking his head, "all undoubtedly true, of course, but without payment now, I regret that I am not allowed to board you."

"I can send a wireless from on board," said the tall woman calmly, assured, "and guarantee payment when we stop in Egypt. There will be banking connections in Port Saïd and Suez."

"I am sorry, ma'am, but the companionway is going up now. We must clear the pier. The next ship is waiting to come in." The man nodded and gestured at Alexander, as if warning him as well. Karlov had noticed a sleek French vessel with two slanted funnels anchored near the mouth of the port. Probably one of the German ships seized by France as war reparations, she was flying the red and white colors of the *Messageries Maritimes*, familiar to anyone from Shanghai. "Final boarding, Count Karlov."

The woman, agitated now, turned and faced Alexander.

He had never seen such eyes. Almost black, flashing bright as signal lamps, shaped like two perfect almonds, they absorbed him and looked back at Alexander as if they were seeing the world. Her face was oval and deep brown like the darkest chocolate, with high cheekbones and a long straight nose like a Karlov. But she had the full generous lips of a different people.

"May I help, ma'am?" he said after a moment. The words of Hak Lee flashed in his mind. Money is always a useful servant.

"No, thank you, sir," said Mrs. Hammond as the bursar put on his cap. "Certainly not."

The steam whistle of the *China Star* blew twice from the side of her single raked funnel.

Karlov turned to the bursar and drew a letter of credit from his pocket. He wondered if he looked foolish with the large binoculars around his neck.

"May I advance something for now to cover the lady's passage to Egypt?" He handed the letter to the bursar. After all, what ship would want an empty cabin?

The officer's demeanor changed. "Of course, Count Karlov," said the Scot.

The woman was beginning to protest when a young officer with a megaphone hollered down at the bursar from the port wing of the bridge. The Scot pointed at the woman's baggage and whistled. Two P & O seamen, dark as the lady herself, hustled her cases and leather hat boxes up the gangway. The Lascars were neat and efficient in their red sashes and matching turbans.

"Really," said Mrs. Hammond a little stiffly, "you shouldn't . . ."

"All aboard!" Passengers and crew were staring down from the decks. Dockhands took positions by the ropes and bumpers.

"After you," said Alexander to the woman, gesturing towards the steps. "If you please, Mrs. Hammond." He was careful not to appear familiar, nor to presume any obligation.

The two climbed the companionway. The bursar donned his cap and followed them up as the whistle blew once more. Karlov tasted the salty breeze as they climbed.

Katia was waiting for her brother at the top of the steep gangway. He had not noticed that her dress was torn, her hair wild. Still distracted, she stumbled against the top edge of the companionway. Her parcel of books fell and tore open.

Das Kapital caught on the first cleat of the steps. Its loose cover fluttered to the edge of the deck. Alexander pinned it down with the tip of his cane. He stared at the book jacket and lifted the cane. His sister exclaimed too late, then bit her lip as Karl Marx blew into the oily sea.

"Oh, let me help you," said the dark woman to Katerina, bending gracefully and gathering up the books. "Allow me." She steadied the Russian girl, taking her by one arm. "Please."

"What did she do in the war, Captain Marden?"

"Same as her two sisters, Mr. Willard. Troop service from Bombay and Cape Town, bringing the Indian Army and the Cape Rifles to the trenches. Hospital ship on the way back." The captain stroked his trim speckled beard. "But the *Singapore Star* and the *Mandalay Star* went down with all hands, and with most of a battalion each. U-boats caught them off the Azores. Too many men for the boats, of course."

"Better than three years of mud and wire in Flanders," replied one of Katerina's neighbors, said to be an important rubber planter from Malaya. "Most of 'em wouldn't have made it home anyway. Sailoring was the best way to survive it."

"With respect, Mr. Walker," said the captain with some asperity, "the P and O lost eighty-five ships in the Great War. Even the Frenchies, the Messageries Maritimes, lost twenty-two." The captain continued in a steady cold voice as if back on the bridge instead of entertaining the cream of First Class. "Mines, raiders, torpedoes. Never room in the boats for the ship's crew, let alone her officers. When the *Mandalay* sank, they say the sea was brown with uniforms, dotted white like a field of cotton with the turbans of the Punjabis."

For a moment the table was silent. Alexander glanced up at the framed picture of the steamer *Medina* hanging behind the captain. He had read the brass plaque while the ladies were being seated. In 1911 the new ship had served as George V's Royal Yacht at the Delhi Durbar. Six years later the 12,000-ton P & O vessel had been torpedoed and sunk by U-31 off Stan Point while transporting men and a few families from India to London. Then the German submarine had surfaced and taken on board as many women and children as she could accommodate. The story made him wonder about his new binoculars.

Alexander was used to a preoccupation with the losses and hardships of Russia's revolution and civil war. But Paris and conversations like this had reminded him of the sufferings of others. They denied him the weakness of feeling sorry for himself.

His own shortened leg and bad knee were nothing to the scars and eye patches, missing limbs and proud flesh he had witnessed every day in France. The wounded armies had retired from the trenches to the boulevards and cafés. In restaurants, without even seeing the veterans themselves, Karlov had learned to recognize men gassed in the field by the long grinding coughs and short staccato gasps he heard from tables behind him.

"Enough of this old war talk," said Katia's other neighbor, a jowly man with quick bright eyes. His flushed round face sat on his white wing collar like a tomato on a plate. His young blond wife, seated next to Alexander, seemed to appreciate her Russian neighbor. "It's all old nonsense to a pretty girl like Countess Kartov here," the husband added.

"Karlov," said Katerina flatly without looking at the portly speaker, a cotton broker from Alexandria. "And I am not a countess."

They don't know what Katia has been through, thought Alexander. His sister had experienced brutality and death to match any soldier. He suspected that even if she had a title, she would never use it.

With her dour remark, the talk at the captain's table changed from one conversation to five as the Goan stewards served prawns in aspic and each man turned to the lady on his left.

As Alexander had learned on the passage west, the first dinner on board was always like this. Some people immediately established their positions for the long voyage, with the captain, with their First Class peers, and with the ship's crew. Others were reserved, assessing, holding back in the English way, lest they open the door of friendship too wide and too hastily and permit early relationships that later they might regret. The social theatre was even more complicated on a voyage such as this, with passengers boarding and disembarking at many ports on three continents. The first passengers, like these Britishers who had boarded at London, considered the ship to be their own. To them, later boarders were transients.

Alexander Karlov himself was neither socially eager nor restrained. After surviving revolution in Russia and poverty in Shanghai, at twenty-two he did not need the British to determine who he was. His father's confident identity was set in his bones. Apart from his sister, there was only one passenger in whom he had an interest.

He smiled at the elderly woman beside him and looked again around the dining cabin. Most of the sixty First Class passengers were seated at a dozen tables of varying size, from singles to the captain's table of ten. No one was said to understand protocol and social harmony like a senior steward of the P & O.

For the fourth meal, Mrs. Derrick Hammond was still not to be seen. The first evening he had not been surprised, merely disappointed. After the *China Star* had cleared Marseilles, dinner was a handsome late buffet, a supper with no seating time or assignments. No one dressed. Not everyone appeared. Alexander and Katia had found crayfish and lobster, mussels and squid and sea urchins, all the salty luxuries of the French coast, waiting in the dining cabin on a sea of ice between chilled bottles of rosé from Provence.

The first morning a passenger list was posted on the ship's notice board next to a chart of the day's route and a schedule of the Royal Mail sailings of the Peninsular & Oriental Steam Navigation Company. Alexander had checked her name, disappointed to see that she was married. But one never knows, Mei-lan had advised him. Every lady is a woman first, and Mrs. Derrick Hammond was alone.

He walked the decks as they steamed past the rocky coasts of Corsica and Sardinia, hoping to see the dark woman in a deck chair, or find her playing shuffleboard or ring toss. He tried to guess at her first name. Something British, despite her race or color. Alice? Caroline? Victoria? He wondered if she thought he was attached to Katerina.

He tipped the deck steward to assign Mrs. Hammond a numbered deck chair beside his own. But she did not appear, neither on deck nor for morning bouillon or lunch or tea. After lunch Alexander rewarded the Goan who had been serving him with special care. Though he must be at home in Portuguese and Urdu, the slight olive-skinned man spoke English nearly as well as Karlov. His white trousers and jacket were starched and pressed sharply enough to have satisfied Alexander's father.

"While the flowers are still fresh, Pedro, send a bouquet of the best to Cabin Nine with this card, if you please." On the back he had written: "With thanks to you for helping my sister collect her books." Beneath that, as best he could, he drew a fierce Russian bear. He watched Pedro wait for the dining cabin to empty before selecting from the tables some flowers from the French coast.

Strolling the deck the second morning reminded Alexander of his flight from Vladivostok to Shanghai four years earlier. But this was not the rough, cold and lonely sea whose waters had parted for the *Murmansk* as she sailed south into the freezing drizzle of the Sea of Japan. That old icebreaker had been crowded with two horses and 340 hungry Hussars and Cossacks, White refugees escaping the Red Revolution.

Instead of a rusting hulk transporting soldiers who had lost their country, this vessel was a proud strand in the web of the world's most powerful empire. The instructors at the Corps des Pages, old officers themselves, had taught that the British empire was the only one to rival their own: absorbing every religion and many races, and accomplishing at sea what Russia did by land, stretching from the Atlantic to the Pacific and from Central Asia to the Arctic. Even in America the two empires had contended, with the czar building trading forts in California before the Anglo-Saxons were established there. The officers were contemptuous of the French. "The British cut them down from Plassey to Quebec, from the Caribbean to the Nile," Alexander's old fencing instructor had told his young swordsmen. "We Russians butchered them in the Crimea, and from the Volga to the Vistula. On their retreat from Moscow the French stripped their wounded of boots and greatcoats and cooked their own dead over camp fires."

Being at sea again reminded Alexander that the shipping lines of the great nations, though they were commercial, were more than that. They were also military, cultural and imperial, not unlike the lonely voyages of the early explorers. He glanced up at the trim white lifeboats that hung from davits above his head, pleased that this was not the Sea of Japan.

Here in the Mediterranean, the breeze was warm, the gentle sea often spotted with coastal fishing boats or occasionally a distant cargo ship. The air was not as salty. On the *China Star* no spray reached the First Class decks. The only sign of her wartime service was one square metal panel secured to a forward deck. Once the base plate for a two-inch gun, it now mounted three wooden posts for ring toss.

Alexander leaned on the starboard railing and looked down on the crowded Second Class deck. He searched for Katerina but did not find her. "I want to see the difference," she had said, opening one of the fire doors used to separate the classes. "Those people were so spoiled and stuffy at dinner last night. It reminded me of our family's old friends at home." His sister seemed embarrassed by what to Alexander were congenial memories of Voskrenoye. "I'll see you at lunch, Sasha."

He hung his cane on the rail and took a dark cheroot from his old case but could not light it in the wind. He turned his back to the sea and tried again with more success.

Lydia, the cotton broker's young wife, stood near him, playing ring toss by herself. She held her hat on with her left hand while she threw the small red rope hoop with her right. Lydia Richards reminded him of Violetta Katkoff.

Lydia's hoop missed the post and slid along the metal plate. She bent to pick it up. Alexander admired the perfect split pear of her derriere.

"Do you play?" she asked with an open smile.

"Not yet." He tossed his cigar into the sea and lifted two blue hoops from a hook.

For a half hour the two threw and flirted until the noon whistle blew.

"Time to dress for lunch, my dear," boomed the cotton broker's bluff deep voice as he emerged around a corner of the housing. "A splendid morning, wouldn't you say, Count Kartov? This salt air makes a chap hungry."

"Richard is always hungry," whispered Lydia as she passed Alexander. Was the poor girl thinking of something else? he wondered.

"Quite right, Mr. Richards." Alexander ignored the misnomer. Only an Englishman could be called Richard Richards.

That evening Alexander Karlov found himself alone on deck again. After dinner Katia had gone back to Second Class.

"It's more interesting," she said before leaving her brother. "And more amusing. Behave yourself, Sasha. All these ladies are after you, especially those English cousins at the next table. They're too old for you, of course, nearly thirty. They're part of the spinster fishing fleet, off to the East to find husbands." He smiled at the phrasing and Katia smiled back. "Do you know what they call the girls who fail to hook a catch and have to sail back alone?"

Her brother shook his head.

"Returned empties."

For a moment the twins shared laughter as they had when they were young.

After Katerina left, he smoked a torpedo and watched a glow of light on the port horizon. The slender crescent moon was not yet large enough to obscure the stars, but clear enough to draw one's spirit. Illuminated by the sparkling night sky, the ocean rolled in smooth silver waves.

Alexander felt alone but not yet lonely. He wished Vita were waiting for him in a cabin. He had given her his address before he left, and a package of little luxuries from Roger & Gallet, so that she would think of him whenever she bathed and soaped her breasts. Violetta had cried when he departed, eager to follow him to Shanghai.

Music floated up from the decks below. First a piano from the First Class music room, then an accordion from a lower deck.

"Are you the Russian bear?" said a clear voice behind him.

"I hope so," said Alexander without turning, though his heart danced. He felt the caress of her eyes. "Who are you?"

"A Burgher girl from Colombo." The voice laughed.

"Mrs. Hammond?" He did not dare to look at her in this magic light.

"You may call me Laila."

She joined him at the rail, gazing first at the ocean, then up at the night sky, not at Alexander.

"*Bon soir*!" called the cheerful French girl with whom Katerina had passed most of the afternoon. "What a pretty dress! Won't you join us?

The second sitting is just over. Soon this dining cabin will become a party room."

"Thank you, Isabelle, I'd love to," said Katerina Karlov.

The three Frenchmen sitting with the young schoolteacher rose and Isabelle introduced them to her.

Katerina was embarrassed that her new dress was too elegant for Second Class. She had dressed as simply as she could for the captain's table. Before slipping through the fire door, she had removed the earrings given her by Sasha. At the same time, Katerina recognized her own weakness: despite her Bolshevik sympathies, she was still her mother's daughter. After the long hardships of Moscow, she had enjoyed the extravagant indulgences of Paris. The first of them, after all, were part of her assignment as a revolutionary. Proselytizing in Second Class could be the next part.

The large low-ceilinged cabin was noisy and crowded. Waiters cleared the tables. The passengers smoked and drank coffee, wine and beer. Some brought out bottles of their own and tipped the waiters to provide glasses. Groups had already formed by language and country, age and family situation.

At one side a party of Goans was chattering in lively Portuguese. Two Indian families from Bombay were crowded together at another nearby table. The patriarchs, wearing dark English suits, cleaned their spectacles and flipped through swatches of cotton, stroking and pinching each with discrimination. Dressed in simple saris, their women gossiped while the children played games with colored beads.

Katerina was relieved to be speaking French. It reminded her of her mother. When she was not playing Mozart on her Pleyel after dinner at Voskrenoye, Countess Karlov used to pass the winter evenings with Molière and Racine. Katerina herself had always been a better student of languages than her brother. But after four years in Shanghai, Sasha spoke English like a colonial. Her own English, like her German, was still a secondary, classroom language. But her German had been useful when she was carrying out her mission in Poland. Again she considered what she had done there. Hardened as she had become, perhaps the horror and guilt of that act had restrained her from killing Viktor.

She found the atmosphere more lively and diverse than in First Class, which of course was more haute bourgeoisie than it was aristocratic, at least by Russian standards. At home the aristocracy had a wild passionate style often not bound by middle-class confinements. She remembered creeping out of bed one night and peeking down through the banisters to the hall below where her father and his friends were sliding bottles and drinks along the floor on trays taken from the pantry. Finally they fenced and fought with canes and shooting sticks, roaring like Cossacks, until one distinguished guest was bloodied and another had cracked the long hall mirror with a thrust. What must they have been like when younger, or on campaign, or on a grand tour abroad?

The British structure seemed more rigid, more defined. Here on board, the officers were British, the seamen Lascars from the Gulf of Kutch, and the engine-room crew other distinct sorts of Indian. Each group of Lascars was said to come from a single maritime village. They were commanded on board and at home by the same *serang* or headman. From the steel compartments of the vessel itself to the distinctions of the crew and passengers, the *China Star* reinforced the finely shaded rankings of empire, whether civil service, military, educational or commercial.

Katerina realized that the extremities of her life now made her comfortable in the worlds of both classes, and beyond. In the Russia of her parents, the divide between privilege and near serfdom was the gap between luxury and misery. The chasm of distinction in Russia had always been Eastern and feudal, not modern European, something like that between the princely classes and the untouchables in India. Perhaps this was why revolution had come first to Russia, though Katia was certain much of Europe needed it as well. She would find a way to do her part.

Here in Second Class, she found much of what Lenin considered the true enemy, the great barrier to upheaval: the solid middle class, the bourgeoisie, and the sense of false opportunity by which this class was used to deceive the masses. At home in the countryside, the same was true of the richer peasants, the kulaks. Some of the strong younger leaders, like Dzerzhinsky and Stalin, recently had proclaimed the need to exterminate these enemies and were already performing that cruel duty. The Decembrists, nearly a hundred years before, had not understood these realities and had paid for their naiveté with death and exile.

"Isabelle says you, too, are going to Shanghai, mademoiselle," said one of the Frenchmen eagerly, pouring Katerina a glass of red and offering her a cigarette.

"Jacques is going to be the athletic director of the Cercle Sportif," said Isabelle. "And Antoine's family lives in Shanghai." The big blond lad smiled at her. "His father is with the police in the French Concession."

"What sports will you teach?" Katerina asked Jacques, disliking the mention of colonial police.

"Tennis, fencing, horsemanship, gymnastics," replied the young instructor, smiling. "Everything except *boule*."

The third Frenchman rose and stepped to the stand-up piano that was secured to the wall between two portholes. He set his wine glass on the bench beside him and ran the keys.

"*Du jazz, Charles!*" called Jacques. "*La musique américaine!*"

Katerina drank wine and smoked Gitanes, indifferent to the attentions she was receiving but welcoming the distraction. At last she could act like a pretty young woman freed of the vicious animal that had dominated her for so long.

Later, when the piano stopped, and before an accordion began to wheeze and play, she thought she heard her own language spoken at a table behind her. Katerina was thrilled, despite the coarseness of the accent and the words. To that, she had become accustomed. She turned and peered through the smoke.

Two men sat alone at a small table set against a bulkhead. Both had the hard worn blocky faces of men who had reason to look older than their years. Both had narrow heads with their eyes set close together like a single lens. The two were drinking from a bottle of clear liquor with no label. A pocket watch lay open on the table between them. The smaller man took a set of dice from a pocket and rolled up his sleeves. He spat into one palm, then rolled the dice across the table against the wall. The larger man closed the watch and carefully put it away. Then he turned up one sleeve to slightly above the wrist and lifted the dice. "*Chóba!*" He shook the dice high in the air in his joined cupped hands. "Again!"

Katerina noticed a tattoo on the man's wrist: a large wolf with the wings of a bat. His neck, both hands and even each finger, were dark with tattoos. A dagger darkened one forefinger.

She looked away and sought to recall what she had heard in the Cheka. Long-serving prisoners used tattoos as a code, especially in the more brutal camps of Siberia. Tattoos were a prison language that was both social and political. On a man's hands and fingers, they constituted a warning to others. There the indelible marks represented a final uncompromising commitment to the criminal life.

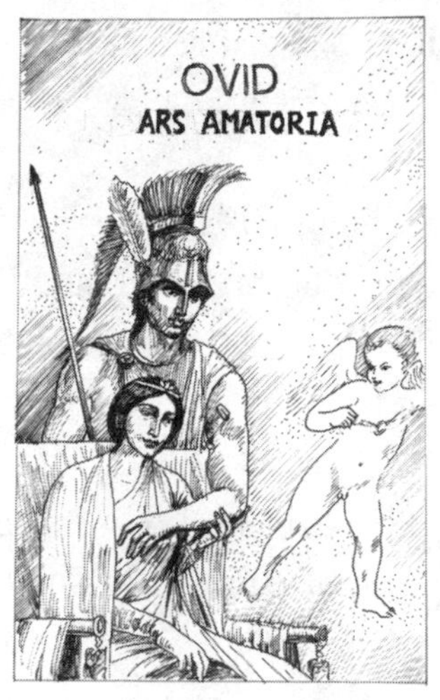

- 17 -

"Thank you for the flowers," said Laila Hammond as she and Alexander left the rail and strolled aft along the starlit deck. "You brought the countryside into my cabin."

"The captain's table has been empty without you." Alexander was dying to unbutton the high white collar of her dress and kiss her smooth dark neck.

"If I am eating alone, generally I prefer to have a tray in my stateroom. Then I can read without people feeling sorry for me or trying to talk to me."

"May I offer you a drink?" He could not imagine her being alone.

"With pleasure," said Mrs. Hammond. "But not in one of the public rooms, if you don't mind." She glanced at him as they walked. "Please understand that I am a married lady, and it is a small world, and a smaller boat."

"That leaves us three choices." Alexander paused as they came to the open deck of the stern, part of the First Class deck promenade. A long wooden bench was built against the rear housing, protecting any seated passengers from the wind.

"Three?"

"Here, or in a stateroom." He smiled before gesturing at the bench, making the more proper choice himself. "Would you mind waiting for me here while I fetch us a drink?"

Laila Hammond sat erect in the center of the bench and drew her thin white shawl around her shoulders. Alexander hurried to a stairway, trying to diminish his limp as he left her.

He returned with a towel and his cane over one arm and a small tray with two glasses and an ice bucket.

"Champagne?" He bowed.

"Please," she said. "You serve so well, you must be Goan."

They drank and talked as the night cooled. Their bench became a moving island in the night.

Alexander first explained how he had come to France to find his sister. He went on to speak of his father and their struggles in Shanghai. His candor surprised him. Mr. Hak Lee and Mei-lan would not have recommended it. Perhaps it was the near darkness, or the champagne, or the isolation of the sea that made him reveal so much. Perhaps it was a need for intimacy. Or was it Laila Hammond herself?

"May I ask what brought you to France?" he asked after a time.

"Yes," she said. "If our conversation is our own."

"Of course."

"I prefer to talk to very few people, but to do so with openness."

He filled their glasses. She had long dark slender fingers and perfect clear nails.

"My husband is not well," she said. "For four years Derrick has been in a clinic in the south of France. After a lifetime in Ceylon, the climate suits him better than England or Switzerland, and the doctors are not much worse." She shivered a bit. "It seems there is little they can do."

Alexander took off his jacket.

"Please don't. You'll be cold," she said as he draped it around her shoulders. "But thank you."

Alexander felt the fresh chill of the night sea. "Is he very ill?"

"Derrick looks well, very well, though he is older than I by sixteen years." She gave Alexander an assessing look. "Even more years, I think, than I am older than you, young Count Karlov." Her voice seemed to smile. He watched her lips.

"You look a bit the way he used to," she said. "Though he was even more handsome."

Slightly annoyed by the comparison, Alexander did not reply.

"Derrick's illness is mental, but he can still be most charming. Some days he is lucid, plausible and very cheerful, perhaps too much so." Laila drank again before continuing. "Others he is wretched, almost silent, angry and even dangerous, perhaps to himself, possibly to others. Sometimes he swings so quickly between euphoria and morbidity."

"Do you see him often?"

"It is difficult," she said with regret, looking at the sea. "Ceylon is so far away. So I have been studying in England and visiting Derrick in France. I always go for his birthday and stay as long as I can. But after a few days I seem to disturb him even more. His temperament, and our problems in Ceylon, finally drive me away or even home. We have no children, though Derrick has a son, Jason, by his first wife. For me, my studies at Oxford are a holiday."

She seemed troubled, and Alexander was relieved to turn to this more hopeful topic. "What have you been studying?"

"What we call *Literae Humaniores*, at LMH, Lady Margaret Hall, for my second degree." She saw his incomprehension. "Greats."

"Greats?"

"Classics. Latin and Greek, for my doctorate."

Alexander was impressed. "May I call you Doctor Hammond?"

"Not until I know the results of my examinations."

"You will pass."

His confidence made her regard him more intently. "Have you been to university?"

"No." Alexander grinned. "I think it's too late. I never finished school."

"Why ever not?"

"They closed my school in St. Petersburg when the revolution came in 'seventeen. It was an old military academy, the Corps des Pages. My father went there as well." Alexander emptied his glass. "Then, in Shanghai, my father died, and there was so much I had to do." Like money and murder, he thought. He poured the last drops of champagne into both glasses. "We need another bottle," he observed.

"Yes," she said without hesitation, standing and handing Alexander his jacket. "I have one in my stateroom." He was astonished by her proposal.

As he followed Laila, his eyes caught the suggestion of her derriere. It carried not the full soft look offered by Violetta or Lydia Richards, but the high firm invitation he had noticed in photographs in Paris of Josephine Baker, "*la Vénus d'ébène.*"

Viktor Polyak shouldered aside another passenger as he pushed forward. At last *Le Karnak* was under way. He forced his way between two men in faded khaki tunics until he stood at the crowded rail of the narrow Third Class deck. Wooden crates with stencilled addresses in Lyons and Haïphong were lashed to stanchions behind them. The men wore white military caps. They were eating black olives from a crumpled scrap of newspaper.

"*Eh, là! Attention!*" exclaimed one of them. A large thick-set man himself, he turned to face Polyak in angry protest. Almost shoulder to shoulder, his face red, he stared up into the eyes of the Commissar. Then he looked down and saw the steel double hook tapping the rail. The man spat a pit into the sea and turned to his companion. "*Noch ein Schwein französisch.*"

Polyak noticed the metal buttons that secured the men's jackets. A grenade with flames bursting from it was embossed on each button. The Foreign Legion. He had seen these oppressors in the French Concession of Shanghai.

The Commissar looked back at the port and saw a black police Citröen hurtle onto the wharf and brake sharply. Two officers stepped out and spoke to a pier boss. The man shrugged and gestured at the departing vessel. Other ships were tied up nearby, stern-to-pier at the busy home port of the Messageries Maritimes, what French sailors called "La Joliette."

Polyak had been fortunate at the last moment to buy a steerage passage to Port Saïd on the *Karnak*, a 10,000-tonner, a "*bateau vite*" with two tall funnels bound for Egypt, the Indian Ocean, Saigon and Shanghai.

For once he had plenty of money, enough to buy a First Class passage to Shanghai or anywhere else. And he had more than money. He had sewn the old bitch's emerald into the lining at the top of his left boot.

He knew he would prefer the anonymity and atmosphere of Third Class. His three cabin mates seemed harmless enough, two French veterans hungry for a new life of opportunity in the East, and the fussy Laotian domestic of a rich imperialist family sailing First Class for Haïphong. The toilet cabinet that they shared with the next cabin contained a small sink with one tap and cold sea water.

Fortunately, the *Karnak* was swifter than the *China Star* and the two ships might share several ports of call before Shanghai. The routes of these vessels always reflected the hopeless distortions of imperialism. This ship would stop somewhere in French North Africa, and later probably at Madagascar, Réunion and Haïphong. The English steamer would favor the British colonies.

The throbbing of the engines lulled him as Polyak closed his eyes and thought of what he must do when he caught the girl.

Despite four years with him, and all that he had done for her, including giving her a child, and after four years of severe re-education, it was now evident that there was some perversity bound inside Katerina Karlov that he could not yet control. Not the ethic of her class and its rotten values, but something more personal, perhaps the proud defiant fibre of her evil family. The Commissar recalled again her father's burning eyes as the old count lay bleeding with his limbs destroyed. He must not rest until the young count, too, was dead and his sister either obedient or dead herself.

Mrs. Hammond's stateroom was much like Alexander's: compact, efficient with tight luxury. The head of the broad bed was set in a depression in the interior wall. Two upholstered chairs and a small round table were centered beneath two portholes. An ice bucket covered by a towel rested on the table beside a basket of fruit. She must have been planning to drink by herself. A shallow escritoire or dressing table was fastened to the wall under a mirror between the bed and the narrow door to the bathroom. Flowered wallpaper and framed colonial scenes of Martinique, Cochin-China and Senegal decorated the walls. A vase of flowers stood on the bedside table. Books were everywhere, on a chair, on both tables and on the bed.

"Please," said Laila Hammond, gesturing at the seat not occupied by books.

Alexander sat, stretching out his leg. There was a moment of silence. Only the steady throbbing of the vessel reminded them where they were. Nervous, he examined the volumes on the table beside him. Thucydides, with Greek on the left-hand pages, and English on the right. Ovid, the verse in Latin and the footnotes in English. Two volumes of ancient Greek, to him incomprehensible.

"Is this sort of scholarship a lonely study?" he said as Laila took the dripping bottle from the bucket of melted ice and handed it to him.

"How did you know?" she asked, not waiting for a reply. "What are you reading?"

Alexander busied himself drying the bottle with the towel while he devised an answer.

"Dumas," he said, careful to keep one palm tight over the cork as he opened the champagne. His father would not forgive him if the cork flew at such a moment. "*The Count of Monte Cristo*. He is an old friend of mine, Edmond Dantès. He was born in Marseilles. Do you know him?"

She cocked her head, following his thought. "No. Would I like him?"

"You might love him. Mercédès always did, though she married his enemy." He filled their glasses. "In the end, the Count sails away with Haydee, a beautiful lady from a distant country." A beautiful dark exotic lady, he thought.

"If you were not here," said Mrs. Hammond, drinking, "I would be reading now. Ovid, I should think, this time of day. Or perhaps Catullus. They're both about *servitium amoris*, you know."

"Servo . . .?"

"Servitium amoris, enslavement to passion." She paused to see if he understood. "I always read at bedtime."

"Please do."

Laila Hammond waited to see if he was jesting, but he extended his hand, encouraging her. She chose a book from the side table and sat on the edge of the bed. She removed her shoes and seated herself gracefully with her long legs extended, as on a chaise longue. She turned on the lamp and sat back against the pillows, taking a sip of champagne before lifting a pair of spectacles from the table and setting them on her long high nose.

Laila seemed to be making few concessions to their flirtation, carrying on in her cabin as she would if alone. She was making him suit her. Alexander did not mind. On the contrary, he felt relieved of the burden of attempted seduction and its dance.

For the first time he observed clearly the shaped firmness of her face, not yet lined but lacking the softness of a younger woman. Could she be thirty? Thirty-five?

"Do you like poetry?" Laila glanced up through her lenses with huge black eyes as she opened the book. Her white skirt covered her legs. Her stockinged feet were like her hands, long and slender and dark against the clothes and the coverlet.

"Poetry?" he said, fearing a more detailed question. "Of course I like poetry."

"Perhaps something from the *Heroides*, then," she said. "They were love letters, of course, from legendary heroines to their lords." She turned to one bookmark after another. "Or perhaps a few verses from *Ars Amatoria*. Ovid was really more Italian than Roman, if you understand what I mean."

Alexander nodded, refilled their glasses and sat down once more. He could not believe that he was here with this older woman in her cabin. Never had he seen anyone so lovely, so compelling.

"'So various are women's hearts, that to catch a thousand takes a thousand arts,'" she read. "'Hearts have as many traits as faces. Like Proteus, the wise man, versatile, adapts.'" Her voice was soft, but her diction crisp. Laila paused and looked at him. "What do you think? Do you like it?"

Alexander rose with the bottle. Proteus? Proteus? Uncertain what to say, intensely aware of her but oblivious to the words, he stepped to the bed and filled her glass.

"Very much," he said. "I would like to hear it again."

She smiled and took his free hand. At her touch a current ran through him. "You have such long fingers," she said, turning his hand and looking at the palm. "Please sit here." She patted the bed.

He sat on the edge of the bed, almost touching her, the bottle still in one hand.

Laila looked at the wine and tapped the image of the sailboat on the label. "Let me read you another verse."

He nodded and she began. "'When the tables are spread, there's more than wine to turn your head. There Love, with soft arms and flushed face, has often given the horns of Bacchus an embrace.'"

She removed her glasses and continued without looking at the book. "'Wine makes all men lovers. Then girls bewitch men with desire, and Venus in the wine is a fire within a fire. Faults overlooked, night turns any woman into a goddess.'"

"These poems could break your heart," he said, hoping that was an adequate response. He set down the empty bottle.

Laila closed the book and placed it on the table. She reached up one hand and touched his cheek.

"They should," she said. Her fingers parted and stroked through the hair at the back of his head. Then again she touched his cheek, regarding him easily, as if her assessment were complete, and her decision was acceptance.

Astonished, sensing the invitation, Alexander leaned forward awkwardly towards her face.

He felt he was diving into her eyes. He closed his as he kissed Laila Hammond and embraced her. She did not resist as he drew her long body against his. Her small breasts were firm against his chest. But she did not embrace him or touch his body with her hands. He felt her body tremble like a tuning fork. He was aware of Laila waving one hand behind her head in some silent struggle with herself, as if she could not decide what to do with it or how to behave. She clenched the hand into a fist, her fingers tight with the tension of self-control. Then she rolled on top of him and suddenly drew back, breathing rapidly through parted lips as she lifted her head from his. He was embarrassed that she must feel the excitement of his body.

Laila rested her hands on his shoulders and looked down at him before she spoke. Her silky hair touched his face.

"I want you," she whispered, "but I cannot have you."

Alexander closed his eyes in resignation.

"You can stay if you wish," she said, disengaging gently as she steadied herself with long breaths, lying to one side, still touching him, careful to present no rejection in her restraint. "But there cannot be more than that."

"Would you like me to stay, Doctor Hammond?"

"Yes, my handsome boy. Yes." She leaned over him and slowly sucked and nibbled his lower lip until it bled. Then her soft lips kissed his mouth as if to taste his blood. Like a lioness cleaning her cub, her tongue licked his lip twice before she spoke again.

"For a long time I have been lonely and alone," she said, her voice barely audible.

She stood and took a white nightgown from the closet before stepping to the bathroom.

Almost dizzy, Alexander rose and removed his jacket, shoes and socks. He opened one porthole, then the other, and breathed in the sea. When she emerged, his back was to her as he stared into the night. He thought she would like that privacy, and perhaps the opportunity for initiative, for defining the degrees of their intimacy.

Laila hung up his jacket and turned off the lights and slipped into bed.

"Your pillow is waiting, Count Karlov."

- 18 -

"Good morning to you, Pedro!" said Alexander brightly. The early light sparkled off the ocean and shone through the porthole onto the small square table set for two. "English breakfast, if you please. And a pot of China tea with a tall glass on a saucer." He was tired of taking his tea in the delicate British way. This was a morning for Russians. He had never imagined the combination of frustration and satisfaction that he had experienced last night, and that Laila Hammond had provided with such dextrous deliberation.

Katia joined him as Pedro removed the bell-shaped silver cover from his plate of sausages, kidneys, grilled tomato and eggs. His twin's smooth short hair was brushed flat and back in the new *coupe garçonne*.

She was wearing tan linen walking-trousers. A modernism, almost mannish, they were cut in a stylish high-belted Parisian manner that favored *la ligne haricot vert* while suggesting an active life and freedom of movement.

The elegant simplicity of this new *silhouette androgyne* suited his sister, and probably her modern politics, but it did not suit Alexander. He recalled the handsome bill from Lanvin. What would their father have said? Extravagance never troubled him, but he was an ox about tradition.

Alexander was pleased that he had made it to the table first. He rose a bit and nodded across the dining cabin to the Richardses as the Goan held his sister's chair. Lydia waved her fingers. Richards smiled back at Karlov, as if pleased with himself. How could the girl sleep with him?

"Were you up late, Katia?" Alexander asked with a touch of paternal concern.

"Yes." She rested two books near the edge of the table. He recognized one as the scandalous new novel of women's emancipation, *La Garçonne*. Victor Margueritte was said to be celebrating a new sort of woman, one who thought for herself, could drive an automobile and smoked in public places. The other book had no cover.

"I was up very late. And you, Sasha?"

"No, I went to bed early."

"What a good boy. You seem so cheerful." She spread her large crisp napkin and stared at his plate. "I'll have the same, please. What wonderful food. They say it's the only meal the British know how to cook."

"Just one more day's steaming to Port Saïd," said Alexander after ordering for Katia before she could speak for herself. He sensed this annoyed his sister, but he was determined to maintain a few traditional male courtesies. "We can have four days in Egypt while the *Star* unloads and takes on cargo, then waits her turn to sail through the Canal to Port Suez."

"I think I'll just stay on board," Katerina said. "Do a little reading and see the Canal. I can always visit Egypt on the way back." Her expression changed. "And I'm still afraid Viktor might follow me to Egypt. He seemed to know where we were going. He has a hideous new metal hand. He looked like an animal fighting in that alley."

A true Bolshevik, thought Alexander as she started on her breakfast.

"Did he ever tell you how he lost his hand?" he asked, annoyed that Katia had already decided she would not remain in Shanghai.

"Only that it happened in China." She frowned. "He never talks about his hand. Except once with fury after a night of drinking. He swore something about 'a hand for a hand.'"

"I think I'd prefer 'a leg for a leg,'" said Alexander, with a tight grimace. "He broke mine on the train in Siberia just before he killed our mother and kidnapped you."

"Are you certain he killed Maman?"

"Yes, Katia. I saw it."

She nodded curtly, not wishing to acknowledge the confirmation. It was too painful, although it seemed so many years ago. "But how did Viktor lose his hand?"

"He and I were fighting on a railroad car platform on the Night Express for Nanking." Alexander decided not to mention that he had freed himself from Polyak's grip by jamming the bowl of the Commissar's burning pipe into the mouth of the Red agent. "He was trying to strangle me when I kicked him off me and he fell between the tracks."

Katerina set down her knife and fork, drawing back. "How horrible."

Could his twin be feeling sorry for Viktor Polyak? he wondered before replying. Was that possible? "Yes," he said, "your calling him an animal is very apt."

Alexander dropped a spoonful of raspberry preserve into his tea and stirred the glass. He sensed that for now she did not want to hear more. He understood. He himself did not wish to learn everything about Katia's old life in Moscow with Polyak and the Bolsheviks.

For the present their intimate sensibilities seemed to be inclining them both towards mutual discretion rather than to mutual disclosure.

He decided not to mention that the bones of Polyak's large left hand, most of them broken, now decorated the bottom of a fish tank in the office of Mr. Hak Lee. After being nibbled clean by the ravenous snakeheads, the bones served as an inspiration to the gang leader's delinquent debtors.

They continued to eat in silence. "I think I'll go up on deck and read," Katerina announced at last.

"Your deck chair is number thirty-two," he said. "Port side."

"What? I have to sit in seat number thirty-two?" Katia rose at once and picked up her books. "Are we back in school? Why must the English always arrange everyone so strictly? It's just another extension of their little social tyrannies."

"Perhaps you can find a more agreeable arrangement belowdecks," said Alexander.

Instead of appreciating what their father and he had achieved in Shanghai, and what it was providing for her now, she was resenting it all as if each detail were one more unearned part of their former privileged life. He guessed Katia resented the English because of their long support for the Whites in the civil war at home.

"What about the new Russia?" he added, knowing he was taking it too far. "Doesn't the Party tell people what to do? Are the peasants less hungry or the workers better sheltered?"

"Alexander," she answered sharply. She turned back and leaned her knuckles on the edge of the table and spoke down at him in a tight controlled voice, though not quietly enough. An elderly English couple stared at her from the adjoining table as Katerina talked in rapid Russian.

"Haven't you learned anything, Sasha? Anything at all?"

He restrained himself at first. Never answer the wrong questions. Ignore what you do not wish to hear, the old count used to teach by his own example. And never argue with a woman.

"If you want to argue, please sit down and do it like a lady," Alexander said with rigid calm. "If you wish to give a lecture, I suggest you stand in the center of the room and raise your voice just a trifle more. You could give everyone a talk on world socialism."

"Do not tell me what to do." Blood rushed to her face. Her voice hardened as her hands trembled.

"Katerina Karlov . . ."

"You are not my father, though you are sounding just like him."

"Thank you."

"Stop it, Sasha! Can't you see that these stupid class distinctions are what made revolution come to Russia, and to France a hundred and fifty years ago?"

"Come, Katia," he scoffed. "Don't your commissars live better than your beloved proletariat? Who do you think is eating the caviar now, while everyone else is starving? Is the Kremlin empty? Who do you think is sleeping in the palaces?"

His sister turned and strode to the door, her hands clenched like an arthritic.

The English woman raised both eyebrows and whispered to her husband.

"Russians, you know, or some such thing. Did you see what he did to his tea?"

"*Occupé!*" barked Viktor Polyak through the bolted door to the next cabin. The latch turned and shook again. "Occupé!"

The neighboring Annamese families were forever hogging the small common bathroom on the *Karnak* and leaving nests of long dark hairs in the sink. Occasionally, the stink of sweet incense came under the door from their cabin. If he was not confined in a ship, he would teach a few lessons to these French Asiatics, especially to one provocative young woman.

Polyak unstrapped his artificial hand and held each part of it under the dribbling salt water. That vile French doctor had not made it to the standard of the smaller British original. The baser metal was already revealing its weakness. It had been adequate for the thin neck of the hag with the emerald, but the smaller hook had bent sideways in the struggle with the czarist sergeant. The swine had not been easy to kill, and there had not been time to watch him die. There would have been no czars without such animals as slavemasters.

While the larger hook pierced the sergeant's cheek, the smaller sharper one had caught awkwardly beneath the bone of the dying man's jaw. Meanwhile Katerina Karlov had been screaming at Polyak before she fled. With a crowd gathering at the head of the alley, there was no time for delicacy. Pressing one knee down on Narodsky's shoulder, the Commissar had ripped the hook roughly from the sergeant's face, tearing it through the hinge of his jaw just below the ear.

In addition, the two hooks were not soundly secured to the base. Polyak was considering taking the implement to the ship's workshop and soliciting assistance from some plumber or mechanic.

He completed the rinsing and dried the hooks on his shirt. He pressed the shirt to his nose, then rinsed it and unbolted the door.

The latch turned. An Annamese woman, young and with a baby sucking at her swollen breast, opened the door he had unbolted. Her shiny straight dark hair hung to her waist.

The woman gasped as she almost blundered into the big Russian and saw him holding his hook in his hand. The baby began to cry. Polyak stood close to her against the sink, smelling her and staring down at her breasts. He saw a bubble of milk on her nipple, and he wanted it.

Entering his cabin, Polyak left the door open behind him. His cabin mates were absent. They hated the throbbing of the ship's engines that were near the steerage cabins.

The Commissar hung his wet shirt on a loose rivet. He lay down on his bunk with his boots braced against the steel bulkhead above the foot of his berth. He watched the woman in the bathroom as she set her naked child in the sink. He sensed her fear as she covered her breasts with one hand and took a quick step into his cabin to grab the edge of the bathroom door and close it behind her before bolting it. These animals were making a sewer of his sink. He smelled the cloying odor of their incense.

Polyak lit a French cigarette and stared through the smoke that clouded against the bottom of the bunk above him. His artificial hand rested beside him on the narrow berth. The loud drumming and vibrations of the engines did not bother him.

He scratched his stump and thought of the work ahead of him in China for the Cheka and the Comintern. His first assignment was liaison with the dockworkers' union and their comrades from the Party recently started by Mao Tse-tung. But he knew Shanghai was not yet ready for a true general strike. Too many desperate unemployed Chinese were willing to slave in the city of greed. He would also be responsible for eliminating any revanchist leaders among the 30,000 White refugees now living mostly in the French section of the Chinese port. That congenial duty might be more readily accomplished, he thought, tapping the hook on his knee. One day all China would be Red and the Party would destroy both the imperialists and the primitive ways of the mandarins and the superstitions of Confucius and the Buddhists.

It was not a bad time to be away from Moscow. Like a wounded hyena, the Revolution had started to devour itself. Dzerzhinsky's Red Terror had identified new enemies. At first only the priests and aristocrats, the merchants and White Guards had answered for their crimes. But now the Trotskyites and anarchists, the socialists and Mensheviks were being arrested in the night, tortured and deported to Siberia. Even Viktor Polyak himself had dangerous enemies in the Cheka.

Although he had missed the *China Star* in Marseilles, at least the Androv brothers were on board and were not known to the Karlovs. Todor was as clever as Oskar was stupid. Even Chekists who did not know Todor Androv admired the Ferret for his reputation. Set him on the hunt, and Todor would pursue his quarry down the longest, darkest, most twisting tunnel. In a celebrated chase, the Ferret, adept in wild country, had hunted down the Siberian villager who had led the revanchist White officers to the secret mine in the forest near Ekaterinburg. There the Reds had dumped the bodies of the czar and his murdered children and covered them with quicklime. There the Ferret had helped the villager and his wife to endure an inspired punishment for their service to the Whites.

The brothers knew their duties and appreciated the efficient and educational role of violence. Polyak envied Todor's specialized training, especially his skills at surveillance, disguise and pursuit. But he was not certain how far the two would carry things forward on their own.

He had told both brothers to secure fresh papers from two other passengers. Beyond that, it might be best to do any rough work ashore, perhaps in Egypt, rather than to risk being trapped on a vessel with no escape if things went wrong.

As for new papers, Polyak must secure some himself. Not from a cabin mate, though he would not mind seeing one of them disappearing into the vessel's wake. Perhaps a Legionnaire. Even the French did not care about them. The mongrel regiment had fought with the Whites and their allies for two years at Archangel. When the Foreign Legion finally left Russia, most Russian Legionnaires had stayed on and joined White units, still with their French uniforms and equipment.

The Commissar sat up on the edge of the berth and wiped his hook on the bed sheet before strapping it on. It was time to begin hunting for a Legionnaire.

Cocktails in the smoking room of the *China Star* provided the opportunity to meet and talk without the hazards of being trapped at a dinner table. To meet, one stood. To be private, one sat.

"What a peculiar drink, if I may say so, Count Katkof," said Richard Richards amiably, rocking on the heels of his black patent leather pumps. "Vodka with Indian tonic water? Wouldn't it stand up better with a double gin?"

"Count Karlov is Russian, dear." Lydia gave Alexander a private smile. "They drink vodka, you see."

"Ah, of course." Richards looked about the room and returned his attention to Alexander. "But there's one thing I know you Russians understand near as well as we do."

"May I ask what that is, sir?" said Karlov, pretending he did not know. Lydia had told him that the old merchant could discuss only one subject. Though Alexander's mind was preoccupied with Laila Hammond, he could not help thinking of Lydia in a bathtub with his soaps, her breasts playful as slick fat dolphins, arcing from the water through the bubbles when she moved.

"Cotton, of course. The world is made of cotton. Everyone needs the stuff. Army uniforms, ladies' underwear, hospital bandages, whatever. The Gypies make the very best, long staple, fibres two inches long. *Gossypium barbadense*. Grows in the Nile Delta on sixty feet of top soil. Yanks and Chinks only have the medium staple, *Gossypium hirsutum*. Sea Island's the exception." Lydia yawned and glanced about the room as her husband settled in.

"Only Egypt has three planting seasons a year, one of 'em for cotton. Key is plenty of sun, just enough water and bone-cheap labor, like India. Mississippi had slaves. In the Egyptian Delta they still have the fedayeen. China and India were never important until the American Civil War cut off the cotton states."

"I believe my family sold our cotton estates shortly after Alexander the Second freed the serfs in 1861." And we were lucky to survive two serf rebellions long before that, thought Alexander.

"You don't say. Russia was always near the top of the market, until the

Reds came along and ruined all your exports. Now they're all starving. Oh, sorry . . ."

Richards paused, but Karlov did not reply.

"The cotton exchange in Alexandria is an absolute cockpit. Better than the Royal Exchange in Manchester. Shows the real market like nowhere else. Futures, puts, calls. Splendid fun. Brokers screaming and bidding, feathers flying. Fortunes lost. Cotton men send their sons from Bombay and Tennessee just to learn the game."

"Really?" said Alexander, watching the door.

"Yes, indeed. One of the sights of Egypt, better than the Sphinx. Why don't you meet me there and take a peek while Lydia goes shopping at the souk? Should still be a few old Russkies in the pit."

"Sounds most interesting, sir."

"Will you and your sister join us for dinner?" cut in Lydia as a steward swung the bell and the passengers began to stream towards the door.

"That would be lovely," said Alexander, looking about. He had not seen Katia since breakfast, or Mrs. Hammond all day. "I hope you don't mind if my sister joins us a bit late."

Katerina seemed to be making the journey on her own, leaving her brother to his own pursuit while she hung about with a French crowd and other new acquaintances she had found below.

Karlov dined and chatted with the Richardses. He found he liked them both. By the time the roast was served, Katerina still had not appeared. He knew she found them tedious.

"Perhaps your sister is not much of a sailor?" said Lydia. "Do you think she is feeling out of sorts?"

"More than likely." Alexander could guess where she was dining. In the lowest place she could find. Then he noticed people at the next table staring at the door.

His breath stopped. He saw Laila Hammond hesitate before being led to a single table against the wall. She was as stunning as he had expected. Elegant ebony, she had the proud carriage and mysterious darkness he would expect of an Ethiopian princess. She was wearing a long silk dress, something like a sari, alluring but dignified. Glancing around the cabin with forthright eyes, she set a book on the table and ordered quickly.

"I say," said Richard Richards, setting back his shoulders. "Who is that?"

"Flan or compote for you, dear?" Lydia replied, annoyed the men were eyeing the exotic beauty.

"You know what I like," answered Richards, adjusting his black bow tie.

"Two plum compotes and one flan, if you please," ordered Alexander, guessing, sorry that Pedro was not serving them. He was careful not to stare, but observed Laila polishing her glasses on her napkin.

Alexander finished his dessert just as Mrs. Hammond was served her first course. He folded his napkin and rose.

"Would you both mind terribly if I went to see how my sister is doing?" he said.

"What a sweet brother," said Lydia Richards.

Alexander gestured at Pedro as he left, not acknowledging Mrs. Hammond. The Goan followed him to the outside passage.

"Two bottles of Heidsieck, Pedro." He slipped some sterling into the man's palm. "One to the Richards' table with my compliments, one for me to take on deck. Two glasses, if you please."

He sat alone on the bench on the upper deck with a cigar in his hand and the champagne on a tray at his feet. Europe lay to port, Africa to starboard. His torpedo burned down as the evening cooled. Then he heard the tapping of a woman's heels and the moment was complete.

"May I borrow your jacket, Count Karlov?"

He set it on her shoulders and turned up the collar.

"Thank you." She touched his cheek with appreciation. "You know what Ovid said."

He raised both eyebrows but did not reply.

"A frivolous mind is won by small attentions."

• • •

Now they were sitting up in bed, with Homer between them. A glass of champagne rested on each narrow bedside table. Laila was wearing a creamy silk nightgown. Her dark skin dotted through the pale lace like the spots on a leopard. Her eyeglasses rested near the tip of her nose. He was wearing only his crisply starched dress shirt and black bow tie. Two gold studs in the shape of tiny Maltese crosses held the shirt together.

It was heaven as it was. Alexander restrained himself, careful not to spoil it.

"It's your turn to read, Alex." Mrs. Hammond passed him *The Iliad.* "This one's for boys. Book Two, please." She removed her spectacles and lifted her glass, then rested her left hand on the bed cover above his leg. "Of course, Paris was Helen's first younger man, you know. Otherwise, Troy would still be standing."

" 'Now slept the gods, and those who fought at Troy,' " he began.

"I must say I'm disappointed that you can behave so well," she interrupted. She undid his tie and slid one hand beneath the covers. "I'm afraid I cannot."

" 'Now slept the gods . . .' ah," he struggled.

"Don't worry," she said as her nails touched his thigh. "You know I'm not going to make love. But I want to please you so much that I will not lose you."

"What about Homer?"

"Do see if you can continue our lesson while I try to be a good hostess and entertain my guest." She removed her spectacles. "Anyway, you're too young to know what to do all by yourself." Laila dipped her head beneath the covers.

" 'Now slept . . .' " Alexander closed his eyes and clenched the book and gasped.

"Not so loud." She raised her head. "Please do not cry out. It will bring a steward."

Chastened, Alexander reached for his glass and moved his other hand along her smooth shoulder as Laila, cat-like, licked him clean.

Calm for the moment, but knowing she was now excited, he wondered when Laila would give him the chance to surprise her with what Lily had taught him during those afternoons at Mei-lan's bordello: how to please a woman. Too young, was he? Had Mrs. Hammond experienced the Devil's Knot?

"Some champagne, please." She sat up and held out her glass.

He filled it, then took one small breast between his hands as if cupping a precious drink of water in both palms. He squeezed her long pointed nipple. It was even darker than the rest of her skin, almost black, somehow too dark, and he found himself hesitating before kissing it.

"Don't make me spill," she said, gently freeing herself. "Please remember that here I am the hostess, so you must do things as I wish. If I come to visit you, in your cabin, there Count Karlov will be the host, and we will do things his way for a time."

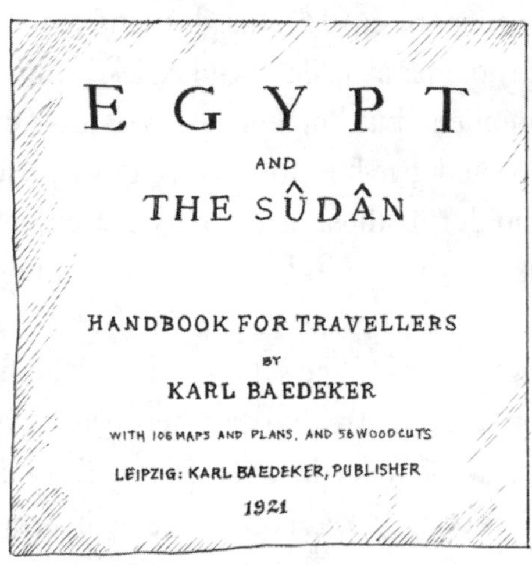
EGYPT

AND

THE SÛDÂN

HANDBOOK FOR TRAVELLERS

BY

KARL BAEDEKER

WITH 106 MAPS AND PLANS, AND 56 WOODCUTS

LEIPZIG: KARL BAEDEKER, PUBLISHER

1921

- 19 -

The starboard rails were crowded when the *China Star* passed the low sand hills of the coast and slipped between the buoys at the entrance to the harbor of Port Saïd. Two massive breakwaters, each thousands of yards long, protected the inner harbor from the muddy effluent of the Nile. Excited passengers pointed at the lighthouse as the crew opened the hatches, unfastened the booms and lowered the gangways. A broad-bellied barge was secured against bumpers to the port side of the *Star*.

Ferdinande de Lesseps waited to receive them near the landward end of one breakwater. The brilliant French engineer stood over twenty feet tall, mounted on an even taller pedestal. His great achievement began somewhere behind his statue.

Alexander recognized the hot dry air of the desert gusting across the busy port, an introduction to the Sahara and the khamsin. He stood at the top of the First Class gangway holding a small leather-and-canvas overnight case. He had arranged to be met by a car and driver to take him to Alexandria for a day in his namesake city before boarding the night train to Cairo. First he would collect Mrs. Hammond at a hotel a short distance from the port.

"Have a lovely time, Sasha," said Katia, friendly again in parting, kissing her twin goodbye. "Say hello to the Sphinx."

"Be careful," he said. "I'll see you Sunday at Suez." He had asked Pedro to look after his sister and report anything alarming to a ship's officer. He was not comfortable with her new friends. "Please have one of your mates watch out for Miss Karlov if she visits Second. I'll be at Mena House in Cairo."

Lighters and barges crossed the thick dark water as the disembarking passengers were helped into small boats waiting at the bottom of the gangways. A giant dredger labored nearby. Native workers swarmed ashore from a stern-wheel steamer. Stripped to the waist, barefoot in baggy trousers and headcloths, dark-skinned navvies and porters worked the piers. Alexander glanced back at the *Star*. First two Austins, then a Bentley were being lifted from her hold on pallets and lowered by the forward boom over the side to the barge. Deckhands hauled on guide ropes to prevent the vehicles from spinning in the air.

Customs officers and the agents of Thomas Cook and various hotels waited to receive the passengers as they stepped from the boats at the Custom House. A thin Egyptian in sandals, loose trousers and a tattered pinstripe jacket with peak lapels pressed towards Alexander.

"I am Nubar Ali, sir, best driver." He seized Karlov's case and handed it to a second man. "You need guide, sir? My brother, big dragoman, Hector Ali here, present to you Alexandria, all Egypt, Aswan, Abu Simbel." As he spoke, the other man touched his forehead and climbed into the front seat of the old Morris. The rear seat had been neatly patched with what appeared to be fragments of a corduroy jacket, pockets and all. The tires, smooth as black balloons, were of different sizes.

"No thank you, Nubar. Just to the Casino Palace, if you please."

"Hector Ali escort you everywhere. Beach, Golf Club, Pompey's Pillar, Royal Yacht Club, Circolo Italiano." Nubar turned to face Alexander, keeping one hand on the wheel. "Esplanade, museum archeologic, Deutscher Club." The car hurtled between a green tram and a broken-down donkey cart piled with onions and carrots. "You so good gentleman, effendi, perhaps require best very young lady for afternoon hotel?"

"Not today, thank you," said Karlov, already feeling more at home than he had in France. The din and scents of the port, the ceaseless importuning, the warm erotic vitality, all the scrambled turmoil of East and West, reminded him of home.

The Morris drew up at the Casino Palace. Before Hector or Alexander could alight, two young beggars leaped onto the narrow running boards on either side of the car. They stretched thin arms in through the windows with open palms. Uniformed in a long *gallabiyyah*, green sash and fez, a stout hotel doorman advanced to the motorcar swinging a short-handled horsehair whip.

"Dogs!" he cried, lashing the legs of the nearest beggar. "Leave my master in peace!" Both boys dashed out of reach while the attendant opened the door for Alexander and passed his case to a bowing porter. The quick use of the *qurbash* reminded him of the knouts long carried by the Cossacks to keep order for the czar. He wondered if this small fierce drama was a routine demonstration of the valuable service provided by the doorman.

Soon Karlov was seated in a tall rattan chair on the hotel's generous veranda, enjoying the sea view while drinking foamy red orange juice and thick coffee and glancing at the headlines of yesterday's *Egyptian Gazette*. "Cotton Market: Bull Movement Continues," he read. "Prince Farûq Celebrates Third Birthday."

"Good morning, Count Karlov." Laila Hammond smiled and joined him. She set her wide-brimmed Panama on an empty seat and touched her hair with one hand. "Are you interested in archeology?" she said, opening her Baedeker.

"Archeology?" said Alexander, more inspired by Nubar's earlier suggestion. "Of course. Fine idea. Let's start by taking a room and reading your guidebook in bed."

"Have we time?" Laila 's eyes brightened. She seemed more carefree than on board, her spirit light as a schoolgirl's. Perhaps the clinic in the south of France was now part of a different world.

An elaborately framed photograph of King Fuad hung on the wall behind the concierge, who was uniformed *à la Suisse* but wearing a fez. Celebrated even in Paris for his 400-room palace and numberless harem, Alexander was confident that the shrewd old king would understand this brief visit to the hotel.

"Have you a room?" he asked at the desk. "Just for the morning. With a good bath, if you please."

"Of course, sir," said the man blandly, accepting his baksheesh with a nod and clapping his hands for a porter.

Upstairs, an ice bucket, a pitcher of blood-orange juice and Karl Baedeker's *Egypt and The Sûdân—Handbook for Travellers* were soon waiting on the bedside table. A mosquito net, unopened, was coiled overhead like a trap set above the bed. Two fans turned slowly beside it, like ancient propellers unable to gain loft.

Immediately Mrs. Hammond undressed and slipped beneath the covers. She was not wearing her spectacles, he noticed. Perhaps she was now intent on pleasing herself rather than Alexander.

He opened the guidebook and climbed into bed. Acting studious, he sat back against the headboard and turned to "History and Topography of Ancient Alexandria."

At first Laila lay on her side, touching him from toe to shoulder. He tried to appear disinterested.

"'Alexandria was founded in three-thirty-one B.CC. by Alexander the Great,'" read Alexander, thinking of softer things, "'and forms a magnificent and lasting memorial of his Egyptian campaign.'"

Laila slowly covered more and more of him with the smooth warm chocolate of her skin as she curled into him like a cat. He skipped a page.

"'Caesar was afterwards conquered by the charms of the Egyptian queen, Cleopatra, but Antony fell more fatally into her toils and spent years of dissipation with her at Alexandria . . .'"

"Have we time for dissipation, Count Karlov?"

"Do I have your attention, Dr. Hammond?" he countered, pretending not to be excited by her attentions though it was evident he was.

"Completely," she whispered. Her lips touched his ear.

"Is this the way you study Greats at Oxford?"

"Don't be impertinent." She squeezed him until he shrieked.

"I lost my place," he said, closing the book.

"Good," she said. "We will have to start again." The curtain of her hair swept from his shoulder down his side to his lower body, tickling him with advancing promise.

Holding her breast with one hand and Karl Baedeker with the other, Alexander closed his eyes and trembled as he enjoyed the deep generosity of her lips.

Whenever Alexander shut his eyes he seemed to smell her more completely. He was uncertain whether it was Laila Hammond herself or some perfume, a faint scent that suggested cinnamon or sandalwood. When he pressed his nose into her skin he imagined it was like coming ashore in a small open boat on a spice island like Pemba or Halmahera where the scented air of the land would overwhelm the sea.

He looked up, the blood hot in his face. "That's it," he said excitedly. "You know what the French say."

"The French?"

"*C'est une question de la peau*, they say. That's how you know if the other person suits you deeply, and they're right. It's a matter of the skin."

He pressed his cheek against the smoothness of her inner thigh and inhaled before he used his tongue.

"I do not know how much more of this I can manage," she said huskily. "I feel like a Catholic schoolgirl, tormented by what I want but will not accept, trying to compensate my lover for what I withhold."

"Oh." Alexander pulled himself up against the pillows. A little more compensation would be welcome. "That sounds awfully complicated, Mrs. Hammond. And I was just getting used to it all."

He put ice and a dash of juice into both glasses and poured the champagne. "But I'm afraid we should get up. Egypt is waiting. Nubar is driving us to Alexandria, and we have things to do there before we take the night train to Cairo."

Laila parted his hair in the center with the fingers of one hand as he spoke, then rose from the bed with her glass. She made no attempt to cover herself as she stepped to the tall French window and gazed at the Mediterranean through the thin white curtain. She turned and faced him.

"I will visit the museum while you meet your friend at the Cotton Bourse."

She sipped champagne and licked red froth from her lower lip as she regarded him. The darkness of her skin outlined her body against the curtain. Her waist was small and tapered. Her derriere was high and tight, a bit generous, round as two halves of a ball, but a bit dimpled in each cheek.

Alexander had never seen anything more beautiful.

"Minet el-Bassal, the Bourse," said Nubar. "I present to you the Cotton Exchange, effendi." Hector Ali held open the car door for Karlov.

Alexander climbed the broad steps of the massive stone building. He advised the doorkeeper that he had come to join Mr. Richards. He passed from the warm bright Egyptian day into the gloom of a wide high-ceilinged entrance hall.

A clamor of voices and shouted orders rolled towards him from the broad open doors of the floor of the Exchange. His eyes adjusted. Servants passed him bearing copper trays loaded with small cups of steaming coffee. Messengers ripped strips of paper from three telegraph machines mounted on pedestals just inside the entrance.

"Aha! Count Katkov!" cried the friendly voice of Richard Richards as the Englishman hurried to his side.

"We have come at a fine time. It is a day for traders! The Exchange is in turmoil." The Englishman carried a small clutch of brown order chits in one hand. His round face was flushed. His eyes shone.

"It seems there are floods in India, a dock strike in America, and in Lower Egypt a plague of pink boll worms and the Jew's Mallow weed." He clapped Karlov's shoulder. "Altogether, a perfect day. There is no cotton. These are the moments that make men poor and rich!"

Richards grasped Alexander's arm. "It is not that the price is too high, boy. It is that some of the traders have obligations, forward contracts, that they cannot meet. It is not so much actual cotton that is being sold, but rather guesses as to its future value, do you see?"

A trader nearby held up two blue seller's tickets in each hand. Well-dressed men in three-piece suits and expensive gallabiyyahs swarmed about him, jostling and grabbing like schoolboys, bidding furiously and making offers for his orders. Throughout the crowded hall, merchants yelled and clamored as two men with long sticks changed the prices posted on a gallery board at the far end of the great hall.

A runner jostled Karlov as he burrowed through the crowds. Annoyed, rocking on his cane, Alexander stepped to the side of the hall. Richards, seeming to relish the madness, became embroiled in the scramble.

A very tall European in a short broad jacket pushed aggressively towards two men standing next to Alexander. He shouted orders in French and Arabic as he approached, evidently desperate to buy. His face was wet with perspiration.

Alexander heard a sharp cry. He looked down into the crowd and saw the back of a young Egyptian boy, richly dressed in a dark suit and a scarlet tarbush. The tall Frenchman knocked the child aside as he advanced, pushing heavily against the youth's shoulder so that he was almost spun around. The trader continued forward, shouting as he advanced, several brown bid tickets held high in his left hand and a cigarette in his right.

Alexander saw the boy's face as he spun and fell forward onto his knees.

It was not a child, but a dwarf.

The little man's face was red with fury. For a moment he hesitated with his hands on the floor and his round bald head raised and swinging from side to side like a turtle's. Vivid raised patches of proud flesh marred his head with pink and white ridges where he must once have suffered burns. His tarbush lay on the floor amid a scattering of precious blue chits.

"How dare you, sir!" the small man cried, scooping together his tickets with both hands as the Frenchman glanced down and nearly stepped on him.

The dwarf's left eye appeared to be made of glass or ivory. His small ears hung in empty loops like the handles of a vase.

Alexander Karlov reached down and offered a hand to the little man. The dwarf did not accept it. Unable to bend his left leg, Alexander lowered himself on one hand and helped to collect the chits. There were not two or three, such as other fortunate traders held, but twenty-five or thirty.

For an instant their faces came close and their eyes locked. The two seemed to be alone in the immense hall. It was like coming face to face with a badger in a tunnel.

Karlov had never seen such intensity. Anger and pride were contained in the dwarf like two explosive elements inside a bomb. His grey eye blazed.

Then the little man's expression altered, as if he saw that behind the offer of assistance there was not pity, but courtesy. His eye blinked once and changed, like an owl adjusting to the dawn.

The dwarf took Alexander's hand and collected himself for a moment before rising with deliberate dignity. Karlov had never felt skin so smooth or a grip so firm. The small man had the skin of a baby and the grip of a Black Sea crab.

The dwarf released his hand.

Alexander heard the voice of the Frenchman and his tone of ridicule.

"*Regarde-moi ça! Quelle horreur!*" The man laughed. "*Quel petit imbécile!*"

The dwarf stood before Alexander in the press and gazed up at Karlov with an assessing eye. Slowly his face grew pale as the blood left his hairless skin. He pulled down his cuffs and adjusted his collar. He settled his tarbush on the smooth dome of his head and moved the red silk tassel until it hung properly to the left. He set back his uneven shoulders. Alexander noticed the perfect English cut of his worsted herringbone suit, artfully tailored to accommodate his deformities.

"I am Olivio Fonseca Alavedo, sir," the dwarf said evenly with a bow. "You are Russian, I perceive."

"I am, indeed, sir." How had he known? Alexander clicked his heels. "Alexander Karlov at your service."

Behind him the Frenchman glanced at the cane and snickered. "*Quelle drôle de théâtre! Deux infirmes du cirque.*"

Alexander clenched his cane and turned to the tall trader. His father's slow cold anger rose within him as if the old count were still alive, armed and eager for a duel.

"I believe you owe this gentleman an apology," said Karlov in educated French.

"'Gentleman?'" The Frenchman stared down at the dwarf as if he had found a slug on a rosebush. The man turned to his companion. "Who are these two? Is this a business exchange or a circus sideshow?"

"My name is Alexander Karlov. Now you owe us two apologies, and I will have them, sir."

"Nonsense." The man turned away. "I have cotton to buy."

"He will buy no cotton today," hissed the dwarf to Karlov. He clapped his hands.

Two Egyptian traders hurried eagerly to his side.

"Effendi?" asked one, touching his tarbush.

"Whenever that Frenchman attempts to make an order, Mamoud, you will place a bid just above his price. You too, Salah."

The dwarf"s voice tightened like a wrench gripping a nut.

"If that man does business today, so much as a single bale, even the cheapest Ashmouni or Gallini, you two and your sons will never do more with me. Your mothers will beg in the alleys. Your sisters will be sold to the camel butchers."

"Of course, effendi. As you wish." Mamoud bowed. He did not seem surprised by what he had heard. "But up to what price the bale? Up to what amount?"

"Until I tell you to desist. For any amount." The dwarf shrugged. "That Frenchman is not a man of money." He handed Alexander an engraved card.

"If it would be helpful," said Karlov to Olivio Alavedo, recalling the Frenchman's reference to himself, "I would be most pleased to place a substantial order for my own account." Mr. Hak Lee would appreciate this sort of business wagering, especially its double purpose.

"Done, sir." The dwarf nodded at Mamoud. "You will buy Mr. Karlov five hundred bales at my own next price."

"Would you like a letter of credit against my order?" asked Alexander. He wondered if the little man was a student of the Count of Monte Cristo, that master of revenge by commerce.

"Not necessary, I would say. By the close of business this afternoon, we will have sold these orders at a profit."

"As you wish. Tomorrow I will be in Cairo, at Mena House."

The dwarf regarded him with increased interest. "Should you have time, Mr. Karlov, please grant me the honor of calling on me in Cairo at my new café. I am in your debt, and I am not comfortable with obligation."

"You have no obligation, sir." Alexander handed him a card. "None at all."

Olivio Alavedo seemed pleased by the gesture. "I have few friends," he said. "Now you are one. If there is any service that you require, it will be done. Faster than you can ask."

"You are most kind, but I don't believe I will need any assistance in Cairo." Other than what Mrs. Hammond might provide, he thought.

Alexander bowed and stepped back against the wall. He bought a cup of coffee from a waiter. After he had finished it, he walked over to Richard Richards as Alavedo turned and whispered to one of his agents.

"Damnedest thing," said Richards. "There's a Frog over there by the price board trying to buy a small amount of cotton to cover his early sales. But the price keeps going up. Every time he bids, some little Gypie agent buys above his bid price. And if the Frog does not meet his contracts, he will be obliged to resign from the Exchange and he will be ruined."

"I think I know the gentleman you mention."

"I thought you might," Richards smiled roundly. "Isn't that the stretched-out Frenchie you and the midget messed about with?"

"Perhaps." Alexander nodded. "I believe the short gentleman you speak of, Mr. Alavedo, is a dwarf, not a midget."

"They tell me he comes from Goa, said to be the bastard grandson of a Portuguese bishop. Nearly burned alive in a fire down in Kenya. The little chap has sugar in Brazil and cork forests and port in Portugal. Now he's building some sort of restaurant or café on a houseboat in Cairo." Richards paused, but the young Russian did not reply.

"You seem to have a hand for getting into mischief, Count Katkof. Can I offer you a drink at the Members' Bar?"

"What a sound idea," said Karlov, following him. "Please call me Alexander."

They stood at the quiet end of the long hardwood bar. Overhead, dark wooden fans turned swiftly, sucking up the smoke in cloudy cones.

"Longest bar in Lower Egypt," said Richards as he paid for two gin and tonics. "Ever seen one like it? In St. James's they don't have the space, or enough members who don't mind drinking with each other. Never get over those old schoolboy hatreds, you know. Who wants to? Where's the fun in that?"

Alexander recognized the colonial spirit: loyal to England in their bones, but appreciative of the distance that gave them a measure of freedom they would never find at home.

The Frenchman suddenly appeared at the doorway to the bar, as if searching for someone.

"I thought he was done with," grumbled Richards, none too quietly. "When will those chaps learn they lost the Battle of the Nile and go back to Toulouse? I'll never understand why everything in Alexandria is still named in French."

The tall man approached Karlov with a wary charm in his eyes. He seemed suspended between pride and some useful social grace.

"Messieurs ..." he began. He clutched his handkerchief in his left hand.

"I am Richard Richards," said the English broker. "May I present you to Count Alexander Kartkof."

"*Enchanté*," said Alexander.

The Frenchman hesitated, evidently uncomfortable that Karlov spoke his language.

"Antoine Lefevre, *à votre service*." He bowed. "*Je suis désolé, monsieur le comte*."

Alexander waved one hand and set down his drink while the man spoke with care, as if hoping to slip sideways through brambles without tearing his coat on a thorn.

"I was rushing to business, and I spoke in haste, jesting, meaning no offense, you understand. Please accept my regrets."

"Meaning no offense?" snapped Karlov incredulously in rapid French, attempting to look the man directly in the eye. "Two cripples in a circus, you called us? Now you are adding dishonesty to insult, sir. Is this a lesson in Gallic diplomacy?"

The man opened his mouth but did not reply.

"To me your words are nothing." Alexander shrugged. He wondered if the man could fence. "It is to Monsieur Olivio Alavedo that a full apology is due at once, sir, before these drinks are finished."

Lefevre hesitated, as if weighing two prices on a scale known only to himself. Money or pride?

"Of course," he said after a moment, making his choice as he watched Richards sip his gin and tap several blue chits on the bar. "I will do so now. You have my word." He wiped his brow as he hurried from the bar.

"The Frenchies never give a true apology, do they? Always edge around it like a snake in the path. That's something they beat into us at school. Only way to learn, really." Richards raised a hand for the bartender's attention, then turned back to Alexander. "But I say, Arthur, if you're hoping to make that Cairo train, you'd best mount up."

- 20 -

The purposeful frenzy of Alexandria's railroad station, the *Gare du Caire*, reminded Karlov of Shanghai's North Station. He was not late, but nearly so.

Steam wafted back along the platform from the long black locomotive of the Egyptian Railway. A shrill whistle blasted from another track. Tall ironwork columns rose like giant palms, spreading at their tops like fronds to support the smoky glass panels of the roof. Not unlike the great hangers of *Les Halles*, Alexander thought, remembering his last dawn breakfast there after a long night of drinking and dancing in Paris.

Immaculate stewards waited beside the steps at the end of each First Class Pullman coach. Hector Ali handed Karlov's valise and ticket to a steward.

"Compartment Seven, sir." The man led him down the spotless carpeted passage and unlocked the door.

"Thank you," said Alexander. "A bottle of champagne, if you please."

Even more than his shipboard cabin, the compartment possessed a tight measure of efficient luxury. Beside the tiny triangular corner sink and panelled mirror stood a narrow door that must lead to the adjoining compartment. Alexander slipped open the bolt and hung his jacket on a brass hook. The comfortable sofa faced forward, with an upper bunk folded against the wall above his head. Small leather nets were secured to the dark wooden walls at either end of the top and lower berths, replacing bedside tables for nighttime conveniences.

Alexander lowered the window by its leather strap and leaned out on his folded arms. The noise and smells of the station filled his compartment. Vendors raised to his window trays laden with fruit, single cigarettes and nuts in paper cones.

A sharp whistle blew. The train puffed from the station as the steward returned with the champagne and a copy of that morning's *Egyptian Gazette*. Dark smoke from the engine clouded past. The gathering intensity of the great steam locomotives always reminded Alexander of a horse preparing for a race. Snorting and building steam, they held back their power and breathed like a massive wheeled animal before the start. A whiff of coal dust entered the cabin. The attendant closed the window.

Green rice fields, tall golden sugarcane and oxen turning water wheels glided slowly by the window like a cinema film of the Egypt that was legend. The short trip to Cairo, a hundred and thirty miles, ensured that the nightly run would be leisurely. Entering the rich Delta of the River Nile, the train crossed canals and passed a lake and clusters of tan clay dwellings crowned by small cupolas. Several light railway lines branched off into the distance.

Alexander sat calmly, an unlit cigar in his hand as the window darkened. Recalling that this railroad had been constructed by an Englishman nearly seventy years earlier, he was astonished again by the backwardness of his own country. Five miles on either side of the Trans-Siberian, most of Russia was a wilderness. How was it possible that, half a century or more ago, France and England had built more in Africa and Asia than his own countrymen ever built at home?

He recalled Katerina promising that the Soviets would create a new and better country. It had been their last argument before he departed for Alexandria. "Instead of making a new America in Siberia," he had replied, "your Red friends are building the world's biggest prison." Irritating as Katia was, however, he was troubled that he had left his sister alone on the ship.

Alexander leaned his head against the rounded headrest in the corner by the window. The clacking of the wheels lulled him.

He was awakened by the tickle of a woman's hair on his neck, her scent in his breath and her lips on his cheek.

"And good evening to you, Doctor Hammond," he murmured, not opening his eyes, holding the moment. He turned to kiss her, sensing a still less-guarded passion in Laila as she unbuttoned his shirt and ran her nails along his sides. Like Ivan Pavlov training a puppy, she had learned how to excite him with just a suggestion of what lay ahead. He felt her tremble.

Then Laila stopped herself, sighed, kissed him lightly and rose.

"Will you take me to the restaurant car while they make up the compartments for the night?"

"If you insist," he said, unable to keep the sulkiness from his voice.

"Then perhaps we will come back to Count Karlov's cabin, and do things his way," Laila added, raising her chin and pouting her lips together as she fixed them in the looking glass.

"Just give me a moment to change my shirt," said Alexander eagerly, hoping he understood her rightly. He hurried to button the garment, then extended his arm to her. "Are we ready?"

• • •

Fortunately, there were two of them to divide the work, thought Todor Androv as he repeated his instructions to his brother before he left the *Star*. Oskar had never been quite the same since he had accidentally electrocuted himself during a particularly troublesome interrogation. Torture was not always the simple one-sided experience that critics of the Cheka claimed.

Todor feared that whatever decisions the two made in his absence, Viktor Polyak would react with fury. Only a hard death for Karlov and the total submission of his sister would satisfy the Commissar. The Ferret watched Oskar's peculiar fingers toy with his pocket watch until it chimed. The steel instrument was the only possession for which his brother cared.

Todor recalled a fundamental lesson of his training: never lose a quarry. The two brothers must now separate, and each must do his duty. Although he was no longer at his best, Oskar was still dependable enough at murder. His unusual appearance would be less noticeable in Cairo than on shipboard. Demonic tattoos might designate some brutal status to a Siberian life-server, but they held little charm for the urban bourgeoisie.

"You will follow that bastard count, Oskar, and dispose of him in Egypt. Cairo is a big city, the biggest in Africa, and we have friends there if you need them."

Polyak would appreciate that choice. In Paris and Shanghai, Count Karlov had the support and protection of other Whites, and friends and sympathetic police who conspired with the revanchists. In Cairo, Karlov would be unsupported, friendless and distracted by his new black whore. In Egypt there would be no one to protect or miss or mourn him.

"If we fail, Oskar, Polyak will make Siberia seem like a summer resort on the Black Sea."

Oskar nodded and rubbed olive oil into his hands, always tingling and painful since he had gone too far with the prison tattoos.

Working on the flesh-less skin of the fingers without proper tools or inks, the Siberian tattooist had damaged the nerves of both hands and introduced poisons that had hardened the sheaths of his tendons until several fingers were permanently curled like the heel talons of a vulture.

"If you lose Karlov, you can be certain of finding him at the most costly and fashionable imperialist establishments. There are two hotels in Cairo where he might stay, one on the Nile in the city, Shepheard's, and its satellite, the Semiramis. The other is by the pyramids, Mena House. For a little money, Oskar, the native staff will do what you ask. They must despise the imperialists."

Todor Androv paused to be certain his brother understood the mission. When Oskar nodded, the Ferret gave him a handful of folded currency.

"When you have finished, try to secure some evidence that you have killed him. Without that, Polyak will never believe us. In the meanwhile, I will watch that suka, that bitch here on board."

"What should I do about the Count's woman?" asked Oskar. "The tall dark one."

"Dispose of his whore as well. Better two dead than one witness." Todor Androv handed his brother the faded passport of an engine-room hand who had possessed the same hairline and almost the same shape of head as Oskar, if not the same eyes and mouth. No one could have Oskar Androv's eyes and still be living.

"I will see you at Suez, brother."

Mrs. Hammond turned off the switch while Alexander bolted the door to the compartment. It had been their first meal together, and they drank to that before they dined.

A perfect avocado from the Delta had been followed by roast lamb and red currant jelly accompanied by a moderate claret. All at a small table in the pink glow of a tiny lamp with a pleated shade, but with starched linen and agreeable service as Egypt slid slowly past. Once she touched his knee with her hand.

Now only a dim blue night-light illuminated the crisp linen of the narrow berth.

Laila sat on the edge of the bed and bent to unstrap her shoes.

"Allow me, Mrs. Hammond." Mindful of her earlier promise, Alexander leaned his cane in the corner and hung his jacket from a hook. He must show that his way would be her pleasure.

"Please let me be your host." He knelt and began to remove her shoes. She sat back and rotated each foot around its ankle when it was freed.

Alexander took her feet one by one, pressing both thumbs into each arch and squeezing the toes together as if he were wringing out a towel or twisting a pepper grinder.

As she relaxed and released herself, he slipped both hands up one calf beneath her skirt. His breathing stopped as he felt her long firm thigh, then the smooth softness inside her upper leg just above the top band of her silk stocking. He unsnapped the top of the stocking from her garter belt and rolled it neatly down her leg as Laila cast back her head and closed her eyes.

Again he ran both hands up that leg, feeling now the open warmth of her skin. He did the same with her other leg, then raised the front of her skirt to her hips. The muscles of her thighs tightened. He reached up and placed one hand on her cheek, with his thumb across her lips. She kissed the thumb and sucked it in between her lips. He drew his hand away and ran it up her leg until his thumb entered her gently. After a moment, Alexander could smell her readiness. He reached under her skirt and gripped a tight round cheek in each hand and moved his head up between her thighs, pressing his nose into her, tickling her with his hair, scratching her with his cheeks.

Laila Hammond twitched once, then grabbed his hair with both hands. Her body twisted and writhed as his lips and tongue kept after her.

Suddenly she squirmed and screamed as if she were being slaughtered.

Someone banged twice against the cabin wall next door.

Alexander stood and took off his shirt and trousers as the few lights of the Delta villages sparkled and passed slowly in the night while his lover removed her clothes. A long tear ran down the back of his shirt where her nails had scratched him through the garment.

Laila lay back with her head against the wall beside the window. She sighed once, deeply, as if emptying herself of all the past, as if her life were beginning once more. Then her quieter breathing was lost in the rhythmic clacking of the wheels.

They were too confined to try the Devil's Knot. Instead he seized one of Laila's feet and pulled her body down towards the foot of the berth. He forced that foot, then the other, into the strong flexible leather netting on the wall above the bottom of the bed.

Without being asked she slipped both her hands into the webbing at the head of the berth. Already the tension of their first lovemaking had been replaced by a mutual complaisance. Soon they would know each other.

Alexander pressed a button and the night-light vanished. He settled on the narrow bunk with his knees tight against her hips. In a moment Mrs. Hammond cried out again. Her body arched and jumped like a fish on a riverbank.

- 21 -

"Whilst in Cairo, Count Karlov is my guest," read the card waiting with the concierge. A gold coffered ceiling and elaborate arabesque details on the walls and moldings received them like an Ottoman palace.

"Welcome to Mena House," said the desk man, passing a large key to the bellboy. "Señor Alavedo, your host, has selected your rooms."

"Our host?" protested Alexander, wary of obligation. "I . . ."

"Everything is provided for, sir." The concierge waved one hand. "Señor Alavedo leaves no choice in such matters."

It was the second surprise of the morning. As they had stepped from the train at Main Station, Hector Ali had been waiting to receive them on the platform with a porter. He must have driven through the night from Alexandria.

"Good morning, effendi. Madame," Hector said without explanation. He cuffed the aged porter on the shoulder and gestured at the bags before bowing to Mrs. Hammond.They had found Nubar Ali outside the station rolling a front wheel to the back of the Morris, a spanner in the other hand. His pinstripe jacket was split partway up the back. The old car was already clean and dusted after its run from Alexandria but had a fresh dent in one front fender. Nubar showed no sign of fatigue as he drove like a rally champion across the English Bridge and down the Shari el-Giza to the grand hotel by the pyramids.

The two rooms were dark and cool. A ceiling fan was turning slowly. The boy drew the heavy curtains and folded back the shutters with a bow and both hands extended, as if presenting a stage in the theatre or at the opera.

The Sphinx reposed before them, a giant lion with the face of a man basking in the bright clear light of the desert morning.

Laila Hammond opened the French doors. She stepped onto the balcony and sat without speaking on a rattan chair with both hands folded in her lap, content as if she had come home.

"Coffee, if you please," said Karlov quietly to the boy. He noticed an envelope in front of three platters of fruit. These were not the tired offerings of hard pears and bruised bananas to be found in most staterooms and hotels, but three perfect pyramids of mangoes, avocados and blood oranges. Alexander felt several avocados and mangoes and found that the riper ones were arranged at the top. He opened the envelope and drew out a card:

The Cataract Café

Please accept this small offering from my farms. With your permission, my motor will call for you at 6:00 and bring you to my café.

Olivio Fonseca Alavedo

A smaller envelope, unsealed, waited inside the first. It contained crisp banknotes, Egyptian pounds, folded around a second card. "With the unwitting compliments of Monsieur Lefevre, your French acquaintance in Alexandria," read the note, in the same compact angular hand as the first.

Later, exhausted by visiting the Citadel and three hours at the *Musée des Antiquités Egyptiennes*, Alexander was prepared for the small comforts of a café. The touring had been more gruelling than a fencing match and, with Dr. Hammond, more mentally taxing than an advanced ballistics examination at the Corps des Pages.

The complexities of dynasties and hieroglyphics were strenuous enough without the added commentaries of Plutarch and Herodotus, who accompanied Laila as if they were still living and whispering at her elbow. For the first time Alexander Karlov had been tempted to use his leg as an excuse for retreat. Only when he dropped his cane in the Graeco-Roman Room of Gallery X did Mrs. Hammond relent.

"I will spare you Ptolemy," she said with the austere exasperation of an unappreciated pedagogue.

Laila and he had bathed alone in their separate bathrooms. She had required some privacy after the intimacies of the previous night. One person often stepped back afterwards, he knew, and Mei-lan had advised him that this was never the moment to demand assurance. The key was to learn what pleased your lover.

He thought of how the extreme darkness of Laila's nipples sometimes disturbed his enthusiasm for the glories of her skin and body. He recalled Mei-lan deploring the cautious lover's habit of searching for imperfection, unwittingly seeking to justify the self-protection of one's own emotional restraint. Wiser lovers would find passion by revelling in each other's finer attributes. With Dr. Hammond, he should not find that difficult.

The telephone rang. Their motorcar was here. Alexander stepped to the half-open bedroom door and knocked.

"Your car is waiting, Mrs. Hammond."

Laila soon emerged, cool as an ice figure, dressed in a suit the color of pale peaches and wearing the ruthless high heels of Paris. Her black skin seemed to shine.

She approached Alexander, put one hand on his cheek and kissed him long on the lips as if she were drawing the world into her. She made no effort to spare or redo her lipstick.

Almost dizzy with surprise and delight, Alexander followed her like a puppy from the room and down the wide hall to the stairs. He did not feel that sense of relaxed mastery that most male animals seem to display after sex, like a lion yawning, or a cock strutting in the barnyard. Perhaps he was not the master. Already the sleeping car seemed a distant adventure. Would it be repeated?

Karlov gripped the stair rail and frowned as he tried to recall more of the intimate wisdom of Mei-lan. The man often acquires ascendancy for a time after the woman has surrendered her power of sexual denial. But some women, instinctive courtesans, retain a different but related influence, establishing inside the man a subtle subservience or dependency, so that his sense of need endures. For almost every man, she said, no matter how otherwise strong and independent, there is one woman who retains that emotional authority and skill. Rarely do both parties simultaneously balance the emotional and the sensual.

This was all too confusing to contemplate just now, thought Alexander, smiling to himself as he hurried to catch up with Laila crossing the marble lobby.

"I am Tariq, sir, Señor Alavedo's driver," said a massive dark-skinned man in a white gallabiyyah standing at the bottom of the hotel's steps. He opened the door to a maroon Daimler as the doorman stepped aside. Nubar and Hector stared at them with desolation from their place with the other guides and drivers at the bottom of the circular drive. Karlov reminded himself to take proper care of both men later. He must also find a way to repay the dwarf.

"Where are we going, Tariq?" asked Laila Hammond, drawing herself forward with the plush cord attached to the back of the front seat as they turned onto the Shari el-Nil.

"To the Embankment, madame, to my lord's Café. It is a new houseboat on the Nile."

The Daimler sailed through the chaos of Cairo traffic like a galleon through a swarm of fishing smacks. Donkeys and buses, hand-drawn carts and camels parted before the gleaming machine.

They drew up beside the broad sidewalk of the limestone embankment. Small boys played and idled on the parapet, staring down at the *feluccas* and *gayyasas* that plied the busy river. Planks, rigging and two barrels were stacked beneath the embankment's eucalyptus trees under the guard of what appeared to be another Tariq. One of the boys found a nail near the boards and slipped it into a pocket of his robe. The big man put his qurbash under one arm. With one eye still on the boys, he opened the door of the Daimler.

"My brother, Haqim, effendi," explained Tariq as they emerged from the car.

An old Ford lorry with a wooden box body pulled up behind the automobile. Two youths with shovels sat on a pile of sand in the back.

Alexander glanced down from the embankment at the partly finished vessel. He was reminded of a naval lecture he had attended at the Corps des Pages. Was it the fifteenth century when the Portuguese set out in their caravels, compact agile ships with three lateen sails and high rounded bows? Sailing down and up two coasts of Africa before crossing the Indian Ocean from Mombasa to Goa and Ceylon, where they built thick-walled stone forts that for centuries flew the blue-and-white flag of Portugal and harbored her language, religion and commerce? Was this little man playing Vasco da Gama on the Nile?

This vessel, though its main deck was incomplete and its masts had not been raised, had the lines and the high bow and stern of a seaworthy caravel. Four shipwrights, adzes and chisels and wooden mallets in hand, their dark chests and shoulders slick with sweat, straddled the thick beams that joined her sides above a deep rounded hold. A gangway with a tan-and-green canvas awning led from the embankment to the ship.

Alexander offered his hand, but Laila Hammond preceded him on her own. The walkway swayed as the caravel was rocked by the movement of the river and the activities on board. The cool musty smell of the river rose around him, reminding Karlov of the more pungent odor of Soochow Creek.

"Aha! Welcome!" cried the dwarf, his smiling face pale and round as the moon.

"Welcome to the Cataract Café!" He climbed down from the high cushioned seat of a formal desk set beneath a large umbrella on the poop deck. A bit unsteady, Alavedo seized the edge of the desk with his tiny hands. "Forgive the agitation of my vessel. Save for one cabin, she is unfinished and in need of ballast."

"Mrs. Hammond," said Alexander, "may I present our host, my friend from Alexandria, Señor Olivio Fonseca Alavedo."

"Olivio, to you both." The dwarf kissed her hand. "At your service, madame." His eye widened and shone with the joy of his inspection. A different man might have made Alexander jealous.

The three sat at a large café table under an umbrella. Silent servants waited on them with trays carried up a ladder from the unfinished waist of the vessel. Fresh mango juice and varied hot samosas were set before them.

"You and I share the tie of Portugal," said the dwarf to Laila Hammond, drawing his two hands apart in the air like a pair of cymbals. "Both our countries were islands colonized by the blood of the Tagus and the Douro, were they not?"

Alexander had the sense that he himself was not present, as if the little man were taking his lady on some magic voyage on which he was not invited. Could sexual energy be entangled with his other surprising powers?

"Indeed they were," replied Mrs. Hammond with her smile. "But my people, or some of them, came to Ceylon with the Dutch in the eighteenth century, not with the Portuguese in the sixteenth."

She sipped her juice and continued without Alavedo's having to encourage her, except with the focus of his expression. It reminded Alexander of another man who had the same attentive concentration with women but a different manner and style. Both appeared to listen as if caring what a woman said. "You must make each lady think she is the only woman in the world," his father had urged, "but never for too long, lest they behave as if they are."

"And on the other side we were Tamils," Laila added. "Dravidians brought from southern India to labor on the plantations in the hills, though we had a written language older than Lisbon or Amsterdam. First we picked coffee beans, until the rust fungus ravaged the island fifty years ago. 'Devastating Emily,' the old planters called the leaf blight, *Hemileia Vastatrix*. Emily nearly ruined them all, but when the coffee died the determined ones saved themselves by planting tea seeds and bushes from Assam. So they put us back to work, and the Tamils bent and planted tea."

The dwarf nodded thoughtfully. "I myself have coffee," he said. "In another Portuguese land, Brazil. Have you an interest in tea or coffee?"

"Not directly, but through my husband." Mrs. Hammond hesitated. "My own family has been in trade and pearls and gemstones."

Alexander realized he had already learned more about Laila than he had the entire week, in bed and out. Nettled, he selected a second mushroom samosa.

Suddenly Haqim cried out from the embankment. The caravel rocked as a barrel of nails was rolled down the gangway, bouncing on each tread. Two men attempted to control its descent.

The barrel broke free. It knocked the lower man into the river and gained speed as it hurtled and bounced down the gangway. At the bottom it left the ramp and pitched out over the open hold like a child flying off the bottom of a slide.

There was an explosive crash belowdecks. Echoing voices from the hold shrieked and wailed. Tariq clambered down. Alexander left his cane on the deck and hurried down a ladder into the hold.

"Idiots!" cried the dwarf, his face red as his tarbush. He scuttled to the rail of the poop deck and stared down. "Fools! This is why the work is never done. Must I do everything myself?"

Alexander walked awkwardly on the thin layer of sand that covered the sloping bottom of the hold. He limped towards a fallen man. The worker lay moaning, surrounded by the splinters of the barrel. One of his shoulders was bloody and open to the bone. His right arm appeared broken in two places. Nails were scattered about in the sand. Alexander bent to help the man. Tariq, knowing the priorities of his master, was inspecting the vessel for damage to the hold.

"Send that wretch to the beggars' clinic!" shrilled the dwarf from above. "The Qasr el-Aini. And have that other idiot down there gather up those costly nails." Alexander glanced up. Only Alavedo's flushed face appeared against the cloudless blue Egyptian sky, like a single shiny mango hanging from a branch.

"What would I do without my Nubians?" Karlov heard his host exclaim more calmly. "These fellahs are useless."

Tariq climbed the ladder. The injured man was draped across his shoulders like the carcass of a deer. A wrist and one ankle were gripped together in Tariq's right hand. Blood spread down his gallabiyyah.

Alexander heard Laila and Olivio laughing as he reappeared on the poop deck. Their chatter ceased as he approached them.

He heard the voice of the man who had fallen in the river, hollering for a rope to be dropped to him from the side. Alexander glanced down, wondering if he should help. He saw the Egyptian paddling amidst the scummy spoiled fruit and river rats that floated between the embankment and the caravel. His robe floated around his head like a lily pad around a water flower. The rats reminded Alexander of the Paris sewers.

"Drop that man no rope, unless it is to hang him!" cried the dwarf, agitated again. “Why would I take him back on board my vessel? For what?” Alavedo’s anger simmered like oil in a pan, popping and spitting with heat. “What does he think this is? A playground? Let him wash down to the public steps.”

Alexander looked up at the Embankment. He saw Tariq settle the injured worker in the back of a donkey cart like a sack of grain. The big Nubian gave the driver a few coins and the man lashed his tired beast.

Ignoring the matter, Haqim was supervising the construction of a wooden chute to funnel the new sand into the ship’s hold.

“The Sahara is my ballast,” explained the dwarf, gentling himself as he regained the attention of his guests. “I apologize for all this foolishness.” He clapped his hands. “Now I think we need something a trifle stronger.” A servant appeared at the head of the stair. “Gin, and a bottle of white wine, Abdul.”

Laila smiled at Alexander before turning again to their host.

“Have you been long in Egypt?” she asked Olivio.

“I came last year,” said the dwarf. “After many years and some difficulties in British East Africa, and after settling various family affairs in Portugal and elsewhere.” He spoke with geniality, his calm regained. “I find Cairo a place of deep interest and opportunity, though it is a city of thieves and rogues. In Egypt everything is precious, even water. There are fortunes waiting, in cotton, sugar, antiquities, gambling. And in time every person of interest passes by.”

- 22 -

"If you'll just wait, please, Alex, while I go upstairs and change my shoes." Laila folded her napkin and touched his hand. The grand Moorish dining room of Mena House was dominated by what lay outside its windows. In the light of the half moon the pyramid of Cheops rose into the night. "All my life I have wanted to climb the Great Pyramid by moonlight."

Alexander smiled and rose from his seat. He knew he could never do the same. He had, nevertheless, purchased two tickets for the ascent. The Beduin guides had offered to carry him up, assuring him that he would not be the first to accept such complete assistance. Most climbers, however fit and active, welcomed some support in case they became giddy or stumbled. The Beduin, working in teams, offered a sort of canvas sling for the more helpless. Infirmity was a business.

He rolled a cigar in his fingers. He was determined to climb unassisted as far as he could, at least far enough to share Mrs. Hammond's scholarly adventure and to have her feel that he participated in her enthusiasm.

She returned soon, smiling like a schoolgirl, her hair in a tight bun, a paisley scarf around her neck, wearing tan trousers and the low leather boots of an Alpine hiker. He gave his jacket to a desk clerk.

They left the hotel and walked hand-in-hand to the Beduin canopy near the base of the pyramid. There the sheikh assigned them five guides, the two sturdiest to Alexander. Several other parties were setting out and returning. By the time they arrived at the north-east corner of the monument, they seemed to be virtually alone. Each side of the pyramid was two hundred and fifty yards long, Laila announced, requiring no guide book. "It is far taller than the tip of St. Peter's dome."

Alexander glanced up. His leg hurt from the strain of walking across the uneven sand and rock. Wind was rising from the Western Desert, stirring the sand just enough to feel its sharpness as it flew. The air itself tasted different than on the river. Cleaner and sharper, as if another Africa were coming to them across the Sahara from the south.

In the clear brightness of the desert night, he could see shadowy figures resting and scuttling like beetles along the face of the pyramid. A few were alone, but most moved in clusters. After the first few levels of the ascent, many travellers accepted the help of three Beduin, one holding each hand and the third pushing or supporting from behind. The descent was said to be more dangerous and fatiguing. A larger group, nine or ten small figures, had collected on the flat platform at the very top.

Laila touched the pyramid with one hand, gauging the height of the tiers. Each stone step was about three feet high. Before the surface limestone covering was removed, the smooth sides must have blazed in the sun.

"Please start," Alexander said, hoping Laila would not notice his awkwardness or feel obliged to share his pace. "Don't wait for me, I'll just go up as best I can."

Relieved by his offer, she kissed his cheek and set off with her three guides.

Alexander handed his cane to one of the remaining Beduin. Both guides climbed the first mammoth stone and reached down with one hand to assist him. He put his good leg forward onto the corner of the stone and they pulled him up by his hands. At the top of each step he paused and glanced up at Laila as she moved steadily up the face. She hesitated occasionally, no doubt enjoying the expanding view of the canals and palm groves that she had already described to him.

By the time he had climbed thirty feet, Alexander was exhausted. He waved off the eager Beduin who waited on the stone above. Instead he sat down against the rock and took a cigar from his silver case.

After a time he looked up and saw Laila at the very top. She appeared to be alone. He thought he saw her guides resting a step or two below, probably deferring to her wishes. Laila waved down at him, her scarf blowing in her hand as she moved it side to side like a naval semaphore. He noticed a single climber moving up nimbly on his own, perhaps halfway in a line directly between the two of them.

Alexander waved back. The sand was rising with the wind. Squinting, he lost sight of her as she disappeared to the other side of the high platform, doubtless viewing the great city in the distance on the Nile.

He sat down and leaned comfortably against the next stone, extending his left leg to the side. Using the sheath knife on his arm, he cut two slits in his torpedo, like the gills of a fish. In the wind he lit the cigar with difficulty.

Suddenly a woman's scream cut the night. Then a second cry, from the top of the Great Pyramid.

Alarmed, Alexander rose and peered up through the blowing sand. Two figures appeared to be fighting on the edge of the platform. He saw another clamber onto the platform as the first two fell together, as if embracing, onto the stone below. A gunshot cracked in the air. The two struggling figures rose to their knees and fell again, out of sight just around the corner angle of the pyramid.

"Quickly!" Alexander reached up his hands. The Beduin assisted him as he began to climb. After a dozen steps, he paused. His leg felt it was being pounded by a maul. Better to go straight across to the corner and look up, he thought. He leaned against the side of the next stone and instructed the guides to help him along the face.

From his new position he saw three figures gathered together a few steps below the top: Laila and two of her guides. A fourth person, standing near them, was shouting down to Alexander's Beduin.

Some levels lower, a burly man was scrambling down towards the eastern face, moving swiftly, like a lizard fleeing across a wall. Leaning against the stone with his left hand, Alexander hobbled to the east as fast as he could manage without his cane. The man changed his route to avoid the interception, descending faster but making less progress eastward. Yelling at his guides, Alexander pointed at him. The Beduin hesitated, probably mindful of the gunshot, but moved forward. The fleeing figure hurried down faster and faster.

By the time Karlov reached the line of his descent, the man was well below him and about to jump down from the last step. Alexander caught his breath and drew his knife. He stood sideways, one foot forward on the edge of the stone step, the other braced against the pyramid. He almost plunged down the face of the monument with the exertion of his throw. In the near darkness, he was unable to follow the flight of the blade to its finish.

The man stumbled as he hit the rocky sand at the base of the pyramid. He rose, limping at first, and made off into the flying sand as fast as he could run.

"One hundred pounds to the man who catches him," hollered Alexander. The two Beduin leaped down in hopeless pursuit.

• • •

Back at Mena House, Alexander paced about the sitting room while the physician and nurse from the Anglo-American Hospital attended to Mrs. Hammond in the bedroom. The police had taken his report downstairs in the hotel office. He sat down at the writing desk and examined the Beretta that one of the Beduin had found on the step where Laila and her attacker had fallen. It was a short-barrelled .38, a practical weapon for close work. Alexander's knife lay beside it. He had recovered the Marseilles blade in the sand near the base of the pyramid, with fresh blood on the tip of the weapon.

Laila had told him that while she was staring across the desert at Cairo she had heard a grunting breath as someone climbed onto the platform behind her. She thought it must be one of the guides attempting to press her for baksheesh. Annoyed, she turned sharply.

Instead there was a thick-set man with a narrow head and skin like she had never seen. His face was so close that she almost touched him when she turned. His neck and lower jaw were covered in tattoos that seemed to extend on below his collar. In the strange light it appeared as if his skin had been bound within a thick spider's web.

She instantly pushed the man from her. He staggered back as if himself dizzy from the climb. Cursing, he almost fell over the edge of the platform. As she screamed for the Beduin, the man drew a pistol. Furious, she struck her attacker with both hands, grabbing his arm as he raised the weapon. Then they struggled and fell as they tumbled roughly down two steps. The gun fired, grazing her right arm. The man had lost the pistol when he reached out to save himself a further fall. As the first guide came near, he fled.

Mrs. Hammond had been fortunate, said the English doctor, stepping out of the bedroom for a moment. "Scrapes and bruises, a twisted ankle and a flesh wound to the arm. Nothing a strong girl won't get over."

There was a knock on the outer door.

"Who is it?" said Karlov.

"It is I, your friend from Alexandria," said a low voice. "Olivio Fonseca Alavedo."

Alexander slipped the Beretta into a drawer and opened the door.

"The hotel informed me," said the little man with true concern, "and I came at once." Tariq stood behind his master, his arms folded across his chest. Alavedo spoke to him in Arabic. The big Nubian remained in the hall and closed the door after the dwarf.

The two sat and Alexander poured gin for his new guest.

"No doubt it was just some robbery gone wrong," said Alexander as the physician entered the sitting room again.

"Unlikely," murmured the dwarf. "The Beduin cannot afford to have their clients robbed. Their sheikh would flay them."

"Why, Señor Alavedo," said the doctor. "How agreeable to see you, sir. Let me thank you for your generosity to the Anglo-American."

"It is nothing." Olivio waved one hand. "How is my friend, Mrs. Hammond?"

"Quite well, but she would like to see you both."

Laila seemed a familiar sight to Alexander. She was sitting up in bed with her spectacles on her nose and Herodotus on the side table. But her right arm was in a sling.

"Did you see this man, my dear?" asked the dwarf as soon as the doctor took his leave.

"Only his face and hands. They were covered in tattoos. Images of knives and chains, and a dog or wolf with its mouth open. That's all I remember."

"Did he say anything?" Alexander's stomach tightened as he thought of Katia alone on shipboard.

"Nothing I understood. But he was enraged, like a wild animal, cursing in some language as we fought."

"Can you remember the language?" said Alexander. "Or any words?"

"Just 'suka,' he kept yelling 'suka!' "

"Russian," nodded Alexander, guessing the worst. "Suka means female dog in Russian." If he and Laila were being hunted, why not Katerina as well?

"May I ask," said the dwarf, "have either of you enemies who should concern us?"

"Not exactly enemies," said Mrs. Hammond carefully, "but there are problems in my life, most of them at home, in Ceylon."

Alexander was enjoying watching his two new friends assess each other.

"And you, Count Karlov? Please remember that you are my guests here. If you are attacked, I am attacked." He smiled in his way before continuing. His thin lips rose at the corners. The smooth burned skin of his face drew tight as hard-drying enamel.

"As to enemies, do not be embarrassed. I myself would not know what to do without them."

"Enemies?" Alexander sat on the foot of the bed, not wishing to look down at their guest.

"For four years, since I was eighteen, I have never been to a place where I have not had enemies. From Siberia to Shanghai, and Paris to Marseilles." He paused and took a long drink. The intensity of his relationships, both with enemies and friends, seemed the substitute for a carefree youth. Since his flight from school, there had been more enemies than playmates.

"May I ask you something, Mr. Alavedo?"

"Olivio," said the dwarf, shaking his head. His shoulders swayed with the smooth dome of his head, as if he had no neck. "You need ask for nothing. Just tell me what you wish to be done."

"In Alexandria you kindly offered your assistance and I declined. Now I ask for it. I wish to return quickly with Mrs. Hammond to the *China Star*, perhaps catching her at Ismailia, before Suez. I am concerned about the safety of my sister who is alone on board. But the police must not delay us here, and I would ask that if you can prevent this tattooed creature from pursuing us, you will kindly do so."

"Done and done," said the dwarf. "I will speak to the police. And early tomorrow Haqim will drive you both to Ismailia in my wife's motor." The little man paused. He raised both hands and his grey eye brightened as he presented the drama of his scheme.

"Meanwhile I will tell the desk and others that I am giving a reception for you tomorrow evening at my new café on the river Nile. It is so much easier to have a villain come to you, like a moth to a flame, than it is to have to hunt him down in a city such as Cairo. As for now, I believe Mrs. Hammond requires a drink."

Alexander made three drinks.

The dwarf stood, leaving his own untouched.

"Goodnight to you both." Olivio Alavedo kissed Laila's hand, his face just over the edge of the bed, cheerful as a doll.

In a moment the little man returned to the door with a stained knife in his hand.

"Is this your work, Count Karlov?" he added approvingly. "Is this the dried blood of that rogue?"

"It is, sir."

"I will make certain that he gives us more," said the dwarf. "Before you drive to Ismailia, please remember to leave a few belongings here. Send something to be pressed or laundered so that the staff at Mena House will believe you have not left. It will be my pleasure to lay the trap."

- 23 -

Everywhere Oskar Androv looked, poverty and privilege were bound together like the misformed bodies of twins connected at birth. From Moscow before the Revolution to Cairo today. While one creature starved, the other grew fat and drained his brother's blood.

The cold of Russia made things even worse. In Egypt the poor went in rags and barefoot without suffering. The beggars seemed light-hearted, as if playing a game, even when they crippled their children to make them better mendicants and celebrated their deformities when they cried for baksheesh.

But in Russia, the long winter meant death. Men bound straw about their feet and often lost their toes. There was no warmth for humor. In such a climate, a body required more food. Alcohol kept men alive and killed them. Behind the palaces in Petrograd families made rubbish fires in the alleys and found frozen bodies under the melting snow. At least now in Moscow everyone was equally poor. Only the apparatchiki and a few Party bosses had adopted the corruptions of the very rich.

Oskar stood some distance down the Embankment under a flowering tree. Its long brown seed pods lay scattered on the stone pavement. He tore a scarlet and yellow flower from a branch and crushed a pod under the metal tip of the sole of his boot. Once again he was alone. Oskar raised his collar. The thick odor of the Nile rose around him from the darkened river. Gripping a cigarette between his teeth, he swung his left leg. The limb had stiffened since the light wound he had received when the bastard's knife struck the outside of his upper thigh as he fled. But it was nothing to the brutal pain of the old injuries in Siberia from mine collapses, prison brawls and beatings by the guards. His poisoned hands hurt worse than his leg.

He watched the shiny cars pull up near the head of the gangway. A large mound of sand stood nearby. Sections of a wooden chute were stacked near the parapet beside the sand. Oskar pushed a button on his pocket watch, the only luxury he carried. It chimed once with the lonely echo of a buoy bell ringing in the fog. A quarter past the hour. The father of a prisoner due for interrogation had given him the dependable steel-cased instrument. It had been a fruitless bribe.

Drivers and attendants held doors and beat back the beggar boys, like Cossacks clearing rabble from the streets. Fat men in uniforms and European suits, others in gallabiyyahs and tarbushes, followed ladies in costly dresses with shawls about their shoulders while they hastened across the Embankment as if hoping their feet need not touch the ground. They gossiped and displayed themselves, disdaining any contact with a different humanity. Only this river and the desert bound their country together.

Oskar surveyed these people with care but saw no black woman nor any crippled count. The two must have arrived early, perhaps to visit in the single chamber that had been built beneath the high forward deck where thirty or forty guests were assembling under the umbrellas. He felt ashamed that he had not disposed of the black whore on the pyramid, but the quick climb had made him strangely weak and dizzy.

He grew hungry and more angry as he watched the pigs pick over the delicacies and order more drinks under the lanterns that hung along the sides of this useless boat. Oskar saw insects and moths as big as birds gathering about the swinging colored lights.

The smell of the trees and the river was overwhelmed by the odors of grilling fat and meat and spices rising from the charcoal fire of a street vendor. Oskar stepped to the painted wheeled cart. He paid for a fruit drink and two hot pastries stuffed with chopped camel meat, easy to eat even with his wretched teeth and rotten gums. He devoured the first in two bites and savored the second slowly, as if it would be his last. This was the sort of food that once he would have killed for, and some men had. As he did every night, he thought of his time in captivity.

In Siberia, the only change after they slaughtered the czar was the transporting of many more prisoners. Oskar recalled the prison train that had been caught in a blizzard only six miles from his camp at Khabarovsk. Thirteen box cars built of open wooden slats, each crammed with men and a few women, all packed like grains of corn pressed in a mill. After days of running east, and nights passed at railroad sidings, they were already starved and half frozen before the train had jammed in an icy Siberian drift. For three days and nights the engine crew and guards hunkered around a fire built from the wood fuel of the locomotive. The first night they heard the screams and moans of the prisoners above the blasting wind of the blizzard. When finally a gang of prisoners from the camp was ordered to open the doors of the box cars there was no sound and no one moved. The bodies looked like long icicles in a frozen waterfall, some colored by the stains of blood or urine. Others, hugging one another more fiercely in death than in life, had to be separated by hatchets. Oskar Androv had found one man with his teeth deep in the frozen shoulder of another.

What could bother him after that? Only the death of the privileged gave him satisfaction.

Oskar sat hunched on the parapet and took his bottle from a pocket. By the time he had finished it, the party seemed to be concluded.

A thin moon rose over the domes and minarets of Cairo. The shiny silver curve of its reflection trembled and sparkled on the moving surface of the river like the bright blade of a scythe pressed against a spinning sharpening stone.

Twice Oskar had observed the dwarf go slowly down some wooden steps and enter the door leading to the private cabin. The treads were only a few inches high, no doubt built to accommodate the little monster. Each time the warped creature had emerged with a lighter step, as if he had just taken a drink with special friends. It must be that aristo bastard and his injured whore.

Oskar knew that if he failed in these killings, his brother Todor would punish him as he would any stranger who disappointed him. Later the Commissar would do the same to Todor, to the Ferret himself. There were no relations in this life, and no excuses. He must strike boldly.

Oskar watched an enormous black man in a turban tour the deck and extinguish the lanterns as lesser servants cleaned up after the party. When the big savage was not watching, several of the others finished the abandoned colored drinks. They stole any food left on the trays or tables.

The midget seemed to be below with his friends. Finally, after all the others had left, the black man climbed the gangway, unlocked a large English automobile and drove away. Oskar waited another half hour, watching the boat rock gently on the Nile. He understood the struggles of the rats he heard scuttling and fighting after scraps in the filthy water by the Embankment.

He threw his empty bottle into the river and drew the new pistol from a pocket. He checked the weapon with his stiff fingers, then bent to pass under the rope secured across the end of the darkened gangway. The boat seemed empty, but he was certain it was not. A thin line of flickering pink light glowed beneath the door to the cabin. He heard a woman's musical voice.

Oskar Androv turned the knob slowly with his left hand. His right held the gun. The knob worked noiselessly. He opened the door into the candlelight.

A heavy-breasted young woman with chains of gold coins around her waist and forehead was erect on her knees upon a wide divan covered in folds of loose silk. She had long black hair. Her skin was the color of tobacco. Her head was cast back. Her eyes were closed. The lids, like her nipples, were covered in a shining silvery paste. Her hips and breasts moved in swift rhythmic circles with the ululations of her voice. At first he thought she was alone.

Oskar's appetite turned from murder to rape. This was what had filled the best of his dreams.

He closed the door and put his gun in a pocket. Though Oskar's damaged nose could not smell it, he noticed the smoke of incense rising from a salver.

Suddenly he saw that he was not alone with the woman. Two small hands gripped pieces of the girl's backside as if clenching the bar of a trapeze and hanging on for life itself.

A very small man with a hard round yellow belly lay on his back amidst the silks. His chin poked up between the woman's thighs. His little bowed legs paddled in the air as she settled onto him, then twitched furiously when she raised herself and settled again and again. Oskar could not see the midget's head. His face was hidden beneath her private body.

Then the Russian heard a slurping sound like a starving swine splashing in a trough of slops.

Oskar's body began to sweat. He stiffened as he approached the divan. Now he would not be obliged to choose between rape and murder. He reached out and touched the woman's breast with one tattooed hand, prepared to fling her aside and butcher the little creature before attending to the harlot.

The girl's eyes opened. She screamed as if struck by a cobra and stood up on the couch with her hands braced against the ceiling.

The dwarf sat up. His mouth was open. His hands leaned on the divan to either side. His little chest, slick with sweat and the woman's sex, pumped as he gasped for breath. His astonishing manhood and his shining wet face were red as a bowl of blood.

"Tariq!" he cried with more rage than alarm.

Oskar reached for the door with one hand and for his gun with the other. Both hands were too late. In that instant he knew he was doomed.

The door banged violently inwards against his reaching arm. A big black man in a turban struck Oskar's other arm aside as if it were a lifeless branch. He seized Oskar's gun hand in his enormous fist and twisted the weapon until two of the intruder's fingers snapped. His other hand grabbed Oskar by the throat and lifted him from the ground.

"Bind his feet and hands, Tariq. Empty his pockets and throw him in the hold." The voice of the dwarf grew calmer. "I will join you shortly."

Oskar heard the little beast speak once more as he was dragged from the cabin.

"Jamilla," said the honeyed but commanding voice, "come to me, child. Resume your song. Slip this gold coin into your navel. Our dance is not yet finished."

Oskar Androv understood confinement. It seemed natural, like finding a harbor on his voyage. Now he lay on his back in the sand of the hold. He stared up through the far open box of the night sky like a grave robber looking up from a tomb. He was surprised the huge black man had not secured him to some post or anchor. One corner of the framed night sky was brighter with the moving moon. The sky, too, had always been a refuge.

He saw his captor approach with a spade. The black man spat in the sand, then began to shovel the granular particles onto Oskar's legs until they covered him to his waist. The man stopped and leaned on the tool. Oskar wiggled as he had seen the still-living do in the tangled depths of mass graves. His feet worked their way lower, but his body came more erect.

The big man spat again and threw more shovels against his torso until Oskar was buried to his chest. His hands, knotted together, rested on the sand before him. Despite his broken fingers, he had almost freed them. There was an art to this sort of thing, and Oskar Androv knew it.

"Tariq," called an imperious voice from above. "Take me down."

"Yes, master." The man climbed to the edge of the hold. Oskar looked up and saw the two standing beside the steps like a child and an ogre. The mouth of a wooden chute leading to the sand pile on the Embankment was secured to the top of the parapet beside them.

Tariq lifted the dwarf like an infant. He settled his master against his chest with one arm and carried him down into the hold.

Olivio Alavedo seated himself comfortably in the sand like a young boy at play on the beach. He lifted some sand and let it run out between both palms. Just out of reach, he studied his prisoner as he might a sick animal in a laboratory cage. The man's posture, his silence, the marks on his skin, the sunken eyes in the narrow head, the still violence of his demeanor, all told Olivio who he was and what his life had been. The dwarf was at home with suffering and revenge. This man and he understood each other.

"Welcome to the Cataract Café," said Alavedo, as if truly pleased with this extension of his hospitality. He held the Russian's watch in his hand.

Oskar Androv made no sound. He felt he had been dead for a lifetime.

"Why did you attack my friends?" Olivio asked.

Oskar had endured too much to respond to such a creature. He thought without regret of the interrogations he himself had conducted for the Cheka. He was confident that his brother and the Commissar would avenge him. He had already retreated into the cave of withdrawn silence that had helped him survive when most other men had perished. He had learned to disappear within himself. Indifference was his armor.

"Why did you attack my friends?"

The words echoed in the hold. The dwarf punched the button on the watch. The timepiece chimed twice in the silence. The little man waited a moment before he spoke again.

"He requires more sand."

Tariq began to shovel.

"No, no, Tariq," Alavedo said crossly. He stood and shook his head. "Not like that. You are shifting the ballast, and making more work for tomorrow. Can you not understand? Do this properly. We are not Italians. Here on board, we must do things 'Royal Navy style.' Ship-shape. Why do you think English ships rule the seas?"

He stretched apart the fingers of his small hands and spread them to left and right in the air, palms down.

"The sand should be even, level in the hold, so. Our little Sahara must be perfect. Otherwise the drinks of my guests will not be level in their glasses. Their martinis will spill. Take me on deck. This man is patient. He understands. We will do this work as it should be done."

While Tariq assembled the chute from the sand pile to the edge of the parapet, Olivio Alavedo settled himself on a step part-way down the ladder to the hold. There he calmed himself in the pleasing privacy of the Egyptian night at sea. Unable to bend his neck, he leaned his head back against the ladder to gaze up at the moon. Even at the White Rhino Hotel, on the equator in Kenya, the heavens were not as bright as in the dry cloudless sky of Egypt.

His boat rocked him gently as a cradle. Rarely did the fierce frenzy of his life permit such an opportunity for peaceful contemplation. The dwarf reflected on all he had survived and accomplished, from poverty in Goa to struggle in Kenya and success in Egypt. Just as he was completing this magic vessel that would draw *le tout Caire* to his Café, he was obliged now to suffer the insult of having a barbarian anti-Christ revolutionist break in and threaten his life during a moment of personal delicacy! Not to mention the attempt to murder his guests. The man had no respect, and he appeared to be slow to learn.

Alavedo, however, had been raised in a Holy Roman orphanage attached to the largest church in Asia, Goa's Cathedral of St. Catherine da Sé. There he had played under the pews and winkled out thin coins between the cracks of the poor boxes. Seeing him scuttling about, the worshipers believed he was a helpless infant, whereas, in truth, he was four or five and already skilled at survival and wise in deception.

While the Nubian toiled above him and the villain struggled in the pit below, the dwarf reflected on the fortifying lessons of his lonely childhood. He recalled the long view taken by the Church of Rome, and the patience of the Franciscan teaching sisters. His first clear memory was of the peculiar intimate attentions given him by a fat nun whenever she bathed his small but precocious body with soft soapy hands. He recalled the scratchy tickling of her mustache on his belly when she kissed him with open lips and herself became astonishingly excited.

It seemed right tonight to give this devil in the sand one more chance at redemption, though Olivio was confident that whatever remained of this creature would not welcome that. A Dominican Inquisitor would not be so generous. Even in Goa, the Inquisition had refreshed the faithful and educated the faithless with ecclesiastical parades and celebrations, culminating in a magnificent two-day *auto-da-fé*, when nonbelievers of every superstition and color were slowly burned alive before the enchanted public.

Golden Goa herself had taught the dwarf that diminutive size was no barrier to riches or power, to women or longevity. Facing the hordes of Islam, the city had once survived a year-long siege, defended only by armed priests, fighting slaves from Mozambique and a few hundred

Portuguese soldiers sickened with cholera. After that, Goa became for a time the most prosperous city in Asia, celebrated for luxury and debauchery, more populous than London. As to the women, intermarriage was rewarded and harems tolerated, civic enthusiasms not neglected by the dwarf himself.

He lowered himself two steps deeper into the hold, thinking now of his young Russian friend, and their unlikely similarities. Like himself, the count seemed to have been hardened by youthful sufferings, while still retaining the energy of optimism.

Alexander Karlov had surprised him with his nimble courage and his magnificent woman. Of course, when a man was young, an older woman might present some charm, but as one aged oneself there was little magic to be found in one's seniors, and less and less to learn from them. After a time, even their increasing efforts could not compensate for the creeping ravages they all struggled to avoid. The dwarf sighed and stared down into the hold.

"Why did you attack my guests?" Alavedo asked once more.

The impudence of no response was answered by Tariq when the Nubian looked down at his small master for instruction.

"The chute is prepared, my lord."

Alavedo gestured with one hand. The shovelling resumed. Sand slid down. A cloud of fine particles dusted up in the hold like a storm in the desert.

Oskar Androv coughed and could not stop. It was the first sound he had allowed himself. Only the coughing connected him to the reality he was ignoring. Was this the beginning of his burial?

The work proceeded as Tariq adjusted the mouth of the chute along the parapet so that the sand filled the hold evenly fore and aft. Slowly the Sahara rose around the captive, who had managed now to liberate his hands. With these he worked to free himself or to extend his time. He pushed the sand back from his body, first with his hands, then upward with both arms.

The level of the sand rose higher than Oskar Androv's head. Only the arms and head of the assassin were visible in the round depression in the ballast.

Alavedo watched the two men at their complementary labors as the rising moon moved the line of shadow across the hold. He admired the skill and the steadiness of each. The conical sand pit that now surrounded the intruder reminded the dwarf of another malignant creature he had observed with respect in East Africa. There an insect had taught him again that ferocity, like power, need not be limited by size.

The ant lion would dig a perfect cone in the sand, perhaps six or eight inches deep. Then the small lace-winged insect would secrete itself inside the sand at the top of this trap. When any smaller insect, often a red ant, slipped down into the conical pit, the ant lion would emerge like lightning and employ its long jaw to tear off one or two of its victim's legs before dragging the immobilized prey to its own nest.

Such simple methods, thought the dwarf, are so often best. Most people in Egypt considered the sand a curse. Like the diminutive ant lion, Olivio Fonseca Alavedo made it a resource.

The level of the ballast was still rising, but the conical pit had reached a geometrical perfection beyond which no man could extend it. It would not allow itself to become more steep.

The dwarf observed that no matter how skillfully the rogue used his peculiar hands and arms, the sand he pushed away would now slide back in to touch his uptilted chin. As in the pit of the ant lion, the sand had reached its angle of repose, the immutable pitch at which it held itself in place.

In time, the last thing to be seen would be the clutching mutilated fingers of the assassin's hands, reaching towards the heavens.

"More sand, master?" called Tariq, doubtless understanding the dynamic in some simpler way.

Should he offer this killer one more question, one more choice? Alavedo considered as he climbed back to the deck. Or does he understand it is time to die?

For a moment the dwarf stood beside his Nubian. He drew the steel watch from his waistcoat and punched the button. The hour chimed. He steadied his breathing after the varied exertions of the evening, mindful of his own unfinished obligation belowdecks.

Alavedo looked down and saw the answer.

The light of the moon reached the marked face of the villain, illuminating the mottled darkness of his countenance and soul.

The dwarf nodded once.

Tariq poured another shovel into the chute.

- 24 -

The clear early-morning light of the desert welcomed them like a curtain rising on a lighted stage. The hard tan landscape separated into rolling slopes and smooth hills as the maroon Daimler advanced along the empty road. The western faces of the hills seemed to darken further as they remained in shadow and contrasted with the eastern slopes that brightened with sharp strokes of the rising light.

Laila took Alexander's hand and held it against the softness of her lips, reminding him of their night and the pleasures they had exchanged. Though he remembered every smell and touch, he had the sense that she felt their lovemaking had not been complete. Both knew their thoughts were distant and distinct. Neither had determined how much of their worlds to bring together.

"Breakfast now, effendi." Tariq pulled the car to a stop. He stepped down, opened their door and went to the back of the automobile. He lowered the boot, bracing the lid open like a table on its hinges. He pulled out a wicker hamper, unfolded a linen cloth and draped it across the lid.

While Laila and Alexander climbed a nearby slope, Tariq set out mangoes, sliced ham and hard-boiled eggs, all from the farms of his master. He waited until they returned to pour rich coffee and blood orange juice from silver thermos bottles.

"We will not be long, Tariq," said Alexander, concerned to return to the boat and make certain Katerina was safe.

"Could that be the *China Star*?" asked Laila as the upper decks and striped funnels of a steamship passed between distant sandy hills with the startling unreality of puppets on a stage. Moving sections of the ship's outline alternated with the chain of hills. Her fragments seemed impossible creatures from a distant world.

"No, Doctor Hammond. She has two funnels. It can't be the *Star*."

As the vessel vanished behind the last hill, Tariq folded back the two sides of the Daimler's long angled bonnet. He wiped sand from the engine. Like an Arab looking after his steed, he poured water into the radiator before drinking himself.

Faster than it seemed possible, the sun climbed and the hills lost their shadows. The heat rose around them with the dense irresistible authority of a flooding tide. Sand covered the route before them in uneven drifts as the Sahara reclaimed the road.

They sat in the back of the motorcar with both doors open, eating and drinking from the walnut shelf tables that dropped from the back of the front seat.

Tariq walked on ahead in his sandals and gallabiyyah, assessing the depth of the drifts, leaving the two passengers to breakfast alone.

Laila put down her cup and moved her hand higher on Alexander's leg. He brushed a sandfly from the front of her blouse. She closed her eyes and leaned her head back against the high upholstered seat.

"What would your sage friend from the Celestial Empire advise you about being entertained by an older lady, one perhaps ten years your senior?" asked Laila Hammond quietly as her body twitched and her pointed nipple hardened between his fingers.

Alexander poured more juice with his other hand, thinking carefully before replying. "As a general matter, I believe Mr. Hak Lee would recommend it as an educational passage in a long adventure, Doctor Hammond. He told me age was important, but not determinative."

"And if it were me?" Her dark fingers rested on his thigh as if his limb were some distant unrelated object, then casually began to unbutton his white cotton trousers, teasing him with her slow approach, resting her still hand on him inside the garment. They were developing the game of feigning indifference and increasing the other's sexual tension while they spoke of different things. "What would he say if it were me, Count Karlov?"

"The Master of the Mountain would warn me to flee and save my heart, then he would try to steal you for himself." Alexander tried to keep his voice neutral, as if he were not excited by her touch. "He would see in you the magic all men search for." He put down his empty glass and slowly unbuttoned Laila's blouse.

"The older a man is, he advised me once, the younger, or more beautiful, or more skilled the woman must be to arouse him. When a man is young, he said, a woman's age matters less. Anything will excite him, even sleep." Alexander took one of her breasts in both hands and pinched the nipple tightly between the knuckles of his thumbs. "He himself favored either old lovers who bear the comfortable gift of familiarity, or extremely young ones who refresh you with the excitement of their youth." He licked the dark volcano of her nipple as he squeezed it.

"Ouch!" Laila cried at last before he closed his eyes and sucked it into his mouth.

Tariq ignored them when he returned. The Sudanese released air from each tire before dusting off the car and driving on. His work provided both passengers time to rearrange themselves. No doubt the driver was jaded by his master's less conventional diversions, thought Alexander, reminding himself to scorn embarrassment like a Russian gentleman of the old days.

"Ismailia, effendi," said the Nubian as the Canal port appeared suddenly before them. In a moment they passed from isolation to turmoil.

"Will we have time to visit the museum and see the Greek and Roman collections before we board?" said Laila. "They have an alabaster Ptolemaic coffin."

"Do they?" said Alexander, unable to feign interest. "We'll see," he added, aware he was annoying Laila with this dismissal, but thinking of his sister and Viktor Polyak.

"Please give this present to Señor Alavedo," said Karlov as they stepped down from the Daimler. He handed Tariq a small parcel and a tip. His only purchase in Cairo had been at Coutsicos, the bookseller near Shepheard's. There on a high dusty shelf the Greek proprietor had found a volume of Alexandre Dumas in the Portuguese translation, *O Conde de Monte Cristo*.

It was so much easier, Todor Androv observed, to pass from First Class to Second, than the reverse. Some sort of imperial steward, with all the arrogance of an empowered servant, had barred his way when the Ferret opened a fire door that separated the classes.

Androv stood on the dock at Ismailia near a man selling bright fragments of alleged antiquities spread out on a worn carpet. Todor lit his last tube cigarette and watched the count's sister lean over the rail of the First Class deck. She stared straight out at the Western Desert through a large pair of black binoculars.

If she would only leave the ship, he might contrive to keep her from reboarding. Then he could detain her until the Commissar's vessel came through the Canal. If Oskar had killed the count, and he delivered the sister, then for once even Viktor Polyak might be satisfied.

As Todor paced about the busy pier, one of those obscene motorcars of the very rich drew up nearby.

A tall driver in a turban opened the rear door of the dark red automobile. The black whore and Karlov emerged, shielding their eyes against the hot glare of the Canal. Was there nothing money could not buy?

Todor looked up and saw the sister wave. The long-nosed young count, dressed in the white suit of a colonial dandy over a Russian shirt, grinned like a fool. He and the black woman waved back.

Where was Oskar? Dead? Murdered? How else could Karlov be here and Oskar be missing?

Once again, alive or dead, his brother's bungling had left the work for him.

As the *Star* left her station in the center of the Canal and prepared to clear Port Suez, Alexander and Laila rose from their deck chairs and walked to the starboard rail to watch Suez recede. He had been relieved to find that his twin was safely on board. The Red Sea and the Indian Ocean lay before them, less than a two-week sail to Colombo.

Alexander passed the field glasses to Mrs. Hammond.

"They're so heavy," she said, "as if you think you're going to war."

He did not reply. They were not going to the opera.

"Look!" She handed them back. "I think it's your little friend, come to wave good-bye."

Alexander focused the bright German lenses. Two maroon Daimlers, spotless as if they knew no Sahara, were parked side by side like a pair of fine carriage horses.

One of the massive Nubians stood before the cars with two creatures in his arms, like a nanny holding twin babies in a nursery. The turbaned giant held a dark infant in his left arm, swaddled in white. In his right, erect as a guardsman, the dwarf was braced in a three-piece tan suit and his scarlet tarbush. A black lady, dramatically voluptuous, stood behind them. The second Sudanese was wiping the door handles with a large shammy cloth.

The little man raised both hands to his lips and blew a kiss towards the vessel. Then he held up his daughter's right hand and the two small creatures both saluted the dwarf's departing friends.

Alexander and Laila waved back, then watched the port captain's launch pull away from the dock and speed to the departing *China Star*. The green flag of Egypt snapped smartly in the wind from a short brass mast. The small boat pulled up beside one of the *Star's* gangways, secured now against the side of the steamer. A parcel was passed across and the launch turned back to Egypt.

They were alone on the starboard deck. The Red Sea had lost its celebrated night-time phosphorescence that made it sparkle as if the waves rolled above a bed of diamonds shifting about on the floor of the ocean. The false dawn was giving way to the rising orange arc of the sun that flared at the edge of the water like a distant sea battle just over the horizon.

Alexander tucked the blue blanket around Mrs. Hammond's toes at the foot of her deck chair. He knew her left arm was still stiff and uncomfortable from her modest wound.

For a short time the night sky and the dawn, the departing coolness and the rising warmth, were in balance. The ship and the ocean were still theirs.

How lovely this would be if he had not the concerns of Viktor Polyak and the troubles awaiting him in Shanghai. But if Mr. Hak Lee required assistance, things must be terrible indeed. To Alexander, and even at times to his father, it had seemed dangerous enough simply being the gangster's friend.

Habituated to the ceaseless commotion of Shanghai, Alexander had come to value these early mornings with Laila Hammond. No matter how early he rose, she was always the first on deck. Leaving her in the middle of the night for his own cabin, he had enjoyed a brief second sleep before dressing and climbing to the tour deck.

There she was, in a sari and shawl with the deck blanket covering her. On the other empty chair beside her, three books waited for the light. A folded blanket rested on the foot of his chair. The blanket bore a stitched number matching that engraved on the oval brass plaque secured to the head of the hard-wood chair. A brass eyelet in one corner of the blanket allowed for a cord to attach the blanket to the chair on blowy days at sea.

Laila reached out and touched Alexander's hand.

"Now that we are learning to visit in each other's cabins," she said, "I should explain that this is an old custom in Kandy, the mountain capital of our ancient kings."

Is she preparing me for Ceylon, only a ten-day run away? thought Alexander. Laila had been injured, her life at risk, due to the hazards of his own life. He felt an obligation, and a curiosity, to assist her with her difficulties if he could.

"There were two types of marriages in Kandy. *Diga* and *bina*. In the first, the wife lives in the husband's dwelling. In bina, he resides in hers. Sometimes a woman married two brothers, each of whom slept with her specified nights of the month." She smiled. "The old men used to jest that in the first years of the marriage, the brothers were jealous, but after a time they were relieved."

I am not your husband's brother, Alexander wanted to say, desiring all of her.

"Did the Portuguese and the Dutch and the English tolerate such customs?" he said instead. Was she explaining a way to make their love acceptable?

"The Portuguese and the Dutch never conquered Kandy. For three hundred years they held only the coasts and ports, and some nearby lands. Only the British conquered Kandy, and they tolerated such polygamy until the last few years."

Alexander leaned back his head and waited quietly, sensing that, at last, as they left Europe astern, she was indeed preparing him for her island.

"We have layers of laws and customs, Alex. Four religions. And animists and devil worshipers. And intensities of love and hate richer than any I have found in France or England."

She raised his hand into the early rays of sunlight that were climbing towards them over the port rail. She freed his fingers and extended her flattened hand beside his to show the contrast.

"My skin is my grandmother's," she said.

"I love your skin."

"She was a hill country Tamil, very dark and dangerously beautiful. Her father was a headman, first employed on a coffee plantation to manage the Tamils from Penable, his village in southern India. She married an elderly Burgher shopkeeper, a widower, half Dutch, half Sinhalese. Her daughter, my mother, was rather pale, with skin the color of forest honey. My uncle looks like a Dutchman, except for his black eyes. I have his nose."

She rested her hand high on the leg of his soft white flannels. Laila had learned how to keep his attention.

"My word," she said, pressing her hand against him. "What is this, young man?"

Alexander pulled a steel pocket watch from his trousers.

"A gift from Olivio Alavedo. It came with a card in that parcel he sent by launch from Port Suez. His note said it was a small remembrance from the Cataract Café, and that our tattooed friend would have no further use for it."

Laila had not yet lifted a book, and Alexander was certain that she wished to resume the direction of their talk.

"If we had a child, Count Karlov, he could be any color."

His stomach tightened. He wondered if Laila meant more than she had said.

Laila paused but continued when he did not reply. They had not discussed age or race.

"But I would hope he had the eyes of my young Slav lover. Even in Ceylon, where everything is confused, no one has one green eye, one blue."

"I know one thing he would have," said Alexander. "A fine strong nose." He leaned and kissed hers.

"I hope you have been listening to me," she said, before closing her eyes and turning her lips to his.

"Good morning, Don Karlov, memsahib," said Pedro from a discreet distance. "Morning tea." He set down a low teak table with a tray already resting on it. There was one glass, one cup and china pots of sugar and jam.

"Good morning to you, Pedro. Soon we will be in Goa." Alexander thought of the letter from Olivio that had been delivered by the launch at Suez. "Will you be pleased to be home, Pedro?"

"I will stay on board, sir. My family is so very complicated. If they know I am back, they will treat me like children pulling apart a string of beads. Everyone will want something." He bowed before leaving. "Blessedly, Don Karlov, the stop is brief."

"My family is very complicated, too," said Mrs. Hammond after Pedro left them. "Not to mention Derrick's. Every tea bush and pearl and palm tree is forever in dispute." She leaned forward and raised the brown china pot.

"Tea, *Camellia sinensis*, is the only thing that you and I, Russia and Ceylon, share." Laila poured. She shook her head and smiled as Alexander stirred a heavy spoonful of blackberry jam into his glass. "But I do not think you understand it."

"May I tell you what my father said to an Englishman at the Shanghai Club who was boasting about his country's long affinity with tea?"

"Do."

" 'England is an island. Russia is two continents,' my father told him.

'The czar's caravans began bringing bricks of tea across central Asia on camelback in the eighteenth century. The tea was compressed into wooden frames in Hankow, then sewn into hides in packs of twelve. The broken leaves and the tea dust were pressed into smaller tablets, hard as wood or stone, that were used as currency in the villages.'"

"I wish I had known your father. Are you like him?"

"My sister says, too much so." He stirred his glass until it darkened with the bittersweet preserve. "The fruit jams we used at home in Voskrenoye came from our estates in the Crimea. My own favorite tea is what they used to call Russian Caravan tea, Lapsang Souchong, a China tea from Fujian and Keemun, I believe."

"You surprise me, Count Karlov. Such scholarship." She raised both eyebrows. "I wish we were drinking a fine Pekoe from our highlands, but at least these deck chairs are from Ceylon. Our island teak, *tectona grandis*. It defies termites at home and salt at sea."

"How do you know, Mrs. Hammond? Couldn't this wood come from Java or Sumatra?"

"By the grain and the smell," she said, sniffing. "Women have a superior sense of smell. With age, of course, it diminishes."

Alexander pointed at his nose and flared his nostrils. Could she be serious?

"If you are raised on a tea estate, you develop the nose of a bloodhound. As a girl near Dimbula, I followed the barefoot women and children as they plucked the buds and the two youngest leaves from each plant and collected them in baskets. Since I was not busy plucking, I amused myself by watching for the deadly snakes that made the work exciting. Every day we killed three or four Russell's vipers as we climbed between the rows of bushes."

Alexander nodded as Laila continued.

"The leaves were spread on bamboo racks in the muster sheds to dry and wither for a day before the rolling and the fermentation. After they were fired over charcoal, I copied the sorters as they sniffed like dogs and graded the leaves into Pekoes and Souchongs. By the time I was eleven, my nose uncorrupted by petrol or tobacco, I could break down the elements of scent and distinguish the aromas better than any tea master. The fragrance comes from the essential oils that are released when the leaves are rolled. I could tell which hills the leaves came from. Only a lifetime in wine or perfume or possibly tobacco could give one such a nose."

"Congratulations," he said and kissed hers once more.

- 25 -

"Better stay inside, Pedro," said Alexander as the steward offered Mrs. Hammond his hand at the head of the gangway. The classicist followed Katerina down the unsteady steps, chatting amiably with her.

The two women had adopted a wary acquaintanceship. At first Alexander hoped this indicated that Laila had grown less interested in concealing her relationship with him. Then he realized that Mrs. Hammond was using her public chats with Katia as a mask of concealment, not friendship. She wished to be perceived as his sister's companion, not his.

With only a few hours in port, and after a grueling day in Bombay, few passengers were going ashore in Goa. The *Star's* launch rolled heavily with the swells. When all the First Class passengers had boarded, the boatswain filled the launch with half a dozen from Second. They sat on a bench opposite the Karlovs and Mrs. Hammond. A European lady was introduced by Katerina to her brother and Mrs. Hammond. The last to board was a middle-aged, thin-faced man in worn trousers and a coarse grey shirt.

A larger craft was coming out from port with a customs officer to take in those passengers permanently disembarking. The *Star's* launch pulled away, making space at the bottom of the gangway for the bigger boat.

Alexander checked that he had in his pocket Olivio Alavedo's letter to his Goan agent.

"How long did you say we had ashore?" Katerina asked the crewman as they entered Aguada Bay.

"Four hours, ma'am."

Alexander took out Androv's heavy pocket watch. When he pressed the button, the steel instrument chimed twice. He looked up and found the European at the stern staring covetously at the unusual timepiece.

The flag of Portugal wrapped itself about the flagpole in the gusty wind as they stepped ashore in the harbor of Panaji. Everywhere were reminders of whose port this was.

A limestone fort shielded the mouth of the harbor with its corner towers and crenellated bastions. Four stumpy cannon and black pyramids of cannonballs occupied positions between the two largest piers. On either side of the artillery pieces stood a stone column carved with the crest of Braganza. Tall palms, their trunks curved landward by long struggle with the sea wind, shaded the entrance to the pastel two-story commercial buildings behind the docks.

"*Bom dia*!" said the uniformed port officer as they stepped ashore. "Welcome to Portugal."

The brisk smell of the sea quickly gave way to the sweet scents of coconut palms, sugarcane and spices. Elephants waved their ears and worked on the next pier, bending their knees with patient swinging strides, shifting logs with their trunks and moving barrels under the direction of bare-chested mahouts.

Guides waited beside rickshaws to help the passengers use their limited time ashore. Katerina declined one of the two-wheeled vehicles and set off on foot with her friend from Second Class.

Alexander handed the dwarf's envelope to a guide and assisted Laila into a rickshaw for the run to the trading house a short distance along the harbor. There they climbed a few steps and entered a high-ceilinged office beside a sign painted "Fonseca-Guimarens." A turbaned Indian sat cross-legged beside the door, his eyes half closed as he used a cord attached to his big toe to wave a broad fan mounted on the ceiling. Alexander passed the envelope to a clerk.

A portly olive-skinned man with his waistcoat unbuttoned hurried towards them, tightening his necktie as he approached.

"I am Reshi Boktoo," he said, bowing. "Welcome to the house of Fonseca." He kissed Laila's hand. "Señor Alavedo puts me at your disposal, Count Karlov. How may I serve you?"

They sat on dark rattan chairs. An office servant brought coffee. The setting made Alexander feel he was almost home.

"Of course the Indians drink tea," said their host. "But here we are in Portugal. Our beans come not from Java but from the hills of Señor Alavedo's *fazendas* in Brazil."

"I have never tasted better," said Alexander, curious about the extent of the holdings of the dwarf.

The sounds of groaning bullocks, grinding cart wheels, automobile horns and the cries of porters and begging children came through the dark lattices of the windows.

"Are we far from the columns of Philipia?" asked Laila Hammond in the cultured voice that Alexander had grown to appreciate. "Count Karlov is named for the Macedonian who conquered India, and I thought he should see some of what the great Alexander left behind."

"Actually, Mrs. Hammond," interrupted Alexander helpfully, "my parents named me after Alexander the First. The czar, of course. Not the old Greek."

"And for whom do you think your czar was named?" said the scholar with her gentle persistence.

Alexander recalled too late his father's injunction: never argue with a woman.

"Alas, madame," said Boktoo when Karlov did not respond, "the Greek ruins are too distant, but perhaps before you depart I can find for you something by which to remember them."

He clapped his hands and the servant returned with a platter of steaming spicy samosas.

"In the meantime, my rickshaw is your rickshaw. With your permission my runner will take you through the Arch of the Viceroys to the Basilica da Bom Jesus. There Señor Alavedo would wish you to enjoy the remains of Saint Francis Xavier, the Conqueror of Souls." Boktoo crossed himself reverently. "Next month we celebrate the three hundredth year of his body reposing here, except for his right arm, which rests at the Vatican, where it assisted in his canonization."

When they returned to the dock two hours later, Boktoo was waiting under a parasol, a wicker basket on his servant's arm.

Alexander tipped the rickshaw runner with sterling. They stepped down and joined the merchant. The smell of fish rose powerfully from wooden planks covered with sparkling rows of mackerel, snapper and king fish. Lobster and tiger prawns wrestled in crowded wooden buckets of sea water.

"Thank you," said Alexander as the *Star*'s boatswain piped his whistle twice. "I'm afraid we must . . ."

"Bless your voyage," said Reshi Boktoo, bowing with a smile, "and please let me present this trifling basket to you with the compliments of Señor Alavedo himself. I have enclosed a letter for our correspondent trader in Colombo. If it pleases you, he will do for you in Ceylon what I have tried to do in Golden Goa."

Katerina and her companion were waiting in the launch, now crowded with travellers' purchases and ship's supplies. Alexander noticed that the thin-faced European seemed to be staring at his twin. The man remained silent as the launch sped to the *Star*. He was passing a pair of yellow dice back and forth from one hand to the other. Alexander became curious as to the nationality of this fellow traveller. Karlov thought he had noticed him watching them intently from a side nave of the Basilica. He looked at the man's feet and thought he had seen heavy thick-soled boots like his somewhere before.

"Why don't we see what's in your basket?" Laila lifted one corner of the starched cotton cloth that covered it.

"Not here, Mrs. Hammond, if you don't mind," admonished Alexander. He was pleased at the rare opportunity to lecture his educated lover. "Our mother taught us to open presents when they can be most appreciated, both for one's own pleasure and to respect the giver."

In an hour they were under way. With India sliding by to port, the *Star* steamed south to make the tip of the subcontinent before turning east for Ceylon.

"Champagne, effendi?" asked Pedro, cheerful again as Goa fell away to stern. As he set down the frosty bucket, Mrs. Hammond lifted the cloth cover from the gift basket set on the deck chair beside hers. She took out a handsome bottle of some golden liquid and passed it to Alexander.

"I think not, Pedro. Why don't we slip this into the ice?" He handed the bottle to the steward. "We'll drink it while Mrs. Hammond ravishes the basket."

"Fontenhas!" exclaimed Pedro, eyeing the bottle. "To a Goan, the drink of the gods. Better than Feni, made from cashews and coconut palms." He turned the bottle in his hands in admiration before opening it and setting it in the ice. "They say that when a woman drinks this, she will love you as if she knew no other."

"And what is this, Pedro?" Mrs. Hammond lifted a smaller square bottle from the basket. Alexander removed a card that had lain beside it.

"Oh. I would not drink that," said the steward with emphasis.

"Please tell us." said Laila firmly. "What is it?"

"This is the devil's drink, Datura, another of our special potions. It helps one sleep. In diluted doses, no doubt such as this, it is what the Indian ladies of Goa would give to their Portuguese husbands and lovers if they wanted to have them sleep, and wished to be free to indulge themselves with younger men." Pedro paused. "Concentrated, Datura can also be a lethal poison. No doubt this was misplaced," he said dismissively, taking his leave.

"I already have my younger man." Laila tossed the small bottle over the side and rummaged to the bottom of the basket.

Alexander read the card and regretted her gesture. He guessed the dwarf had arranged for this drink in case it might be useful if they were pursued by another enemy.

"Chorizo," she said, glancing up. "A Portuguese sausage. But what is this?" Laila lifted out a small square box made of a rich wood. She raised the box to her nose and sniffed, then lifted the lid.

A coin rested in a bed of pale silk.

"Greek, and very old," Laila said with admiration. "A head of Alexander. Made of silver and some less precious metals." She lifted out the coin to examine it more closely. There was a single dent in its thick rounded edge. She turned it over.

An elephant adorned the other side of the coin. The animal had the short ears and rounded shoulders of the Indian species.

"Your little friend is most generous," she said as Alexander poured the Fontenhas.

"To Olivio Fonseca Alavedo," said Count Karlov, touching her glass.

Laila Hammond drank, then held up the coin beside Alexander's head.

"He has your nose," she said.

• • •

There were many Port Saïds, but Viktor Polyak knew which one would lure the Foreign Legionnaires. This time he would observe his own instructions, and take a life where it would not be missed.

The *Karnak* was a swift steamer, but she made several ports and passage at Suez could be slow. While French automobiles and wine were being unloaded, one company of the Legion was allowed ashore at a time. Meanwhile, the ship would take her turn at the coaling station and then make passage through the busy canal.

The papers of a fellow Russian would serve him best. Polyak had identified a knot of Russian Legionnaires, the usual defeated veterans who had joined *La Légion Etrangère* after their own cause was lost. On board the *Karnak*, this meant Germans, Austrians, Bulgarians and the Russians, White survivors of the bitter revanchist campaigns of Kolchak and Denikin and Wrangel.

The Commissar followed the men into a sailor's bar in the old quarter. Alcohol would come first. Women next.

Viktor Polyak sat on a corner bench in the back of La Poule de Luxe. The wooden seat was greasy and sticky from old beer. He bought a glass of cheap sailor's gin, the next best thing to what he wanted, and added his own smoke to the tobacco that layered the air like morning fog in a coal town.

A party of English seamen drank and roared at the dented round table beside him. Within an hour, the Russian Legionnaires, their sobriety purged, had caught up to the Britishers. Brandy was their drink, as if they were finishing the day rather than beginning it.

"We could have won, Vladimir," said one. Though his words were slurred and senseless, the Legionnaire spoke the proper Russian of an educated man. "If only we'd had one campaign instead of four. We were always fighting on the edges while they held the center, Moscow and St. Petersburg."

"We should have butchered those godless bastards," nodded his companion. "We nearly caught them before Moscow in the fall of 'nineteen.

All they had were armed peasants, *tachanka* machine-gun carts and those leather-jacketed Latvians. Whenever they broke and ran, their commissars killed more of them than we did."

Polyak had learned to focus his hatreds, not disperse them. He relaxed and did so now. He comforted himself with the words of Feliks Dzerzinsky. "I am not able to hate in half measures," said the founder of the Cheka. "The proletariat will drown the bourgeoisie in their own blood."

When the two Whites staggered from the Poule, arms over each other's shoulders like boys at a drinking party, the Commissar followed them into the famous Night Alley of Port Saïd. Pimps and thieves and painted boys and girls hung about the stalls and doorways, common as cobblestones.

He himself had no use for a woman today, though he might have to buy one to stay close to the soldiers. The Commissar continued to follow the two Russians along the narrow winding street. He saw them hesitate between several doorways on either side of Night Alley.

One entrance had an Eastern curtain of colored hanging beads. Red lamps, incense and laughter issued out between the swinging beads. But a balcony hung over the narrow alley from the other side. Loop earrings and a green shawl framed a very young face with large silver-painted eyes. The girl smiled down and waved her fingers like the petals of a flower.

The Russians accepted the invitation.

Polyak waited long enough, then followed the two inside. He ignored the protesting fat robed creature inside the door, whether a madam or a eunuch, he could not tell. He pushed past and climbed the narrow sloping stair.

The two Legionnaires were at work in a small room, half naked amidst piles of bolsters and soiled spangled cushions that covered the floor. The dim red light came from an oil lantern that hung on a hook from the center of the low ceiling. The walls were draped with cheap cloth like the inside of a Moorish tent. The uniform trousers of both men lay crumpled on a wooden stool near the doorway.

Polyak lifted the stool by a leg and clubbed one soldier across the face as the man attempted to rise. The Legionnaire's neck snapped. His head fell back on one shoulder as he collapsed.

Polyak dropped the broken stool and lifted the metal lantern from its hook in the center of the hanging cloths.

"*Svinia!*" screamed the second soldier, rising and attempting to cast his shrieking clinging girl to one side. "Swine!"

The Commissar swung the lantern into the face of the young Russian. Burning oil covered the soldier's face and dripped flaming to the cushions. The man screamed and fell howling on his knees, clawing at his face and hair. The girls yelled and rushed to the balcony. Fire flashed along the hanging walls.

Polyak grabbed both sets of trousers and bolted down the stairs and into Night Alley as smoke clouded from the shutters of the balcony.

He hurried down one passage and alley after another, finally pausing in a doorway and searching the pockets of the trousers. He gathered the money, letters, photographs and identity papers and stuffed them into his own pockets before hurrying back to the pier by a different route. There he took a place on the *Karnak's* waiting launch. But he stepped ashore again when the boatswain grumbled that there had been some trouble at the coaling station, an accident or a battle between gangs of coal coolies, delaying the ship's passage into the one-hundred-mile Canal.

Polyak paid a guide and made his way to the office of the Peninsular & Oriental Steam Navigation Company.

"I have friends on board the *China Star*," he said to a native clerk, another of those proud pretentious pawns who accepted his colonial enslavement as if it were a privilege.

"The *Star* should be off Goa just now, sir. Permit me to give you her ports and schedule."

The Commissar accepted the paper and stepped outside into the shade of the long arcade.

"Finished," he said, dismissing the guide with his last French coins and waving his hook. "Leave me."

The Egyptian began the usual patter of entreaty. There was so much to see in Port Saïd, so many opportunities for a gentleman. The dragoman looked eagerly into Polyak's face as he began. Then his speech wound down like a dying engine and the man hurried from the corner.

Polyak sat under the tattered awning of a café. He heard the urgent rattle of dice and the clack-clack of backgammon pieces. He smelled the thick coffee and the powerful scent of charcoal and tobacco as the mouth of a hookah was passed from man to man. He ordered tea and spread before him the itineraries and schedules of the two ships. Soon the *Karnak* would be leaving for Ismailia, making for the Bitter Lakes and Suez. With fewer stops and less port time than the *Star*, the *Karnak* should be in Shanghai before the Karlovs.

No matter where the two went, and when, he would catch them, provided they survived the attentions of the Androv brothers. But in his belly Viktor Polyak was certain he would have the opportunity to settle with both twins himself.

- 26 -

"Not tonight, not now, Alex," she said as he bent over Laila from behind her chair, clasping and raising her breasts with both hands in a way that had become a signal between them, her nipples tight between his fingers. "Oh. Please." She hunched her shoulders forward but pressed her cheek against his hand as she discouraged him. "I can't go to bed. I wouldn't be able to sleep."

"Well," said Alexander, emptying the bottle into their glasses in the candlelight. "We could still . . . or we could go to my cabin . . ." He had thought of nothing but being with her.

"No." Laila shook her head. "Let's spend the night on deck. I want to see the first change of light. I want to be the first to see my island, to smell it. You don't know what that means. Bring your binoculars."

Never argue with a woman. Alexander kissed her cheek and retreated to the cabin door. He wondered how she would treat him once they arrived in Ceylon. How much discretion, how much separation, would she require?

"In an hour," she said as he left her cabin.

He was waiting when she arrived. There were two deck blankets on each chair. The Beychevelle was open next to a plate of English biscuits and the field glasses.

Alexander leaned against the port rail, his collar up and a long cigar glowing in the moonlight. He tossed the cork into the sea. It had become the way Mei-lan told him it should be with the right woman. Each time you see her, you should be both comfortable and excited. He felt so again.

Mrs. Hammond was wearing a pale suit and a white cotton shawl around her head and shoulders. The darkness of her face and legs seemed to glow from within in the light of the moon. She came up and put her arms about his waist. Her black eyes were alight with the night shine of the sea.

"Thank you," she whispered before kissing him. "Our bed is wherever we are."

She took his hand and they strolled slowly astern, then back up the starboard side as they had done each day. Laila drew him into a corner of the superstructure behind a lifeboat.

"In the old days," she said, "when the first passenger ships arrived, they used to sprinkle cinnamon oil on the decks so the visitors would catch the special smell of Ceylon, or Serendib, as the Arabs called it, the island of serendipity, the home of Sinbad the Sailor."

Then she held his face between her hands and stroked his lips with her fingers. Alexander rested his cane in the corner and gripped her bottom in both hands. He closed his eyes as Laila kissed him and raised his hands to her breasts. He felt her tremble. Her nipples were firm as cherry pits. He loosened her sash and opened Laila's sari while she unbuttoned his trousers.

He had never expected to find a woman to share the sense of

abandon that he had always imagined but thought he might never experience.

"It's time I told you about Ceylon," she said later. Laila spoke softly, her head against his chest, the silk of her hair against his cheek. "About the hill country and Leopard Gate and the troubles of my family, and Derrick's." She snuggled closer under the blanket and pressed two fingers across his lips when Alexander began to protest.

"You've told me so much about Shanghai and your father, I could close my eyes and be riding or fencing at the Salle d'Armes," she whispered. "But I've told you nothing about tea and pearls and devil worship and hunting in the jungle."

"I think I'll need a drink." Alexander reached across her and filled both glasses, bracing himself to receive instruction.

"I wish you knew more about tea," she said.

"Tea? I told you, my family's been drinking tea for two hundred years."

"You don't understand," she demurred. "Coffee is an African drink, from the highlands of Abyssinia. As it cools, you taste its bitterness. That is why it suits the French. Alcohol is for everyone, but no one drowns in it like the English and you Russians." Alexander bridled at this but let her carry on. "Tea, tea is for the civilized, whether poor or rich. From Lhasa to London, in Japan and India, Russia and China. Only the Americans and the French do not drink it."

Alexander put down his wine. "The water must be boiling," he said as he slipped one hand between her legs. "Otherwise, the tea water will change color, but the leaves will not be cooked."

"And it is not merely a drink," she said, accepting his gesture as a concession necessary to retain his attention. "In Siam they eat tea, boiled into balls mixed with fish, oil and garlic."

He nodded with some interest. Tea was a more congenial subject than Ovid or Catullus.

"But it's even more important as a medicine," she persisted. "Cold tea leaves heal burns. The tannic acid in boiled tea fights dysentery, cholera and typhoid, all the waterborne diseases."

"Really?" He paused to drink his wine. "Please tell me how your family, your husband's family, became planters."

"In Ceylon, the Tamils, like my mother's family, do the work, and the English, like my husband's family, own the plantations. We Burghers are somewhere awkward in between."

"Someone has to do the work." He kissed her cheek. "Someone has to own the plantations."

She pushed his hand away. "Derrick's family has been at it for generations. His grandfather left the East India Company eighty years ago and planted tea in Assam that he had smuggled out of China, bribing some Han with opium from India. First Mr. Hammond cleared the jungle, unwittingly destroying trees of fine indigenous Indian tea. His brother, my husband's great-uncle, was an importer in London, with an office on Mincing Lane, where they held the tea auctions. Derrick's father was a younger brother who sailed from Madras to Colombo and began his own plantation after an ugly family dispute. He insisted that the indigenous Assam teas were finer than the imported Chinese. Stronger, with more caffeine, good tannin and more fragrant essential oils." Laila ignored Alexander when his hand settled between her legs again.

"His elder brother beat him with a pruning staff, nearly killed him when he returned to India from leave in England and found that Derrick's father was unlearning the Chinese methods and replacing the Chinese plants with native Assam bushes. But later, in Ceylon, Derrick's father was free to plant what he wanted, the finest Orange Pekoe in the world."

She paused and drank. "Perhaps you have heard of Professor Krassnow?"

"I don't think so."

"He was a Russian, like my young lover, but better educated. From Kharkoff University."

Alexander lifted his glass, as if he had not heard her. What could she know of the Corps des Pages?

"Your czar directed Andreas Krassnow to visit each of the world's tea-growing countries. After years of study, the professor wrote that the tea plant is native to the entire monsoon region of Asia, but has only two true *jats* or varieties, Chinese and Assam."

"Both kinds should be served from samovars into teapots, of course, then into glasses," said Alexander, thinking of the battered samovar the Russian refugees had given his father in gratitude for his hospitality at the Salle d'Armes. "With no milk, no lemon, no sugar. Just a spoonful of thick dark jam. A fine preserve is both sweet and tart."

Laila glanced at him sternly before resuming the lesson.

"A tropical climate is best. High and warm and moist, like a steamy jungle. Of course, all the Hammonds thought they knew more about tea than anyone else, but in every generation a family fight nearly destroyed their business. Now, with Derrick ill, it is all happening again." Her voice hardened as she reached the contemporary part of the tale.

"His son Jason, by his first wife, Clelia, has had himself appointed administrator while Derrick is incapacitated in the clinic in France. You should know that Jason hates me. To him, I'm embarrassing and expensive. He's trying to sell everything in Ceylon and live like a lord in Gloucestershire. It's become a feast for the solicitors in London and the proctors in Colombo. But Leopard Gate is mine as well, and I am fighting him."

"Is that your plantation?"

"It was when I left. A pantheon of hills near Ella's Gap, a few miles from Bandarawela and Nuwara Eliya, covered with bushes of *Camellia thea*, the finest Assam indigenous plants. A steep undulating rainy tea garden where the water drains without washing away the soil. Some years we get six hundred pounds of tea an acre, nearly half again the average. The estate backs onto the jungle near two great rocks where Derrick's father once lay out all night with his rifle and shot a giant leopard that had killed his favorite mastiff, right on the steps of the verandah. He always said it was the long-tailed forest monkeys that helped him hunt the leopard, their natural enemy."

Alexander had grown interested. "Everyone has one."

She smiled at this male interest in the details of hunting. "You could never see or hear the leopard, but one could hear the monkeys, howling as they swung through the jungle canopy above the cat. Mr. Hammond was nodding asleep just before sunrise after a long night on one of the rocks that stand like giant gateposts where the forest meets the verge of the plantation. Then the monkeys began crying at the edge of the forest. For the first time he heard the sawing cough of the leopard as it answered them. The cat finally stepped out between the base of the rocks below him. He said it was the most beautiful creature he had ever seen. More than nine feet long, nose to tail. Nearly black, since its spots almost came together."

"Did he kill it?"

"Mr. Hammond blew a hole through its shoulder with his Holland, the old four-fifty, his elephant gun. But the leopard got away. Being English, he took a long drink from his flask and spun a gold sovereign in the air. It came up heads, Queen Victoria. He reloaded the empty barrel and followed the blood trail into the jungle with one of the plantation boys. He should have used the dogs and waited for the cat to bleed out, because if you wound a leopard, it will always hunt you. Always. But he hurried in and the leopard sprang on him and knocked him down as he fired again. The cat died there on top of him, but his arm and shoulder were never the same."

Laila shifted her position, uncomfortable with the memory. "Nor the rest of him either. The infection went on forever. The arm never healed properly. It was always painful. He drank himself silly for the next fifteen years, and taught Derrick to do the same."

"I see . . ."

"And my side of the family is not much better." Laila held out her glass and waited for Alexander to fill it. They had learned how to drink together.

"In my case, it was not trading in sapphires and other gems, or the little chain of village shops that divided the family, or even our tangles of race and color. It was the pearl fishing." She paused and stared up at the stars. "Every year the British opened a pearl season in the Gulf of Mannar. Eight thousand divers would gather, half on dhows from the Persian Gulf, and half our own Tamils with lungs like blowfish and bubbles of air trapped in the blood between their ears. All they wore was a leather necklace that held the bone clip that pinched their nostrils like a clothespin. For six weeks the divers lived in a temporary village of palm-thatch huts pitched up on the beach among twenty thousand other men who lived off their diving."

She spread her hands, describing the scene. "Jewelers and traders, criminals and shopkeepers. The divers went down at first light, each man standing on a heavy flat stone with a rope through its center tied to his boat. The stones dropped them quickly to the bottom, where they shoveled the *pinctadas*, the pearl oysters, into baskets, over one million each day. At night, thieves and fights and fires waited for them on shore."

Alexander listened, imagining what that life was like, wondering if he could have made those dives.

"For three generations there were always one or two divers in my family. The head of the family paid for the boat and supported the divers the rest of the year. My grandfather began diving when he was fourteen. He dove for nineteen years, until you could hear him breathing at night, sighing like a leaking bellows with a torn seam. Each year he sold his catch on the market run by the British. But every year he withheld one pearl, usually his finest, and the family could never agree on the relative value of what he had sold and the pearl he had kept. Each one was a lustrous ivory with a rose tone and the smooth silky skin of a baby, and the rounded shape of a full moon."

She paused, almost breathless with intensity, and he dared not voice his admiration.

"When my grandfather could no longer dive, he made those nineteen into a necklace which he gave to my grandmother when they married. It was the only work of his lifetime. Among our people, the number nineteen signifies a harmony of nature. There was nothing like it in the hill country, and few like it in Colombo. In the center is one black pearl, the darkest grey, very unusual in our waters. Most black pearls come from the South Seas. It is iridescent, like a peacock, with a cast of aubergine and a sheen of blue and green and pink."

"Where is the necklace now?" Alexander thought of the eighteen white pearls against her skin, and the single dark one that would be part of her. "It would be so lovely on you."

Important jewelry emphasizes a woman's essential appearance, Mei-lan had told him once, whether that be her beauty or her age. It does not make an older woman more attractive, she had said in self-disparagement, though it may comfort the wearer and stir envy in others.

"My mother gave me the necklace when I married," Laila replied. "It was being kept in the old safe in the estate office at Leopard Gate, but when I opened the safe to take it to London last year, the box was empty. I always travelled with it, because pearls are like living things and must be worn against the skin to keep their sense of life."

"Living things?"

"Of course. Their skin is porous, like ours. Pearls breathe. Pearls survive on the oil of the skin of the woman who wears them. A sapphire can be polished if it is scratched. A pearl dies if it is not worn."

Laila spoke with impatience, almost severity, as if Alexander had expressed a denial she had been obliged to repudiate before.

"Gemstones come to us as precious minerals from the earth. Coral and ivory are living things, but they are not gems. Only pearls are gems that come from a living creature. Stones like diamonds and rubies are for glory, glamour and distinction. Pearls are for emotions. They must be loved and nourished."

For an instant Alexander thought of the emerald necklace Katerina had worn one night in Paris and how that display had shamed them both.

"Who knew the combination to the safe?" he asked quietly. "Besides you."

"Only Derrick and his first wife also knew it. Their son, Jason, must have stolen the pearls after his mother gave him the combination."

"If one were to sell such a thing in Ceylon," he said, disturbed at her loss, "where would you sell it?"

She had considered this as well. "At the Colombo sales, either as it is, or perhaps pearl by pearl to conceal the provenance." She shook her head, discounting that scheme. "But then you would lose the premium for the rarity of the necklace and the value of the matching pairs in their perfect graduation of size. If one wished to sell the necklace as one piece of jewelry, or in a bigger market somewhere in the East, the place to sell it would be where the money is, where very rich people with no country collect such things as a bank of value. For that, there is only one city."

"Where do you mean?" Alexander asked, though he thought he knew.

"Shanghai."

The *China Star* steamed steadily on, with India somewhere over the horizon off her port beam.

Laila lay on her side in the deck chair, tight in Alexander's arms but seeming to grow more contained and private as the night lengthened. Both knew their idyll together was over. He thought of the decisions he must make in Colombo. The *Star* would be lying in port for several nights, bunkering and taking on minor cargo, most likely tea and rubber, perhaps some cinnamon and sugar.

But he knew that Laila's problems would take her more than two days. She had never asked him to stay on, or to assist her, though he hoped she wished for both. He closed his eyes for a moment, then came awake when he felt her stir.

A faint dome of light was rising in the east. The ship shuddered slightly as she swung onto her new course and turned to meet the morning. They must have passed the tip of India and begun steaming northeast for Ceylon.

Freed of his embrace, Laila stood and walked forward with a blanket around her shoulders, stopping where the end of the port rail met the raised steel side of the ship's bow. She lifted the binoculars and stared at the horizon. Alexander sat on the foot of the chair with the last glass of wine cupped in both hands. He gazed at her back and thought of all the people he had lost forever. His schoolmates, the estate staff and their neighbors, his mother, his father, even Andrei Yeltsov, the first friend of his flight across Siberia to Vladivostok and Shanghai. He did not want to be alone again.

The sea itself seemed to burn. A belt of orange light scorched the horizon beneath a layer of low cloud. Alexander rose and walked to the bow with an unlit cigar in his hand. He stood close to Laila without touching her. He did not smell the sea or see the sky. He sensed only her.

The clouds gathered densely in the center of the horizon as the sun rose. The light brightened to north and south, but the sun itself was blocked. The sea was running in long rolling swells, sparkling with light on the crests and grey with the depth of the ocean in the dips. The island was directly before them, obscured by morning fog and cloud. Pink and orange light rose all around it like a mango-colored fan opening wider and higher.

"Adam's Peak," murmured Laila as one mountaintop, then a range of others, appeared above the thinning clouds. Slowly their blue cast turned to green as the lower elevations of the island were exposed like a row of descending ledges. Then the mountains were lost in the distance. The mists thinned with the rising rays of the sun, revealing a sandy palm-fringed shore.

"The mountains always protected us," said Laila. "That is where our unconquered kings held out against the Portuguese and Dutch. But those beaches and our harbors were our undoing."

"They are an invitation," said Alexander, for the first time eager to go ashore. "Like Eden." He thought of the contrast with the bleak grey outline of Siberia as Russia disappeared into the frozen mist and the battered icebreaker made for the Sea of Japan.

"The sea and our perfect harbors have brought Ceylon all our troubles and invaders. Jaffna brought the Indians. Then the Portuguese and Dutch used Galle. Now Colombo and Trincomalee serve the English."

A scattering of native fishing boats worked the water before them, like skirmishers screening the heavy forces of the steamships anchored in the harbor roads. The high wooden bows and blunt sterns of the brightly painted fishing craft rode lightly on the sea. Lean dark fishermen sat on the edges of the narrow boats handling ropes and nets. Outriggers skimmed the water, secured to one side of each boat by two long arching poles.

The surface calmed as the *China Star* entered the island waters. A line of vessels was moored like sentries on a wall where the sea changed from deep blue-grey to a pale hazy green. He had never seen such water.

Two motor launches sped towards the P & O vessel as she approached the roadstead. The Royal Mail launch reached her first. A Union Jack fluttered on her sternmast. Canvas sacks bearing the lion and unicorn stencil waited on the platform at the bottom of the lowered gangway of the *Star*. Each bag was secured at the throat with a heavy cord and seal. The launch was quickly loaded and set off for shore as the second one replaced her at the gangway. The pilot and the P & O agent stepped aboard and prepared to clear the vessel in for port.

The *China Star* slowed inside the breakwater as she slid gently into her place behind the *Tokushima Maru*. Two anchors ran down from her bow while her stern was secured to a buoy. Alexander recognized the flag of the Nippon Yusen line from the Shanghai trade: the horizontal red stripes of the rising sun, the banner of the Japanese fleet that had sunk eight Russian battleships in 1905. The *Tokushima Maru* rode high in the water. Her deck hands were securing the booms of her forward masts. Each year Japan's trade was growing, secure and prosperous beneath the umbrella of her Anglo-French allies of the Great War.

Alexander thought of his fencing mate, Hideo Tanaka, the only schoolboy swordsman other than himself who had contributed something to the fencing *piste* besides enthusiasm and the excitement of a sport based on mortal combat. Both had brought a disciplined ferocity to the schoolboy tournaments. Alexander had been emboldened by the training of his military academy and the lessons of Siberian survival in his flight across Russia. *Bushido*, the cult of the warrior, guided each of Hideo's ripostes and lunges.

Laila touched his arm. "We must disembark separately, Alex. Where will you be staying in Colombo, the Grand Oriental?"

"No, Katia and I will be at the Galle Face." He tried to keep the disappointment from his voice. She had become cautious, needing to establish a distance between them.

"I will stop first at our house in town," she added. "Perhaps later I can call on you at the hotel."

Alexander had no choice but acceptance. He remained on the upper deck as Laila descended and prepared to board the sleek passenger launch that was now steaming towards the *Star*. A canvas awning covered her forward deck. The rear deck was enclosed with a long windowed cabin that protected passengers from the black smoke pouring from a tall raked funnel amidships.

He watched Mrs. Hammond board, then descended to find his sister. But Katia had preceded him and was just stepping into the crowded P & O launch herself. She waved and smiled as the trim vessel pulled away.

The previous afternoon Alexander had knocked on the door of Katerina's cabin.

"You have been so occupied, Sasha." She smiled as he entered. "You seem to have our father's charm, but a different taste. What the French call *le goût mûr*."

Feeling guilty for not defending Laila, he ignored the provocation and restrained himself from asking Katia about her own adventures in Second Class. At times he had not seen her for several days.

"I may stay on for a week or two in Ceylon," he had replied, now confident his sister would be safe aboard the *Star*. "And catch a later steamer for Shanghai. Papa's stable Cossack, Ivan Semyonov, will look after you at the Salle d'Armes. He will need no letter to know who you are." He handed her both envelopes. "But these letters are for two special friends who will help you in every way they can. Jessica James, the daughter of American missionaries, and Mr. Hak Lee." He had thought it best not to introduce Katerina to Madame Mei-lan Wong.

"Who is Mr. Lee?"

"A Chinese man of business. A man of many interests, one might say." Opium and women, thought Alexander. Kidnapping and murder. "He is a sort of partner in the Salle d'Armes, and he has been a true friend to me." Hunting Reds, he did not add.

- 27 -

Laila Hammond offered the jetty sergeant her gloved hand and accepted his assistance as she stepped from the boat and climbed the steps to the covered deck of the passenger pier. She noticed rows of wheel sets and steel base frames lined up on the next pier, waiting to be assembled into railroad carriages at the Colombo workshops. She was proud that the island's First Class carriages were renowned as among the finest in the world. The outsides of each coach would be made of varnished teak. Inside, each cabin was panelled with halmilla and huriyamara wood inlaid with satinwood, and furnished with brass fittings and fine upholstery.

Laila ignored the solicitations of the licensed guides, trim in their dark blue coats with green facings. She walked past the Customs House to the corner of York and Church Streets. There she passed between two mighty columns and entered the high-ceilinged dark lobby of the Grand Oriental Hotel. Laila chose a table against the back wall and ordered a cup of tea while she waited for her baggage to be unloaded.

Surprised glances from two European ladies seated nearby reminded her that she was a dark Burgher girl returning to her country. No doubt her smart French suit and shoes, and her lofty demeanor, would add female jealousy to class resentment, fortifying their need to keep others in their place.

For most Burghers, social distinctions were both important and precarious. Mixed blood was an entitlement in some situations and a barrier in others. The more European a Burgher appeared, the greater were his own assumptions and sensitivities. Even when their mixed backgrounds were English on neither side, but perhaps Dutch or Portuguese, too many of her Burgher friends wished to be perceived as English, or as close to that as possible.

Laila ignored the admiring smiles of a gentleman at another table and pretended to study the plaque on the wall behind her, which noted that the hotel structure had been built as a British army barrack in 1837.

"Your baggage is here, ma'am," said a hall boy. "Would you care for a carriage or a motorcar?"

"Two jinrickshaws, please. Mine with rubber wheels, if there is one."

As he departed, she remembered the excitement of crossing Colombo by herself as a girl. Her family forbade her to appear on a bicycle on a public street in town, but the dusty busy streets were like candy to her. Instead of suffering the awkward divided identity that troubled most of her young Burgher friends, Laila had enjoyed both worlds, most of all along Colombo's roads and avenues, where the frantic energy of the East jostled with the order of the Europeans.

Once the boy returned to fetch her, she climbed into the first rickshaw as her baggage was piled into the second. "Cinnamon Gardens, please," she said to the puller, pleased to be speaking Sinhalese again. "Six Horton Place."

The rickshaw coolie trotted through the crush of tram cars, lorries and bullock carts, past the arcades of York Street and the emporiums of Cargill's and Millers, then across Slave Island and by the Town Hall. For a moment they were stuck behind a bullock cart loaded with large sacks. As they passed, she saw that each bore the mark of the government salt monopoly. The carter was asleep on the small shelf that served as a bench between the front shafts of his cart. His right foot was extended forward into the bullock's crotch, where its jiggling movements encouraged the animal to quicken its pace.

When they entered Alexandra Place, Laila closed her eyes and smelled the dry dust and the blossoms as the morning warmed. Everywhere she went, she seemed to find namesakes of her young lover. She opened her eyes as the rickshaw slowed and entered Horton Place.

There her father had built a house with money from the manufacture of tea chests from attonia wood at Morutuma and from the production of thick sacking used to export the precious four-foot quills of cinnamon bark. As a girl, she had been excited by the scandalous romance of Horton Place, named for the governor whose wife's affair with Lord Byron had inspired the poet to write Laila's favorite lines of English verse: "She walks in beauty, like the night . . . Of cloudless climes and starry skies."

They stopped before an ironwork gate. The flowering shrubs and creepers that climbed the low wall seemed more lush than ever, almost wild. Long fronds of tall palms hung over the wall from inside the garden. Curved husks of dead palm leaves lay rotting on the ground.

Laila stepped down and tried to open the gate but found it secured by a chain and padlock. Reality replaced her girlhood dreams.

She gripped a bar in each hand and stared at the single-story cream-colored villa with its red tiled roof. A deep verandah ran all the way around it. Four pillars supported the porch that covered the driveway where it curved before the center of the house. To the right, set back in the garden, she could just see one end of the tennis court. It had no lines. To the left she saw the stable. The tops of the stall doors were closed. Temple flowers, white and yellow frangipani, bloomed on all sides.

"Mano!" she called briskly, impatient with the barrier to her own house. "Mano!"

A thin dark man with white hair and a face lined like old bark finally emerged from one side of the garden and smiled at her through the bars. His large ears extended directly to the sides.

"Missie Laila!" Pleasure and anguish seemed joined in his voice. He bowed and peaked his fingertips together.

"Please open the gate, Mano." She remembered him running barefoot beside her, one protective hand pressed flat against her back as she learned to ride a bicycle.

"Missie, I cannot. The house has left the family."

"Open this gate, Mano," she said again, the authority of privilege in her tone. "I was born in this house." The villa had been her dowry.

"I cannot." Mano shook his head and gripped his hands behind his back. "Mr. Hammond has sold the house to Cockford's, the property agent." He shook the keys at his waist and tapped the lock with a knuckle. "They have even the keys. To this new lock I have no key."

"My husband did not sell the house. Mr. Hammond is ill in France." She watched Mano shake his head as she spoke. "He cannot have sold it."

"His son has sold it, Mr. Jason. Everything, missie. Furniture, the lot." Mano fluttered his hands high, like two birds taking wing. "Gone. Gone. And I believe, Missie Laila, that the tea garden, Leopard Gate, is being sold as well."

Laila turned to the rickshaw boys. "Queen's Street, number twenty-seven," she said sharply. The two pullers were squatting by the wall, chewing betel leaves, shavings of areca nuts and bits of tobacco leaf and spitting out the red juice. "Cartwright and da Souza, the lawyers."

The indignity burned within her all the way there. How dare Jason sell her own house?

Carter Cartwright had died on Laila's last visit to Colombo, collapsing on the courthouse steps with thick briefs in his hand and old madeira in his liver. The da Souza brothers now sat on the two opposite sides of the massive partners' desk that had once accommodated both their own father and Carter Cartwright. The Burgher and the Englishman had made a useful partnership. Now their portraits faced each other across the desk. Their glass decanters stood empty on the sideboard.

Whatever else, the two brothers were skilled proctors, as solicitors were called here.

Lucas da Souza, the brighter and less attractive of the brothers, had once presumed to court her, no doubt thinking that his skin, lighter than her own, was a substitute for looks or humor. He rose now as if welcoming an old love.

"Why, Laila Hammond!" said the proctor. "More lovely than ever. How Colombo has missed you. Will you take tea with us?" He clapped his hands.

"Please," said Laila, removing her gloves slowly rather than shaking hands. "But I have come to you on business, gentlemen. In the past you assisted me with the difficulties of my own family, but now I need your help to protect my husband's interests, and my own, both here and up-country."

The lawyers understood at once the nature of her problem. "These matters have become very costly, especially when vigorously disputed." Ralph da Souza shook his head. "So costly."

"And there is the matter of the outstanding account," noted Lucas. "From all the old troubles. For us to study these new problems and brief an advocate, a barrister, we must first close our account on the earlier files."

For the first time, Laila felt the sickening weakness of inadequate finances. How would she find the money to reimburse Alexander for the voyage and to settle these accounts?

"Hold on," interrupted Ralph da Souza. "Was not Horton Place your dowry?"

"It was," she said with force.

"And was not one of your parents a Tamil, what the law calls 'a Malabar inhabitant of the province of Jaffna?' " Ralph removed his spectacles and held up one hand to restrain the intervention of his brother. "So that Tamil law would apply?"

"My mother was Tamil."

"Then Thesawalami, Tamil law, applies," nodded Ralph. "And so on your marriage, your husband automatically owned one half of your dowry, Horton Place. But the other half is still yours, and so Jason Hammond, even though appointed administrator due to his father's incompetence, could not lawfully sell the villa without your consent."

Encouraged by this interpretation of the law and by the possibility of payment, the three discussed strategy. The afternoon had passed by the time Laila Hammond crossed the arcade and climbed into the first rickshaw. Both pullers were seated against the wall of the arcade eating *roti* and rice and curry with their fingers.

"The Galle Face Hotel, please." She leaned back under the shelter of the canopy, angry and exhausted. The joy of her voyage had already been replaced by the bitterness of family conflict and the insecurity of her situation.

Alexander Karlov sat alone on the black-and-white checkered central terrace before the verandah of the old hotel. He had seen only one other terrace like it: Peter the Great's four immense marble chessboards at Peterhoff, the czar's country palace outside St. Petersburg designed as a rival to Versailles. Visiting as a court page from his academy, Alexander had looked down from that terrace and admired the carved heads of the Chinese dragons whose mouths served as fountains in the formal French gardens. They were his first sight of the saurian symbol that later he had found everywhere in Shanghai.

Karlov appreciated the solid colonial magnificence of the Galle Face.

It reminded him of the grand villas and hotels of the Black Sea resorts. He regretted that Katia had not joined him. Her place was still set. But his thoughts were of a different woman, and of her touch and skin and smell.

A few feet away, white lines of surf crashed against the high seawall as if on the edge of storm. The tall waving palms were black sentinels against the clear night sky.

Alexander's white jacket was folded on the chair beside him. He had dined well on fish curry and wild pig. His wine was almost finished. His cigar glowed, friendly in the darkness, as he considered whether he should reboard the *Star* in the morning or linger in Ceylon. There were many reasons to hasten to Shanghai, and one to remain in Colombo.

"May I borrow your jacket?" asked Laila, resting both hands on his shoulders. The current of her touch refreshed him. Alexander had not heard her steps against the din of the surf. He covered her left hand with his as the fingers of her right slipped between the widely spaced buttons of his Russian shirt.

She drank from his glass, then sat beside Alexander and told him all she could as her dinner was ordered and served. They shared dense chocolate mousse from a single spoon.

"I understand what it means to lose your house and land," he said. "If you were required to choose between the house and Leopard Gate, which would you keep?"

"I was born at Horton Place," she said, her eyes on the dark void of the ocean, "but I would like to die at Leopard Gate."

It was the reply for which he had hoped. He wished to help her, without being ruined. A tea estate was at least a business and would be congenial to a Russian in exile. He tried to think of what Mr. Hak Lee would do, or better yet, the dwarf of Cairo, Olivio Fonseca Alavedo. Mercy would have no part in their solutions, but perhaps he should find a gentler plan. His father had trained him with an instinct for action and decision, but not for calculation and shrewd manipulation. Now he must learn to think ahead. He must play chess with life.

"Then we should have your lawyers tie up the house with the claim that half is yours," he said. "That would maintain your interest without the cost of buying the other half. And if you wish a Russian partner in the tea business, then you and I might buy the estate ourselves. A conflict over the house might discourage buyers of both properties." He found himself thinking like the dwarf.

She seemed delighted by his offer. He was pleased with his cunning.

"Your stepson, Jason, will find it difficult to sell a lawsuit."

"May I ask you a question, Count Karlov?" said Laila when they were resting during the night. She had been unusually lazy in their love-making. Not indifferent or unresponsive, but without her usual activity and intensity. More like a cat enjoying having its belly scratched.

The tall windows and wooden shutters were spread open. The rhythm of the sea pounded the wall beneath them. White dots of water rose from the surf like sparks. They could not see the moon, but the cone of its beam moved slowly across the room as if searching for their tangled bodies.

"You're so young, Alex. You must be careful," she continued when he did not reply. "You know what Ovid said. 'Mature experienced women are as common as blackberries.'"

"Perhaps that is why the Romans exiled him," Alexander said, raising his head. At least he remembered that much. "But I like berries."

Laila slapped his bottom sharply. "May I ask you a question?" she said again.

"Perhaps," answered Alexander, his cheek on the impossible softness of her inner thigh, her scent close to him.

"Would you ever consider making an older woman your countess?"

He grew alert, like a hare in a clearing in the forest.

"That would depend on who this lady was, and how well she behaved, or misbehaved."

"Perhaps a scholar, a lady of refined intelligence with a fine high derriere."

"Could she cook and sew?"

"Let us assume that she could command a household."

"Or a battleship." Alexander turned his head and drew her damp softness into his mouth with a long kiss.

"Your brother has left us," said Captain Walker, smiling at Katerina Karlov after he gestured to the steward to bring on the Stilton and pears and port. "But I understand the Count left most of his baggage on board for Shanghai." Already the green island was lost on the horizon astern. "May I ask if he has found business in Ceylon?"

"Possibly," said Katerina, slightly irritated by the question, and thinking Alexander had found something even more hazardous than commerce. One of the few traits she still shared with her twin was their father's reluctance to follow another's line of enquiry, a habit reinforced by her training with the Cheka.

She was also growing comfortable with a certain sartorial arrogance, common to her father and brother. Her mother, to the contrary, as Madame Lanvin had reminded her, was invariably dressed suitably for both time and place. But Katia had observed that her twin, perhaps socially hardened in Shanghai, was indifferent to the British codes of dress. He wore boots and Russian shirts whenever he chose, generally disdaining neckties. His clothes, of course, were of the best. She now cared little herself. Instead of changing to suit conventions, she dressed as she pleased, in the simplest of the elegant clothes that Alexander had bought for her in Paris. She no longer minded being underdressed for First Class and overdressed for Second.

"You always retire so early, mademoiselle," said a French lady from across the table. "It's such a shame you do not play bezique, or even cribbage."

"I believe Miss Karlov tours the ship after dinner," said the woman's husband, chipping clumsily at the round fortress of the blue-veined

English cheese, doubtless habituated to the sticky softness of his country's offerings. "I would not make so bold as to ask the reason."

"The drinks are better here," said Katerina easily, ignoring the snide undertone. She had enjoyed the change of spending several days ashore. "But I find the conversation broader in Second."

"*Sans doute*," said the lady, peeling her pear without touching the fruit with her hands. "No doubt one would."

In half an hour Katerina was seated in the crowded lounge on the deck below, smoking a Gitane and considering what to drink. She looked around the smoky cabin, nodding at acquaintances and noting who was missing, a habit from her Cheka training.

The passengers in Second seemed to have changed more than those in First. Greeks and Copts had gone ashore at Port Saïd. Muslims at Aden, and all the Indians at Bombay and Goa. A few of the lower ranks of civil servants had debarked at Colombo. The French were still on board, most bound for Annam and Cochin-China. Both Russians were absent. One she had not noticed since Egypt, the larger silent one with the tattooed hands, but the other had gone ashore in the launch at Goa, and then again in Colombo.

Katerina thought about the two absent Russians. She recalled what Alexander had said regarding his fight at the pyramid in Giza with a man who might have been Russian. After that conflict, only one of the Russians had been on board. She thought of the contained hard manner of the two, and of the sort of men she had met during her own training with the Cheka. Her skin prickled as she recalled how the smaller one had watched her brother as he left the launch in Goa and had walked after him and Mrs. Hammond while they strolled ashore. Once again, the small Russian seemed to be doing the same as Alexander. The Cheka had taught her never to accept coincidence.

With her twin still in Ceylon, Katerina now seemed to be the only Russian on board. She knew there would be many thousand in Shanghai, White refugees fled the Revolution, escaping through Vladivostok and Harbin.

Alexander had spoken of the Russian bakeries and churches in the French quarter of the great Chinese port. 'Little Russia,' some called the district. Distinguished officers worked as bodyguards for Chinese gangsters, or as gigolos if they were fortunate. Grand ladies gave piano and language lessons while their daughters worked as dance hall girls or worse. She regretted missing the service for her father. Shanghai's Orthodox cathedral had overflowed with mourners, Alexander told her. Men and women waited in line to bend over the casket and kiss his scarred cheek or cold lips.

But much as she felt attached to memories of family, particularly to her mother, and much as she despised Viktor, Katerina was still committed to the need for change and revolution. At least in China, there were now leaders, both Soviet agents like Mikhail Borodin and Chinese patriots like Mao Tse-tung, and others who would give their lives to make a difference. Somehow she must find a way to participate that was acceptable, and that would give her credit with the Bolsheviks so that one day she might recover her son, with or without Viktor Polyak. No matter what they did with Leon, she would always know him by his Karlov eyes.

At that moment her patient admirer, the young French sports instructor bound for Shanghai, approached with a bottle of calvados and two glasses. She thought of Sasha and his Burgher girl. Perhaps it was time for her own shipboard adventure, something temporary to distance her from the ugly attentions of Viktor in her past. She felt this voyage had softened her. Now she yearned for her share of romance when she lay awake at night. At the same time, the unusual man she needed to find would have to learn to tolerate her strength and at least understand her ideas.

"Un petit *calva*?" said Jacques, filling both glasses before he sat down. For once Katerina Karlov returned the young man's smile.

- 28 -

"Have you taken many train rides?" said Laila as they settled into their panelled cabin. Smoke gusted past the open window as the black locomotive pulled the six passenger coaches from Fort Station in Colombo.

"Too many," said Alexander quickly, setting his steel watch and silver cigar case on the window ledge. He had not spoken to her fully of his other, more brutal rides. "Though along the Nile I was pleasurably surprised, Mrs. Hammond, if you don't mind my saying so." He opened the watch. It chimed the hour.

"I believe our railway is the finest in the world," said Laila. "From the point of view of engineering, interiors and service. Here the English use the less educated Burghers to run the railroad."

"On the Trans-Siberian, we have a library," said Alexander. "At least there used to be." He appreciated her campaign to enhance his interest in her island. In Shanghai, where his countrymen were frequently pimps or tarts, he tried to do the same for Russia.

"Ceylon's railway has the most beautiful and difficult ascents," she continued. "And at Pattipola, the highest station in the world. One could look down at Berne or Zurich."

Laila dropped a cushion onto the floor between them. "Tell me about your other rides."

"Twice I fought Viktor Polyak on a train. First in Siberia, when he murdered my mother and kidnapped Katerina, and once in China, when I thought I had killed him."

"Then we had better lock the door." She rose and slipped the long brass bolt. "I will try to give you a finer memory of our railway, and receive you in my country like a Sinhalese girl comforting a prince in the old days, not like a Burgher lady struggling to be Victorian."

Laila knelt on the cushion and raised her chin. "But sadly for you, I am not as beautiful as the maidens on the rock paintings at Sigiriya, our ancient mountain fortress."

"Of course you are," said Alexander, meaning it, though he had not seen them. "Who could be more lovely?"

"No." Laila shook her head and sat up straight and arched her back. "Perhaps I have their eyes, and even their derriere, but not their tiny waists and magnificent breasts."

"I cannot believe they had your skin or scent."

She smiled up at him and took his right boot in one hand. "For a time I will do my best to serve you as they would have done."

Laila pulled at his boot as Alexander quickly raised his good leg.

"This will be the highest ride of your life, Count Karlov."

She removed the boot expertly, pulling hard until it was nearly off, then hesitating and drawing it gently towards her as it came free.

Alexander thought of Boris, the son of a serf, who always boned their boots after polishing them with thick English paste, and waited to pull them off at the top of the steps when the riders returned from the stables painted with dust or splashed with mud. Boris's special reward each year was a colored Easter egg for his family.

"No," said Alexander, "please, you shouldn't." He removed the second boot himself, certain she had noticed its thicker sole and taller heel.

"Does your leg hurt you?" she asked for the first time.

"Only when I do too much with it, or sometimes not enough." He pulled off his socks and set his feet side by side, no longer ashamed when she saw that the left one was narrower and far shorter.

Laila took a jar of Lundborg's French skin cream from her case, then sat on the cushion and lifted his left foot. Her slender hands were dark against the pale skin of his feet as she separated and stretched his toes. He gazed out at the country while she spoiled him. The top of the window was pleasantly shaded from the heat and the sun by a slanting wooden screen mounted on the outside of the train.

Alexander was relieved to see the activity of Colombo replaced by the serenity of sparkling green paddy fields and heavy black water buffalo, by coconut plantations and small villages lined with shack shops with thatched roofs. He watched one young boy using a switch to drive two buffalo in slow circles as they stirred the muddy soil of a rice paddy. The lush flat land perspired with tropical warmth and fertility. They passed thick jungle forest and several large artificial lakes, each one contained by broad berms of earth covered in wild plants and grasses.

"Most of these tanks and canals were built two thousand years ago to provide water for the paddies and the villages," said Laila, noticing his interest. "The bunds that hold them in have become paths and roadways. Higher up, the tanks are smaller. As each overflows, it fills the tank below. If the monsoon is good, every tank is full."

"I wonder what we were making in Russia two thousand years ago."

"Stone axes?" she said. "Now please help me slip off your trousers, Count Karlov. I cannot do everything by myself." Soon the stimulation of her attentions overcame his embarrassment at the unavoidable display of his damaged limb.

After a time they dressed and Alexander suggested a drink and lunch in the dining car. The train began to climb as the track curved through steep green hills.

"Why don't we lunch here in the cabin?" she said.

"In Egypt you told me meals were always better served in the dining car," said Alexander, already at the door.

As they made their way between the cars, the train stopped at Polgahawela, where a second rail line led north to Jaffna.

"Polgahawela means 'Field of Coconuts,'" said Laila as they stepped down onto the busy platform. The schedules and stops were painted neatly on hanging boards in English and Sinhalese. "Refreshment room," said a sign beside a door in the station wall.

A quiet group of slender dark men in ragged cotton robes was waiting at the far end of the platform.

"A gang of Indian coolies," explained Laila, "waiting to be taken to a tea plantation. These men work in the tea factories. The women and children do the plucking."

On the platform, barefoot women in saris were lifting panniers of plantains and mangoes up to the open windows of the trains. Insects hummed in the scented air. A barefoot boy with a bundle of coconuts hanging from his shoulder chopped the top off one with a machete and handed the bottom part to Karlov.

"Drink it," said Laila. "It's *thambili*, coconut water, from unripe coconuts."

Alexander was surprised by the cool clean taste. He paid the boy a few rupees and Laila drank as well before they crossed the platform and walked through the station to the dusty roadway.

Three men were struggling with the broken wheel of a bullock cart that had collapsed under the weight of a giant stone mortar and pestle secured in the back of the wagon. A yellow pariah dog lay scratching itself nearby. As the men labored, a second cart drew up, drawn by an elephant bound in a complex harness of leather, rope and chains. The dog rose and limped away. The driver leading the elephant stopped and haggled with the other cart men about transferring the stone burden to his heavier wagon.

"That elephant has no tusks," said Alexander, thinking of old prints and photographs. "And it seems shorter than African elephants, with a rounder body and smaller ears."

"Unlike Africa, our females have no tusks," said Laila, "and most males have small ones, *tushes*, we call them. In the old days the Sinhalese used elephants for many purposes. Forestry and construction, war and ceremony, and of course our kings used them as executioners."

"Executioners?"

She pointed towards the elephant. "Sharp iron tips were fitted onto their tusks before they speared a condemned man to the ground. Then the mahout guided them as they braced one foot against the man's chest and used their trunks to tear off his legs and arms like branches from a tree."

"Your gentle Buddhists are worse than the Cheka."

"I am Church of England, Count Karlov, not Buddhist," said Laila sternly. "But gentle religions have their own cruelties," she added as Alexander watched the carters struggling with the huge mortar and pestle. "Stone mills like that one in the wagon are used to press oil from the coconuts. A big stone *chekku* like that will support a family for generations."

An open carriage stopped at the station. A heavyset European and a large brown and white dog sat erect side-by-side on the back seat. The man stepped down, carrying a gun case and leading the long-haired dog on a leather leash. Some sort of bastard hound, guessed Alexander. The man's turbanned driver followed with a bamboo cage that he placed on a red freight scale at the entrance to the station. Behind them, the carriage horse began to stamp and raise its head as the mahout used a long hook to urge the elephant to back up his cart towards the collapsed vehicle nearby.

"Thank you, Ahmed," said the Englishman. "You best leave at once before that ellie agitates the horse." He encouraged the dog to enter the cage and started to unfasten its collar. As he worked the buckle, the dog barked once and bolted from the cage, tearing through the station garden and out onto the road facing the elephant.

The immense beast shifted its weight and trumpeted before raising a front foot and swinging its trunk towards the barking rushing dog.

Alexander stamped his right foot onto the trailing leash as if he were lunging on a fencing piste. The dog was pulled from its feet by the arrested momentum of its dash. Karlov pinned the lead to the ground with the tip of his cane while the dog strained and yelped at the elephant.

"Lucifer!" hollered the Englishman. "Down, Lucy!" He lifted the leash and led the dog back to the cage. Alexander held the cage door as the dog calmed. He noticed the manufacturer's name on the handsomely built scale: "W. & T. Avery, Makers, London & Birmingham." The scale rested on four squat steel wheels.

The dog's owner adjusted the iron balance along the arm of the scale and squinted through his spectacles at the numbers along the bar before announcing the weight to the watching station-master. "Three stone, four pounds. That's a lot for Lucy. Your scale's tipping a bit heavy, if you don't mind my saying so."

"Our scale is perfect, sir," said the station master, a smartly uniformed Burgher. "Would you like me to get the testing weights?" Without waiting for a reply, he recorded the weight and wrote down the charge for the animal as he continued. "Parcel rates for dogs, mongooses and monkeys. There should also be something due for your hound's tearing up the garden, sir. Polgahawela won the prize last year, you know, for the finest station garden in Ceylon."

The Englishman removed his glasses and pinched his nose. He stared at the station-master as if inspecting some unknown creature from the forest. "My dear fellow . . ."

"Double parcel rates, sir, paid in advance, if you intend taking the dog into a passenger car, which may only be done with the concurrence of all fellow passengers." Enjoying his authority, the Burgher spoke firmly, as if educating a child.

"Lucifer always rides with me."

"No refund if other passengers do object, of course. All regulations, sir."

The two were still disputing when Alexander turned to rejoin Laila and they walked together towards the dining car.

"No Englishman would take such care for his child," said Laila as Alexander helped her up the steps. "Though one nanny or lady's maid accompanying her mistress is permitted to travel in First Class at half fare."

These English rules were not as bizarre as they might seem, thought Alexander, though his sister would despise them. He recalled old family friends complaining about the difficulties of travelling with servants while insisting on the necessity of having them at hand when one arrived.

Their dining table was one of six with a cane-backed seat for two on either side. Across the narrow aisle, smaller tables were set for one or two. Only one other place was occupied, by a grey-haired European lady seated alone, her gloves folded neatly on the table and a book open between her knife and fork. She surveyed the two arrivals with careful neutral eyes before removing her bookmark from its place and setting it beside the gloves. Her lips tightened when the waiter took the wood-framed menu from her table and set it between Karlov and Mrs. Hammond.

Perhaps this was why Laila would have preferred to eat privately in their cabin, thought Alexander.

"Please try one of our island drinks, made from coconut palms," suggested Laila. "Either arrack if you want spirits, or toddy if you'd prefer something long."

"Arrack, I think," said Alexander, liking the strong name. "That was my first elephant."

They drank and ate slowly. The drink reminded him of Pernod and licorice. Alexander stared down at the precipices and waterfalls. Several times he could see the rear car as it climbed after them around the curving edges of steep mountains.

"Floods and earth slips and cave-ins keep them busy on this line," Laila noted. She gave him the story of each town where they stopped. Rambukkana, Kadugannawa, Peradeniya. Then south through Gampola and Ulapane to Nawalapitiya, where a second locomotive was added at the rear to assist with the final ascents. He could not master the difficult romantic names.

The train proceeded more and more slowly as it climbed the tight winding turns.

"I'll be getting off at Ella," Laila reminded him when the train stopped at Hatton. "Ella is the last stop before yours, Bandarawela. It's a shame we don't have time to get down here. Hatton's only a few miles from Adam's Peak, a pilgrimage for three religions who want to see the giant sacred stone footprint where the first man stepped onto the world."

As they stood to leave the restaurant car, Lucifer's owner entered and removed his hat. The leash was bound tightly around his other hand. The dog followed quietly at his heel. Nodding at the single lady, he ordered a double whisky as the waiter drew back his chair at another table.

"Does anyone mind if Lucy sits under my table while I dine?" he enquired amiably.

"Dogs in the refreshment car?" said the woman sharply as the waiter turned away. "Dogs? I should think not."

"Mind? No, of course not," said Alexander at the same instant. "Lucifer's most welcome." He thought of his father, after drinking with his friends, unleashing his wild borzois to thunder through the halls and pee in the planters, to the dismay of his mother and the servants in the morning. "No bother at all."

The woman stared at Karlov as if the young man had just been ill across the dinner table.

"Are there no rules?" she asked tartly, looking about for the waiter, who had disappeared at the far end of the carriage.

"Of course there are rules, madam," declared Lucy's owner. "And I will tell you what they are." His voice filled the restaurant car. "Dogs, once their carriage is paid for, are acceptable to the railway in the passenger cars provided that no traveller objects. No one ever objects. Up here, we all have dogs. How could you live without one?"

Without sitting down, he turned to Alexander and bowed to Laila. Lucy rubbed himself against Alexander's leg as his master clapped Karlov on the shoulder.

"Young man, you saved my best hound. Lucifer's the finest seizer in the mountains. Never lets go once he has a hold. Never. He's all courage. He'll hang on to a boar or bear until one of 'em is dead. That elephant would've killed him. Please permit me to stand you both a drink. Name's Palliser." He handed Alexander a card. "Percy Palliser."

"You're most kind," said Karlov, sensing that Laila was keen to get away without an introduction. "But we were just leaving." He gave the Englishman a card of his own.

He heard the woman's continuing protests, and Palliser's immediate response, as he followed Laila from the car.

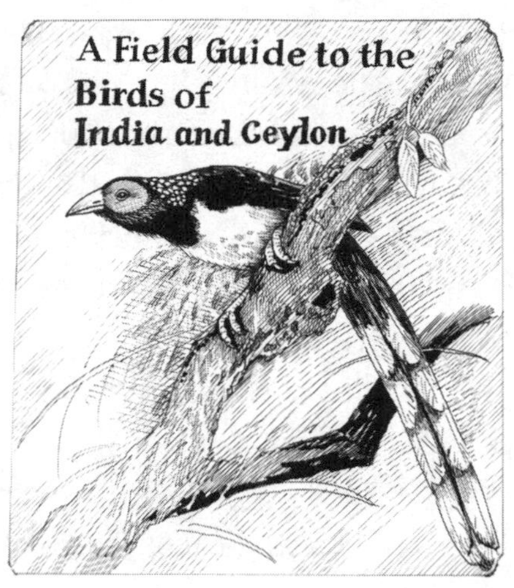

- 29 -

It had been the same when Oskar and he were boys in Kazan, the sense that each of them was alone against the world.

Their mother, old at thirty-five, had died giving birth to Oskar. Todor remembered when there was no work and no money. His mother would chew a crust of moldy black bread, then wrap the dark mess in a scrap of cloth and give it to him to suck on. Their father had abandoned the two boys with his brother and sought employment as a metal worker in Piter, as he called St. Petersburg. Later they heard he had been killed during a strike when the Guards fired on the workers in Winter Palace Square on Bloody Sunday, the first day the crowds had howled, "We have no Czar! We have no Czar!"

Uncle Pavel made a living at the match works, but the sulphur dust and phosphorus fumes had been killing him each fourteen-hour day. At night he sounded as if he were not sleeping, but dying.

Todor Androv thought about those times as he waited for the doorman to inform him that the black whore's rickshaw was back at the Grand Oriental. These uniformed servants of the bourgeoisie always annoyed him. It was still worse when their obsequious manner seemed sincere. But he sensed that this hotel man, even when bribed, regarded Todor's worn black jacket and coarse dark shirt as the harness of a laborer.

He turned his dice in one hand as he thought back to that moment on the launch in Goa. Seeing Oskar's watch in the hands of the enemy his brother was meant to kill had persuaded the Ferret that his missing sibling must be dead.

As the elder, and for ten years the larger brother, Todor had been able to bully Oskar and to take the best food when their uncle pushed a single bowl of buckwheat groats or watery cabbage soup between them, sometimes with a handful of raw onions or pickled cucumbers.

But by fourteen Oskar was becoming larger and stronger. Only their heads were similar, narrow with small close-set eyes. "Fish heads," some boys called the two, until they no longer dared. Fearing retribution himself, Todor had become more restrained and respectful as his brother grew. Later he was surprised that Oskar never repaid him for the blows and hunger of his early years. Instead, Oskar was generous for a time, sharing his bread and protecting his older, smaller brother from the rail yard gangs, occasionally even taking a beating or punishment in his stead.

After his first imprisonment, however, Oskar was not the same. And after his second, he was the vicious and vengeful creature he would be until he died. The beatings and perversion seemed to remain inside him like organs in his body. Sentiment and generosity had become strangers to Oskar Androv, replaced by the tattoos of wolves and daggers that darkened his hands and body. Todor knew that death would not have much mattered to his brother. Oskar would wish only for vengeance, not for sympathy or affectionate regard.

As boys, their play had always some connection to survival. Theft, trickery and brawling were their games. The rail yard had been their school, freight cars and looted storehouses their classrooms. When the two finally had fled their uncle's rough care, Oskar had taken the bastard's boots, and Todor had pocketed his ivory dice, probably once stolen by the old man himself.

Following Oskar's first arrest, Todor, alone and fearful of the gangs and rail guards, sought different opportunities. He explored on his own, jumping down from trains some miles to the east, first at Arsk, then at Shemordan and Kukmor. There he had learned to steal from the village markets, until a burly kulak caught him and tied him to a cattle post. The farm louts spat on him and reviled him as they passed. One paused and stole the boots that he himself had taken from a drunken soldier lying in a gutter in Kazan. It was a loss that Todor Androv had not forgotten.

In the summer months, he wandered in the countryside, living as he could, sleeping in the forest, astonished that he found pleasure in the voices of the birds, especially owls, preferring them to men. Without knowing their species or distinctions, he learned to imitate the calls and whistles of certain birds, especially the vibrant churring of the nightjars that came with darkness, and the bulbuls that announced each dawn. Todor wondered if this skill might be related to his ease with languages. His French and English were already passable.

He respected the abilities of owls to hunt when their prey could neither see nor hear them. Their huge eyes gave them superior night vision. Their contour feathers were soft and velvety, muffling the sound of their flapping wings. Their hearing was so sensitive that they could detect a mouse or rat rustling in the leaves or brush. He was certain that their large heads held large brains. Though Todor's own eyes were small, he shared their aptitude for the solitary hunt.

Loneliness, foresters, even the angry gamekeepers did not disturb him. Only a bear once frightened him.

Defending himself at night with a flaming branch, Todor thought he recognized death itself in the small red eyes and primitive fury of the shaggy beast. Occasionally the raging animal haunted his sleep. Todor would awaken just as the bear rose on its hind legs and clawed for his face and throat. Once he had encountered a forester whose skull was covered with dry yellow skin, patchy as if partly glazed in a baker's oven. A bear had clawed off the man's scalp and hair.

The coming of the Revolution meant loss and death for many. But for the Androv brothers, both back in Kazan as Mother Russia burned, it was a new life. The old rules of class and money, power and proper behavior, meant nothing. Only carving out a place in the ranks of the Bolsheviks mattered, particularly in the instruments of authority and terror, the Cheka and its collaterals. Even more than courage and determination and luck, success in that ambition required special qualities that were congenial to both brothers.

The Cheka became a family for both Androvs. Their aptitudes and demeanor, elsewhere punished and detested, were welcomed and rewarded. Todor was soon celebrated for his cunning and relentlessness in hunting enemies of the Reds. He earned his name: the Ferret. His early successes allowed him to secure his brother's freedom. For Oskar, cruelty and prison stigmata were now credentials.

The urgency of the Revolution and the tenacity of its adversaries on every front had allowed no time for training and preparation. In the early days, Cheka recruits and agents were trained by their assignments, and by the enemies they survived.

Todor wondered how his own experience would serve him now in Ceylon and later in Shanghai, settings dominated by English imperialists and defined by two ancient cultures. He reminded himself that he must present a gentler, less memorable demeanor, that this could be a long pursuit, like an animal trail in the forest. But a successful hunt for the young count would satisfy all his masters: the Cheka, Viktor Polyak and his personal need for fraternal vengeance. Recovering Oskar's pocket watch would affirm that he had done his duty to all three.

Commissar Polyak himself was the only man whom Todor Androv feared. Whatever fuel it was that fired Todor's own ferocity burned still deeper and still hotter in Viktor Polyak.

"Sir!" cried the hotel doorman, interrupting his reflections. "Sir! Your puller is back. If you pay him good, he will take you where he took the lady."

First, Androv had the rickshaw take him to a clothier and general store, Cargill's on York Street. There he asked to buy what would be suitable for visiting the plantation country high in the interior. He had never seen such varieties of goods assembled under a single roof, everything from school materials to weapons. He purchased a pair of binoculars and two books. One on the history of the tea business, the other *A Field Guide to the Birds of India and Ceylon*. Both would also serve to advance his English. Androv looked forward to imitating the calls of the island's owls.

He left Cargill's carrying a small canvas suitcase, and dressed in a crisp blue shirt and tan cotton trousers, but still wearing his own comfortable sturdy boots. On his face was a pair of round spectacles of plain glass, very slightly tinted.

So this is where the Portuguese imprisoned the working class, thought the Ferret as the rickshaw crossed Slave Island. A paradise compared to Siberia. Soon they stopped in Cinnamon Gardens. He stepped down and called for assistance at the gate of the grand residence at 6 Horton Place. An old man appeared.

"What was the woman doing who was here before?" asked Androv after a brief exchange.

"Sir?" asked the man, feigning incomprehension, his wrinkled face close to the gate as he turned his large right ear towards the visitor.

"The black woman," said the Russian, holding out a coin. "The one who was here yesterday. What did she want?"

"Mrs. Hammond?" The man looked at the coin but did not attempt to take it. "Sir, I do not know." He shrugged and seemed about to turn away.

Androv, slight as he was, reached through the steel bars and seized the old man by his prominent ears with both hands. Using the weight of his own body, he leaned back and slammed the servant's head against the bars, then shook it from side to side as blood leaked from the man's broken nose.

"I . . ." The servant spat a tooth between the bars. "I know nothing, sir."

Androv cursed. He flung down the Ceylonese and turned to the rickshaw puller.

"Take me to the woman's hotel. The Galle Face, you said."

There he learned that Mrs. Hammond and Count Karlov had already departed. "The Count made his arrangements at the travel desk," said the concierge loftily.

Some rich woman, perhaps an American, stood beside Androv at the reception counter complaining about her rooms. Piles of leather luggage, trunks and hat boxes, all covered in First Class baggage tags and the stickers of shipping lines and grand hotels, were being moved about by hall boys and eager porters who pretended they enjoyed their toil.

Annoyed, touched by a sense of contamination, Todor walked across the high-ceilinged lobby and glanced at the majestic colonnaded courtyard that opened to the sea. It was worse than being in an Orthodox church, stinking with incense and crowded with idolators. Wherever he looked, bustling waiters in white sarongs and white jackets with brass buttons were serving the hotel's guests. He paused to admire numerous large-billed black crows that leapt about and hovered at the water's edge seeking scraps from the sea and the terraces. Like the staff, these birds had learned to live off the rich.

Todor returned to the lobby and stepped to the travel desk to resume his enquiries. He forced himself to be patient as he smiled through his glasses and deferred to a young Englishman asking about arranging a shikar or safari for elephant and crocodile. The hunter was disappointed that there were no lion, tiger or rhinoceros on the island.

"No bloody lion? Isn't the lion the symbol of Ceylon?" the visitor protested as he turned away. "Doesn't 'sinhal' mean lion in Sinhalese? What?"

The clerk turned to Androv and accepted a florin as the Russian questioned him.

"Yes, sir, Count Karlov left Fort Station on the morning train for Bandarawela," he said. "First Class, of course."

Of course, thought Androv with contempt. "Show me the schedule."

He considered whether he should make contact with the two young Ceylonese identified by the Cheka as possible revolutionaries, sympathizers of the Comintern, which last year had held its Third Congress in Petrograd. Bourgeois island intellectuals of mixed blood, so-called Burghers, the two Ceylonese were said to be recent graduates of some costly English university with a fashion for treasonous sympathy with the Reds. In Ceylon, said the Comintern's experts, revolution might come through organizing the plantation workers, mostly Tamils, reportedly poor dark people from nearby India. Men such as these two Burghers, disgruntled by their own uncertain middling status, might be encouraged to take the lead.

Such briefings and lectures on world revolution by the Comintern and the Cheka had been the high point of Todor Androv's education. One day revolution would come to India itself, a Party lecturer had explained, for there two corrupt religions supported a class system more inescapable and brutal than any on earth. The opiate of these two purportedly gentle spiritual philosophies maintained the slaveries of caste while despising and slaughtering the followers of different gods. These ancient dark-faced bigotries had been transported like infections from India to Ceylon, where they had been brutalized in turn by the better-armed followers of Christ.

Todor Androv decided to ignore the troubles of Ceylon. It was his mission to help carry out Lenin's demand for the extermination of all dangerous Russian émigrés wherever they might hide.

"How much is one Third Class ticket to Bandara?" Androv asked the clerk. He would use the train ride to study his new books and prepare himself for what he must do.

"Bandarawela, sir. In rupees, standard Third Class fare is two and two thirds cents a mile. First Class would be eight cents the mile. Both are a bit more for the Hill section above Nawalapitiya, where the train requires a second locomotive. One hundred cents to the rupee, sir. Fifteen rupees to the sovereign."

"What is the next stop after Bandarawela?" When hunting or following a man, another Chekist had taught him, it is often best not to copy his footsteps too precisely.

"The next stop is Ella, only six miles further on."

Viktor Polyak leaned over the crowded rail and spat into the deepening wake as the *Karnak* steamed from Aden, yet another stolen colonial bastion of the domineering British. The fast French vessel had bunkered quickly at the busy coaling station and would be turning south in the Arabian Sea for the Indian Ocean and Tananarive.

Only a pair of Arab traders had boarded at Aden. Said to be bound for the pearl fisheries in Ceylon, they were hawk-faced saturnine men in long cotton robes who sat in a corner of the smoking cabin with their backs to the deck as they waited for the *Karnak* to sail. The Commissar had watched several First Class passengers go briefly ashore. They returned with their clothes wrinkled and the exhausted sweaty faces of people not used to labor or discomfort but who believed they had endured some hardship. Their guide carried a rolled-up rug and a basket of trinkets and long-handled knives.

The Foreign Legionnaires had been kept on board. No doubt their officers feared losing more men to drunkenness and desertion. The soldiers were scattered in knots along the steerage deck, smoking and bellowing in German and French. As the steamship had left Suez and entered the Red Sea, he had heard several Russian Legionnaires asking if their comrades had seen the pair Viktor had murdered in Port Saïd.

A couple stood close behind him now, speaking in French of their future on a rubber plantation in Cochin-China. Polyak understood snatches of the lies the red-faced plantation manager was telling his scrawny young bride about the glories of a life with servants at a bungalow in the jungle. The Commissar grunted to himself and spat again as he thought of how the French girl would enjoy the second year and the next, when she was feverish or pregnant and her middle-aged husband had taken up again with his dark native mistresses.

The woman's voice reminded him of Katerina Karlov. Viktor thought angrily of how she always resisted him before succumbing, whether in Siberia, Petrograd or Paris. Why were women so false, in both protest and submission? But, like a good Chekist, she had taught him one thing. Thanks to her, now he knew what could control a woman when nothing else served: fear for her child. He wondered if his vigor had succeeded in getting her pregnant again in Paris. He could imagine her dismay when she became aware of her condition. There would be no finer way to bind her to the Party and to him, and to enfuriate her bastard brother when he learned of it.

The thought of that, and the gropings of the couple behind him, turned Polyak's mind to the heavy-breasted young woman in the neighboring cabin below. Too busy with his duties, there had been no time to take a whore in Egypt. He thought for a moment of the drunken twelve-year-old prostitutes available in the factory districts of Moscow.

The Commissar turned his back to the sea and roughly pushed his way through the passengers on the deck behind him. As he passed, he managed to rub against the scrawny French woman. She pretended to ignore the attention and smiled out to sea as the rubber man fondled her. Her sweet perfume reminded Polyak of the stinking incense that would be waiting below.

The low-ceilinged Third Class passage smelled of oil, salt, sweat and old tobacco smoke. The slippery steel deck trembled beneath his feet as he opened the narrow door to his cabin. He heard activity in the common bathroom and wondered if the woman had thought to bolt the door. He set his ear against it and was careful not to knock the steel with his hook. He heard water running and the baby whining. He pulled sharply at the handle and opened the door before she could react. Perhaps the woman was tired of her small dark man and had been hoping to see him again. Quickly Polyak bolted the other door that led into her own cabin.

He snatched the naked child from the woman's bosom. She protested and stretched out her arms in pleading as he placed the baby on the second of the low bunks in his own cabin. White bubbles of milk spotted the woman's full brown breast. The infant squealed but lay still, as if in shock. For an instant Polyak recalled his own child reacting in this way. Frozen in silence, little Leon had responded to his first experience of animal fear with instinctive infantile wisdom, sensing it was a moment to avoid attention, not demand it. Fear was a universal tool.

Thinking of the boy reminded Polyak that it might be time to change his child's name. With Trotsky losing favor, a different name might have more advantage. Perhaps Feliks or Josef. A change would also make it more difficult for Katerina to find the child.

Polyak closed the door to the bathroom. He grabbed the Annamese woman's hair tight against the back of her head and forced her down onto his bunk. He pressed the flat of his hook against the soft balloon of her chest while he unbuttoned. The prick of the pointed metal reduced her to obedience like an edged bit forced into the mouth of a difficult horse.

He tasted the warm thick sweetness of her milk when he bit her breast. Then he tore apart the folds of her sari and pressed himself into her. She made no sound. She seemed used to the practicality of submission. But her eyes stared wildly at the child rolling about on the other berth. When he was finished he stood and the Indian turned to the wall with her knees raised to her belly. No doubt she had enjoyed him.

Polyak lifted the child and set it down like a doll between her and the wall. It stared up at him with unblinking eyes. He pinched the infant once under the chin. It was like switching on a light bulb. The small dark creature wiggled its legs and gurgled. Viktor wanted this woman to know that no harm would come to her or the baby, provided she obliged him. Then she would not speak of these events to her family, thinking also that if she did so her husband would forever reject her as unclean.

He opened the bathroom door and rinsed himself while she rocked with her child on the bed. Then he dropped a few francs onto the disordered blanket beside her. It would be a long voyage for all of them.

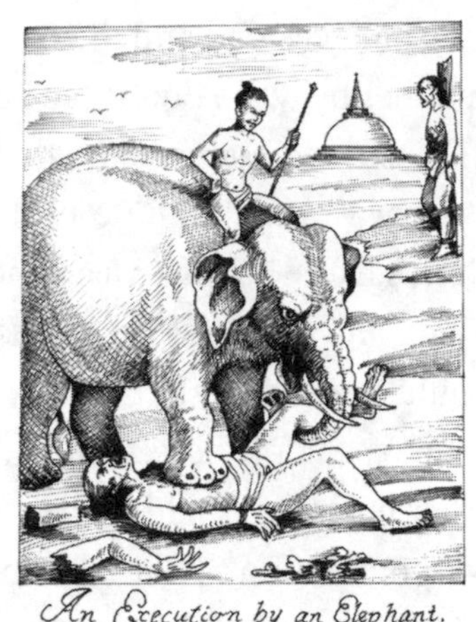

An Execution by an Elephant.

- 30 -

"Your stop, sir," said the cabin boy, lifting Alexander's case. "Bandarawela."

The train slowed as it passed a rail switch and water tower. The track curved gently towards the station garden. A sweeper was brushing off the platform as the train slid to a stop. Car doors opened. A mail sack was hurled to the platform before Karlov tipped the cabin boy and stepped down. He smelled frangipani and mountain flowers and breathed the crisp air of Ceylon's hill country instead of the steaming heat of the plains and paddies.

"Bandarawela, 4,036 Feet," read the station sign above the platform.

He walked under the corrugated tin roof through the short passage that separated the ticket office from the waiting room.

A slight older man with an upturned white mustache waited beside the hexagonal red column of the mail box. "VR" was picked out in fresh gold paint below the letter slot. "Bandarawela Hotel" was stitched on the breast pocket of the elderly man's stiff white jacket. Several saddle horses, one open motorcar, a carriage and a canopied hackery drawn by a bull waited outside the station.

The hotel man saluted Karlov and took his case. Alexander watched the lady from the dining car step into the waiting automobile.

The stout carriage pony seemed to need no direction as it descended to the town and entered the large circular drive of the hotel before stopping under the entry porch and turning its head towards the white-helmeted doorman in his white shorts and polished cross-belt. A long single-story facade stretched to either side beneath a steep tiled roof with red brick chimneys. England? thought Alexander.

The doorman took a carrot from a pocket of his shorts. The pony sniffed him and ruffled its upper lip.

Alexander's rooms were at the end of a long corridor that led past a lounge and painted notice boards saying "Members' Bar" and "Billiard Room." He heard the rumble of loud voices and the banging of a gavel through the closed door of the billiard room as he followed the room boy down the hall.

A mosquito net was furled in a ropy knot above the large brass bed. Doors led from his sitting room and bath onto a small garden with one round table, two chairs and a green canvas umbrella.

He unlocked the sitting room door and stepped down into the garden. It was enclosed on one side by a dense blossoming hedge and on the other by a curving brick wall overhung by tall trees. The shadow of a monkey flitted in the branches. Karlov picked a small white flower and ate several juicy blackberries he took from a bush that was growing vigorously amidst the hedge.

Suddenly he was startled by the rustle of some creature on the ground. He looked down to see the prickly arched back of a porcupine retreating into a small passage through the hedge. The rodent snorted once and withdrew until he could no longer hear the faint rattle of its quills.

Alexander smiled. Perfect, he thought, even if I am alone. Laila Hammond had told him that this was where he would be staying while they were in the tea country. Until recently the Bandarawela Hotel had been the Planters Club, and, she had explained, in certain regards it retained its old customs and adornments.

He bathed, shaved and changed into a dark suit and a starched white Russian shirt before setting the flower in his buttonhole and walking to the empty bar.

"Sorry, sir, no vodka," the white-gloved barman advised him. The gloves reminded Alexander of the White Guards officer murdered in Shanghai. His Chekist killer, probably Viktor Polyak, had cut the skin all the way around the old man's wrists and then plunged his hands into boiling water before flaying them. It was the usual Bolshevik punishment when they captured an officer of the Guards regiment celebrated for its white gloves and fierce loyalty to the czar.

A pair of old hunting rifles, their firing mechanisms missing, hung on the wall above the crowded drinks shelf. Nearby, between two sets of three-pointed mounted antlers, hung the framed drawing of a hunter in tight trousers and a tall tweed cap firing into a herd of elephant, with one animal already dead beside him. "Sir Samuel Baker in 1854," read the inscription. "Discoverer of the source of the Nile. Builder of Nuwara Eliya." Ceylon's common link with Africa seemed to be elephants and Englishmen.

"Gin, sir?" asked the barman.

"No, thank you," said Alexander, glancing at a print apparently taken from the autobiography of an English sailor imprisoned on Ceylon in the seventeenth century. "Arrack, if you please." The picture depicted an executioner elephant ripping the limbs from a prisoner, much as Laila had described that traditional ceremony to him.

He drank the small British serving of the powerful drink and ordered another while he studied the framed scenes of early planter life. Hunting, coffee and horses. Wild boar, sloth bear, sambur elk, leopard and elephant. Not bad, thought Alexander, hoping he would have the opportunity to try some sport himself, though he knew he would have to do it mostly from the saddle, which might be impossible in the steeper rocky country broken by so many streams and waterfalls.

"Is the bar always this quiet?" asked Alexander in the stillness.

"No, sir. Most of the old members are gathered in the Billiard Room for a meeting of the Ceylon Fishing Club. They'll be setting the release date for this year's raised trout. The starters were brought from Scotland, I believe."

At that moment a clamor of voices and laughter approached. A dozen men entered. Most set their empty glasses on the bar and called for more. Several were dressed in dinner jackets, others in tweed suits or crested blazers.

"Young chap's not wearing a tie," huffed one red-faced man to another as he tapped his glass on the bar. "Getting away with anything these days."

"Wretched place is gone to hell," nodded the other. "Wouldn't believe what they're letting into the Golf Club these days. If the caddies weren't barefoot, you couldn't tell which are which. Some of the little brown buggers even play better golf. Caught a couple of 'em at it early one morning on fourteen. Using some dead member's irons, and our lost balls from the streams and flooded ditches. Damned if they weren't pitching and chipping like Mungo Park or Harry Vardon."

"At least we've one proper club left at Nuwara Eliya," said the first. "The Hill Club still doesn't put up with this sort of slack nonsense."

Who do these English farmers think they are? thought Alexander Karlov with a flash of his father's ready indignation. Not much more than kulaks, really. It takes more than a servant to make a gentleman, the old Hussar once had told him. "Bad behavior is one thing. Bad manners is something else."

"Why, good evening," said Karlov's acquaintance from the train, extending his hand to Alexander. "Let me stand you a drink. Help you catch up with the rest of this sodden lot. Whisky?"

"Arrack, if you please," said Alexander, still simmering. "How is Lucifer?"

"Keen for a sambur hunt, I'd say," said Percival Palliser.

"This is the gentleman who looked after old Lucy on the train," the Englishman added to a short portly companion in a rumpled tweed suit and striped tie spotted with ashes. The man's thick sandy eyebrows met in the center of his face like a hedge dividing two fields. "First he saved Lucy from an angry elephant, then from that hideous old dragon, Arabella Hartshorn."

Palliser drank before completing the introduction. "Alexander Karlov, Robbie Knox."

"Well done, lad," said Knox. His suit was as thick and rough and well used as the old blood-stained carpet in the hunting lodge at Voskrenoye. "Hard to say which one I'd shoot first. Of course the ellie would look better on the wall. Hate to have to mount old lady Hartshorn, though one of her legs would make a fine umbrella stand."

"I say, Palliser," said another member helpfully, "why don't you lend your young friend a necktie? Then the rest of these fellows wouldn't be so jumpy."

"Mr. Karlov is from Russia," said Palliser. "When the czar of all the Russias came to Kandy with the governor some years back, the governor received him in full tropical kit, white plume and all. Czar Nicholas, a cousin of King George, you know, was dressed like this gentleman here. Seemed to be good enough for the governor," persisted Palliser, enjoying his point. "Probably good enough for the King, come to that."

"All the same . . ." muttered the planter, turning away with his dark double sherry. "Trouble with Palliser," he grumbled to a friend, "hasn't changed since school. Makes everything a debate. Just can't stop once he starts in. Like a mule going home down hill."

"All we think about up here is trout, tea and billiards," said Palliser cheerfully to Alexander.

"And horses and birds," added Knox. "The best birding in the East. Over four hundred birds on the island, half of them residents. Twenty-six endemics, all our own. Think of it!" His eyes shone. "My favorite migrant is the blue-tailed bee-eater. Come swarming over from India, like the Tamils. They love dragon flies. Gobble 'em up like Christmas pudding."

"Yes, Robbie," said Palliser.

"We're the last stop for the migrants, you understand. After Ceylon, it's all water. They come all the way from China and Tibet. We even get a few of yours, Karlov, winging down from Siberia."

"Yes, Robert, of course. Birds." Palliser tapped the bar with his empty glass. "Then we have the races at Nuwara Eliya. All sorts of riders, from grooms to gents. Most of the horses come from India or Australia. The Madras ponies seem to run better at our altitude, over six thousand foot. Some damn fine sprinters. Knox here has one of the best, Magpie, if he trained him properly. Too much over-feeding, like his master. He's a butterball."

"Rubbish," said Knox. "Magpie's fit as a cheetah. None better at five furlongs."

"How long is the track?" asked Alexander.

"Mile and a quarter. The big race is ten furlongs," said Knox. "The Planters Cup, on in a fortnight. Do you ride?" Then his eyes slipped to Alexander's cane. "Oh, sorry."

"Sometimes," said Karlov. He had not raced since he rode his beloved Mongolian mare in the Griffin Handicap in Shanghai. Startled by a dog rushing onto the track, Taiga had gone down with a broken leg and he had been obliged to shoot her where she fell.

They drank at the bar until Alexander felt dizzy and desperate to dine. Finally he shared a table for five, enjoying the venison, boiled cabbage and roast potatoes. He was relieved that the English social habit of putting *froideur* before curiosity discouraged the others from asking him too much about himself. All but Knox seemed satisfied to know that he was White Russian and resident in Shanghai, with a possible interest in shooting or the tea business in the hill country.

"A telegram for you, Count Karlov," interrupted a hotel boy, presenting a small envelope on a plate. One of the Englishmen raised his eyebrows at the mention of the Russian's title.

"Excuse me, gentlemen." Alexander slit open the envelope with a table knife. The message was from Katerina, evidently sent from the Grand Oriental in the harbor just before she reboarded the *Star*.

ABOUT TO SAIL FOR SHANGHAI STOP
RUSSIAN FROM BOAT MAY BE ON ISLAND
HUNTING FOR YOU STOP BE CAREFUL SASHA
STOP PLEASE JOIN ME IN SHANGHAI STOP
KATIA

Later Alexander lay on his back, enjoying the cool night, with no need to use the mosquito net knotted above him. He closed his eyes, still tasting the arrack and after-dinner brandy. Thoughts of Cairo and Shanghai clouded in his mind as sleep took him.

An hour later he awoke. His skin prickled as he listened for the noise that had disturbed him at the garden door. Had he locked it?

He reached across the bed and slipped the sword from his cane as he rose. A door handle turned. Alexander stood against the wall by the doorway that led to the sitting room and garden. He felt a cool draft as the garden door opened. A light step stroked the plank floor of the sitting room. He raised the tip of his sword.

A dark shadow filled the doorway. Alexander was prepared to lunge when a breath of perfume caught him. Sandalwood. He lowered the weapon.

"Laila." Her body trembled when he hugged her. He kissed her face and led her to the bed.

"No," she said. "If we use your bed, the room boy will smell it and know you were not alone. They always sniff the beds."

She unwrapped her shawl and sari and spread them carefully on the bedroom carpet before lying down on her stomach.

"If they establish adultery, they will deny my claim to my husband's property," she said quietly. "I would not wish to be obliged to choose between Count Karlov and a tea garden."

Unable to see her face, Alexander did not know if Laila was smiling as she spoke.

"Please keep still, Doctor Hammond," he said, stroking her back, feeling the hidden warmth of the cleft between her smooth rounded cheeks. "You are my guest. It is my turn."

He drew back a curtain until the moonlight touched her body. Then he knelt on one knee and massaged her neck and back and high hard derriere. Mrs. Hammond parted her legs slightly.

Alexander accepted the invitation. He moistened his fingertips with his tongue, then touched her steadily with two long fingers until she moaned and drew up her knees and raised her brown bottom towards him like the two halves of a pear covered in warm dark chocolate. He was reminded of the rich dessert he had not eaten at the dinner of the Corps des Pages in Paris: *poire belle Hélène.*

- 31 -

Katerina Karlov stood near the broad open doorway of the Salle d'Armes. She counted the baggage as the Chinese driver unloaded the taxi. The *Star* had anchored in Shanghai ahead of schedule, and Katia had said her brief goodbyes and not waited to see if anyone would be meeting her.

What had surprised her on the way to the Salle d'Armes was not the frenzy of the Chinese port but the pervasive Gallic influence as they motored through the French Concession. Was this China or Toulouse? Street names, shops and gendarmes in the uniforms of Paris all reminded her of the powerful colonial entanglement. In St. Petersburg, now Petrograd, Peter the Great had chosen to import French influence to make Russia look to the West instead of to the East. Here in Shanghai, Katia was certain the Chinese had enjoyed no choice.

The posted name of one street had changed from the Avenue Edward VII on the International Settlement side of the road to l'avenue Edouard VII on the French Concession side. The policemen changed with it, from a massive dark turbanned Sikh to small olive-skinned men in French uniforms and conical straw hats. But the dense chaos of porters and barrow boys, motorcars and rickshaws, pedlars and street cooks and mendicants remained the same.

She was embarrassed by the number of cases and hat boxes that were piled at the door of the Salle d'Armes beside the foot locker that contained her favorite new clothes from Poiret and Lanvin. Before the German war, of course, her mother had always returned from Paris in time for the Christmas season with two steamer trunks crowded with her new hanging clothes. Katia used to wait as eagerly for the huge trunks as for her maman. She would help the maid unpack before spreading the two open face-to-face and removing the deep drawers from the right side of each trunk. Then she would make a doll's house of the tall enclosing structure with its leather edges, wooden bands and brass corners.

Katerina reminded herself not to be embarrassed by the contrast between her appreciation of little luxuries and the fervor of her social ideals. She was her mother's daughter. Why could one not live well and still believe in social justice? Did not even Rousseau himself love small comforts, food and beauty? The great libertarian *philosophe* may have died insane, but he gave the world its finest battle cry, the only one for which to die: *Liberté! Égalité! Fraternité!*

"Thank you," she said, tipping the driver generously and stepping back as two horsemen dressed *à l'anglaise* rode out into the dusty sunlight through the tall doorway. One touched his hat to her as he passed and encouraged his horse into a trot. The two riders posted easily as they set off down the Chemin St. Bernard.

The open yard across the street seemed to be some sort of factory for rickshaws, a form of conveyance that she had rejected with horror in Goa and Colombo.

Katia stepped inside the door of her brother's enterprise and let her eyes adjust. The immense space contained a sawdust riding ring, two carpeted fencing pistes, and several straw and canvas-covered targets suitable for varied weapons. A boxing ring was in a far corner near punching bags and a wooden polo horse. Two barefoot men in white tunics and dark sashes were performing some form of combat practice on a thick canvas mat halfway along one wall.

A chill touched her as she realized how much the high-ceilinged hall reminded her of a training center for the Cheka. Only the polo horse and the hanging flags of czarist regiments disturbed the memory. The torn banners reminded her of the cruel struggle for her country. She thought of the relentless determination of the Chekists and worried that Viktor might have taken another boat for Shanghai.

A large red-haired man in loose wrinkled boots stood nearby with his back to her as he checked a rack of sabres, foils and epées.

"Excuse me," said Katerina.

The man turned to her with a sabre and a cleaning cloth in his thick hands.

"Yes, miss?" The rough pudding of the Cossack face opened in a grin. "You are Katerina? Miss Karlov?"

Before she could reply, the man embraced her, almost tearful with his joy. She smelled old sweat and fresh alcohol.

"I am Ivan Semyonov, *hetman* of Cossacks to your father, and now to young Count Alexander. I was going to meet you at the boat." He tapped the sabre before he racked it. "Your brother is the finest fencer on the China Coast."

"How can he . . ."

"With that stiff leg, Alexander Karlov can do everything except retreat, Miss." Semyonov clapped his hands. Two Chinese came forward, one a woman, and gathered in her baggage.

"I am Chung." The woman bowed. "This my husband, Li, the cook."

Katia followed the two up a narrow set of stairs at one side of the old warehouse. She felt eager to snoop and learn how the men of her family had lived when on their own.

She entered a simple windowless room, something like an officer's quarters in a barrack. Riding breeches, dinner jackets, tweeds and one frayed uniform of the 5th Hussars hung from hooks along one wall. Polished boots and shoes with wooden trees lined the opposing wall. She identified Sasha's by the smaller left feet. The tall soft boots reminded her of home. She stroked the worn scarlet braid of her father's tunic and thought of all the useless battles he must have fought from the Crimea to Siberia. She guessed that Alexander would now be big enough to wear his clothes. He seemed to have their father's impulsiveness and his excessive charm with women, but not quite his enthusiastic extravagance. Katerina envied their gift for friendship and wondered if that were easier for men.

She sat on the bed and took off her shoes before stepping to the bureau. There she saw three photographs, a pair of silver-backed brushes with no handles and the enamel Maltese Cross of the Corps des Pages. The military hairbrushes were engraved with the double-headed bear of her family's crest. Two medals hung on ribbons from a corner of the looking glass. She recognized the Order of St. George.

One picture was of a young woman standing near a line of Chinese girls dressed in the uniform smocks of what she took to be some mission school. The initials "J.J." were penned in one corner beneath a heart. The girl had the fresh unlined attractiveness of youth but without true beauty, as Countess Karlov would have said with no malice. The second was of Katia's father as a handsome young lieutenant with his brother officers. All dead, she guessed. She peered more closely at her father's features. She had not realized how much her twin had come to resemble him. The third photograph made her want to cry: Sasha and her with their parents on a special picnic at Voskrenoye. She remembered thinking on that midsummer's night that her mother and father loved each other still.

"Tea, missy?" Chung gestured towards the door, out of breath after helping to carry the foot locker up the stairs.

"Thank you." Katerina pulled on brocade slippers and followed her down. She was feeling slightly nauseous and thought some tea might do her good. The two women, tall and short, walked along the side of the riding ring and past the canvas mat.

One combatant grunted painfully as the two men grappled. The more slender man, Japanese she guessed, had a lean handsome face and a tight body sculpted like a suit of armor. He held one arm extended straight before him with the palm and fingers raised at a sharp angle like a two-handed broadsword poised for attack. His copper face was smooth and dry beneath the white cotton band that crossed the top of his forehead. She had never seen such concentration as in his eyes. Broader and heavier, his face glistening with sweat, his adversary matched his circling movements to the left. The two men seemed not to see her pass.

The far end of the hall opened onto a courtyard where she found an open kitchen, a dining table and sideboard, and a thatched hut with bamboo walls edged with a garden where vegetables and flowers grew together. An old samovar stood steaming on the sideboard with a brown teapot warming on top of it. Tall glasses in lacework silver holders were set beside it near two bottles of vodka. A child of three or four was playing with an old cavalry boot beneath the side table.

She joined Semyonov at the dining table. Li served them two glasses of tea, and Ivan pushed a pot of thick red jam towards her. She served herself, then used her long spoon to take a bit more of the preserve. She bent down and offered the dripping spoon to the little boy. The child dropped the boot and grabbed the spoon with dusty fingers. His round face smiled up at her. Jam soon smeared one dimpled cheek.

"Old Count Karlov always played with baby Lu," said Chung with fondness.

Katerina felt a stab of painful loss. How was Leon, her own son? Where was he now? Guilt blossomed within her. She had learned to protect her heart by putting the child in a separate corner of her mind.

"Have my brother or I received any telegrams or messages from the Refugee Society in Paris, from a Boris Androvich or a Madame Kulikovski?"

Semyonov tried to place the names but could not. "Nothing like that from Paris." The big man grinned at her. "Just one thick scented letter for Count Alexander from a Mademoiselle Katkoff on the rue Bonaparte."

A scream echoed towards them from the Salle d'Armes. Katia stood instantly as if expecting some attack. Ivan rose and turned to face the doorway. The Japanese combatant appeared before them.

"I am Hideo Tanaka." He bowed his head to Katerina and addressed Semyonov. "I fear I have broken your instructor's arm."

The other combatant stood behind him, moaning and biting his lip, his face running wet.

"Let me help," said Katerina, hurrying to the injured man and examining his arm. "Cut off his sleeve and rest this arm flat across the table." She turned to Semyonov. The Cossack sipped his tea, untroubled, as if he had seen too many things more serious than this. "Bring me something for a sling, then we must get him to a hospital."

"I will take him," said Tanaka. "The consulate car will be here in a moment." He turned to his instructor. "It was my fault, Nikita. I should have released your wrist before you fell. After a few moments I always forget we are not fighting."

"*Da, da,*" muttered the instructor.

"I am Katerina Karlov . . ."

"I see that," Hideo said more gently, almost smiling. "When is your brother coming home?"

"Alexander should be arriving soon, I hope." Katia swept back her hair with one hand. The Japanese was looking down into her eyes as if he saw nothing else. She wished she had taken a few moments over her appearance. "But something has detained him in Ceylon."

"His friends are asking for him," said Tanaka, his eyes still holding hers.

"Especially Mr. Hak Lee," added Semyonov. "Partner to your late father, Count Dimitri."

That reminded her. "I have a letter for Mr. Lee from my brother," said Katerina. And another for Jessica James, she thought, the J.J. of that photograph.

"The old devil is very ill," said Semyonov. "Mr. Hak Lee's enemies are circling like hyenas around a crippled lion. Each one wants the first bite without being the lion's last kill."

A Japanese driver in shining boots and dark uniform of breeches and high-buttoned jacket bowed at the doorway with his gloves and cap in both hands. "Tanaka-san," he said.

"May my driver deliver your letter for you, Miss Karlov?" asked Hideo Tanaka.

"That would be lovely." She hurried to fetch it while Semyonov and Tanaka helped Nikita to the waiting Rolls-Royce. Ivan held the door as the two entered the car. Hideo's fingers touched Katia's as she handed him the letter. His touch lingered with her.

The rising sun of Japan flew from a small mast on the bonnet as the car pulled away.

Several workers from the rickshaw shop pointed at the vehicle and spat into the street. Katerina saw one bowlegged Chinese who stared at her rather than at the departing car. Her training had taught her to notice and memorize such things but never to react.

"Hot tea?" asked Semyonov when they sat down once more at the dining table.

"Thank you." Katia said. She must catch up and make the most of Shanghai before her brother arrived. Handing over her glass, she regarded Semyonov steadily.

"Alexander said you can tell me how our father died."

"I will tell you," the Cossack said, subdued. He rubbed his eyes and pinched his nose before reaching to the sideboard for the open bottle of vodka. "I was nearby when that bastard killed the Major on the lake," he began. "But I could not help him. My own boat was drifting away."

Ivan Semyonov told the tale as he drank. Old Count Karlov had died with courage, but alone and on a boat without his boots on. Commissar Polyak gave him the second barrel of his shotgun while the major was already gravely wounded and helpless at his feet. Katerina's heart hardened as she listened. She resolved to fight Viktor in every way and to help kill him if she could. To her the details were more shocking than surprising. If any two men would hate each other, it would have been those two. As the Cossack filled his glass, she looked up. Ivan's red eyes were weeping as he told the end.

"Finally Polyak bent down and broke the Major's neck as he was dying." Semyonov stared at Katerina and shook his head. "There was nothing I could do."

- 32 -

"A birder are you, sir?" asked the desk clerk. "ELLA REST HOUSE, 6900 FEET," read the sign on the wall beside the man.

"What?" said Todor Androv, writing his chosen name in the register of the government hotel. He had decided it best to go one stop further than Karlov's station at Bandarawela and to stay at a modest nearby hotel. "A bird man?" He glanced up through his spectacles.

"I mean you seem interested in birds, sir, if I may say so. A bird-watcher. That book, Mr. Anders, and your field glasses."

The Cheka agent confirmed the pretext. "Yes, that is why I am here." Slightly uncomfortable, Androv reached into a pocket and ground his dice in one hand.

"We get so many birders, sir. Ella is right on the flyway from India for all the migrants. They fly through Ella Gap on their way to the plains and the coast. But no Indian pittas so far this year, so we will have a late monsoon and many many worms and insects before the pittas fly to us from Nepal." The man pointed to his left along the open walkway. "If you step out onto the terrace you should be able to see all the way south down to the sea through Ella's Gap, if it's clear enough this afternoon."

"Can you arrange a guide, someone to show me the best places for bird-watching, and to take me perhaps into the forest? I have some friends I might wish to follow and catch up with."

"Of course, sir." The clerk smiled in pleasure. "The guides know all the best camping places, where there is water and often old Vedda caves for shelter in foul weather. If you learn where your friends are going, a guide will take you to them with no trouble. Some are especially good for birding. Here is a map of the hill country."

Androv set his ivory dice on the counter and perused the map, and not just for killing purposes. He looked forward to the forest, especially at night. This island had eleven species of owl, he had read, the order of *Strigiformes*. Most were small night hunters, like the oriental scops. Only one was unique to Ceylon, the tiny chestnut-backed owlet. But another, the largest, had attracted his keen attention. The spot-bellied eagle owl was reportedly feared by the forest people for the horrific human cries it made at night. Todor looked forward like a boy to seeing how well he would imitate its call.

"Do you wish a walking trip, Mr. Anders?" The clerk hesitated when the Ferret took a moment to answer. "On foot, sir, or by horseback?"

"I will walk. Perhaps a guide with a rifle, a hunter, so I can do a little shooting."

"A capital idea, sir. A rifle can be very useful in the jungle, with all the elephant and leopard. Sometimes very dangerous."

As long as there were no bear, Androv thought before he replied. "Please arrange for this."

The small Russian was gratified that he was learning to take advantage of these colonial facilities and their lackeys. At the same time, he reminded himself, he must retain his sense of purpose and remember who he was, and whom he served. He thought of Viktor Polyak. The Commissar embodied Trotsky's demand for the permanent revolution: the need to abjure any softening, the obligation to maintain the intensity of the days when the Revolution was young and hungry, eager to devour its enemies.

Todor Androv passed the clerk some coins and gathered up his dice.

"Thank you, sir. I should also mention that the Nuwara Eliya branch of the Ceylon Bird Club is meeting here tomorrow afternoon, and I am certain they would be pleased to assist you. They always welcome visiting birders." He lowered his voice and leaned across the counter. "And for a small fee, you may join the Club."

"Good morning, sir." The elderly waiter had a lean dark handsome face. "Tea or coffee?"

"A pot of tea and a tall glass, if you please," said Karlov.

"Porridge or eggs, sir?"

"Both. Two hoppers with poached eggs."

He took out Mrs. Hammond's note and with it a hand-drawn map showing the route from Bandarawela to Leopard Gate. "Please try hoppers for breakfast," he read again. "Akbar and Hindoo will call for you at nine."

The hotel dining room was nearly empty. This must be what the English mean by "Tudor," Alexander judged as he noticed the three long ceiling beams and the wooden elements of the plaster walls.

"Forest honey from the jungle, sir." The waiter set down a small bowl beside his porridge. "The Veddas gather it to trade at the markets for tobacco."

"Is that right?" Alexander had thought these ancient forest dwellers, the Bushmen or aborigines of Ceylon, to be long dead.

He ate the nubbly hot cereal until he scraped the last dark honey from the sides of the bowl. Bits of crystalized sugar and waxy comb thickened each bite.

"Egg hoppers and *pol sambol*, sir." The waiter presented a large covered plate. He lifted the metal lid. Fragrant heat rose from the dish of two bowl-shaped rice pancakes. Each had high crisp edges and a poached egg in the center. Small mounds of grated coconut, red chili and spices rested on the side of the plate. "Maldive fish curry and *hodhi* gravy, sir," said the waiter, setting down two more plates. "And buffalo curd yoghurt with wood apple jam."

It was almost nine. Alexander set to work as Robbie Knox and another of the previous evening's dinner companions entered. Knox was smoking a pipe. The other, older man carried a large foamy glass of what appeared to be thick dark beer.

"Morning to you, Karlov," said Knox, his pipe still caught between his long yellow teeth. Ashes dusted his lapels. "Tucking in already, eh?"

"Good morning." The Russian stood, unable to remember the other man's name. As they were English, he did not impose by suggesting that they join him.

"Going native, are we, lad?" grunted the older man as he squinted down at Alexander's plates and shook his head. "But up here one needs a proper breakfast. Sausage and bacon would give you a stronger kick-off. And a glass of black velvet. Nothing like champagne and stout to launch the day."

"By the way," said Knox, coughing, "there's a little Moorman asking for you at the door. Think he used to be a jockey, back in Bombay or some such. He's holding a horse. Big handsome brute, bit edgy, seventeen hands or more. Outstanding for a grey. Think I've seen 'im before."

A few minutes later Alexander stood outside the covered entrance of the Hotel Bandarawela.

"I am Akbar, sir," said a small dark man in old jodhpurs and a turban. He held a prancing horse by the bridle. The big stallion had a fine head and white hind stockings. "This is Hindoo. No one's been on him in some time, I'm afraid, sir. But Mrs. Hammond said you could ride him."

"How old is he?" Alexander looked Hindoo in the eye. The animal lifted his head and shifted his feet as Karlov hushed him and tried to place one hand on his cheek.

"Ten, sir." Akbar gestured at a smaller horse that bent to nibble the thick grass in the center of the drive. "If you prefer, you could try Sandy."

Alexander stroked Hindoo's powerful shoulder and lengthened the left stirrup. If he made the stirrup long enough to be comfortable, he would have no balance on a long ride. Posting was impossible. The stiff leg was too short when he walked and too long when he rode. He guessed the stallion might not take it well when he mounted from the off side. He looked across the saddle and saw Knox watching from the window of the dining room.

The white-helmeted doorman walked over from his post and spoke to Akbar. He drew two small feathery carrots from a pocket and handed both to Karlov.

Alexander ran one hand along the horse's neck and held the carrots near his nose. Hindoo did not react. Karlov ate one himself and held out the other on the flat of his palm. The stallion twitched his nostrils and pinched the carrot between his soft lips. Handing his cane to Akbar, Karlov took the reins and asked the Muslim to release the bridle. Then he mounted from the right and swung his left boot over Hindoo into the long stirrup. The big grey made no difficulty.

Karlov turned the horse's head to face the open drive when he saw Akbar on the short mare. Alexander felt the contained energy building in his mount as they walked out the drive and along the narrow streets of the busy mountain village. He sawed gently on the reins with short repeated movements of alternating hands as he felt Hindoo struggling to catch the bit forward between his teeth.

The crisp morning air reminded Alexander of early rides at home. They rode by men who were unloading carts and setting up a streetside market with pyramids of vegetables and fruit. Akbar tapped Sandy's flank with the black cane. Hindoo seemed not to mind as the mare walked past him where the dirt road climbed and roughened at the edge of town. The stallion calmed as they walked along the quiet road.

Steep slopes covered in neat horizontal rows of bright green tea bushes fell sharply from the roadside into deep winding valleys. Five-petalled white flowers bloomed on the plants. Here and there rows of dark women and a few children bent low over the bushes, gathering the shiny pointed leaves into bamboo baskets. Hard work, Alexander reckoned. Even walking erect would be difficult on these hillsides.

He thought of the last time he had seen the surly faces of the peasants at home. The women, exhausted and early-aged. The men, *frontoviki* back from the trenches, worn and gaunt, angry survivors of the German war. Here cheerful women, old and young, often looked up and even waved one hand as the two men rode past. Instead of being trapped in frozen villages like feudal serfs, these Tamils had journeyed far to find this work. Some pluckers carried baskets on their backs by leather straps that crossed their foreheads. The women had dark eyes and fine glossy hair. Most wore bright head scarves, colorful robes and silver necklaces, bracelets and hoop earrings.

Unlike other plants, Akbar told him, tea bushes were picked continually rather than harvested seasonally. The woman and children would be picking a bud and two leaves from the end of each shoot. The bushes, kept down to three or four feet, were planted so close together that the farther slopes became an emerald carpet.

The morning mist cleared from the hills and valleys as they rode. In the distance the wild edge of the forest jungle pressed close against the orderly green of the bushes. Karlov had the sense that the jungle and the cultivation were fighting a long battle of their own.

Twice they passed neat painted signs. "DWALINGONG TEA ESTATE, MANAGER'S BUNGALOW." "PONDICHERRY ESTATES, HILL THREE."

Alexander thought of how his father would have loved this. "I will be riding with you every day," the old soldier once had told him.

They came to a wide path that led from the edge of the road between two estates. Hindoo sniffed the air and grew more lively. His ears twitched. He was ready to run. Akbar paused and nodded at Karlov, gesturing forward with the head of the cane.

The black outline of a leopard was painted on a white wooden sign mounted on two stakes. "LEOPARD GATE" was lettered in peeling paint beneath the image of the spotted cat.

Hindoo stiffened, then passed the mare and began to trot down an easy descent. Ahead, the path became a narrower trail that wound upward through long slopes covered with vivid green bushes of young tea. A shadow crossed the path before them. Alexander glanced up and saw a broad-winged hawk or eagle gliding in an arc high above them, perhaps watching for a snake or rodent.

Karlov knew what Hindoo wished to do and he did not mind. He thought of his first wild ride on Taiga as snow clouds opened above the hills of Mongolia and they galloped across the plain into the blinding frozen whiteness. Alexander loosened the reins and leaned over the horse's shoulders as they came to the bottom of the dip in the path. He tightened his upper legs and relaxed his hands.

Hindoo burst forward like an arrow released from a bow.

Alexander felt the power of his stretching muscles as the horse galloped up along the side of the first long slope, then down a bit and up the next one and the next. "*Ura!*" he yelled. "Charge!" Small birds flew up from the bushes as they hurtled past. The rhythm of the stallion's run steadied as he passed from plunging nervous release to smooth swinging stride.

Alexander breathed the wind. His body eased. He felt at home. He could be galloping in Russia.

He glanced up the steep shining slope above him on his right. A broad bungalow with a stone foundation was built into the side of the hill. A deep verandah surrounded it as far as he could see. A place for breakfast and sunset drinks. A garden spread below the bungalow like an apron. To either side, stands of trees separated the house from the tea of Leopard Gate. Then he was past it. He knew Laila Hammond would not invite him home until that was appropriate.

At the far edge of the next hill, he saw the rough green edge of the jungle and the shadowy openings of the tunnels of darkness that led into it. Two massive boulders stood like sentinels at the end of the final hillside of tea bushes. Down to his left, the descending hills and valleys were lost in a distant blue haze that Alexander thought might even be the sea. His leg began to ache.

He considered where to turn or slow Hindoo as they galloped towards the end of the trail at the final plantation hillside. To go down would be too steep at speed. To turn up would mean breaking into the bushes and damaging the tea.

Suddenly Hindoo shuddered and plunged, almost bucking as he pulled stiffly, first right and then to the left.

A large bull elephant stepped forward from the forest in front of them and advanced into the tea bushes with a steady slow pace. The sun shone on its stumpy pointed ivory as the immense animal turned its head and waved two torn uneven ears. Three more elephants, a cow and two young bulls, followed it from the jungle.

Hindoo raised his head and snorted. He plunged downhill, bursting through row after row of thick bushes. Alexander leaned back and braced his feet against the raised stirrups, fighting to lift the stallion's head and pull him to one side into the slope.

Hindoo stumbled violently on one knee. Almost falling, the big grey pitched his rider from his back and galloped away with stirrups flying. Alexander rolled to the right to spare his leg. Stunned, for a moment he saw nothing as he fell and crashed to the ground between two rows of plants.

The bull trumpeted as Alexander sat up against a tea bush and stared at the herd of elephant as they advanced towards him along the hillside. Now eight or ten or more, they seemed to act as if he were not there. Dignified, they walked slowly forward through the bushes as if reclaiming their land. Only the big male seemed vigilant. Disturbed by Karlov, it strode directly for him, raising its trunk and extending its ears to the sides.

The bull paused, curled its trunk around a bush and ripped the plant whole from the ground. With the bush tight in the coil of its trunk like a bunch of daisies in the fist of a child, the elephant took another stride towards Alexander.

He could see the few long lashes of its small eyes when it hesitated a few paces from him and stared down, calmly swinging its head from side to side.

Alexander knew better than to move. The decision would be the animal's. He gazed up steadily into the huge face of the elephant, not breathing as he leaned back on his hands, one against the slope, the other awkwardly downhill. His leg had passed from numb to tortured, with a wire-like hot pain that he remembered from another day. He feared that he had broken it once again.

The two young bulls moved forward until they were almost shoulder to shoulder with their leader. The smaller one seemed dangerously adventurous, on the edge of aggression as it came even closer with its ears cocked and its tail erect. Then the big bull trumpeted once and the small elephant stopped. The leader raised its trunk and slowly scratched its shoulders with the clenched bush. Alexander could hear the rough scrapes as the small branches broke against the animal's skin. He was close enough to smell the rising dusty odor of the soil and the elephants.

The big bull flung down the bush and raised its trunk, curling the tip towards Alexander. The decision seemed to be made. The animal calmly turned uphill and led his herd between the two boulders and back to the trees.

Alexander felt the pain more sharply as his own breathing steadied. Soon he could not see the elephants. He heard a tree crack somewhere in the jungle, then only the wind that gusted up the hillside. He reached into his pocket for the map and wondered if he could bear to stand and to make his way back on foot.

When he flattened the map on the ground between two bushes, he noticed the white spiral shell of a snail near the woody stem of one plant. As he reached to lift it, he saw the thick patterned grey-green body of a long snake slide slowly behind the bushes.

Karlov drew back both hands as he felt his body freeze. The section of the snake that he could see twisted and doubled into two coiling curves. Finally the creature, too, stopped moving.

A wide flat head rose above the nearest bush. It swung slightly from left to right. A forked tongue flicked along its lower lip.

Alexander looked into the smooth reflecting amber of its slitted eyes.

Laila's map rose in the breeze and fluttered between them.

The snake struck the floating paper like a javelin piercing a light leather shield. For an instant the reptile's upper body seemed to hover above the bushes. Then the serpent collapsed behind them and was gone.

Alexander closed his eyes and gasped. A viper or a cobra, he wondered, wiping the sweat from his face. He glanced up the steep hillside and down over the green bushes that seemed to run on forever towards the sea. He seized the hard stiff stem of a bush above him and rose slowly on his good leg. He unbuttoned and relieved himself.

His entire body trembled when he tested a bit of weight on his left leg. He exclaimed sharply, then bit his lip and tried to hobble one step between the plants.

"Alexander!" called a clear voice. "Alex!"

He waved and saw Laila on horseback on the trail, with Akbar behind her leading Hindoo. The stallion's mane ruffled in the wind. The horse shone with the sweat of his run.

Alexander set his good leg downhill and wiped his face on a sleeve as they approached. Then he put his hands on his hips and watched his lover ride towards him through the tea with the sapphire sky behind her.

Hindoo nuzzled his belly as Alexander took the reins and turned the horse so he could mount from the uphill side.

"Perhaps now you understand, Count Karlov, that every day will be a challenge in Ceylon," smiled Laila.

"I learned that on shipboard, Mrs. Hammond," he said, kicking Hindoo into a trot.

- 33 -

"Good afternoon, sir." The door steward bowed after Alexander slowly climbed the steps of the substantial stone and wood building and entered the dark lobby of the Hill Club. Two British campaign medals were pinned above the breast pocket of the man's high-collared white tunic. A pale wide scar crossed one cheek like partially erased chalk on a blackboard. A small green and red cockade decorated the left side of his turban. Indian Army, Alexander guessed, the men who had defended the North-West Frontier for their British masters and kept his own country out of Afghanistan.

"May I ask, sir, are you a member or a guest?" said the old havildar in a polite firm voice.

Karlov glanced down the hall before replying. The glassy eyes of a boar stared down at him over long yellow tusks. A massive set of buffalo horns reached out like craggy eyebrows above two dim lamps that illuminated the notice board. An umbrella stand made from the hollowed-out foot of an elephant stood near the front desk, its wide toenails glossy as tortoise shell.

"A guest," replied Karlov, entering his name in the register, slightly annoyed with himself for the vulgarism of including his modest title.

This club, Laila Hammond had explained, was the ultimate refuge of the tea planters, the keep of their mountain fortress, where they created a distant England of servants and exclusion such as some of them might never have known at home.

"These Britishers don't mind being without their children, but they can't live without their clubs," his father once said after an English friend saw his three sons off on a boat for a year of boarding school in Wiltshire, the youngest eight years old. "They join their clubs to avoid people they don't know. Inside them, they avoid people they know too well."

"And the member's name, Count?" enquired the steward, evidently expert at reading the entry ledger upside-down.

"Hammond," said Alexander, trying to keep the weight off his aching ankle.

The fractured joint was taped in a thick wrap of khaki bandaging that Nuwara Eliya's retired army surgeon had found in his old wartime medical kit. Alexander and Laila had chased the doctor down, finding him at the sanatorium being built for veterans of the Great War at the foot of Ceylon's highest mountain, Pidurutalaga. Fortunate men, Karlov thought. In Shanghai, the czar's old soldiers were starving in the alleys or lying drunk in rags. The doctor said he had seen worse fractures, but he recommended an operation on the old knee injury. It was not an original suggestion. Alexander had nodded and refused a crutch. The cane was bad enough.

"Mr. Hammond has not yet arrived, sir," said the doorman, as if surprised to hear the name. "Perhaps you would care to wait in the Guests and Ladies Lounge, the mixed bar." He gestured down the hall to the left. "Second door."

"Thank you." Alexander nodded and limped down the polished plank floor of the corridor. He paused and peeked inside the Billiard Room before he came to the lounge. Two ocean-like tables on massive dark legs were shrouded under canvas covers. Standing ashtrays waited between cue racks. Ivory balls rested in hinged wooden boxes with their lids open. Antlers, tusks and horns guarded all four walls beneath the heavy dark beams that crowned the room beneath the steep gabled ceiling.

Alexander was reminded of the uncured skins of wolves and bears nailed roughly to the frosty walls of his father's barracks in Siberia. Then he read a framed sign hanging near the door.

For the Convenience
of
PLAYERS
SILENCE
in
The Billiard Room
is
ESSENTIAL

Alexander entered the lounge. A waiter was alone in the shadowy room, snoring, grunting like a pig stuck in a swamp. His bald brown head rested on a folded napkin on the bar.

"So sorry, sir," said the club servant, straightening up with a jerk as if struck in the throat. "Beg pardon, sir." He turned aside and blew his nose on the napkin. "What may I serve you, sir?"

"A glass of that soda water, if you please."

The barman pressed the tall silver siphon, then pushed the glass and a drinks chit across the bar.

Karlov took the glass and limped over to the wall of photographs mounted on either side of the tall stone fireplace. "CEYLON MOUNTED RIFLES, 1914," read the caption of a photograph of four rows of officers in spiked white pith helmets. Alexander looked more closely and discerned a tea leaf centered in their regimental crest. He spotted Lieutenants Knox and Palliser standing in the first row behind the seated senior officers. How erect and young and fit they looked.

"FIRST MEMBERS DINNER, THE HILL CLUB, NUWARA ELIYA, 21 DECEMBER 1876," read the caption beneath a picture of eighteen men at table in black tie. They had the faces of hard-living durable outdoor men, like cattle drovers or sergeant majors or first mates, rather than coddled colonial aristocrats. A line of white-jacketed servants, hands clasped before their dark sashes, stood against the wall behind the members. Cigar boxes, wine bottles and a multitude of glasses covered the long table.

Was not that the time of the catastrophic coffee blight, wondered Karlov, when the most determined of the desperate planters sought to shift from coffee beans to tea leaves, abandoning the plants of Ethiopia and Jamaica for those of Assam and Hunan?

A row of six presidents was framed on the other side of the mantlepiece. "EDWIN ROSLING, FOUNDING MEMBER AND FIRST CLUB PRESIDENT," said one. "LIONEL HAMMOND," said the next. "FOUNDING MEMBER AND CLUB PRESIDENT 1899–1909."

Alexander heard slow steps behind him and turned to face the door.

"Good afternoon to you, madame," he said softly with a bow.

"Good evening," replied a sharp voice he recognized from the train. It was Lucy's enemy, the lady from the dining car. Mrs. Hartland, or was it Hartshaw?

She took what he guessed was her customary leather armchair in the corner. The barman served a glass of pale sherry. The lady nodded to the servant and opened her book.

Laila Hammond appeared in the doorway, wearing a long skirt and fitted linen jacket. Why not a sari? thought Alexander, favoring defiance.

"Good evening, Count Karlov," she said, selecting a seat beside the photograph of her father-in-law, Lionel Hammond. "Won't you join me?"

They spoke quietly, as if in church, but perhaps not quietly enough.

"These pictures make it all look easy," said Laila. "But when the first coffee planters started in the eighteen twenties, they worked harder than any Tamil. They lived in mud huts with roofs of *cajan* thatch, the dried leaves of coconut palms. In fifty years the Tamils still lived in crowded huts, and the planters were in stone bungalows. Then the coffee died."

Laila had already explained that her presence would be a challenge to the club, a bitter dilemma for its social jurists. Members' wives, and their guests, were welcome at the Hill Club, or at least accepted, and no members were more senior than the Hammonds. But, of course, there were no Burgher members, let alone Sinhalese or Tamils, and Mrs. Derrick Hammond herself was darker than most Burghers.

Worse still, she was as if "separated" from her husband, in a sense perhaps now not fully married, with the Hammond tea estate possibly for sale, and her guest was a young male stranger. Nor would this outpost of English farmers welcome a foreign planter in their valleys.

While they spoke, Mrs. Hartshorn asked the barman for some notepaper and an envelope. She rested the paper on her book and swiftly wrote a note which she handed to the servant. The man nodded and left the lounge.

"I wish I could have worn my pearls," said Laila.

"We will find them." Alexander hoped he spoke the truth.

"Excuse me," said a thin elderly European who had just entered. The man wore a tight dark suit and gripped a small blue booklet in one hand with his thumb between the pages. The sharp creases of his trousers were thin and shiny where they had been pressed too often. Some sort of exhausted British civil servant, guessed Karlov, now still a captive in retirement.

"I am Chilling, ma'am, the manager, and it is my duty to point out that only members and their wives and guests are permitted in the Hill Club."

Alexander's face darkened. He observed the English lady intently reading her book as if she were a stranger to the scene.

"My husband, Mr. Hammond, is a member. Count Karlov is our guest." Laila Hammond spoke evenly, glancing at the nearby photograph. "My father-in-law founded this club."

"With respect, ma'am, forgive me, but actually Mr. Hammond is not presently a member in good standing, so regrettably you and your guest may not use the Club. The rules provide that if a member's account is not settled within eighteen months, then his membership is suspended. After three years, it is cancelled."

Chilling squinted down and opened the booklet in his hand. "Regrettably, it is now nearly two years that Mr. Hammond's bill has gone unpaid, ma'am."

Careful, thought Alexander, restraining himself. This is not your club, and not your fight. By now his father would have intervened in rage, as if chasing wild camp dogs from the body of a dead Hussar.

Alexander smelled pipe smoke.

Percy Palliser entered the room with Robbie Knox.

"Evening, Karlov," nodded Knox, stuffing a bird guide into a pocket and tapping out his pipe at the bar with loud knocks as he squinted around the room. The three lower buttons of his vest were open over a tight shirt. He scratched his eyebrows and groaned when he saw who was seated in the corner. "Two double whiskies, Aturi."

"Sir . . ." began the manager.

"What's the fuss here?" said Palliser to Chilling, bowing respectfully to Mrs. Hammond.

"The club rules, Mr. Palliser, provide that only a member in good standing, and his wife and their guests may . . ."

"Rules, man! The devil this nonsense! Count Karlov and this lady are my guests. In 'seventy-six, Mrs. Hammond's father-in-law stood on the cornerstone in a rain storm and drank the first bottle of champagne with old Rosling and my uncle." Palliser clapped one hand on the bar. "A bottle of our coldest champagne, please, Aturi, and be quick about it. Chop-chop!"

"Who's ever looked at the rules?" said Knox. "I've been on the Rules Committee for ten years and we've never had a meeting, unless you count drinking together at the bar." He waved the manager away.

Chilling turned and left the room as Aturi set an ice bucket before them.

"Cigar?" Alexander held out his open case. "Percival, Mr. Knox?"

In a moment the champagne was poured. Pungent smoke enriched the air.

Mrs. Hartshorn coughed as if gagging down the dense black smoke of a steam engine.

"I understand that Leopard Gate may be for sale," said Palliser to Laila Hammond as Mrs. Hartshorn closed her book and left the room.

"Perhaps," said Laila. "At least an interest in it."

"I'm considering buying," drawled Alexander in the English way. "That's why I'm up here." He sensed that Laila was grateful for his intervention. "My family always liked tea, particularly Russian Caravan Tea, Lapsang Souchong."

"You don't say?" Knox raised his eyebrows. "Best Lapsang used to come from Fujian, in the Wuyi mountains, sometimes blended with a little Keemun." The planter's face softened with remembrance. "The Chinamen dried the leaves in bamboo baskets over pine fires to give Lapsang that special smoky flavor and aroma."

Knox paused and pointed to his glass as Palliser poured. He seemed to be enjoying his own expertise. Showing off for Laila? wondered Alexander as he struggled to recall what his father had taught him about the tea trade. Knox drank and continued.

"Lapsang's a black tea, of course, fully oxidized, or fermented, as we call it. We make the world's finest high-grown black teas right here. Green tea comes from the same plants, you know, just never gets fermented. Green is mostly for the North African market, and for the Americans, who call black tea 'English Breakfast Tea.' They seem to think the two teas from the same leaves are altogether different and come from different plants. Strange people, those Americans, never quite know what they're about, but they're always at it anyway. 'High grown' hereabouts goes for everything three thousand five hundred foot or higher, right up to eight thousand."

"In the old days," said Alexander, aware he had Laila's attention, "the Chinese used to pack the tea for the Russian trade into dense bricks for the camel caravans. They stitched the tablets into moist hides, which tightened as they dried." He hoped he had it right.

"What sort of place did your family have in Russia?" asked Knox. "I've about five hundred acres up here, mostly under tea. All of it over four thousand foot."

"I don't know how much land there was," said Karlov, thinking of Voskrenoye, the Crimea and the estate in Poland. "Nearly five thousand souls. That was the way everyone used to measure, you know, by the number of people in your villages." He did not mention that for several generations the Karlovs had been increasingly in debt, selling off bits of Poland and the Ukraine. At Voskrenoye, maps of the old estates were pinned like wallpaper along the basement corridor that led to the wine cellar. Alexander wondered what the properties were like now, with the kulaks and priests butchered and the village churches burned down by the Reds.

"Don't know how some of the chaps would take to having a Russian tea garden up here," chuckled Knox. "Most of 'em didn't even want a Scotsman when my pa first arrived. Course in those days some of the older chaps had fought you Russkies to the death at Balaclava and Sevastopol, or at least they said they had."

"When my grandfather bought our estates in Poland," said Karlov, "some of the Poles weren't too pleased either."

"You don't say," said Percival.

"I understand that old Palliser here will be taking you into the jungle for a little *shikar*." Knox tamped down his pipe and picked a bit of tobacco from his tongue before continuing.

"I'd take my own rations along if I were you, boy. His cook's another of his filthy Moormen. Malays, most of 'em. Disgusting. Worse than bloody Hindus. Nothing but yesterday's greasy lamb and stale flat bread. If you kill anything, you'll be better off cooking it yourself." He paused as another idea came to him. "Bring along your own marmite to tart everything up."

"I never saw you leave anything on the bone at my table, Knox. Usually feed like a starving python," said Palliser. "Poor Mohammed's spent years trying to cook something you won't eat, so there'll be something left for the boys."

"I was always just being a good guest, Percival." Knox patted his own ample midriff. "Please don't confuse manners with pleasure."

"Welcome to the Celestial Kingdom, Miss Karlov. Welcome to Shanghai." The old Chinese sighed like a gust of wind passing through an icy gorge. His long pointed amber-colored nails scraped open an abscess in the hanging lobe of his remarkably large left ear.

Katerina had seen suffering, devastation and people she wished never to see again, but she had never seen anyone like this Shanghainese. Nor had she hoped or imagined that she would. This tall gaunt creature with a bald egg-shaped head was the man Sasha said was known as Big Ear, the Master of the Mountain.

Mr. Hak Lee had sent a large black American car to collect her at the Salle d'Armes. Now she was not certain where she was, only that it was one of the man's establishments somewhere in the International Settlement near Soochow Creek. It seemed to be some sort of counting house or private lending bank. Lines of whispering Chinese waited in the outer room near two grilled windows, fingering the money that they either paid in or received. Most wore round skull hats and loose black *samfoos* with the light cotton jackets hanging open above baggy trousers or over blue gowns. Others wore fedoras and the frayed vest or jacket of a European suit. Katerina had felt slightly dizzy as she passed through the smoky room. Here in her host's private room the soothing smell of sandalwood rose from a bronze brazier that smoked gently in one corner. She saw a bowl of wood chips and shavings waiting on a pedestal beside it.

"Until the young count arrives," said Mr. Hak Lee, "you must permit me to be your protector in Shanghai."

"I doubt that will be . . ."

"We have no choice. It is my obligation." Big Ear's long fingers hovered above the round tins of tobacco that lay on his black desk. "ABDULLA EGYPTIAN SPECIAL, BRAND NO. 16, 173 NEW BOND STREET, CIGARETTE SPECIALISTS," read the side of one tin between images of Turkish soldiers and palm trees. "ZAREMA," read another. "THE CIGARETTE OF THE CONNOISSEUR. MADE OF THE FINEST YANIDJE TOBACCO. LET YOUR PALATE BE THE JUDGE." A very long pipe with an ivory mouthpiece and a copper stem and bowl lay nearby.

"A cigarette?" He removed the lid of one tin and tilted it towards her.

"No, thank you." With her Chekist training pressing her for insight, Katerina looked into his black eyes but saw nothing.

"Your brother's letter speaks of danger," said the Chinese. "I will provide you with an attendant to protect you." He took out several cigarettes and crushed them in his hands. Tobacco scattered on the desk as he cupped his palms over his nose one by one.

"I understand you were my father's friend."

"I was your father's partner. Not his friend." Hak Lee's thin body trembled in his blue silk robe as he suppressed a cough. "I am your brother's friend, and his partner."

Since Viktor had kidnapped her on the train four years before,

Katerina had not possessed a single friend. The Cheka, Polyak and survival had not allowed for friendship.

"Some years ago your brother saved the life of a lady who once saved mine," Big Ear added quietly when she did not reply. Katerina reflected on how little she and her twin had told each other.

Hak Lee's lips formed a circle. He leaned forward, breathed in sharply and groaned as if something were trying to escape from his body. His long face seemed to shrink and concentrate as if struggling to deny pain or its appearance. She guessed that the pipe was not for tobacco, that the Master of the Mountain required something stronger.

Katerina examined the man more closely and realized that there was something in his face that she had seen in Russia when things were at their worst, when the lakes and rivers were frozen black and the markets and granaries were empty. It was the gaze and gauntness of a particular kind of suffering: starvation.

But how could that be with a man so rich and powerful?

"May I take you to the theatre or the cinema?" asked Hideo Tanaka that afternoon over a pastry and pot of tea at the Chocolate Factory. Having seen Hideo fighting on the training mat, Katerina had joined him without bringing along the male servant Hak Lee had given her as a guardian. But she wondered if she was being watched.

"I'd love to see a motion picture. What is playing?" Katerina found that she was comfortable with the bamboo color of Hideo's skin and the disciplined intensity of his demeanor. She thought his knobby cheekbones and the angular planes of his cheeks and jaw gave his face a handsome force. In Moscow, seeing a film would have been a fantasy, an unimaginable luxury of time and opportunity. "What language are they in?"

"English, and a few in French. Here, let us see." Tanaka opened that morning's *North-China Daily News.*

"At the Carlton they're showing Douglas Fairbanks in *The Nut*. Or we could see *Mad Love* with that Polish actress, Pola Negri, at the Victoria. She's also in *One Arabian Night* at the Apollo. 'A spicy tale of the scandals of an Oriental Court,' it says." Hideo glanced at her, smiling, before he turned the page. "Then there are the new Chinese films at the open-air cinemas. Here is one: *The Bell of Quong Foo*. Or, if you'd like something more serious, we could go to the Olympic."

"What are they showing?"

"The Shanghai Zionist Association is presenting *The New Palestine Film*," he read from the advertisement. " 'The history of the Zionist Movement from the first landing of the Pioneers. The development of Palestine through the Reborn Jewish Nation and the Aegis of Great Britain will be one of the Greatest Achievements of the Twentieth Century.' "

Katerina shook her head. She did not require more political education. "I'd rather see *Mad Love*," she said.

Her Japanese companion approved of the choice. "Then we can dine at the Trocadero and dance at the Vienna Garden Ballroom on Bubbling Well Road. Would you like that?"

"Yes, I would."

Patience was the first duty of a watcher, but Viktor Polyak possessed little of it. Frustrated and hungry again, he crouched back under the canopy of his man's rickshaw and watched the gaudy entrance of the Vienna Garden from the corner of Majestic Road. Signs outside the ballroom advertised "LOVELY DANCE PARTNERS," a "NEW WEE GOLF COURSE" and "THE TUNEFUL RHYTHM OF CELIS' ALL-STAR ORCHESTRA."

It was already two in the morning. Once again Katerina Karlov was slipping back into the corruptions of the privileged rich, thought Polyak as he drank from the square bottle of cheap sailors' gin he had bought as a substitute for vodka. How quickly she had abandoned all the self-respect he had taught her. He felt like a great teacher who sees his favored pupil stumble back into unthinking idleness. Unfortunately, it would not be intelligent to snatch her before her brother had returned unsuspecting to Shanghai. The dangerous young bastard must be dealt with first. Alone and unsupported, her obedience would come more easily.

From time to time the doors spread open and a buzzing nest of spoiled half-drunken patrons stumbled towards their waiting motor-cars, occasionally dancing across the sidewalk as if they were still displaying themselves in the gilded ballroom. Some men wore white silk scarves hanging unevenly around their necks. Most of the women were Chinese, dressed either in provocative cheongsams or in the sort of excessive fashions he had seen in Paris. But the most glamorous, and the most eager to please, he recognized with bitterness, were the young Russian girls, professional taxi dancers leaving with their richest clients.

Polyak leaned forward and spat out the side of the rickshaw before finishing the gin and dropping the bottle into the gutter.

At that moment the doors opened and Katia emerged. Her companion was not a sloppy European inebriate as he had expected. He appeared to be a Japanese in English formal clothes. Slender but solid, he was unusually tall for a Japanese. The two held hands as a large black automobile pulled forward and received them. Sickened with jealousy and anger, Polyak observed that the vehicle bore the flag and diplomatic license plate of the Empire of Japan.

- 34 -

"The boys have gone ahead to make camp, Karlov," said Percy Palliser. "Can trust them with everything except the dogs and guns. And drink, of course. Never does to leave an open bottle in camp." He moved around to the left side of his stocky mare and tightened the girth. "Easy, Nellie." He punched the horse hard in the belly before he heaved on the cinch. "That's my girl."

Lucifer and several other dogs ran about, rushing off towards the entrance to the rear courtyard of the bungalow, then dashing back to their master, scampering around his feet, lowering their heads and whining. Only Heidi, a short-haired short-legged brown dog with a long tubular body, remained close to her master.

An old woman was minding a large open black kettle in one corner of the courtyard, throwing in handfuls of long grass from a large pile at her side, then skimming off the oily surface with a wooden spoon and pouring the oil into an open pan at the edge of the fire.

"I always prefer these stockman's saddles for jungle riding." Palliser handed one to Alexander. "Aussies know what they're about in the bush. Never tell what you'll come across on these game trails. But they say that big grey of yours is fairly steady."

Rather like a cavalry saddle, thought Alexander as he settled it on Hindoo's back. Heavier than an English hunting saddle, and higher in the front and back, it had two brass loops for attaching equipment. A saddlebag was secured to Nellie's loops.

Percy passed Alexander a double rifle and a handful of copper cartridges. "Hope this old Holland suits you. Three seventy-five. Stops most things if you shoot her straight." He assessed Alexander, then said, "May be a bit short in the stock for a tall lad like you. The old governor had arms like tree stumps."

Karlov opened the well-oiled weapon and stared down both rifled barrels at the sky. "My grandfather left me a pair of these," he said. "They were his favorites for bear." This rifle even had the same front sight, tipped with platinum to make it bright for shooting in poor light.

Palliser slid his own weapon into a leather rifle holster and buckled shut the cover. "I had two of these saddle holsters made up after I saw one in an American cowboy film. 'Virginia,' I think it was. Or 'The Virginians,' if I'm not mistaken." He helped Karlov secure the second holster on Hindoo.

Alexander had never seen an American motion picture about cowboys. But the idea reminded him that by now Lily must be a film star in Shanghai, with even less time for him than when she was working as Mei-lan's most desirable and expensive pheasant. He thought of her waiting for him in the bathtub that first time. Lily's slick bronze skin and puffy red lips floating above the scented bubbles in the candlelight. He had believed his life would never be the same again.

Karlov lengthened Hindoo's left stirrup and tried to keep the weight off his leg as he moved around the big grey. He slipped the black cane into the holster beside the Holland as Lucy rubbed himself against Alexander's good leg.

Palliser walked over to the corner, nodded at the woman and dipped a rag into the pan. He wiped his face, neck and wrists with the warm oily cloth. "Citronella oil," he said. "From that lemon grass. Discourages the ticks. They're no bigger than a grain of gunpowder but they'll get in everywhere and drive you mad. Only other thing for it is coconut oil." He dipped the rag again and handed it to Alexander.

"If we're lucky, we'll shoot something for the pot along the way," said Percival as he mounted up and the dogs leapt and barked. "Venison for preference. Make the boys glad to see us." Alexander was enjoying the company.

They rode east from Nuwara Eliya as the morning opened. The valley clouds thinned to haze above the tea gardens on the slopes. Skylarks soared and warbled high above them. Palliser chose the way. Fresh, comfortable with each other, the two horses trotted steadily in line along the path between different estates.

After an hour they paused at Robbie Knox's bungalow for morning tea. "Time for tiffin," said Palliser as he dismounted.

The planter waved a greeting from his seat on the broad verandah, apparently bird-watching and drinking while he reviewed the morning's work with his *cangany*. The Burgher foreman stood when he saw Knox's guests approach. "Off you go, Voort," said Knox. "Don't forget your stick. Keep those coolies at it. Plenty of weeding and pruning."

Palliser and Karlov handed their reins to a houseboy. Before Alexander could draw his cane from the holster, Palliser held out a solid arm as if nothing could be more natural. Alexander was startled by the gesture, though he was aware that since the Great War, the world had become used to cripples. In France and England, Germany and Russia, no one had come home the way they left.

"Leave your stick, Karlov. Just hang on to this. I'm used to giving an arm to half these old farmers when they stagger out of the club."

"Thank you." He accepted Palliser's assistance to the steps.

"Two glasses for my guests, Max," Knox told a Ceylonese servant. His own glass was nearly empty beside an open bottle of madeira and a round tin of Dundee shortbread. Binoculars hung from his neck. A thick notebook lay open face down on the table. "Bird Diary" was written boldly on the cover.

"I gave your camp boys a sack of Jennifer's turnips and red cabbages when they passed through, Palliser," said Reggie Knox. "Just to make sure you didn't starve this poor lad in the jungle. Here, help yourself, Karlov."

"May I ask, Mr. Knox, how many pounds of tea an acre you take in here?" Alexander enquired, taking a thick wedge of shortbread. "And how many pluckers you employ?"

"Not enough, and too many, is your answer, Karlov. Sounds like you're getting a bit keener about all our tea nonsense. Don't bother with it. I'd stick to the hunting and riding if I were you."

Knox poured the golden wine, then elaborated. "Tea's not worth it, even with this high-grown Pekoe. Each plant requires twelve square feet. That's three thousand, six hundred and thirty bushes an acre. And each plant needs fussing over, worse than a woman." Knox rolled his eyes. "Every season they have a new enemy. White ants, caterpillars, borers, mites, thread blight."

Palliser yawned without covering his mouth but Alexander was giving Knox his full attention. He liked the idea of owning some land of his own, and sharing it with Laila, but he was concerned about the improvidence that seemed in his family's blood. Everything he possessed was in Shanghai, and there he had inherited two things with the Salle d'Armes: debts and a partner who terrified most men.

"The blasted tea work never ends," added Knox. "Plucking, withering, rolling, fermenting, firing, drying, grading, packing, shipping." He rose and lowered the brown wooden blinds at one end of the verandah, cutting off the direct sun and breeze. "And these plantation Tamils will drive you mad. Many of the women and children come over from India every year for the money. One needs masses of them. They're cheap enough, mind you, but full of superstition. Never leave you any time for birding or hunting or fishing." He coughed and handed a glass to Palliser before resuming.

"Hunting should be pretty fair now, Percy. Plenty of big boar, *sus scrofa*. That half-dachshund bitch of yours, Heidi, ought to be handy going in after them once you're into the thick stuff." Knox turned back to Karlov as if addressing a pupil. "Hogs have damned sensitive ears. That Heidi of his always goes for an ear and hangs on like a freight car hitch. Must hurt like hell if you're a pig. Takes a lot of the fight out of 'em."

"Any elephant about?" asked Palliser.

"Not this year. No good bulls. Just a couple of tame ones at the bottom of the valley, moving boulders and logs around to build a dam. They're nearly clever enough to do it on their own."

"Used to be so many elephants crashing about and trampling crops that the government paid a bounty to shoot them. Seven shillings a tail," said Palliser to Alexander. "Only stopped because it cost too much. But it was the end of the big herds. Blasted natives with their cheap rifles shot the youngsters and pregnant females so they could cut off the tails and collect the seven bob."

"But we still have plenty of those vicious sloth bear, especially one nasty brute that's scaring all the villagers along the edge of the jungle," said Knox. "*Ursus ursinus*. More dangerous than leopard. This one ripped off a girl's face when she was doing her family's washing in the stream. Proper neat job of it, too, just like a surgeon stripping off burned skin. Must have been his fishing spot." He paused to refill the glasses. Even Russians rarely drank in the morning, thought Alexander.

"The headman says it's the same big bear that killed a honey gatherer from his village last month. Probably weighs three hundred pounds or more. The boy was standing on a stump scooping honey out of a hollow *palu* tree with a coconut shell. The bear stood up and tore his belly open like an oyster. The villagers say it was an angry old bastard with a patchy coat and grey face. One gimpy foreleg. Probably crippled by one of those beastly native traps." He popped a piece of shortbread in his mouth. "Must've been hungry, poor sod. I'd be cross myself."

Knox offered the shortbread tin to his younger guest, then took out the last crumbly wedge himself. He spoke as if he were talking only to Alexander.

"What's left of the Veddas make some mighty nasty traps. They use vines, logs, pits, old bits of sawtooth metal, whatever they can find. Except for bows and arrows, most of them have nothing else for heavy game. Harry Houdini himself couldn't escape from one of their snares. Have to keep a sharp eye out on the animal trails, boy. Don't let old Palliser get stuck in one."

"No worries about us, Knox," said Percival dismissively. "We'll be camping in the usual spot and going out hunting from there."

Alexander found himself excited by the conversation, and enjoying the rich fortified wine and the sugary shortbread.

"By the way, Karlov," said Knox, wiping pale crumbs from his binoculars. "That old Moor jockey I saw you with at Bandarawela told my stable boy you were the best rider he'd ever seen up here. Until you fell off, of course." He smiled and drank. "Perhaps you ought to have a crack at the Planters Cup, if you survive your jungle days with Palliser. Couldn't you borrow that big stallion I see you're riding again today? Doesn't he belong to . . ."

"Excuse me, Mr. Knox, but I was hoping to meet your wife before we leave," interrupted Alexander. Laila had already suggested he borrow Hindoo for the race if his ankle was up to it. "Or is your lady away in town?"

"No. Jennifer's fussing over her vegetables and roses. But she never speaks to me until the afternoon. Says that's what saves our marriage. Until teatime Jennie speaks only to her flowers. Seems they never talk back." He grunted and licked crumbs of shortbread from his fingertips.

"Look at Palliser, for example. His wife couldn't stand his arguing. Now she prefers to freeze on her own in Cornwall. Who could blame her? Isn't that so, Percy?" Knox leaned towards his friend and raised his eyebrows. "I say, isn't that so, Percival?"

Palliser shrugged. "The moody weather suits her."

"Hope you're taking along some field glasses," said Knox, "so young Karlov can learn something about our birds, at least."

"I'm afraid mine are on the way to Shanghai," said Alexander as Palliser shook his head. "I left them on board the *Star*."

"Shame. You'll both miss so much," said Knox. "We had a splendid meeting of the Bird Club yesterday. At the old Rest House. Chaps came from all over with their field notes. Someone claimed he'd spotted a whistling thrush. Bright blue shoulder patch and all, running about by a stream, spreading and closing its tail, again and again. No one believed him, of course. Nobody's seen a whistling thrush hereabouts since 'aught-two."

"Probably flew in with a case of gin." Palliser put down his empty glass. "Time we got started, Karlov. The madeira's flowing like glue."

"One little chap even showed up from Germany, or some such place, maybe Poland," continued Robbie Knox as his guests rose and made for the steps. "An owl man, very serious, keen to see or hear one of our spot-bellied eagle owls, *Bubo nipalensis*. Known as the *Ulama* to the villagers, the shrieking Devil Bird," he told Alexander. "The fellow promised to stop by and do a little birding with me. He looks rather like a white-bellied drongo himself. Eyes set close together like two young peas in a pod. Said he'd probably be catching up with some friends in the bush."

"This is what the natives call *mukalana*, high jungle," said Palliser, turning in the saddle, speaking to Karlov in the new quiet voice he had been using since they entered the wild country. "*Landa*, the low jungle near the coast, is thick and hot. Altogether different. Full of peacocks and crocodile, buffalo and spotted deer."

He leaned low as Nellie passed under a branch. "Up here it can be more like a wood at home, often clear like this under the trees, with fast water instead of all those tanks and bunds built by the old kings in the lower country. Even the birds and snakes are different. Only the leeches and the big game are the same. Elephant and bear and leopard. But up here we get no buff and more sambur and spotted deer."

Alexander nodded, loving the silence of the forest as they followed an elephant path.

"In the low country the leeches swarm about in the long grass," added Percival in his soft forest voice. "Up in the jungle here, they're waiting for you on the leaves. Pull 'em off the wrong way and you'll bleed to death."

Karlov stroked Hindoo's neck whenever the stallion started or grew nervous. Twice Palliser dismounted to find easier fords across the mountain streams that often led to steep ravines and tall misting waterfalls. The slippery smooth river stones were awkward enough for the horses. Both men knew that crossing on foot would be more than tricky for Alexander with his bad leg and ankle. Each time, Percy led his own horse across, then came back and offered to do the same with Hindoo after checking the banks for spoor.

They rode on as the forest grew thicker and darker. Thorny bushes and ropey vines clinging to old trees were interrupted by occasional overgrown *chenas*, small abandoned fields where jungle villagers had once cleared patches of land and planted millet, maize and vegetables. Palliser identified cassia flowers, gooseberries and morra fruit as he encouraged the dogs rushing about ahead of them while they flushed birds and chased the scents of the forest floor. Occasionally grey monkeys swung overhead like flitting shadows. Once they heard the bell-like bark of a male deer.

"No, Lucifer, no, straight on," Palliser repeated to the large hound whenever the dog flushed wood pigeon. Meanwhile, Heidi trotted along steadily with her nose down, often under the feet of Nellie or Alexander's horse.

Suddenly there was a rushing sound in the bush ahead of them. Lucy's deep bark was followed by snorts and squeals. Heidi tore forward to join the other dogs.

"Pigs!" yelled Palliser, drawing his rifle as his horse pranced sideways. Hindoo snorted and stamped, but Karlov held him in.

Alexander saw Heidi dashing about beneath the branches of the thickest bushes through the tangled underwood. Soon the boar and the dogs were lost far ahead, snapping and barking as the pigs sought the refuge of the deeper bush.

Palliser and Karlov forced their reluctant mounts through the heavy thorny branches that scratched their shoulders as they pressed forward. Soon Alexander saw two young pink-bellied boar, dead and bloody, chewed up where the hounds had caught them.

The clamor ahead of them changed as they approached a tall outcropping of overgrown boulders. Deep snarls were followed by the yelping and whining of what had to be an injured dog.

Palliser dismounted and threw his reins to Alexander. "Stay up," he said as he forced his way into a small rough clearing at the base of the rocks.

The big sow was bayed. Her long snout was ripped. Pointed pink teats stuck through her matted black hair. Six or seven piglets trembled and squealed behind her in a cleft of the rocks. The floor of the clearing was torn up where the pigs had rooted for tubers and worms.

Lucifer was on his side, twitching and whimpering. Blood pumped from his carotid artery. A tangled mess of his torn intestines hung from his belly. He rose on his front legs and tried to drag himself towards his master when he saw Palliser enter the clearing. Heidi was hanging onto the sow's right ear by her teeth, being flung to left and right as the pig tossed her head and tried to fight off two dogs who were going for her hind parts.

Alexander drew the Holland, but Hindoo was too wild to permit a shot. He jumped down and released the horses. Flipping off the safety, he tried to spot the male whose tusks must have caught Lucy.

Palliser fired. The sow fell. Heidi released her and went for the young pigs. She seized one by the back of the neck and swung the squealing baby violently back and forth against the rocks.

At that instant a giant grizzled boar broke from the bush with a dog after him. The big hog charged at Palliser as Lucifer struggled to get between them. Long yellow tusks curled forward from the mouth of the wild pig.

"Percival!" Alexander hollered as he raised the rifle in a snap-shot and fired both barrels.

The big boar struck Palliser's legs and knocked down the hunter. Percy grunted as he fell on his back against a rock, but he held onto his rifle with one hand. The massive dying boar staggered on a few more steps before collapsing on top of Lucy as Alexander reloaded. The hog's tusks were chipped and uneven, with angled concave edges and streaks of discoloration running their length.

Palliser crawled to Lucifer and took the dog's head in his lap. "Lucy, old boy," he whispered as he rocked and wept. "Lucy."

"Damned hog must weigh twenty stone," said Palliser later as Alexander helped him up into the saddle. Lucifer lay nearby under a mound of rocks. "You killed that boar twice. Who taught you to shoot like that?"

"My father, and my grandfather," said Alexander. And our game-keepers, and summer military camps with the Corps des Pages, and instructing at the Salle d'Armes, he reflected.

"Brandy?" The Englishman took a leather-bound silver flask from his saddlebag and offered it to Karlov. His lap and right boot were slick with two different kinds of blood.

"After you."

Alexander drank after Palliser, then ripped open the Englishman's torn right trouser. He splashed brandy on the planter's deep bleeding cut. "This needs a little attention, Percival."

"Damned waste of good drink," said Palliser. "Would it take you long to cut something off that sow for supper?"

Alexander drew his Marseilles knife, slit open the animal's belly, cleaned out the guts and cut off the head.

"Will one of these horses mind carrying the rest?" he asked, wiping his hands on some leaves. With the legs still on, the body would be heavy, but his slender knife, now dulled, was too light to saw them off.

"My Nellie's used to it. She'll carry anything, living or dead. But that Hindoo would never stand the stink or the fresh blood. Doesn't like other animals. There's a scrap of canvas and a strip of hide in my saddlebag." Percival untied the bag behind him and tossed the canvas and the rawhide to Alexander.

"Wrap up that carcass and pitch her on behind me. You take the saddlebag," added Palliser as Karlov cleaned his knife. "Then we'll find the camp and drink ourselves silly while the boys roast the pig. Of course, it's the only thing my Moormen won't eat. But I'll skin the little brown bastards myself if the fire isn't ready when we get there."

"Almost home," said Percy two hours later as they crossed another small swift stream in the fading light. Hindoo was avoiding walking with his head too close to Nellie. When Alexander happened to glance downstream into the breeze, he spotted a reddish-brown deer with a white belly drinking at a pool. The slender creature raised its head when Alexander drew his Holland. He fired as the animal turned to look upstream and twitched its ears, prepared to bolt. The deer must not have heard the horses over the running water. It was a lot of bullet for an animal less than three feet at the shoulder.

"Chital, spotted deer," said Palliser after it fell. "We'll send the boys right back for him. Leave him out here after dark and a leopard will be into him before the boys have a chance for a bite."

The horses were tired but nervous as they rode on in the near darkness. Alexander held one hand before his face to keep off the branches he could barely see.

A violent slurping sucking sound rose far to their right. Agitated, Hindoo pressed forward into some thorn bushes on the left.

"Sloth bear," said Palliser, stopping Nellie for a moment. "You can hear them for miles when they're sucking out termites with those long ugly muzzles. The Lord gave them three-inch hooked claws to climb trees and rip open termite mounds, and long rough sticky tongues with which to go in after them. Kill more natives every year than buffalo or elephant or crocs."

Finally a glow of light shone through the forest. Lean dark men in turbans ran up and salaamed, welcoming them to camp. Two dashed back along the trail to collect their dinner.

Palliser and Karlov soon sat drinking whisky by the fire while the pig and spotted deer roasted. Alexander had cleaned his friend's wound and wrapped it in linen torn from a clean shirt. Then he had looked after the horses while Palliser checked the dogs and picked a leech from Heidi's nostril.

Famished, Alexander was intoxicated by the smell of the cooking pig and venison. He pushed aside the voice of his father telling him that burned human flesh smelled like pork. Cabbage and turnips and wild onions were steaming in a black pot resting on the coals at the fire's edge. Wood apples were frying in the inverted lid of the iron pot.

"I have never eaten better," said Alexander later as their fire dimmed and the two shared another drink, seated on a stretch of canvas that would become their shelter if it rained. He scratched at some ticks and heard laughter from the second fire. He nibbled at another scrap of crisp pork and sucked his fingers clean. The camp boys were gorging on the young deer, rice and a curry of chillies, pumpkins and sweet potatoes.

Palliser did not reply. The whisky bottle empty, his back against a tree, the Englishman was asleep.

Alexander heard the long tremulous hoot of an owl. He rose and placed a saddle near his friend. He lowered Percival's head onto the leather pillow and stretched out his legs before spreading a blanket over him. Then he walked over and checked the horses.

Finally he lay down himself, hands under his head as he stared up into the jungle canopy, unable to see a single star. Alexander turned on his side and stared when he noticed a different constellation sparkling between two trees.

A score of small lights twinkled brightly, fireflies caught in an enormous spreading spider web.

- 35 -

"Owls your specialty, are they?" said Robbie Knox as the intense little man and his guide caught up with the planter at the edge of the jungle. The fellow's narrow head and pointed face now reminded him of a slaty-breasted rail. Knox sat on a boulder and opened his pocket flask as he prompted for an answer. "Owls, eh?"

"Yes. Yes, that is right." The foreigner removed his spectacles and wiped them on a red kerchief tied about his neck. "Owls. I believe in Ceylon only one of yours is a migrant, the short-eared owl?"

"Right you are, Mr. Anders, the *Asio flammeus*," said Knox. "The bugger's very hard to spot, even when he's there. But a proper short-eared killer at dusk or dawn. He can hear and snatch a mole under a pile of leaves."

"And I am so most interested in your spot-bellied or forest eagle owl. Is not that the biggest one?"

"Quite right. *Bubo nipalensis*." Knox passed over the flask and raised his eyebrows as the little man continued drinking deeply. "Stands over two foot tall, if you ever see one. They rest all day, hiding in the foliage of a tall forest tree." He saw Anders lift the end of his scarf to wipe his lips after he returned the flask. "They're even more nocturnal and elusive than the others. Like every good hunter, the eagle owl keeps out of sight himself."

Knox watched Anders remove his kerchief to clean the lenses of his field glasses.

He glanced at Chester. The visitor's old Sinhalese guide stood a few yards away, spitting betel and scratching his neck. Chester carried his sturdy army service rifle, a Lee Enfield .303, as if it were part of his arm. A proper stopper, one wouldn't want to get hit by it, thought Robbie Knox. The fastest bolt-action rifle in the world, with a rate of fire of eight aimed rounds per minute, these weapons had killed a lot of Huns in the Great War, though never enough. A rucksack and a patched canvas satchel rested near the guide's feet.

Robbie Knox was struck by the sharpness of Anders' interest as he told him more about the giant nocturnal hunter. "Villagers call them the Devil Bird, the Ulama. The eagle owl has a cry like a dying child. No one can ever hear it and go back to sleep. They say that whatever suffering you have had in your life, their howling screaming call will bring that pain back to you again."

Knox shook the flask and screwed on the cap, uncertain whether the foreigner had understood him. "Of course, there are so many diurnals to see here by daylight. Bee-eaters, babblers, bulbuls, hanging parrots, paradise-flycatchers. Did you bring your notebook?"

Androv lifted his bird guide from a side pocket. "Book?"

"No, no, Anders," said Knox with a suggestion of impatience. "Your own notebook, your field book, for sketches and recording sightings. You know, every birder carries one."

Hoping to hide his ignorance, Anders shook his head. He removed his spectacles and set the field glasses to his eyes, attempting to follow a brown bird of prey soaring on an updraft.

"Well, I'll walk you into the forest to get you on the right trail where your Russian friend has gone, then we'll have a spot of lunch and I'll leave you to go on and find him with Chester. Be jolly for young Karlov to be surprised and see an old friend up here. Chester knows the way, but he's a bit lazy at the walking these days and not much for company."

Knox pulled out his watch. "I have to get back to give Magpie some oats and have tea with my Jennifer. Best part of my day, if you don't mind my saying so."

The planter looked over at the guide and raised his voice. "I say there, Chester. Chester! Get that pack off the ground, will you? I don't want those red ants eating my lunch. That's it, boy, keep the knapsack on your shoulder where it belongs."

Knox was surprised that Anders was not doing a better job of following the crested hawk-eagle with his field glasses. In his opinion, the binoculars had too much magnification and therefore too small a field for proper birding. But the little chap was a damned good fast walker, and that always helped.

They parted after lunch. Androv and Chester continued on the elephant path while Robbie Knox turned back towards his tea plantation.

"You'll find your friend easily now," said Knox as he departed. "Just straight along this trail."

After they had walked another mile, Androv tapped Chester on the shoulder.

"You stay here until I come back," he said slowly, pointing at the ground. "Stay here by these rocks. I must go back and catch Mr. Knox and give him something. Soon I return here and we go on." He turned away, then paused. He had already paid for one other thing besides the guide himself.

"Give me the rifle in case I see some game."

Todor Androv walked swiftly back until he was out of sight.

At last he was alone in the trees once more. He thought of what Viktor Polyak and his brother would expect of him. He paused and drew back the smooth sliding bolt of the rifle and checked the ten-round detachable box magazine. Only five rimmed cartridges. The bullets must be precious, he thought. Of course, the rifle he knew well. England had sent thousands of these Lee Enfields to Russia during the German war. The older model, of course, the Mark One. Scowling at that, he chambered a round.

The Ferret began to trot back through the jungle, the weapon in his right hand. He paused once when he heard a bird call that he could not identify, perhaps some sort of thrush or flycatcher. He considered stopping to check his bird book, but he decided to run on.

Androv slowed when he thought he had nearly caught up with the colonial Englishman. His footsteps became quieter, but the short fat man had moved more rapidly than he anticipated. The planter was nearly out of the forest by the time the Russian spotted him. He was singing to himself, disturbing the peace of the forest with some British marching song.

Taking a shorter route than they had earlier, Knox was picking his way across a rocky stream that flowed down to a jungle waterfall. He was using a long stick like a staff, balancing himself on the slippery stones and measuring the depth of the water ahead.

With his prey in range, Androv knelt and rested the rifle on a branch. The singing annoyed and distracted him as he settled the open sights on the left side of the man's broad back. He waited until Knox hesitated and stood still at the edge of a pool, glancing downstream at the sparkling mist rising from the waterfall.

The planter's voice rose as he sang for himself. "From Hector and Lysander, and such great men as these . . ."

Todor Androv held his breath and fired. The Englishman cried once and fell on his face into the water with a loud splash.

The Ferret ran to him. He leaned the rifle against a tree and waded into the cold stream. Knox was struggling gently as if paddling slowly face down. Androv knelt with his knee on the back of the dying man and pressed his face into the pool until the heavy body no longer trembled. Methodically he pocketed the planter's money, watch and flask.

As if shaking hands, the Russian took the body by the right hand with his own. He dragged the heavy floating figure easily downstream as it slipped along behind him with the force of the current. The stream grew narrower and faster as they approached the waterfall.

Androv stopped when the current became demanding. The water came to the tops of his boots. The body pressed against his legs as if wanting to continue on its own. He released the bloody hand.

As the corpse rushed to the falls, Todor bent and cleaned his hands in the clear chilly water. By the time the dead man was found downstream, he should be on his way back to Colombo.

Now for the other witness.

The old guide was asleep when Androv returned to him. Chester was curled up between two boulders, gasping for air and whistling as he snored. Red, betel-stained saliva dribbled from his lower lip and chin. Empty nut shells were sprinkled on the ground around him.

The Ferret carefully sat down beside him. Stretching his legs, he opened his long clasp knife. He brought the blade to Chester's throat, but then changed his mind. It should appear that they had fought after the guide killed Knox.

He drew back the knife and plunged it into the man's chest to the hilt.

Chester screamed once as he awoke. His mouth opened in a circle. His eyes stared like a hungry bird in a nest. Androv twisted the knife as he kept it pressed against the thin body of the guide.

The old man died faster than the Russian expected. His eyes rolled up in their sockets. Blood covered his lean chest and belly. His arms waved once. His hands settled gently against Androv's face as if he were stroking the cheeks of a child and saying goodbye. Then he grew still.

Androv slipped Knox's watch, some of his money and the spent cartridge into Chester's pocket. He opened the flask and drank what remained before leaving it open beside the body. The leopards or bears could have this one. Now he must find Count Karlov.

He walked on for an hour, until he came to an overgrown clearing and two abandoned huts that Knox had mentioned as being near the camp site. He settled by some boulders and waited for dusk before approaching closer to the camp. For animals, especially owls, this was the time of the hunter.

Todor Androv was hungry, but he was used to that. At least his old boots were now dry. So far it had all gone well. One less British imperialist. One less slavish colonial servant. But Androv knew that Viktor Polyak and the Cheka would not yet be satisfied. He checked the rifle and chambered a round in the rapidly fading light.

At length the Russian rose and began to walk slowly along the trail. He squinted ahead to discern the path. He was pleased he had his round spectacles to save his eyes from the branches that scratched his face as he proceeded. The trail appeared only as a lighter grey tunnel inside the near-total darkness of the surrounding jungle.

As he moved he thought of all he had seen since leaving Russia. Paris and Marseilles, Port Saïd and Cairo, Goa and Colombo. The travels of a rich man's honeymoon. The Cheka had been his bride and she had given him the world. Yet this island jungle, so far away, shared much with the deep lonely forests at home. Especially at night.

Suddenly Androv felt himself plunging forward. Something was wrapped firmly around his legs. The Enfield flew from his hand as he stumbled. A falling log struck his right shoulder and he collapsed into a tight pit.

The Ferret cursed and tried to turn and move his arms and legs. But his right arm was pinned beneath the heavy log, probably a tree trunk. His legs were snared in some sort of net inside a pit, tight as a coffin, that held him up to his belly. He attempted to reach down with his left arm, but his body was pressed against that side of the pit by the log that pinned his other arm. He thought that arm was broken.

As he struggled, a weird sound echoed through the jungle air. A long shrill hooting became the wail of a tortured beast. Androv cocked his head. The Ulama, the Devil Bird, of course. For a moment he appreciated the thrill of the call.

It was succeeded by the silence of the forest. He tried to free his right arm and grope around beneath the heavy log, but all he felt was sharpening pain from his elbow to his neck. He could not feel his hand or any motion in his fingers.

A branch snapped behind him. He felt the chill of fear.

Androv tried to twist his upper body and turn his head but still he could not see far enough in the direction of the noise. With his left hand he searched the forest floor all around him but he found no rifle. Nor could he reach down to grasp his pocket knife.

The hooting wail rose again, louder and more shrill, for a moment becoming almost a high-pitched whining sob, the tortured cry of a tormented suffering child. Twice it stopped, then began again and grew more horrible before it stilled.

Despite his predicament, Todor Androv pursed his lips and closed his eyes. He must imitate that call. His throat trembled as he made the simple slow hooting call common to many forest owls. Then he concentrated, putting aside the distraction of his fear. He adopted a child's pain from his own as he emitted a thinner anguished cry. He was pleased with his effort, but there was no answer to his call.

Androv imagined the great eagle owl hunting for a roosting jungle fowl, or perhaps a young jackal or a hare, its all-seeing eyes piercing the night, its broad soft wings spreading like a shroud as it glided in the darkness, then dove with claws extended.

His musing was broken by the sounds of heavy movement in the brush behind him. Leopard, he thought as his body froze. No, that would be quieter, more cat-like.

His brother would have known what to do. He had always been unmoved by either fear or pain. Oskar could endure anything, and he had. Todor Androv wished he had been able to talk more with his younger brother, awkward as that always was. His only fraternal pleasure had come from cheating Oskar at dice.

Struggling harder, fighting off the intense pain, the Ferret managed to squeeze and wiggle his left hand down into the edge of the pit beside his leg. Twisting his upper body, he was able to plunge his hand into a pocket and clutch his clasp knife. He pulled it up and tried without success to open it with one hand. He clenched the closed side of the knife between his teeth and extended the blade with his left hand. At last he had a weapon.

As he lifted his arm in front of him with the knife in hand he heard a guttural breathing, a thick low growl deep in the back of some creature's throat. A massive black shadow passed close by and stopped somewhere in front of him.

He smelled the rank odor of a large omnivorous beast. Androv thought of the dark forest at home and he knew what it must be. But this time he had no fire, no flaming branch to protect him.

Something scraped along the ground as the animal moved.

The bear turned and faced him. Todor saw two red eyes close to his own. He smelled the hot foul breath of rotten meat and old fish.

Androv swung the knife back and forth before him as he heard a long mournful screaming cut the darkness.

The bear shuffled closer, sounding pained as it moved. Todor could just discern the long pale muzzle approaching him. The animal forced out a low groaning growl.

The Ferret lunged and the tip of his knife struck the creature's snout. He felt the rough patchy hair of the beast's thin coat as the bear snarled.

A powerful blow clubbed his shoulder, almost ripping off his left arm as long claws cut to the bone. He felt the overwhelming pain that he had always feared. The animal grunted and took his upper arm in its teeth, pulling and tearing at the limb as it tried to drag him from the pit. Todor was living the hell he had long imagined.

The bear then released his arm and licked his face with a long tongue like gummy sand paper. With one slow stroke it clawed off his face from scalp to chin. The last scream of Todor Androv joined the sad shrill cry of the forest eagle owl.

- 36 -

"Didn't leave much to bury," said Palliser after one of the camp boys had led them to the remains.

"Hardly enough to recognize. Only his field glasses, that Enfield and his boots, and those look like they've had a lot of use," he continued, inspecting what could be identified in the bloody debris. "Reckon that sloth bear struggled against these blasted native snares. Tracks show he's that bastard with a bad front leg. Must have been thrilled to find such an easy supper."

Karlov examined the English army rifle, then picked up one of the thick-soled boots. Both hob-nailed heels were badly worn down on the insides. He tried to remember where recently he had seen another pair quite like them. They could well be Russian, the heavy black leather service boots of any junior officer who could not afford to buy his own. Thick broad bands of reinforcing leather ran down both side seams. They had been patched and restitched more than once. Torn pages of a bird book and a pair of dice were scattered on the ground near the other boot.

Alexander bit his lip in concentration and knelt to examine the severed head. The bloodstained mouth was open. He shifted the head with a stick and looked at the steel teeth in the back of the mouth. Russian, he was certain, the best known example of Soviet medical care, said to be available one day to all his countrymen. Another of Polyak's agents, he reckoned, probably from the *China Star*. He tried to recall when he had last seen a man playing with some dice.

"We'll wrap what's left in the canvas, and Nellie can carry the poor chap back," said Palliser as Alexander, distracted, picked up the yellowed ivory dice. "A little walking will loosen up my leg," added Percival, smiling. "Wouldn't want to end up with one like yours."

If this dead man had been after him, Alexander realized, and with Polyak still alive, he and his sister had not escaped pursuit. It was time to shorten his visit to Ceylon.

Two hours later, one of the boys who had gone on ahead came running back towards them on the trail.

"More trouble," said Palliser after conversing with the excited man in Sinhalese. He shifted the remains of the body to the back of his saddle and groaned as he swung his leg over the canvas and mounted up. Alexander saw fresh blood on his friend's trousers.

They found the second body between some boulders.

"I know this fellow," said the planter. "He's an old guide, Chester." He patted the dead man once on the shoulder, almost with affection. "Everyone knows him."

Palliser lifted the empty flask and sniffed it. "That's odd. It's Knox's old pocket flask. Robbie used it every day." He shook his head and screwed on the cap. "And Chester never drank, so what's it doing here?"

Percival knelt by the nearby tracks and traced the shape of the pads with his fingertips. "Some young leopard got him," he said evenly. "Clawed up his neck and chest, then started feasting on the buttocks but didn't have time to come back for a second helping."

Alexander recognized the calm that seemed to have settled over Palliser. The demeanor, steady and wry, came from the war, from losing friends and surviving. His father and the other old Russian veterans in Shanghai had appeared the same whenever there was trouble.

Palliser stood and looked up at Karlov. He rested one hand on Hindoo's shoulder. "It's a bloody mystery. I'm surprised Chester didn't have his rifle. Never without it. Bet that was his Enfield we found back by the pit."

Alexander considered who might have killed Chester before the leopard got to him.

The planter knelt again and shook out the dead man's leather pouch. Betel leaves, areca nuts, a few rupees and a handful of rough tobacco fell on the ground. Palliser emptied the pockets. "Lot of money for a native. One empty cartridge, and look at this." He opened the lid of a gold pocket watch and squinted at the engraved date. His voice changed. "That's Robbie's wedding day."

There was not enough canvas to wrap the second body properly.

"Hindoo is just going to have to put up with one of them," said Palliser, untying and shifting the first body to the stallion with the help of one of the boys. "Hold him in, Karlov, while I tie this first chap on behind you. At least Hindoo won't think it's a wild animal."

Alexander was surprised to see a uniformed European police officer staring down from the steps of the Knox bungalow as they rode up. A stout handsome woman with short wavy grey hair stood on the verandah behind the officer. She wore a green gardener's smock with large front pockets and a trimming clipper in a leather holster at her waist.

"I am Jennifer Knox," the woman said to Alexander in a tight contained voice after he dismounted. "Robbie told me so much about you."

He noticed that the table beside her was set for tea, with an unopened tin of shortbread between two plates and cups. Several pipes rested in the bowl of a coconut shell.

"Oh, Percy," she said, turning to Palliser as he leaned the Enfield against the railing and hurried to climb the steps and hug her.

"Jennie," he said as tears and sobs overwhelmed her. "Jennie."

The police officer lifted the rifle and examined the weapon while the two comforted each other.

"What am I going to do, Percy? What am I going to tell Robert?" Jennifer Knox asked, leaning back but still in Palliser's arms. Alexander heard age in her voice. "He's at school in Devon. He's only ten. What can I do? What am I to say to him?"

"The plantation manager downstream found Mr. Knox and brought him back here," said the officer in a quiet voice. "He was shot once in the back. I shall have to ask you both some questions, gentlemen." He stared at what was packed on the horses before he spoke again. "And what is this?"

"Can we spare Mrs. Knox, Superintendent, and perhaps do this in the garden behind the bungalow?" Palliser went down the steps and took both horses by their heads.

Alexander followed them. He had already decided not to mention where he thought he might have seen the unknown dead man's boots and the dice. It was on the launch in Goa. He recalled the warning in his sister's telegram.

Polyak was behind all this. It was time he sailed for Shanghai.

"I am sorry you have had such a terrible visit," said Laila at dinner that evening at the Hotel Bandarawela. "Now you will never want to return."

"I will, because of you." He rested his hand over hers. "If you join me in Shanghai, we will come here often, to visit our plantation."

"Leopard Gate?" Her face seemed frozen as she imagined the possibility. "Do you mean it?"

"Now I know why you love it. Who could not? The waves of hills, the verandah on the bungalow, those sunsets."

He could feel the excitement in her fingers as she turned her hand to clasp his. It was time for a serving of poire belle Hélène.

"I placed my bid with the agent this morning. I told him I wanted the horses and all the livestock. One price for everything." Somehow he would have to find the money in Shanghai. Never had he felt more like his father than in making this wild plunge into debt. "I doubt that anyone will offer more."

"No! You . . ."

"One price for everything, I told him." Alexander smiled for the first time that evening. "Including the lady of the house."

She smiled back and stroked his leg with hers. "You have her already, Count Karlov."

He released Laila's hand and filled their glasses.

"But I must leave the day after tomorrow, to catch the *Angkor* for Shanghai. She's French, Messageries Maritimes, their first steamer with oil-fired heating. I want you to come with me."

"I doubt if I can leave so soon." She saw Alexander's disappointment and quickly offered, "But can we have a picnic tomorrow?"

He knew she was doing her best. "Of course, a light one, please." He coughed to get the slight burr out of his voice. "Tomorrow I am riding your Hindoo in the Planters Cup before I catch the night train for Colombo. I'd like to drop below one seventy-five before the race."

"You weren't meant to be a jockey." Laila shook her head. "You're perfect as you are."

He shook his head, knowing better. "Every one and a half pounds is worth one length over a mile and a quarter. Six pounds means a disadvantage of four lengths in this race."

"Hindoo is still fast enough," she said. "But he hasn't raced in years, and there are always some real runners up from Galle and Colombo."

Alexander dismissed the problem with a wave. "Akbar says that if the track is dry, he should run well. I'm giving him some early exercise tomorrow. Before we have that picnic."

He knew this was Laila's favorite spot on the island, with a dramatic plunging view thousands of feet down through Ella's Gap across the green plains to the sea. At first he saw sunlight sparkling on the distant water, but clouds were streaming from the northwest and the prospect was not as clear as he had hoped.

They found a narrow platform of soft flat ground at the verge of a eucalyptus forest. Below them the ground fell away in wavy ledges past shiny slopes of tea. To their left a narrow white stream rushed down a rocky channel jammed with boulders that threw bright spray into the air like surf on the sea wall of the Galle Face Hotel. The clouds were thickening above them.

"So, how will Hindoo run tomorrow?" said Laila as she lifted the picnic from a saddlebag. She took out an old striped cotton sari and spread it over the ground like a fisherman casting a net. A cloud of small white butterflies rose as the cloth settled near them.

"Hindoo will start like the wind." Alexander loosened the girths and left the horses to graze on the tall wild grasses at the edge of the forest. He took a bottle of wine and two enamel cups from his bag. He tried not to limp as he carried them over. "But I can't say how he'll finish." He did not add that Hindoo was hard to handle once he became excited.

Tomorrow would be Alexander's last day in the hill country before he took the night train. He had been asking Laila to come with him, repeating his request although he knew it would make no difference. Her troubles in Ceylon were far from finished. Laila said she would join him on the China Coast when she could, and she had asked him to watch for her pearl necklace at the sales in Shanghai. Eighteen large white graduated pearls, with a single magnificent black one in the center.

If he found the courage, although it was too soon, he wanted to ask her one other question, a question for a lifetime.

"You really shouldn't be riding at all, Alexander. The doctor said you will only make that ankle worse. And he told Percy he doesn't want to see you if anything more happens to that knee of yours. He thinks you need an operation, maybe two. Said he had done enough messy work in Flanders and it has taken him five years to get over it."

Alexander sat on the blanket facing the sea, his legs stretched before him. He opened the wine and stared at Laila against the moving sky as she set out the food. The afternoon sun lit one side of her face. He felt he was seeing her for the first time.

She was wearing tight riding breeches sculpted to her backside, a pale blue linen shirt and what he guessed was the vest of an old brown tweed suit. Her profile was strong and dark, but her face seemed softer. Her thick silky hair hung below her collar. He could not believe that he was with her, or that he was leaving her.

"While you are away," she said, conscious of his inspection, "I am going to resume my studies. You have made Livy and Catullus wait longer than they are used to."

"Will you do one other thing as well?" He filled the cups and tasted the red wine.

"What?"

"Ask your husband for a divorce." It was not the question he had intended to ask her. "Or sue for one."

Surprised, Laila looked at him closely before replying. Seeing his seriousness, she nodded. "Yes, I mean to." She hesitated. "But I think not until his son has arranged to sell Leopard Gate. Then we can buy it." She touched his cheek. "Can you be patient with me?"

"No."

"I will do my best." She placed one hand on his shoulder as she bent over him to arrange cold duck and her own sweet ambarella chutney on a plate.

Alexander took her derriere in both hands and pressed his face into the front of her trousers, moving his mouth and nose against her until he could smell her rising scent.

"Oh, Alex," she murmured, running long fingers through his hair. "That Karlov nose."

He bit the front of her breeches and held them in his teeth so that she could not draw back as he pulled out her shirt with both hands. He unbuttoned it with hasty fingers before releasing her trousers and kissing and nibbling her warm smooth belly as he stroked the cleft at the back of her breeches.

Laila raised her chin into the breeze and gulped the air with her eyes closed. "Please, may I have some wine?"

He poured and she sat between his legs, leaning back against his chest as they both stared down at the sea through Ella's Gap. They ate radishes and duck and mangoes from one plate.

While she drank he held her breasts inside her open shirt and burrowed his face into her hair to kiss her neck. He felt her nipples harden between his fingers.

"Shouldn't we take off our boots?" she asked, before kneeling to pull his off.

When they were naked, Laila sat down again as she had before. He kissed her shoulders and stroked her breasts and belly from behind as they drank and fed each other the pulpy fruit. Then she leaned forward on her hands and rose briefly before lowering herself onto him, first incompletely once or twice as if a welcoming tease, then settling down fully, absorbing him as he gasped and clasped her against him, her back damp against his chest. For a long moment they were perfectly quiet and still. He felt her body tighten as if she would never release him.

Alexander reached to the side and emptied the wine into her cup. They finished it and dropped the cup as their bodies trembled together.

Finally she collapsed with her chin on her chest and her hair falling over her face. He kissed her neck and sucked it in small pieces. He reached one hand along her cheek to her lips. She kissed the insides of his fingers and he felt the tears on her face as Laila's body began to shake with silent weeping.

- 37 -

"Might just squeeze in the first two races before the heavens open, Percy," said the white-haired club secretary, gin in hand. His double-breasted blazer was tight above his slightly-yellowed thick white flannels as he welcomed members and racing friends to the grassy enclosure before the clubhouse of the Nuwara Eliya Turf Club.

Two long rows of whitewashed stalls extended behind the single-story Tudor building. One shed had a thatched roof, the other faded red tiles. Grooms and stable boys and jockeys were carrying buckets and harness. Some led nervous horses by their bridles or short leads. On the other side of the enclosure, a tall viewing stand separated the clubhouse from the oval track.

"Who's your money on in the Planters Cup?" added the secretary.

"My young Russian friend, Karlov."

"You don't say, Palliser." The red-cheeked secretary raised his thin white eyebrows and accepted another drink. "I hear the chap thinks he's going to be a planter. Wonder if he knows what he's about. These foreigners always think it will be easy."

"His family's been drinking tea a lot longer than the Windsors, Ralphie. Ah, here he comes now." Palliser smiled through the crowd and raised his furled umbrella to catch Alexander's eye.

"Let me introduce you two. Count Karlov, Ralph Sedgwick, our club secretary and a racer once himself in better days."

"Welcome to the Nuwara Eliya Turf Club." Sedgwick glanced at Karlov's cane, then at his muscular appearance. "I understand you'll be riding old Hindoo in the Cup. Bit tall and solid for a jockey, aren't you?"

"Yes, sir," said Alexander. "I imagine we'll be the heaviest pair on the track."

"You wouldn't want to bow him," Sedgwick warned. "Be a shame to ruin Hindoo's tendons, rupture a sheath or whatever."

"I don't think Karlov needs a riding lesson, Ralph," said Palliser quickly, sensing his young friend's annoyance. "The Count has his own stable in Shanghai. His family bred cavalry horses for the czar."

Sedgwick seemed unimpressed by any Russian heritage. "You know what they say," persisted the secretary. "God punishes horses who carry too much weight."

Alexander looked away, grateful to Percy and trying not to get upset before the race. What did he care for the opinions of an English country farmer? He noticed Arabella Hartshorn conversing nearby. She and Sedgwick would make a tidy pair. Then he saw Laila enter the enclosure and wave at Palliser. Mrs. Hartshorn arched her shoulders and turned her back as Mrs. Hammond walked past her.

"Quite a crowded field for our little race. Fourteen horses," Sedgwick noted. "Three all the way from Colombo, including last year's winner,

Hurlingham. But I'd keep my eye on Malabar, that young Arabian my friends the Hartshorns have brought up here for a bit of training. Their nephew is riding him. The lad's just come out from London."

"His aunt Arabella will trim his allowance if he loses to Karlov," said Palliser in a loud voice. "Look at her. That flowery hat probably suited her before Crimea."

"All the same, Malabar's meant to be the first of a better blood line out here," said Sedgwick. "Be good for the colony."

"You know Mrs. Hammond, Ralph," said Percival as Laila joined the three.

"Of course." Sedgwick bowed stiffly. "How do you do, ma'am. How is Derrick getting on?"

"I'm afraid Derrick is still not himself," said Laila Hammond. "He's at the same clinic in Villefranche."

"At least the weather's better there."

Sedgwick continued drinking and nodding to passing friends. The women wore flowered print frocks or suits with shawls or sweaters. Many of the men carried field glasses and umbrellas. "Morning, Arthur. Madeleine, dear, how are you?"

All replied to Sedgwick but most did not stop as they passed by. Alexander wondered if they were deliberately avoiding Mrs. Hammond and her new friend. He shrugged and took two glasses of Pimm's from a passing tray and handed one to her. Two hundred people crowded the enclosure and plundered the buffet table as the first racegoers strolled towards the steep stand beside the track.

"Don't disappoint old Knox, my lad," said Palliser gruffly when Alexander excused himself. "Robbie was going to bet everything on you to win."

Karlov walked to Hindoo's stall and found Akbar brushing down the big stallion.

"How does he look?" asked the Russian, cupping Hindoo's soft nose and hushing him.

"He will run well for his age," nodded Akbar without smiling. "*Inshallah.*"

Alexander ran his hands down both forelegs from elbow to fetlock.

The noise of the moving crowd echoed inside the plaster walls of the stall. The stands were filling for the first race, five furlongs for the young sprinters. Robbie Knox's Magpie would be one of them. Several men stood on wooden boxes behind the grandstand, taking bets and exchanging wagering tickets for rupees and sterling. Each bookmaker or turf accountant was covered by an open umbrella attached to a bamboo pole nailed to his box. Touts paused by their stands to whisper in their ears.

Avoiding the jockeys' changing room, Alexander hung his jacket on a hook and buttoned on a racing shirt, slightly annoyed to be wearing the Hammond colors. He sat on an inverted tin bucket and pulled on his right boot. He used his knife to cut a five-inch slit in the bend of the left boot to accommodate the swollen knob at the front of his ankle.

A loud buzz reached them from the stands, then wild cheering and huzzahs as the first race finished to cries of "Magpie! Magpie!"

Alexander walked to the Dutch door of the stall. He glanced up through its open top at the darkening sky as a light sprinkle began to fall.

He was tightening the straps that held the number four secured to his back when Akbar spoke.

"You must watch for three horses, effendi." He held up three fingers. "Hurlingham, of course. He is like Hindoo, big and fast and so keen to go, sir. Blue-and-white checks, number six." Akbar spoke slowly, careful with the words he had prepared. "Vasco is the finest horse in Galle. A chestnut, very steady, fine pace, a good finisher, number ten. Red stripes. Best rider, professional jockey from India. The third is Malabar, a three-year-old colt, from an old English family of rich traders in Colombo. I do not know his colors, but he is black with a fine Arabian head. Number eleven. They say he will be the best horse on the island."

The rain fell more steadily. The crowd grew noisier again as the second race began, eight furlongs for the Sir Samuel Baker Plate.

Alexander wondered where Laila was in the stands. She would be with Percy, he guessed. He was more worried about his leg than about the race. The ankle was still stiff and wrapped but no longer too painful. He thought of his last race in Shanghai and shooting Taiga after she went down. He held Hindoo by the bridle as Akbar set the saddle well forward and tightened the girth.

Wild cheering rose from the stands while Akbar led Hindoo from the stall. Alexander donned his cap and mounted from the right. When Akbar handed him his whip, Karlov looked down the shed row and saw a tall black horse step from a stall onto the damp ground. The powerful animal had the long elegant head of a fine Arabian. He seemed a monument of sleek black muscle. A blond young Englishman mounted gracefully. A fox hunter at home, guessed Alexander.

Grooms led the fourteen horses past one side of the grandstand onto the track between the starting posts. The starter stood near the outside post with an umbrella in one hand and a short-barrelled pistol in the other as the horses assembled unevenly for the walk-up start.

The narrow grandstand rose in nine steep levels, with one box in the center for the officials of the Turf Club. Two long wooden benches in the front row were painted with the word, "MEMBERS." A slanting roof extended over the top rows of seats, but umbrellas covered every inch of the busy space. Several thousand people crowded forward at both sides of the stands.

Alexander knew the drill. Once the starter thought the horses were as close to even as they would get, he would fire his .22 blank cartridge and the horses would be off on the ten-furlong race.

In the meantime, the fourteen animals were turning and twisting in their positions, each one intense with coiled energy. They pressed forward or shied backward as their riders held them in. Some turned completely around or sideways towards the inside or outside rail. Only Vasco seemed calm, as if understanding the steady murmuring of his jockey's voice.

Hindoo kicked out as another tall stallion passed too close behind him.

"Steady there, number four!" yelled the starter as the other jockey cursed. Number six, Karlov noticed, Hurlingham. The starter ignored Hindoo as horses and jockeys fussed and disturbed each other while they sought positions on the softening track. It would be another moment before all the horses were roughly in line.

Hurlingham stood one horse away from Hindoo, prancing nervously, shouldering hard against the smaller horse that separated him from Karlov's mount. Alexander felt the agitation disturb Hindoo. He let the ten-year-old face backward as he tossed his head. Knowing the advantage of keeping his weight off his horse's back before the start, Alexander braced his right foot on the inside rail and lifted his weight from the animal.

"Number four!" yelled the starter, impatient as the rain fell harder.

"Sorry, sir!" Alexander turned his horse about and rode the few steps to the line. The movement bothered Hurlingham and a nearby gelding.

As the pistol fired, Hurlingham bolted forward with Hindoo first after him. The dozen others tore after them as the crowd roared.

"Steady, boy, steady." Alexander knew Hindoo was now used to his uneven stirrups, but that the imbalance would add strain to his run. With his whip hand he pulled his cap lower over his eyes as the rain slanted down. Hurlingham, perhaps two lengths ahead, tight on the inside rail, was kicking up wet clods of grass and mud. Three horses seemed close behind the leaders.

So far Hindoo was running the race Alexander had feared, breaking on top, giving it all from the start. But with number six running so strongly, it might be for the best. Karlov looked down past his right shoulder and saw the black three-year-old gaining, moving up on the horses who had been the front followers. Alexander tried to get his mount to relax, hoping to have something in reserve in the mile-and-one-quarter race. Hindoo settled into stride.

Alexander Karlov felt he was himself again, exhilarated and at home with the wind and rain in his face. He was ready to gallop on, across the

Mongolian grasslands, through the endless dark forests of Siberia and home to Voskrenoye.

As they passed the five-eighths pole, the black Arabian came up beside Hindoo. Perhaps sensing the challenge, Hurlingham stretched and pulled away. Alexander saw the mud on the lean face of Malabar's jockey as the Englishman crouched forward and used his whip.

The crowd cheered as the young black moved up and the leaders passed the quarter pole. Alexander felt Hindoo work harder as the three-year-old moved past. He saw the number eleven on the jockey's back. Hindoo held his place, almost nose to tail. Karlov was careful to keep him out of line. If the two horses clipped heels, the animal following would fall. Alexander guessed Hindoo was not happy on the worsening slippery track. His own leg began to throb as he leaned forward more and pressed back against the stirrups.

Then another smaller horse gained on the leaders, running steadily a bit outside Vasco. The jockey rode high and forward, his hands low, his whip held in both hands across the chestnut's neck. The small dark man caught Karlov's eye.

With three furlongs to go the rain fell harder. The horses seemed settled in two packs as they made a wide turn on the irregular track: four in the front chasing Hurlingham and the other nine riding a tight race of their own behind.

It was time to make his run. Alexander did his best to center his weight. He straightened his good leg and rose higher above the saddle with his body bent forward, parallel to the ground. He began to use the whip. His ankle burned. He felt Hindoo's muscles tighten and stretch as the big stallion fought Malabar for the second inside position.

The two raced alone, slipping and sliding with every stride as they matched each other shoulder to shoulder. The other rider knocked Karlov's left stirrup and the young jockey yelled a curse into the wind. A bolt of pain ran up Alexander's leg. But Hindoo slowly pulled away, with Vasco now closing in.

Only Hurlingham was ahead of them. Big splashes of mud rose from his hooves and struck Alexander as Hindoo began to close the spread. Two lengths, then one. A wall of noise struck them as they came around the final turn into the stretch.

Cheers exploded as the stands rushed towards them. For an instant Alexander thought of Taiga and his father. He was not riding alone. He ignored his leg and braced against the stirrups and used the whip.

Hindoo moved up, passing between the finish posts dead even with Hurlingham.

The race was over. The horses slowed on the muddy track and turned and trotted back towards the finish line. Alexander stared at the sea of black umbrellas but could not make out any faces. He was not certain who had won. Hindoo was hot and puffing between his legs, steaming in the rain.

Ralph Sedgwick stood at the inside finishing post with a long green megaphone in his hand. His white trouser cuffs were muddy. A Moorman held an umbrella above the secretary's head. The official looked up at the gathering horses and turned to face the grandstand with his megaphone.

"Number ten, Vasco, is the winner," Sedgwick announced. "Malabar, number eleven, is runner-up. Four and six are disqualified for starting early." He handed the megaphone to the Moorman and walked back to the stands. The dark attendant hurried after him, tilting the umbrella forward against the driving rain.

For a moment Alexander lingered on the track, indignant at the result, but knowing not to challenge the club secretary, ill-disposed as he had been. Hurlingham's rider hesitated as well, staring at Karlov and shaking his head as if Hindoo's movements before the race had caused their fast start.

Alexander dismounted near the open stable door. His left leg was numb and trembling, the ankle swelling against its wrap. He was relieved to find Akbar waiting to unsaddle and walk the steaming stallion. He raised his leg and leaned for a moment against the outside wall of the long stable. He closed his eyes before lifting the reins over Hindoo's head and handing them to Akbar. Karlov stroked Hindoo's cheek. The groom removed the saddle and replaced the bridle with a halter.

Alexander watched Akbar sponge down the stallion with two buckets of warm water. When Hindoo was slick with sweat and water, the groom started near his head and used the concave side of a long metal scraper to remove the extra moisture from his body. He splashed the last quarter bucket onto the big grey's genitals.

While Akbar spread a light cloth cooler over his back, Hindoo lowered his head and nuzzled his nose into Alexander's chest as if worried for his rider. Then the Moorman began to walk the stallion around the long shed row to cool him out. It would be some time before Akbar would return Hindoo to his stall to remove his cooler and dry him with a rub rag.

Laila was standing in one corner of the stall. Her long wet skirt clung to her. Her hat and umbrella hung from a tack hook. Light rain slanted in over the open half of the door.

"You won," she said, pressing her soft mouth against his before he could reply. She loosened the straps of his number and lifted the cloth over his head. "Are you all right? Let me help. You're so wet."

"Just one moment." He swung the upper half of the door until it was nearly closed. He felt her eyes on him in the darkened stall.

Laila took a towel from a hook and rubbed his hair as if she were drying a child's head. He closed his eyes and she wiped his face.

Laila's damp blouse hung loose and open when he cleared his eyes and looked at her again. She unbuttoned his wet shirt and helped him out of it before reversing the towel and drying him back and front.

"You smell of horse and mud." Her hands caressed his sides and she kissed his chest before loosening his belt. "It's time my jockey entertained his mistress."

Mrs. Hammond raised her skirt. Alexander forgot his leg and pressed her hard against he wall.

The platform was damp and grey in the early evening as Alexander waited with his bag at the Bandarawela station. Although she had not promised, he had hoped that Laila would be there to see him off.

The short train pulled up a few moments early, but he waited to board until the last moment. Once in his compartment he lowered the window and leaned out, cold with disappointment. He gazed back until the train had left the platform and he could no longer see Bandarawela. Then he ordered a bottle of arrack, a sandwich and mustard.

The train slowed as it drew into the Nuwara Eliya station. Alexander waited for his drink as he listened to the bustle of the hill station platform and thought of his last two train rides with the lady of his heart. The whistle blew twice. The train pulled away. He felt empty. He was alone again.

"Come in," he called brusquely when he heard a knocking on the cabin door. Impatient for his tray and drink, he stood and opened the door himself.

"May I join you to Colombo?" asked Mrs. Hammond.

- 38 -

The agents of the French police had been following him for three days, making it difficult for Viktor Polyak to connect with the young Reds of Shanghai and the provinces.

China's Communist Party had held another secret meeting in Shanghai. Because Lenin's agent, Mikhail Borodin, had been assigned to work with the Nationalists of Sun Yat-sen and Chiang Kai-shek, the Cheka was concerned that Russia might lose influence with the country's Communists. The Soviets needed a second major revolution, either in Germany or China. It must be Bolshevik. It must be tied to Moscow.

But today Polyak was focused on more immediate concerns. He must either escape his pursuers or kill them. Both were short and slight, dressed in the cheap grey suits of French detectives. One was an Annamite, small and yellow as a young summer squash.

Twice the Commissar had nearly lost them, once at the docks and once in the six-story chaos of the Great World Amusement Palace on the avenue Edouard VII.

Polyak had forced his way to the staircase through the seething crowd of magicians, acrobats and bird sellers. He had dashed up the crowded steps past the barbers, midwives and pimps of the second floor. On the third floor he hesitated behind the line of young men waiting to lower their trousers in public and pay to use the exposed modern flush toilets that required a higher posture than was traditional in China. But his followers had spotted him again on the next floor amidst the revolving wheels, acupuncture cabinets and fan-tan tables. The French detective would have lost him had the Indochinese not spotted him. Once again it was the damned fancy count who had been Polyak's curse, for the bright double hook of the Commissar's artificial hand was difficult to hide.

To turn on the men following him here in the French Concession was too dangerous. The French police and their Annamese and Chinese running dogs were everywhere. Preserving French authority was their job. Suppressing revolutionary politics was their duty. If they caught you they did not share the British weakness for restraint and discipline. They did not fuss with serious crime except as an opportunity for extortion and corruption. There were seven hundred brothels in the Concession. The French police chief ran the drug trade.

Polyak led the two across Soochow Creek into Chapei, Chinese Shanghai, then into a narrow lane off Sinkian Road. He paused by a line of street cooks. His nose distracted him with the smell of food. Onions and garlic sizzled in giant woks over smoky beds of charcoal. Pans of duck feet and pots of eels waited beside bowls of chillies and pickles.

Hunger had been a companion of Viktor Polyak all his life. As a boy in St. Petersburg scraping onions and rotten cabbages from the bottoms of old sacks in the corner of his father's windowless room near the docks. As one of a band of Bolshevik revolutionaries roaming from village to village exhorting peasants, murdering kulaks and burning churches. Even as a Commissar stiffening units of the Red Army from Omsk to Vladivostok, the men half-starved and half-clothed as they fought the Whites back and forth across Siberia. Finally as a Chekist hunting Whites and renegade Bolsheviks in Harbin and Tientsin. Always hunger. Like a lean animal in hard dry country, he had learned to eat when he could.

The Commissar bought six meat dumplings, his favorite Chinese fare, and ate them slowly from a scrap of newspaper. As he savored each one, he lowered his head to look back beneath the lines of laundry that hung across the alley. He peered between long strips of white cotton, bandages for binding the feet of women. For a moment his view was obscured by clumps of live ducks suspended by their feet from the bamboo shoulder poles of two porters. Then he saw the Indochinese wriggling through the crowd with the French detective a few steps behind him.

Polyak flung aside the greasy scrap of newsprint and continued into a warren of smaller alleys where the second floors of mud brick dwellings nearly met above the narrow lanes. A yellow dog with one ear and a long thin tail whined as he approached, then slunk behind a pile of sacks.

The Russian pressed himself against a wall to avoid a stinking two-wheeled cart loaded with night soil on its way to the countryside for sale to the farmers. He did not look back. Two peasants with straw sandals leaned into the work, grunting and staring at the ground as their thin legs strained to haul the filthy weight. Leather straps were bound about their chests and shoulders like the harness of a team of oxen.

These slaves should be the fodder of revolution. But like the *narod* at home, the "dark people," the illiterate peasant masses, these Chinese seemed shrouded with resignation, fatalism and superstition. No wonder such men lost themselves on the bunks of opium dens whenever they had a few coins. They reminded Polyak of his father's agony as a naval stevedore in St. Petersburg, caring only to lose himself in a state of *zapoi*, an obliterating drunken stupor. Opium was the vodka of the Chinese, their insensate refuge from despair. No wonder the old serf rebellions had never succeeded centuries ago. Misery was not enough. Lenin was correct. Disciplined professional revolutionaries were required, men who did not fear the use of terror.

One long curving alley ended in a cul-de-sac against a brick wall. The open space at the end was like the center of a country village.

A small tea-house opened near the end of the alley. Old men sat talking on rough benches sipping watery *cha* made from tea dust. Some smoked tobacco from the metal bowls of long-stemmed bamboo pipes. Nearby a quilt restorer slit open filthy worn sleeping covers and extracted the cotton stuffing. Another man, coughing like a Siberian miner, fluffed up the soiled material to prepare it to be used again. Baked rice cakes waited on woven platters at a bamboo stall where a man was grinding flour and mixing the dough that fermented behind him in ceramic pots.

Polyak sat on the end of a barrel with his back against the wall as he waited to be served a cup of green tea.

An ear picker labored nearby. His pointed metal cleaning tools and duck-feather brushes were arrayed beside the head of an elderly client which rested on one cheek set on a tall stool. The old man's eyes were tightly closed as if he feared some pain. He gripped a cigarette in his left hand. Smoke poured from his nostrils as the ear picker wiped a sharp tool on a small cloth pad and examined the orange wax before lifting it to his nose and sniffing loudly.

Sparrows flitted busily around the thatch above the overhanging eaves of the tea-house.

As Polyak waited, considering the sense of village life that seemed so much richer than the bitter Russia of his youth, the Commissar pondered what to do about the Karlovs. Todor Androv's last message said only that he believed Oskar had been murdered in Egypt and that Katerina Karlov had sailed for Shanghai while her brother stayed on in Ceylon with his black whore. Polyak had a Chinaman watching the Salle d'Armes, waiting for the count's return and reporting daily on the sister. Soon he must attend to Katerina and remind her whose she was, but to do so now would be to warn both Karlovs. In due course, it might be best to seize the girl and then trap the brother when he came for her.

Polyak knew he must be careful. Shanghai swarmed with enemies. Thirty thousand White Russians were harboring in the city, with five Orthodox churches, two daily newspapers, their own bakeries and cafés and, more dangerous, associations of veterans of the five-year civil war at home. Hundreds of these revanchist soldiers were armed and formed into the Russian Regiment, paid by the municipal government of the International Settlement as protection for the colonial masters of Shanghai. Many of these men were Cossacks, the same savages whose knouts and sabres had cut down mobs of workers for the czar. There were twenty-two other units in the Shanghai Volunteer Corps, including the American Machine Gun Company and the Public School Cadet Company of the English. All these other formations, whether Portuguese, Jewish or Scottish, served only as unpaid volunteers to suppress the Chinese masses in times of crisis.

There was so much for him to do, and money had become a difficulty. One day the Reds would build a society in which money did not matter. In the meantime, he was still a prisoner of this poison of the bourgeoisie. It was time to sell the green stone he had recovered from the hag in Paris. He reached down and pinched the top of his boot. The necklace was still sewn into the lining. He squeezed the rectangular emerald between his fingers. He must sell the bauble where he could find the highest price.

The waiter bowed and served him. The nearby customers seemed nervous at the sound of Polyak's hook clattering against the side of the small cup that had no handle. He himself was not embarrassed by the device. He had learned to make an advantage of the discomfort of others. Fear was part of his trade. At first he had been concerned that the loss of a hand would be perceived as weakness. But he had learned that this metal hand had the opposite effect. Only stranglings were more difficult. Polyak gave the tea server a coin and blew on his steaming drink as he recalled the dandified British major whose prosthesis he had stolen.

The Commissar did not look up as the two men tracking him suddenly appeared. The French detective sat at a nearby table while the Annamese entered the tea shop.

Polyak rose holding his cup. He flung the hot tea into the face of the seated Frenchman. Then he dropped the cup and seized a long metal probe from the ear cleaner's set. Blinded by the scalding liquid, the detective cried out and leaned forward, rubbing both eyes with his fists. Polyak pressed the flat of his hook against the left side of the Frenchman's head and jammed the long pick into the man's right ear. Then he slammed the wooden knob at the end of the instrument with the side of his fist.

The Frenchman jerked in a spasm, then rose screaming. The end of the pick was tight against his ear hole. He groped for the knob as blood flooded down his neck. Polyak ran for the wall. Hearing the cries, the Annamite hurried back to his colleague. Horrified, he pulled the bloody tool from his partner's ear.

Polyak stepped onto the barrel and forced one foot into a crack between the bricks. He flung himself over the wall as he heard a shot and a bullet struck near the top. He leaped down on the far side. There the ground was higher and littered with waste and garbage. Instead of running, he flattened himself against the wall. A babble of Chinese voices rose from the other side. He looked up and waited. A hand appeared and clutched the top edge of the wall as the detective climbed. The head and shoulders of the Annamese policeman appeared over the top as he prepared to jump down.

Polyak plunged his hook through the center of the exposed hand that gripped the corner of the brick. The policeman shrieked in pain. The Commissar took advantage of the man's momentum to pull him over the wall by his hooked hand. A black automatic pistol clattered to the ground. The hook came free as the body crashed at Polyak's feet onto some broken earthenware crockery. He knelt on the small man's chest. He was certain no one else would cross the wall.

"Do you know who I am?" he asked as the yellow man struggled and groaned. The Commissar lifted the pistol. "*Vous me connaissez?*"

"*Agent* . . ." the policeman gasped. "*Agent communiste* . . ."

Polyak heard several teeth break as he rammed the weapon into the man's mouth and pulled the trigger.

- 39 -

"Soyez sage, monsieur le comte." The old doctor shook his head. "Be smart. *Le bon Dieu* gave you two legs. I have said you must not stand on that one."

The French physician had boarded at Haïphong and would soon be serving as surgeon-in-chief at the Hôpital Sainte Marie in the French Concession of Shanghai. Hervé du Moulin had the bald dented head and liver-spotted hands of an old man. But his eyes were clear and bright.

"If you do not listen to me, *jeune homme*, I will not be your surgeon." He fitted a cigarette into a short ivory holder.

"*Pardonnez-moi, Docteur*," said Alexander without taking his eyes from the approaching harbor. "I will do my best, sir." Conversing with the doctor reminded him of home. His mother had insisted that French was occasionally the language of the house in order to prepare her children for St. Petersburg society and the world.

During the warm evenings the physician and Alexander had played backgammon in the panelled smoking salon as the *Angkor* steamed up the South China Sea. Several experienced French travellers politely declined to play with du Moulin. Warned, Alexander was careful to avoid high stakes. The doctor himself disdained the use of a leather cup and always threw the dice from his hand as he spoke to Karlov about the old days in Beirut, Tananarive and Dalat.

"Do you mind if I play with my own dice, Doctor?" Alexander asked the second time they played, bringing out the dice he had found near the body of Todor Androv. "I've never had a chance to use them."

"Of course, if you permit me first to throw them several times myself," replied du Moulin, examining the two yellow ivory cubes. He rolled them four times. Three times one of the die showed a six. "Interesting, but we will not play with these." The doctor shook his head and returned the dice to Karlov. "May I ask where you found them?"

"In the jungle in Ceylon."

"They could get a man killed."

"Perhaps they did," said Karlov without further explanation.

Alexander rarely won, but he enjoyed watching the proper ivory cubes slip from the physician's elegant mottled hand and tumble across the colored cork triangles, always settling into the same corner of the board. Du Moulin had the long strong fingers of a pianist. "*Comme la vie*, backgammon is not a game of chance," the Frenchman remarked one evening, nodding as Alexander declined the doubled cube.

"*L'heure verte*," the doctor would say late each afternoon, drumming his fingers as the hour approached for the steward to serve him a chilled *pastis* without being asked. "Before the magic green liqueur was outlawed during the war," du Moulin explained the first time, "the aperitif hour was named for the green fairy, '*la fée verte*,' as we called absinthe, or wormwood at the old cafés." He shrugged. "Now we use these anise drinks as a pale substitute."

The two had gone ashore together in Macau. The physician invited Alexander to the Clube Militar on the broad Avenida de Praia Grande. There they drank with a Portuguese colonel, a former patient of the doctor's, posted to the East after arduous service in Mozambique. They dined lavishly on Alexander's losses, finishing with Sirocco, a Fonseca white port. The wine reminded the Russian of his little friend in Cairo, Olivio Fonseca Alavedo.

After dinner Alexander had declined an introduction to a celebrated house of flowers. It was more satisfying to be faithful. But he and the doctor visited two casinos before reboarding. Du Moulin lost modestly at roulette, tipped the croupiers generously and prospered against other guests at baccarat.

By the end of the evening the surgeon was pale save for flushed spots on each cheek. His hands were still steady and his eyes bloodshot but alert. He never explained why he was moving to Shanghai. Alexander wondered if the doctor possessed the sort of complicated history that drove so many to the ultimate city of refuge and perilous opportunity.

Karlov himself had drunk enough to make any Russian proud. Enough Singapore gin slings, wine and port to embolden a troop of Cossacks. Late in the evening he had confided in the doctor his own limited experience with women and his infatuation with one ten years older, married and too well educated. The old physician asked for details before dispensing his wisdom. Alexander gave them too generously, his first romantic confidences since his long afternoon teas with Madame Mei-lan Wong.

"There is no reason in these things, *mon petit*. Just please yourself and learn what you can. But recognize when you have found the lady who you believe will be good to you the longest. Never let that one slip away. Once the equilibrium of mutual enthusiasm is lost, it can never be the same again. That was my mistake when I was young and spoiled." The Frenchman rattled the ice in his glass. "I was, perhaps, a bit like you."

"I'll do my best, sir," said Alexander intently, frowning with concentration as du Moulin continued.

"Women, you see, are relational. We men are physiological. Women are made for attachment, men for competition. *C'est ça le problème*. The difficulty is for men and women to appreciate those qualities in each other." He leaned towards Alexander and tapped his long fingers on the table. "That appreciation is the understanding you must build with the right woman."

Alexander's head boiled with questions and the effort to apply these principles to his own life. But before he could speak, the doctor held up one hand and continued.

"Boys like you express this male thirst for competition in games. Look at you. Why else would you fence and race with that crippled leg? *Ridicule*." He shrugged. "And of course the women employ sex to secure the affection and all the other things they think they need."

"I see," nodded Alexander, flushed and dizzy with wine and wisdom. "Have you yourself ever . . ."

"As for me, the wiser I become, the less able I am to exploit my wisdom." Du Moulin closed his eyes and pinched the bridge of his nose. His face seemed older now, more deeply wrinkled. "But now you have a chance to use what I have learned when I cannot."

Alexander sat back and tried to recall what Edmond Dantès had been taught by the old *abbé* in the adjoining cell at the Château d'If.

Late the next morning Alexander found du Moulin in the smoking room, bent over a soup plate as he splashed water from it into his eyes. The doctor looked up and blinked.

"Parsley water," he said. "Refreshes the eyes, clears away the red. Just simmer three sprigs of parsley in water and let it cool." He wiped his face with a dinner napkin. "I always use it before I operate, or if I need to charm a lady."

Alexander dined well on board and enjoyed having time to consider the excitement of his problems. But the damage to his ankle aggravated the pain and stiffness of his leg.

"How much does it bother you?" du Moulin asked one afternoon. They were strolling the First Class deck and watching the coast of China slip past. The surgeon was wearing one of his high-collared formal jackets that reminded Alexander of the sketches of fashionable scenes from the *Deuxième Empire* that hung behind his mother's piano in her sitting room at Voskrenoye.

"Hardly at all, Doctor," said Alexander, though the bump on the front of his ankle felt like a large marble under his sock.

"Give me your stick, boy." The physician extended his hand and took the cane from Alexander. "Now walk very quickly to that ring toss post and back. *Vas-y! En vitesse*."

Karlov started off gamely. His left shoulder rocked down and up as he limped more and more heavily. The pain ground into every step. He made no sound but his jaw was clenched and his face white when he rejoined du Moulin. The Frenchman found little difficulty in persuading him that the time for surgery was at once.

Obeying instructions, Alexander now put all the weight he could onto his cane and right leg. But he was too excited not to stand with other passengers near the bow of the *Angkor* as she entered the Yangtze delta and approached Shanghai. The tricolor and the flag of the Messageries Maritimes flew from the stern of the steamer.

Alexander glanced down at his feet, pleased that he had polished his boots and honed his weapons. After breakfast he had taken a few drops of olive oil down to his cabin and used his stone and strop to sharpen his razor, the Marseilles knife and his short sword.

Shanghai rose before him like a daydream. The early morning haze of fog and coal dust hung in a flat cloud above the oily water of the great harbor at the bend of the Whangpu River. The majestic towers of the European buildings of the Bund floated above the haze as if they were the golden battlements of a heavenly city. They sparkled in the rising sunlight that struck them like the directed light of a magic lantern. Karlov recognized the upper floors of the Custom House, the Shanghai Club, Jardine's and the Astor House Hotel, where Lily had been kept by her Scottish taipan.

He had come home.

Eager to go ashore, Alexander felt like a puppy straining against its master's leash. His bag was packed and waiting by the companionway. He had sent only one telegram announcing his arrival. He wondered if he would be met.

The *Angkor* slid to her mooring between a French gunboat and the *Diana Dollar*, an American passenger-freighter with an immense white dollar sign painted on her black funnel. Karlov heard the anchor chain rattle down as a breeze gusted out from shore. The fog faded.

Seagoing junks, the warships of many nations and a score of freighters were moored in the deeper waters. Small motor and sailing vessels swarmed about inshore. Sampans with bamboo canopies and cooking fires burning in pans on their decks were tied side to side in busy floating villages. Laundry and fish and paper lanterns painted with Chinese characters hung from each boat. The fresh salty air of the China Sea was replaced by the odors of charcoal and oil, garlic and fish.

He recalled his first arrival in Shanghai several years earlier. Three hundred soldiers were trapped on the Siberian icebreaker unable to land because of the costly formalities imposed by the French. His father had ordered him to sneak ashore and seek assistance. Alexander had lived a lifetime in one day. Robbed, seduced and assaulted, he had been intoxicated by the frenzied port. "What am I to do here?" his father had asked him the next day, as usual not wanting a reply. "I know only two things, Sasha. Riding and killing. If we wait, we will be like all these Russian beggars. Dying slowly, selling their medals in the street." That evening the old cavalryman touched his son's glass with his before he spoke again. "Better to die in the saddle." They started their business the next day and made their way together like two brothers on campaign. They borrowed money, lived too well and taught the arts of horsemanship and fencing.

The launch of the Messageries Maritimes carried the landing passengers to the stone quay at the end of the French Bund. A throng of greeters waited behind the barrier of the port authorities.

Spouses, friends and household servants, consular staff, chauffeurs and porters from the grand hotels, all waved and smiled for the attention of the arrivals. A thick-set man with a short red beard stood still amidst them. Arms crossed, he waited like a boulder in a stream as others moved around him. The man wore a rumpled pin-striped suit, a loose Russian blouse and a brown Chicago hat set low over a block-like face. Alexander recognized Serge, the debt collector who had become a bodyguard.

Karlov retrieved his passport and waved goodbye to du Moulin. He stepped into the crowd.

"*Dobry outra, Graf,*" said a hard voice. The Russian took Alexander's case and led him to a pair of black Chryslers. Two other burly men, Chinese but similarly dressed, stood wiping the two automobiles with large shammy cloths. The rear window of the second car rolled down.

Alexander Karlov lowered his head and smiled. All he could see was the long oval of a bald copper-skinned head. A driver opened the door.

"Mr. Hak Lee," said Alexander with happy respect, entering the car. "How are you, sir?" He knew better than to attempt to shake the old man's hand.

"It is time you came back, my son," sighed the familiar quiet voice as the two vehicles pulled away, with Serge on the running board of Hak Lee's car, holding on his hat by the brim. "You were missed and needed." The words were warm but the tone was cold. "In the meantime I have cared for your sister, Miss Katerina. I have sent her a guardian, working as her servant. Now you must care for me."

"Of course." Alexander felt the dark veined eyes assess him. He himself did the same. Both were aware of the origin of their friendship and their partnership. On Alexander's first day in Shanghai he had saved the life of Mei-lan Wong, a former lover of Hak Lee's and a woman who herself had once saved the Master of the Mountain from his enemies. Since then the young Russian and the old Chinese had formed an occasionally complicitous relationship of their own.

The pitted face and the bony shoulders of the tall man seemed even more thin than before. But the amber two-inch fingernails, the blue silk robe fastened at the side and the black American boots had not changed.

"You are more like your father," said the Chinese, using a sharp nail to open a packet of Senior Service. "Bigger, more confident." Hak Lee withdrew two cigarettes and slit the paper of each from end to end with the corner of his nail. He dropped the papers and rolled the tobacco between his hands.

"I have a small present for you, sir." Alexander drew back his cuff and unstrapped the sheath knife from his wrist. He presented the weapon to Mr. Hak Lee.

"I thank you." The gangster drew the blade and tested the edge against one long dark nail. "Admirable. I trust you have used it well."

"I tried. In Egypt."

Hak Lee slid the knife back into its sheath and set it aside. "Tell me what concerns you, Count Karlov." He picked at the inflamed sore on his ear. "Then I will speak to you of my problems."

Alexander was accustomed to Hak Lee's direct manner, and he had prepared an answer. "I have three, sir, in addition to the situation of my sister and a small matter involving a necklace." He paused and glanced out as they turned left from the avenue Edouard VII. A rickshaw coolie spat after them as the Chrysler nearly ran him down.

"A necklace? That is nothing. Stones, gold, pearls. Every four weeks we hold jewelry sales in the small dining room of the Astor House Hotel. Of course it is a bazaar for the stolen jewelry of the world. In every other great city, thieves must sell their jewelry secretly for one fifth its value. In Shanghai, with little concern for stolen goods, we sell openly and they fetch two or three times as much." Hak Lee glanced down at the tobacco flaking in his hands. "So it all comes here to us. And waiting in Shanghai are always rich buyers in transit, seeking compact forms of value other than currency to carry with them. Now tell me what is disturbing you, Count Karlov."

Big Ear did not respond when Alexander revealed that his sister had a son held in Moscow, the child of her abduction by the Commissar. The old man's eyes brightened when Karlov turned to business.

"I need money to buy a tea plantation in Ceylon. The finest Orange Pekoe in the world, high in the mountains in the tea country. And I must have an operation on my leg."

"The first I can arrange. If you wish a partner, the plantation will cost you nothing, since I desire to purchase property outside China. Both the Communists and the Japanese are threatening everything we have built here. But if you want only money, it will be a debt."

"A partner," said Alexander, not entirely truthfully but knowing Hak Lee was not offering him a choice. "In the tea country of Ceylon, sir, you will truly be the master of the mountain."

Hak Lee nodded with appreciation, then dropped the tobacco between the pointed toes of his boots and pinched his nose between his hands. He sniffed twice before inhaling deeply. "An operation? I, too, am suffering a medical difficulty."

Opium, or age? wondered Alexander. Perhaps an old wound?

"And the third matter?" Big Ear began to cough until his body rocked forward on the upholstered seat.

"I must find Viktor Polyak."

The Master of the Mountain had expected that. "Our old friend. The butcher who would bring the Red bear to China. Your Commissar's left hand is still in my fish bowl, nibbled clean by the snakeheads. His bones serve every day as an inspiration to the debtors who call on me." He sniffed one palm. "How much more of him do you now require?"

"All."

Hak Lee's eyes and lips moved, forming what might be a smile on another man.

The automobile approached the chemin St. Bernard.

"Drop me at the corner, if you please." Alexander Karlov wished to arrive at the Salle d'Armes on his own. The gangster's twin motorcars were too well known.

"Of course." The older man nodded before he instructed the driver accordingly in Cantonese.

"May I call on you tomorrow at the tea-house, sir?"

The Chinaman nodded and coughed as Alexander stepped from the car into the bright dusty street. Serge handed him his leather case.

Karlov gazed down the chemin St. Bernard, seeing it almost as though for the first time. The modest side street was busier than he remembered it. Scores of rickshaws, some broken down, were crowded near an open workshop. Not the sort of enterprise to draw rich clients to the Salle.

He crossed to the other side and limped slowly along the street, recalling the morning he and his father had opened their new enterprise. The old opium warehouse had been cheap enough. A musty sweet smell had hung in the air near the wall racks where thousands of balls of opium, each the size of a large melon, had been stored after arriving from Madras and Calcutta in exchange for the tea of Fujian and Jiangxi.

For two weeks the Karlovs had received more guests than clients. Scores of White emigrés had called on the major for shelter, loans, food, employment and protection. A few, the best received, placed dignity before desperation. They offered their compliments, accepted a glass of tea and asked for nothing. Count Karlov gave each what he could. Shelter for two nights, a bowl of thick borscht, perhaps a few days of work.

In time the fencing classes, gymkhanas, pony school, dressage training and sporting competitions brought prosperity. Boxing, knife throwing and the martial arts kept the Salle d'Armes busy in the evenings.

Alexander regretted that they could not accommodate the American game of baseball, introduced to him by Jessica James in matches between United States Marines from the Yangtze gunboats, the Shanghai Amateur Baseball Club and Japanese ballplayers from the South Manchurian Railway. Horse races and paper chase hunting were also popular in Shanghai. After one season the Karlovs were training both men and horses. As the business flourished, the count had hired his old Hussars as trainers and fencing masters.

The inter-fleet boxing matches drew every visiting admiral and passing sailor, filling the great hall with cheers and hollering in a dozen languages. The Japanese always won the lighter weight classes, until the Americans produced a small but fierce Filipino ship's steward who punched above his weight.

At important events gambling was always a second and more hazardous sport. Then the Cossacks kept order for Count Karlov. After the first pickpocket left with broken hands, there was little of the petty crime that employed so many in the great port city. The quiet partnership of Mr. Hak Lee kept more serious criminals at a respectful distance.

Alexander paused before the entrance and set down his case. He inhaled the familiar odors of sawdust and horses as he bent to sweep the dirt from his boots. Like a cavalry officer, albeit a poor one, he had polished them from toe to top before coming ashore.

He looked across the way where the swarm of damaged rickshaws littered the street in front of the workshop. A number were not the cheap vehicles of the public pullers but the elegant finely made carriages of rich families or costly pheasants. A dozen men were replacing spokes, darning cushions and patching canopies. The long shafts of many were being replaced. The handles of some were being bound with leather strapping.

One bowlegged worker, less active than the others, looked back at Alexander. An old puller was haggling tearfully with the proprietor about the cost of repairs to his battered vehicle. Another sat on the edge of the street picking at his callused scaly feet with a splinter of bamboo.

Alexander lifted his case and squinted as he stepped inside the dark Salle from the brightness of the street. The whistle and clash of blades and the snorting of horses welcomed him home. He set down his bag and let his eyes adjust to the vast shadowy space. The tattered flags and pennants of lost regiments hung limply from the long high walls. The Horse Guards, the 5th Hussars, the Litovski Lancers. Two riders were trotting in line, posting easily as they performed figure eights in the open ring.

The first rider pulled up, then walked her mount towards him.

"Sasha!" cried his sister, jumping down and embracing him. "Everyone has been waiting for you."

She seemed different, warmer than when Alexander last had seen her.

"I must talk to you at once, Katia," he said quietly as the other rider slowed his horse. "One of the Russians from the *Star* followed me in Ceylon, just like you warned in your telegram. He killed a friend of mine and then died himself in a hunting accident." Alexander took his sister's arm. "Do you know where Polyak is?"

"No, Sasha." She shook her head as the other horseman dismounted close beside her.

"Alexander-san!" The handsome young Japanese bowed formally before shaking hands. The hard angles of his face broke in a smile beneath his cheekbones. He pointed at the sword rack. "Shall we fence?"

Katerina laughed. "He just arrived."

"Hideo Tanaka," said Alexander, surprised to sense an intimacy between the two. "In the saddle, at last."

"Your sister is my instructor." His old schoolmate spoke quickly. "And I am teaching her Japanese."

"We met here," Katerina added. "Hideo came to ask when you were returning."

"Count Karlov!" boomed the deep Russian voice of Ivan Semyonov from the far end of the hall.

The old Cossack strode to Alexander and crushed him in a hug. Then they gripped each other's shoulders as they examined one another.

There was more grey in Ivan's red beard and more red in his cheeks and nose. He did not seem quite as large and hard as Alexander remembered him.

The four walked to the open kitchen and outdoor dining table at the other end of the Salle d'Armes. On the way they passed a young man half standing in the stirrups of a wooden horse. The sportsman was swinging a mallet as if playing the chukker of his life. He grunted with each blow as he drove the white wooden balls into a canvas screen hanging in the corner.

"Arm straight, Billie," instructed Alexander as they passed.

Chung stood grinning beside Gregori, the old military servant of Alexander's father, himself the veteran of a dozen campaigns from Rumania to Vladivostok. The cook bowed and pumped the samovar with an upside-down boot that he placed over its top. He handed Alexander a steaming glass of tea.

"Welcome home, Count Karlov." Gregori's lean face wrinkled with delight. He straightened his shoulders and removed his spectacles as he put aside a copy of one of the city's Slavic newspapers, *Slovo*, with its listing of new Russian arrivals in Shanghai.

"This is Jin Min," said Katia, introducing a young servant with a white skull cap. "Your friend Mr. Hak Lee sent him to look after me." Jin Min bowed twice.

Alexander was pleased that his sister's politics permitted such an indulgence. He took his father's seat at the head of the table and stretched out his leg as Gregori set down glasses and wine and vodka. A brown teapot was warming on top of the samovar. The talk grew loud and genial. Clouds of smoke rose from tube cigarettes. Chung and Jin Min served blinis and steaming dumplings and platters of zakuski. Alexander beamed, proud of his Russian hospitality as he ate the herrings in wine, pickled mushrooms and liver paste. He wished only that Laila Hammond were beside him, her hand on his leg beneath the table.

- 40 -

"They will eat anything, but they prefer fresh red meat." Mr. Hak Lee dropped a morsel of spicy ginger beef into the immense fish tank from his ivory chopsticks.

The young snakeheads dove for the rare meat in a tight arrow-shaped pack, arcing through the water like a single animal rather than swimming in an open pattern like a school of fish. The Chinese ate another piece himself before dropping the last bite into the roiling water.

Karlov gazed at the second tank resting on another large red lacquered table. Two mature snakeheads, perhaps three feet long, undulated slowly, expectantly. Their bodies rippled as they waited for their living lunch. Alexander noticed the long row of thin pointed teeth that extended from narrow lips to hinged jaw. It was no wonder the English called these creatures "Frankenfish."

"Please drop a few of those sandalwood shavings on the coals," asked Big Ear, pointing at a smoldering brazier in one corner of the room.

Aware that Hak Lee's ancient brazier had not once grown cold in scores of years, Alexander obliged as the Master of the Mountain groaned and turned his back. Karlov thought he heard his partner regurgitate his food. He saw him drop something more into the tank before expectorating directly into it. A pink cloud discolored the water. The fish swam about in frenzy.

A bamboo cage rocked nearby as layers of fat frogs struggled against each other in their confinement. Karlov noticed a long opium pipe on the table beside the cage. A wooden sieve hung from a nearby peg. He knew that each amphibian had one broken leg to ensure that it could not escape its purpose. Alexander trusted that his own injury would not work so well against him. Tomorrow he would have his operation.

Karlov limped over to the second tank to give his host a moment to recover. He stared at the bottom of the scummy glass container. Instead of a miniature bridge or painted mermaid, his partner had found a more purposeful decoration: the bones of Viktor Polyak's large left hand.

"I see you enjoy my debt collectors," sighed Big Ear after wiping his lips on his sleeve and settling behind his lustrous black desk.

"My snakeheads have so much to teach us. They eat everything, especially their own young. They devour waterbirds and creatures bigger than themselves. They mate only with ones of equal size. If they find a smaller partner, they will eat her. Once they have emptied their ponds of other living creatures, they will slither overland for a mile or more in search of food."

The old Chinese paused as violent coughs seized him. He leaned forward on his arms, both fists on his desk near a round open tin of Pickwick Virginia Cigarettes. The beaming benevolent face of Mr. Pickwick smiled through his round spectacles from the side of the tin. Hak Lee's own head hung low between his shoulders like a vulture's in repose. He closed his eyes and put one hand to his mouth as several drops of blood fell to the desk.

"Are you all right, sir?" Alexander came to his side and placed one hand on the man's thin shoulder despite the gangster's celebrated aversion to being touched. "Can I do anything? Should we send for a doctor?"

Hak Lee shook his head and collapsed into his carved blackwood chair. He opened his mouth and took small sharp breaths. After a moment he regained himself.

"At first, when I cabled you in Paris, I thought they were poisoning me, that at last one of my enemies had learned a way to reach me. I was obliged to have my own chef questioned until he could no longer speak or cook. But his pain was useless to me. It was not him." The gangster paused and covered his mouth. "There is no one I can trust, of course. No one but you." His black eyes almost sparkled as if he had found some humor.

"Now the European doctors tell me that this enemy is inside me." He pointed at his throat and belly. "Cancers." He reached to his shoulder and covered his guest's hand with his own. Alexander had never felt a touch so cold. "They cannot tell me how much time I have. Now nothing that I eat stays with me."

"I'm sorry . . ."

The gaunt Chinese raised his hand and waved away regret. "In the meantime I am collecting what I can, converting properties into simpler riches."

He pointed at a wide shadowy alcove in the wall behind his desk. It was the only alteration that Alexander noticed here in his partner's office behind the Green Dragon Teahouse.

In the front room of the teahouse itself, old men still smoked and gambled as a mama-san paraded her silent painted twelve-year-olds between the tables for their selection. The girls were mute as dolls. Even their smiles were made of paint. Long wooden boxes were still stacked on the rue Lafayette outside the coffin-maker's shop next door. But now a small black safe stood beside a long rectangular pit perhaps three feet deep in the center of this recess in Big Ear's office.

"In a few days my new safe from London will be fixed securely in a cement base in the center of that depression. That is where I have already begun to store my treasures. When I become too ill, I will give only you the combination and my instructions."

Alexander tried not to reveal his astonishment. "As you wish, sir."

"I desire only that while we are both here, you and I will do all we can to assist each other in our struggles."

"Of course." Alexander heard a double knock at the door.

"Perhaps, my son, I may serve you by doing something that is better if not done by you yourself," Mr. Hak Lee added quickly.

A Chinese voice announced a guest as the door opened. A short soft-faced man in a three-piece nailhead suit entered. His waistcoat had the small lapels of an overly tailored English suit. His hair was dark and glossy. Alexander glanced at the man's feet. His heels were a trifle high.

The man was followed by a little woman with bound feet and a tight embroidered silk dress, bearing a tray of tea. Beaded blue butterflies were sown onto the tops of her four-inch shoes. Their wings moved freely as she glided with short graceful steps, as if her feet were fluttering from flower to flower.

Alexander recalled the Manchu legend that, when they died, ladies with long fingernails and bound feet would be received in heaven as members of the privileged class. He wondered which traditional celestial pleasures Hak Lee drew from this woman's feet. Did he nibble and nip the tiny shrivelled toes and heels of his concubine, sucking their soft flesh into his mouth? Or did he prefer "Eating Steamed Dumplings in Pure Water," as licking the feet during bathing was called? Did he drink from her tiny shoes, savoring their odor as a Frenchman might his wine?

"Ah, Mr. Lee," said the sort of smooth educated English voice that had always irritated Alexander's father. "So very kind of you to receive me."

"Count Karlov, I present Mr. Astern." Hak Lee steepled his fingers above his desk.

"Aspern," said the man, looking about the room, then sitting on a high blackwood stool across the desk from Hak Lee and accepting a steaming cup of tea. "It is 'Aspern,' sir, Jock Aspern. A-S-P-E-R-N."

"He comes to us from Singapore and Hong Kong to be the auctioneer at next week's jewelry sales at the Astor House Hotel, where he is always my guest." Hak Lee spoke as if he were addressing only Alexander. "They say the best auctioneers are English." The shoulders of the Chinese shrugged and shook like the rags of a scarecrow blowing in the wind. "No one understands the reason."

Perhaps they provide a false presumption of authority and integrity, surmised the Russian, and a dash of snobbish charm.

"Thank you," said Aspern, looking about from his perch but finding no place to rest his cup, not daring to set it on his host's antique desk. "Please let me know how I may be of service, Mr. Lee."

"You will oblige me by obliging Count Karlov." Hak Lee looked his young friend in the eye and nodded towards the frog cage. The two had learned to share the pleasing utility of small dramas.

Karlov removed the bamboo lid, reached in with the long-handled sieve, lifted out a stout crippled frog and dropped the pop-eyed twitching animal into the tank between the two large fish.

The Englishman gasped and leaned forward. They always care for animals, thought Karlov.

Both snakeheads bent double, their long mouths open as they turned to seize the amphibian that breast-stroked desperately between them. One snapped its mouth shut across the body of the frog. Only two webbed feet escaped, reminding Alexander of the pedals of a piano as they settled deeper into the water on their own. The feet were instantly devoured by the second fish.

"My God," gasped Aspern. His small cup rattled in its saucer.

"Frankenfish, you know," said Alexander cheerfully. He sipped his tea and set his cup on the desk. "May I ask if you expect any pearl necklaces at the next auction?"

The auctioneer took a moment to recover his voice. "We usually have pearls, sometimes as earrings, often these days set in brooches." Aspern stopped speaking as his eyes focused on the skeletal decoration at the bottom of the tank. He quickly looked away and adjusted the overlarge knot of his necktie before continuing. "Are you looking for anything special, Count Karlov?"

"I am." Karlov sat down on the adjacent stool. "A necklace of nineteen graduated Ceylonese pearls with one large very dark grey pearl set in the center."

Aspern hesitated. Alexander was certain he had knowledge of it.

"When you assist Count Karlov, you assist me," urged Hak Lee softly. He dipped his head over the tobacco tin and breathed in deeply.

Aspern glanced at the fishtank. "I believe we have just such a necklace on its way out from England." His round face smiled. "The owner is expected at the Astor House tomorrow." The Englishman lowered his voice as he violated the confidence of auction. "A young Mr. Hammond, I understand. Jason Hammond. His people are planters from Ceylon."

Hak Lee nodded at Alexander's signal. "Before you open the sales room for public display, I will expect you to show the collections to Count Karlov and myself." The Chinese held a messy handkerchief to his mouth. He began to breath quickly before he coughed.

"Of course, Mr. Lee. A private showing for you will be my pleasure, sir."

"It was as I feared," said Dr. du Moulin at his patient's bedside the next evening. "I could not do everything that we wished. We worked only on your ankle. The talus had become unseated."

"My talus?" Alexander spoke slowly, groggy with the soft comfort of the drug. He remembered the painful knobby bump on the front of his ankle. He felt helpless with his left leg raised and suspended by a small wooden pulley anchored to the ceiling. His black cane rested in the corner by the bed. He had been dreaming of Laila and distant green hills when the doctor entered. Alexander had just unbuttoned the high collar of her shirt to discover luminous white pearls shining against the deep darkness of her skin. The dream vanished as the doctor spoke.

"The talus, young man, is a free-floating bone in the front center of the ankle. If it pops and is not reset at once, the surrounding tendons and ligaments will tear and snap. Yours had popped. I was obliged to reseat it and to stitch the tendons."

The surgeon felt Alexander's forehead, then raised one eyelid with the side of his thumb as he examined the extent of the pupil's dilation. "As to the rest, your knee, that was all too old and difficult. You cannot raise a soufflé twice." Hervé du Moulin shrugged and lit a cigarette. "You will have to live with it, like any old *grognard*, another *mutilé de guerre*." Alexander winced, remembering that sorry title from the reserved-seat signs posted in the autobuses of Paris. Crippled veterans were as common there as plane trees.

"How long will I be here like this?" Karlov blinked as he looked around at the walls of the windowless white room. He offered the physician a chocolate from the box beside his bed, the gift of Lily. The young film actress must have been informed by Mei-lan, her former madam. No name was on the message card, just the scarlet lined imprint of the puffy lips he had adored. She had been his first, and, with those lips, the best.

"Perhaps a week. It will be very painful for another day or two, so we will keep you happy in the arms of Morpheus," replied the surgeon. "By this evening we will move you to a finer room, just next door, with a view of the Whangpu and the harbor. But first we have to air it out. We lost a patient there last night."

"*Pardon, Docteur du Moulin*," said a French nun from the doorway. "We have prepared Count Karlov's room."

Alexander had been hoping for a different visitor, perhaps even Lily.

His other old girl, Jesse James, was away, saving the Chinese at her mission in Nanking. Today he wanted the pampering comfort of a woman.

The nun forced a wooden wedge beneath the door to hold it open while two Chinese nurses entered to free the pulley and move the bed. He felt helpless as they wheeled him into the adjoining room.

Alexander Karlov awoke in the early evening, his mind floating distantly from more morphine. The glow of a dying sunset filtered dimly through the curtains. He opened his eyes when there was some movement by the door.

He turned his head and thought he saw a short slender figure removing a cloak and hanging it behind the closed door. It seemed to be a woman, another Chinese nurse in a crisp white uniform and small starched cap set in her dark hair. He was not certain if she was real, or some apparition of his hazy dreams.

Alexander closed his eyes, annoyed by the frequent fussing of the staff that interrupted his reveries. He heard the sharp tap of a woman's heels approach his bed. He was surprised by the richness of the attendant's perfume as she rearranged the covers on both sides. A warm hand touched his cheek. Another caressed his chest and moved down his belly beneath the sheet as his eyes opened.

"Lily!"

"Hush. Hush. You would be so proud of me," she said excitedly. "The French newspaper calls me a *vedette. Le Journal* loved me in *Village Girl Loses Her Way*. It is showing now at the Carlton, you know."

She pirouetted once beside the bed as Alexander, annoyed by her self-concern, struggled to focus his attention.

"This is one of my costumes for the short films about the lives of farm girls when they come to Shanghai to find work and send money home to their families. In the studio we have garments for every trade."

The pleated white skirt barely covered her derriere. He grew more interested.

"Do you like it?" She studied herself in the small mirror that hung above the bedside table.

"Let me see." But his head was spinning. He closed his eyes again.

He reached under the skirt and cupped one naked plump tight buttock. Though he could not see it, he recognized the perfect smooth copper of her skin, without pores, like a baby. In a moment she was wet.

"Do you think you can stay still?" she whispered, unbuttoning the top of her uniform.

"Have I a choice?"

"I gave the night nurse a box of caramels and two tickets to the Carlton." Lily bent by the door and jammed the doorstop in place.

She returned and folded the covers down neatly to the foot of the bed. She unbelted his hospital gown and pulled it open on each side until Alexander lay naked save for the bandages on his leg and the cast on his ankle. She walked back to the door and hung her uniform on a hanger after removing a small curved implement from one pocket. She kicked the doorstop more tightly in place. Then Lily returned to the bedside wearing only her cap and high-heeled white shoes.

She leaned over the small table with her face close to the looking glass. The actress held one eye closed at a time and gripped her lashes with the eyelash-curler.

Alexander smelled her. He reached out until his fingers were wet. The film star seemed to ignore his attentions as she turned her head from side to side and batted her eyelashes demurely in the mirror, studying herself from the corner of each eye.

Lily climbed onto the bed, graceful and light as a cat. She pressed her feet against the wall above his shoulders, one leg on either side of his head, and lowered her stomach onto his as she gripped his hips and her cap scraped his thigh.

"*Mon dieu!*" she exclaimed softly after a moment, raising her head. "*Bravo, mon petit!*"

He closed his eyes, overwhelmed by her moist scent and the smooth slick movement of those lips.

In the middle of the night he awoke once more. Lily had left him. The sheet was folded neatly beneath his chin. He smelled the sweet breath of the girl's perfume and remembered her last words. "How often can you break an ankle?"

Something banged against the other side of the thin wall behind his bed, a disturbance from his former room, as if the hospital bed were being pushed into the corner. He heard a whimpered exclamation, like the yelp of a puppy when someone steps on it by accident. Alexander opened his eyes when he heard a long moan, then the deep gargling sound of a man desperate to spit and breathe. Alarmed, he rose awkwardly from his prone position. Should he holler for a nurse? Once again the bed next door was knocked forcefully against the wall. Then the night was quiet.

"*Infirmière!*" yelled Alexander. "Nurse!"

He heard hurried steps in the corridor but no one came to his door. He sensed the presence of a violent predator. He recalled what the old gamekeeper had told him one morning in the forest at Voskrenoye. Marksmanship, tracking and patience are not sufficient. At the critical moment a great hunter depends on instinct.

"Nurse!" Karlov screamed louder, struggling unsuccessfully to reach his cane.

Then he heard a woman's cry from the doorway to his old room.

"*Mon dieu! Monsieur est mort, étranglé. Assassin! Assassin! Au secours!*"

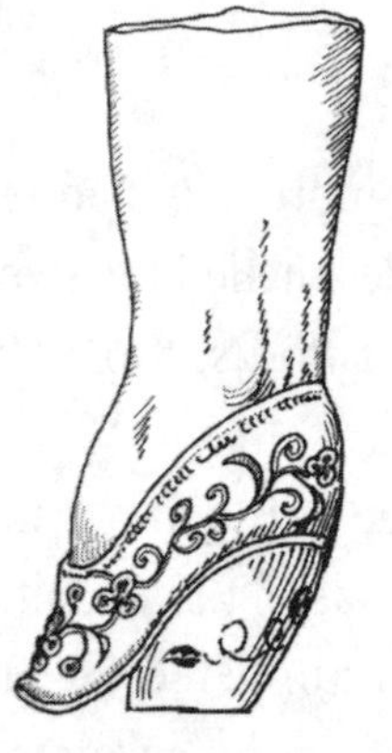 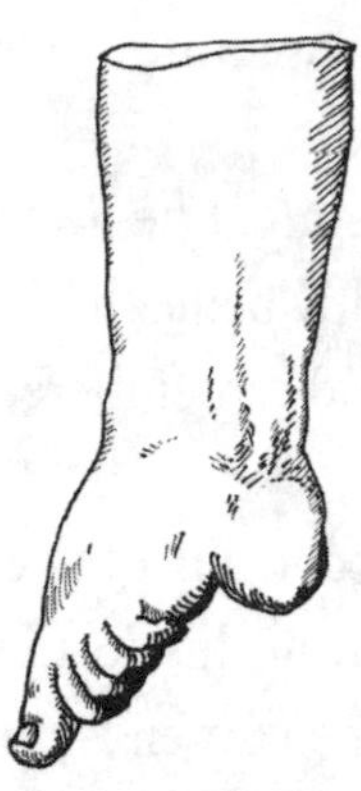

- 41 -

"Hot ginger and dynamite, there's nothing but that at night," crooned the singer. His slick black hair seemed to glow. An open pink rose was pinned to the shawl collar of his white dinner jacket. He closed his eyes and snapped his fingers as the nine-man Filipino band played and swayed behind him while he sang the popular American tune. His voice spread like warm oil across the dance floor of the Cercle Sportif.

"Back in Nagasaki where the fellers chew tobaccy and the women wicky wacky woo."

"I trust he is not singing that one for you, Hideo," smiled Alexander. He glanced at Katerina and thought of the anti-Japanese riots that were erupting in China's Treaty Ports. Following the Versailles peace conference, over the protests of the Chinese delegation, the German port of Shantung had been transferred to Japan as a reward for fighting with the allies during the Great War. Now, in a second wave of protest, Japanese goods were again being boycotted all across China. In Shanghai, Japanese stores had been looted and warehouses destroyed.

"I doubt it, Alexander-san," said Hideo stiffly. There was no one else he would permit to speak to him in such a manner. "My father has been recalled to Tokyo for meetings with the Minister. We are told not to fly our flag on the consular cars. It is shameful," he said, frowning. "People will think we are afraid. I will not ride in my country's Rolls without one. If the police and the Volunteer Corps do not keep order in Shanghai, one day our Marines will have to land here and regulate the city."

None of the three mentioned that it was only seventeen years since Japan had humiliated imperial Russia by sea and land. Finally the Japanese had sunk twenty of the Czar's major warships at Tsushima Straits, despite the protection of the special icons that each vessel had been given by the Czarina and the holy water that had been sprinkled on their guns, the same fluid that had been the principal medicine for the peasants in most hamlets on the Karlov family estates.

Alexander recalled a lunch party at the Japanese official residence when an American missionary had deplored the cruelty of foot binding. Hideo's father, the Consul-General, had answered proudly that to celebrate the first twenty years of the Japanese occupation of Formosa, in 1915 the governor of the island had ended that barbaric Chinese custom. No one had dared reply, though many guests were aware of the added suffering of the 700,000 island women whose feet were then unbound, leaving each a crippling mess of tiny brittle broken bones and flesh soft as flour cakes.

"Do you mind if Hideo and I dance, Sasha?" said Katerina, touching her brother's hand. Alexander's crutches leaned against the corner behind their favored table in the great ballroom of the French club. "We are learning the new American dances."

"Not at all," he said. Better to dance with a Japanese than to be a Marxist and not dance at all. He thought his sister had not been feeling quite herself, but this evening she seemed happy and lively and remarkably taken with Tanaka. Alexander wished only that Laila were already in Shanghai. He had invited Lily to join them at the French club, just to have a fourth for dinner, but the starlet said she had so many invitations for the evening and probably would not be able to attend. He was disturbed by what had happened between them when he was groggy with morphine at the hospital. Now Lily seemed to think that he was hers again, although he had advised her of his sentiments for another woman.

The jewelry auction was only two days away and Alexander still prayed that Laila would arrive in time for that. "I will come to Shanghai," she had said on the train, "if you will come back to Ceylon."

Alexander missed her in his bones. Each time he awoke, whether during the night or in the morning, he imagined her warmth and smell and skin.

He had already engaged Mr. Hak Lee's Scottish solicitor to represent Mrs. Hammond in an attempt to reclaim her property. Even if that effort did not succeed, it might lower the price of the necklace at auction. Failing her arrival and testimony, he would have to buy it himself, although his Chinese partner said he had a different notion. Big Ear seemed also to be taking a close interest in dealing with Viktor Polyak. A fine match, in Karlov's opinion. Alexander was certain that he himself had been the intended victim of the murder in the hospital.

A mixed party of young French and elegant Chinese were enjoying themselves at the adjacent table with laughing conversation, American tobacco and trays of Singapore slings. Karlov thought he had overheard something snide about the presence of a Japanese, a "monkey child." He guessed that Katia had wanted to get Hideo onto the large oval dance floor before the Japanese became incensed. Alexander had seen Tanaka's cold fury on the fencing piste, and he could imagine his ferocity if he or his nation were insulted.

Karlov finished the bottle of Heidsieck and glanced about the crowded ballroom for a waiter. He noticed Aspern dining at a table of half a dozen Europeans. The auctioneer smiled brightly and lifted a glass when he caught Alexander's eye, then leaned over to speak privately to the ruddy-faced young man beside him.

Alexander began the second bottle and lit a torpedo as he considered what the next days might hold. His ankle was better but still painful, and he preferred alcohol to drugs. He felt alone and deep in obligations. As he drank he thought of Ceylon and a picnic in the tea country with the ocean in the distance and clouds racing across the sky. He remembered the touch of a woman's hands as she removed his shirt and her confident ease as Laila undressed herself. He sometimes thought he would never see her again. "So few women truly look better without clothes," Mei-lan had advised him. "Those are the blessed ones."

"May I have the next dance, Count Karlov?" A hand touched his neck. His heart stopped.

Alexander turned his head and struggled to rise, but was obliged to lean forward on the table with both hands.

Laila kissed his cheek, then saw his cast. She was wearing a white silk dress and no jewelry.

For a moment he could not speak.

He shook his head. "Not tonight, Doctor Hammond. But I will save my first dance for you." He had the sense that all eyes saw only what he saw, that every diner and most dancers were regarding only her. No one could match her dark elegance.

"I stopped at the Salle d'Armes," she said, "and was told that you were here."

The waiter brought another glass. The two sat and ignored the room.

"My sister is here," he said. "With her beau."

"My stepson is here as well," she said, resting one hand on his leg, "at that table across the floor." Her touch made him feel they were naked and alone.

"Don't look now," she continued quietly, "but you can tell him by his red face. By eighteen Jason Hammond had drunk enough whisky to match the senior alcoholic in any club in London. He has expensive tastes, many of which come from a bottle or a silver flask, and he has been stealing from his father and me to pay for them."

Alexander glanced across the dance floor, certain it was Jason Hammond seated beside the auctioneer.

As he looked over he saw Lily standing in a tight scarlet cheongsam at the entrance to the ballroom near the head of the great spiral staircase. He felt his face redden. He lowered his head and returned his full attention to Laila Hammond as he awaited the catastrophe.

The starlet hesitated at the edge of the dance floor until she had drawn as many eyes as possible. She then walked directly across towards their table, passing it and greeting a party of guests seated nearby. The eyes of the young actress crossed Alexander's with a steady neutral gaze.

Karlov knew who had saved him. Madame Mei-lan Wong trained her young pheasants never to embarrass a client, whether in public or in bed. Jealous, Lily might be, but awkward, never.

Katerina and Hideo returned to the table. Alexander had never seen his twin so attentive, or Hideo so animated. The Japanese still spoke sparingly with crisp courtesy, but Katia attended to each word as if poised either to laugh or to urge him to continue. It struck him that she was behaving like a lady intent on matrimony. She was giving the young man the promise of her attention.

The four dined richly on warm foie gras, *hommard en croute* and venison from Huangshan. They drank too much white burgundy and Beychevelle.

At the entrance door downstairs they chose rickshaws and parted as couples.

"The Astor House Hotel, if you please," said Alexander to their puller.

"No, if you don't mind," said Laila, "Everyone is staying there. Can't we go to the Salle d'Armes? I would prefer to stay where you live."

"As you wish." Pleased, Alexander turned to wave good night at Hideo and Katia. The two were entering a canopied rickshaw drawn by a sturdy young puller, and they did not seem aware of his goodbye.

"The Golden Den," instructed Hideo Tanaka as he took Katerina's hand to assist her. "In Blood Alley." The illuminated fountain sparkled in the center of the club's immense lawn as they left the broad curving driveway of the Cercle Sportif.

Distracted by each other, it was a time before the two noticed where they were going.

"Stop!" Tanaka leaned forward as the puller ran past the Golden Den and turned down a narrow dark lane. "You have passed it!"

Katerina was thrown forward when the puller stopped abruptly by some bales stacked in the alley. Two heavyset Chinese in European trousers and dark shirts rushed towards the rickshaw. One, holding a short heavy cord in his hand, grabbed for Katerina's arm.

Hideo leaped down like a dancer onto a stage. He pivoted sideways and swung with all his body as he struck the rickshaw puller in the front of the neck with the edge of one hand while the man was still between the traces. The puller collapsed where he stood.

Katerina Karlov felt herself change into an animal of survival as the lessons of the Cheka rushed back to her. The assassin replaced the debutante. All she needed was a weapon. She clawed her attacker's face with her free hand, cutting him across his eye from forehead to cheekbone. Shouting in pained surprise, the Chinese released her. He stared at her for an instant before trying to seize her again.

Katerina screamed and kicked the enraged man in the belly as he climbed into the vehicle. Her cry was one of anger and effort rather than fear. She ripped a two-foot bamboo strut from the frame of the canopy and jumped down on the other side of the rickshaw as Hideo turned to assist her.

The shorter assailant, thickly built, with a broad scarred face, spread his feet and swung a long cosh at Tanaka as the Japanese stepped towards him. Katia thought she heard a bone break as the heavy weapon struck Hideo's left arm above the elbow. Tanaka appeared not to feel the injury as he raised his right knee and extended the foot in a movement of violent precision, kicking the squat Chinaman between the legs with the force of a football goalie clearing the ball, almost lifting the man from his feet. The attacker grunted deeply and fell on his knees, his hands braced on the filthy ground. Tanaka brought his good arm back to his side and exhaled deeply through pursed lips. Then, as the man vomited, Tanaka extended the arm and kicked the man under his chin.

Katerina turned her body sideways as the taller man came at her. She lifted one arm across her chest with the pointed bamboo clenched in her fist. As the Chinese attacked, she straightened her arm and stabbed at his head with her body behind the thrust. Just as the man grabbed her shoulder, the bamboo pierced his throat. He staggered back against the wall with the tubular shard stuck in his neck.

Hideo hurried to her side with the cosh in his good hand. "Are you all right?" His eyes blazed. She had never seen such a concentration of ferocity.

"Hideo!" she cried as the rickshaw puller rose and rushed at them. "Behind you!"

Tanaka spun and struck the man across the face with the lead-filled weapon.

The assailant fell onto his back and lay still.

The Japanese stepped over to the heavy kneeling man and clubbed him in the temple.

The third attacker leaned against the wall, gargling and drooling blood as dark stains ran down his chest. He struggled with bloody hands to remove the splintery bamboo lodged in his throat.

Katerina thought it best to dispose of this one as well. "Never leave a wounded enemy," the instructors always said. But Hideo stepped in before her as if completing a bushido drill. He reached up and pulled aside the wounded man's hands. Then he gripped the forward end of the bamboo and rammed it backward until the point touched the wall behind his adversary. He pinned it there until the man hung from it like meat on a butcher's hook, his head to one side, his eyes twitching.

Katerina almost felt they had been in competition. For Hideo it had resembled a fierce ballet. For her it had been survival. She watched him wipe his hands on the seat of the rickshaw before he went through the trouser pockets of each man. His left arm seemed paralyzed.

"Where did you learn to fight like that?" he asked, casting on the ground all the coins and currency he had found but keeping a folded piece of paper in his hand.

"I was just trying to defend myself. Is your arm all right?"

"They had your name and your description and where you would be tonight," he replied, passing her a note in Chinese characters. "This was no incidental robbery. They must have been trying to capture you. We must tell your brother."

Viktor, she thought. She should have shot him in Marseilles.

"We would not wish the French police to find that note, or us," said Hideo, still breathing quickly. He flexed the fingers of his left hand. "In Shanghai, the Japanese and the White Russians have troubles enough."

Hideo calmed himself and smoothed down his hair before giving her his right arm.

"Please join me for a drink at the Golden Den," he said with a bow, seemingly unaware that his dinner jacket was ripped up the back seam. "Then everyone will know we were there tonight."

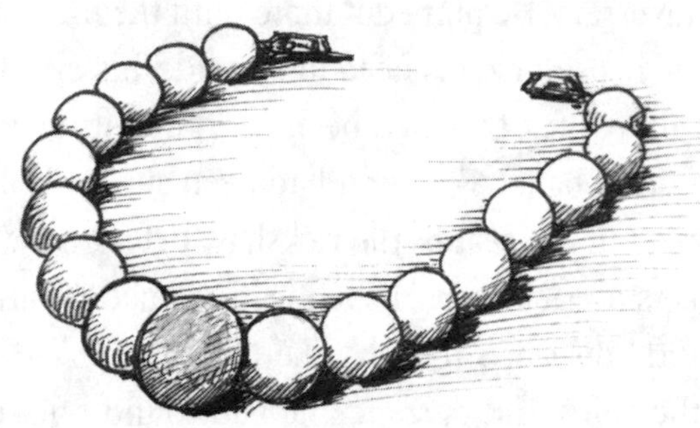

- 42 -

"Won't you come this way, Mr. Lee," said Jock Aspern from the door of the gangster's apartment at the Astor House. The auctioneer glanced doubtfully at Alexander, Katerina and Laila, who were all seated and taking morning tea with Hak Lee. A linen handkerchief dripped from the Englishman's cuff. His hair shone with brilliantine.

"We'll just take a quick peek in the sales room at the more important pieces." Aspern's round face smiled as he ignored the other three. "I have never seen such interest in a sale out here, Mr. Lee."

"My friends will join me."

The Englishman straightened up instantly. "Ah, I see. Of course."

Alexander, now on his cane again, offered to assist his partner, but the old man ignored both him and his own bodyguard. The copper of his pitted skin seemed tinged with grey, as if in shadow. He rocked back in his seat, then stood with the returning momentum. The four followed Aspern along the wide carpeted corridor and down one flight to the second dining room. The doorkeeper acknowledged the party and they entered the high-ceilinged rectangular room.

Eight glass vitrines were positioned along the two side walls. A central aisle led between rows of small chairs to a platform and rostrum at the end of the room. A potted palm was set in each corner. A guard stood when they entered, hastily extinguishing his cigarette. Alexander nodded at the Russian as they passed. He either recognized the man or had seen too many old soldiers just like him.

Hundreds of them had filled the Cathedral of St. Boris at his father's service in Shanghai, holding candles amidst the clouds of incense, kissing Count Karlov on the lips as they bent over the partly open coffin that concealed the absence of his limbs. The major was buried without his legs, but wore the Maltese Cross of the Corps des Pages. His cavalry boots lay beside him, properly polished and boned by his son.

"Graf," returned the guard in a deep voice that sounded of tobacco and the steppes.

A Filipino stood behind a small bar in a rear corner of the room busily straining lemon juice and separating egg whites. Buckets of cracked ice and tall wine goblets stood on the bar between bottles of cognac, maraschino, absinthe and club soda.

Katerina and Aspern crossed the room to the cabinets on the far wall while Mr. Hak Lee took one of two seats reserved for him in the back row on the aisle. His bodyguard stood behind him, having pushed aside two adjoining chairs.

Alexander followed Laila as she checked the shelves of the first vitrine. Silver cigarette cases, gold compacts, pocket watches and platinum studs and cufflinks filled the cabinet. Sapphires and diamonds dominated the second. Each object was accompanied by a lot number. They strolled to the third cabinet.

Laila squeezed Alexander's hand and touched the glass with a fingernail.

The necklace rested on a black velvet cushion in the middle of the second shelf. It was as magnificent as she had said. Powerful yet soft, eighteen graduated white pearls centered by one large black pearl. Alexander imagined the ornament where it belonged, brought to full life on the neck of Laila Hammond, illuminating her beauty with its own.

He took her by the hand. They walked over and chose seats directly in front of Mr. Hak Lee. The Master of the Mountain had already heard the story. Now the owner of the necklace was confirming its provenance. Laila handed him two sheets of paper, one notarized in Colombo, the other in London.

"Mr. Astern," said the Chinese quietly in the stillness of the large room.

"Aspern, sir." The Englishman smiled. "Is there a piece on which you wish to place an early starting bid? Perhaps . . ."

Hak Lee held up one hand. "I will tell you what it is I wish."

"Yes, sir. Of course."

"Open cabinet number three."

"Ah, Mr. Lee." Aspern pulled his handkerchief from his cuff. "I cannot do that, sir."

"Do you know who owns these cabinets?" A guttural rattling sound came from Hak Lee's chest.

"It is not a matter of the vitrines, sir. But that is one thing I may not do until after the sales. These objects are not mine."

"Serge," sighed Hak Lee. The bodyguard stepped before him.

"Get me Cunningham, the assistant manager. Tell him to bring his keys."

Serge left without speaking. Five minutes later the bodyguard returned with an elderly man in black striped trousers, a black waistcoat and wing collar. Alexander recognized Cunningham as a man known for one skill, hotel keeping, and one weakness, the races.

"Open cabinet number three."

"Yes, sir," said Cunningham. Doubtless in debt, thought Alexander. Hak Lee followed the assistant manager to the vitrine as the man unlocked the wooden framing with a small brass key. Hak Lee lifted out the velvet cushion. The nails of his long thin fingers showed like glazed amber beside the white purity of the pearls. He turned to Laila Hammond as Katerina watched from across the room.

"Mrs. Hammond." The old Chinese bowed. "Do I have your word that this necklace is yours? For a friend of Count Karlov's, that will be sufficient."

"My grandfather dove for each one of these pearls in the Gulf of Mannar."

"Count Karlov," said Mr. Hak Lee as Aspern hurried to them, his face shining. "Be so good as to place this on the neck of Mrs. Hammond." He began to cough.

"My pleasure, sir," said Alexander as Laila turned her back to him.

"No! Please, this is impossible," protested Aspern, a shrill edge in his voice. "That necklace is lot thirty-one." Hak Lee's bodyguard stepped towards the auctioneer. Aspern lowered his voice. "It is the property of an important client from London. It is part of the auction."

"Mr. Cunningham," said Alexander's partner, handing the notarized papers to the assistant manager. "Do you sell stolen properties in your hotel?"

"Of course not, sir. That would be a crime."

There is nothing that has not been sold at the Astor House Hotel, thought Karlov. Including his first woman.

Cunningham took a monocle from a vest pocket and read the two documents before he spoke again. "These papers are from a well-known jeweler in Colombo and from P. J. Phillips of Bond Street," he began, his right eye huge through the glass. "They list the dates the firms restrung these pearls for Mrs. Hammond and her late parents. They confirm that this necklace is her property."

Alexander lifted the necklace and placed it around Laila's neck before securing the marquise old-mine diamond clasp. He felt the cool smooth white pearls settle on the dark warmth of his lover's neck. It was as if they shared one skin.

Karlov recognized his father's tone in his own voice when he turned and spoke to Jock Aspern.

"Mrs. Hammond's solicitor will be here in half an hour, sir, when the auction is underway. You might care to take this matter up with him. But first you may wish to advise Jason Hammond that if he speaks once of this, once, to anyone, we will pursue him for theft in the courts of three cities."

Aspern did not reply. Hak Lee nodded with appreciation.

The doorkeeper entered and spoke to the auctioneer. "The bidders are waiting in the hall, Mr. Aspern."

"Open the doors." The Englishman wiped his face.

"Good Lord!" exclaimed Katerina Karlov at the same instant from the far vitrine. "Madame Malakov's emerald!"

Alexander joined his sister at the last cabinet. "You are right," he said, astonished, after studying the necklace. It was the choker Katia had worn and surrendered to the elderly lady at the Polish embassy party in Paris. He recalled the woman's aged dignity as she reclaimed her family's treasure.

Laila and the twins took their seats in front of Mr. Hak Lee. Both Karlovs turned to talk with him in whispers.

The room filled. Bidders clustered at the vitrines while others scrambled to claim their favored seats. Two Chinese waiters in tight white jackets passed trays from the bar. Gamblers and widows, gangsters and aristocrats, shipowners and courtesans crowded the room. A maharani and the San Franciscan madam of a Shanghai bordello celebrated for its exclusively American staff bickered over two front seats. To Alexander it seemed an assembly of the most rich and diverse citizens of the China Coast.

Jock Aspern stepped to the rostrum and knocked twice with the gavel, smiling pleasantly with his flushed round face. He nodded agreeably to old clients as they enjoyed their powerful pink drinks. The lights dimmed as if for dinner rather than lunch, save for those illuminating the podium and the cabinets. The gavel banged once more.

As the room hushed, a small elderly woman in Chinese silks and tiny shoes entered with fluttering steps and took the seat beside Mr. Hak Lee. Alexander turned. He rose and kissed the hand of Mei-lan Wong as the first lot was put for sale. Though they had no opportunity to speak, he saw their old friendship and understanding in her eyes. Mei-lan wore a necklace of jade beads, each one the size of a large pearl and the fresh green of nature in springtime. Her black hair seemed lacquered to her head.

"I have an opening bid of fifteen hundred dollars for a fine gold-and-enamel lady's compact from Cartier of Paris," cried Aspern in his most elegant tone, his confidence restored. "Fifteen hundred, fifteen hundred." He pointed across the room, then back and forth. His eyes twinkled. He seemed larger, taller. "Sixteen hundred. Seventeen, seventeen. Do I have eighteen? Yes, eighteen hundred."

Jock Aspern raised the gavel and gestured from side to side. "Eighteen, eighteen. Sold to the gentleman there for eighteen hundred dollars." The gavel banged. Aspern grinned and waved his fingers. "Next lot. A set of platinum studs and cufflinks by Fabergé. Many are interested. I am starting at seven hundred."

Alexander was a bit surprised, impressed to see a man who was so good at what he did. The auctioneer's irritating mannerisms became advantages when he worked, rather like a rough soldier once he took the field.

Hands rose. Bids were made. Lots sold. Aspern's assistant sat at a small round table by the door, executing the procedures of the auction house: noting names, reconciling bids and payments, arranging for collection or delivery.

Alexander enjoyed the drama but could not help turning to stare at Laila, relaxed and resplendent in her necklace. The pearls seemed more lustrous on her neck.

Karlov watched for Jason Hammond but did not see him. When this was over, he must urge Laila to proceed with her divorce. He thought of the future as he heard the voices of Mei-lan and her old lover murmuring behind him.

He considered how the emerald choker might have found its way to Shanghai and to this auction. The Cheka had entrusted it to Polyak for sale in Paris, Katerina had admitted. There Madame Malakov had been robbed and murdered. Yesterday Katia had been assaulted and nearly kidnapped. Alexander's skin prickled as he thought of his father and mother and the Commissar. Who but Polyak could be selling this treasure?

Alexander took two drinks and passed one to Laila.

"Delicious!" she whispered, licking a touch of pink froth from her upper lip. "What is it?"

"The Astor House Special. Absinthe and brandy encourage bidding."

"Sold!" called Aspern. "Next, lot eighty-six."

Only fifteen more lots until the emerald, thought Alexander. He turned and whispered to Mr. Hak Lee and Mei-lan Wong. They understood their roles and they were ready when the moment approached.

"Lot one hundred and one, one hundred and one. A magnificent emerald necklace from the land of the Incas and the court of the czar." Aspern glanced around the room and smiled as if they were all with him at Tsarskoe Selo. "A single Colombian emerald of thirty-three and one half carats. What do I hear?"

At first there was silence. Then numerous hands were raised and bids presented. Fewer hands went up as the price rose. Finally only three bidders were left, the maharani and two others. One was a dealer, the other a shipowner. All three seemed known to Aspern.

The auctioneer had no need to press for higher bids. The bids flew back and forth like a shuttlecock. A nod from the shipowner, a movement of the maharani's fingertips, a blink from the dealer were sufficient. There seemed to be a silent language of the eyes that connected the auctioneer and the principal bidders. Occasionally one stared with the neutral gaze of a gambler playing at cards, yet the auctioneer appeared to know who was still on board.

"Fifty-five. Sixty. Sixty-five." Aspern seemed to come alive, to grow. "For an emerald gem stone of thirty-three and one half carats." He spoke with precise clarity, pleasure and excitement in his smooth voice as his eyes danced from bidder to bidder.

Suddenly Aspern pointed as if at Karlov. But it was to the lady behind him.

"Seventy thousand dollars. I have seventy thousand from the lady in the back row . . ."

People turned in their seats to stare at the small woman in the back row. Mei-lan never spoke, using slight movements of her folded fan to indicate her rising bids. Mr. Hak Lee sat beside her, still as a Buddha, his hands tucked into his sleeves.

"No," said Aspern, shaking his head at the maharani, rejecting the cut in his increment. "I will not take seventy-two thousand." He smiled down at the Indian princess. "But I will take seventy-five with pleasure. Do I have seventy-five thousand?"

The Indian lady, her face shrouded in a head scarf, inclined the bejeweled fingers of one hand.

"Seventy-five thousand! I have seventy-five thousand. Seventy-five. Do we have eighty?"

The bidding continued in fierce but subtle competition as tension held the room. Alexander wondered how many were aware that Mei-lan was bidding for Mr. Hak Lee. The old Chinese was coughing more and more violently. Alexander feared he would be ill.

"I have ninety-five thousand. Do I see one hundred? One hundred? No?" Aspern raised the gavel and held it in the air as he looked from one silent bidder to another. "Fair warning. I shall sell it for ninety-five thousand dollars. Last chance." The room was quiet.

"Sold then to the lady in the back row for ninety-five thousand dollars." The gavel banged down. "Four more lots, ladies and gentlemen." The atmosphere calmed as bidders whispered and exchanged glances around the room.

Mr. Hak Lee rose with the back of his hand against his mouth, followed closely by Mei-lan. Alexander, Katerina and Laila stood as well. Big Ear walked slowly to a potted palm in a rear corner of the room. He gripped its trunk in his left hand and held back his robe with his right. He bent and coughed and spat into the soil-filled pot. Over and over again. Bidders in the back row turned and whispered. Serge stared back at each one with hard challenging eyes while his master coughed and sighed and spat once more. Then the Chinese stood erect and wiped blood onto the back of his hand before walking slowly to the table by the door.

"Send Madame Wong's emerald to my room at six o'clock this evening. The seller may bring it himself if he chooses," said the Master of the Mountain, presuming it was in the private interest of both parties to bypass the conventions of the auction house. "Apartment two zero one. We will have payment waiting there."

Mr. Hak Lee's friends and bodyguard followed him to the elevator.

- 43 -

Big Ear sat alone in the darkened hotel room. Narrow stripes of light filtered in between the slats of the brown wooden blinds. The door to the adjoining room was closed.

Four stacks of thick envelopes rested beside a leather satchel on the long low table before him. The black velvet cushion on which the pearls had been displayed lay between the satchel and an open round can of Three Castle Virginia Cigarettes. The tobacco seemed appropriate. It was identified with the fierce sea dog Sir Francis Drake, butcher of Spaniards, hailed in the advertisements in *The North-China Daily News* for "inspiring fear into his enemies."

A teapot, cups, two pairs of chopsticks and a platter covered with a lid were set on the other end of the table. Both pot and platter rested on a rack over a low brazier of grey charcoal.

Hak Lee scraped at the abscess on his ear as he reflected how to use his days. The devil in his belly was denying him food. Now he could not hold down even his favorite watercress and snakehead broth. But he continued to eat and drink in the hope of drawing some nourishment before each violent regurgitation.

The Master of the Mountain had seen too much of death and life to believe in ancestors. Family was just another expense, a personal theatre for the most intimate forms of greed and selfishness. The conventions and obligations of culture and society meant nothing to him. Methods were not material. Friendship, courage and respect were the currencies he favored, though he was at ease with certain others.

He thought for a moment of his friend, and the future troubles it might cause the count if the young Russian were to kill the father of his nephew. Family feasts were always difficult enough without having to answer for a murder, no matter how appropriate the killing might have been.

The Chinese employed the nails of his other hand to clear away the scrapings of scabs and puss he had taken from his ear. Then he reached into the tobacco tin and lifted out several cigarettes.

Two knocks struck the door, then two more. Serge, announcing two visitors. A Cantonese voice Mr. Hak Lee did not recognize called out his name with respectful address.

Big Ear crushed the cigarettes between his hands and did not reply.

Two more knocks.

"Enter," he called before dropping the tobacco to the floor and pinching his nose between his hands as he snorted. A flake of Three Castle clung to one nostril.

The door opened.

In the light from the hall Hak Lee made out two men standing next to Serge: a hard-looking Chinese with bow legs clothed in the running trousers of a rickshaw coolie and a tall thick-set European with powerful shoulders and short dark hair. Big Ear could not discern the large man's face but the light of the hall struck something bright at the end of the visitor's left arm.

"Do come in," said the Master of the Mountain. "There is no need for introduction. Leave your man outside with mine. You and I will complete our business alone."

The big man entered the room. Hak Lee recognized him from the sketch that he once had circulated to assist his young Russian friend in finding the killer of the boy's father. If anything, the man's face was harder, his demeanor more menacing, than the image the artist had created two years before. The Red agent carried a square leather box in his hand. He looked around as the door closed behind him and his eyes adjusted to the gloom.

"Do sit down." The gangster removed his hands from his sleeves and gestured at the seat across the table. Something in his stomach began to throb.

The Commissar glanced at the stacked envelopes. Before taking the chair, he stepped to the side door and closed the brass bolt that separated the two hotel rooms. Now he was alone with this old man and his money.

"Is that my money?" Polyak asked, still holding the leather box. "Ninety-five thousand dollars, Mexican dollars or equivalent."

"If the necklace is mine," nodded his host, "the money is yours. But first, do join me in a cup of tea. We are in China."

Careful, thought the Commissar as he set down the box beside the satchel. He watched Hak Lee fill two cups and hold one out to him between both hands.

The Russian accepted the tea but waited for the Chinese to drink first. The tea had a rich smoky smell, quite unlike the cheap pale fluids he had been drinking.

"Permit me to advise you to be careful with all this money in Shanghai," Hak Lee said as he coughed and gasped for air. "I had no time to draw on a single currency, but you may find the variety of dollars, and their small denomination, of some utility in your work. Each envelope contains only one currency, Japanese, Belgian, German or Netherlands, all based on the Mexican dollar. And some American."

"First I will count it." Polyak put down his cup. Too many currencies, he thought. One day this colonial chaos would be replaced with Marxist order. He sniffed and smelled something agreeable other than tea. It was rising from a covered platter by the tea setting. He had not eaten since buying a bowl of congee from a street vendor as he changed lodgings early in the morning. After he had the money, he would not want anyone to be able to identify where he was staying.

"May I see my stone?" said Hak Lee. "Then you may count your dollars."

The Commissar opened the box and passed it across the table. He watched his host switch on a standing lamp at his elbow.

The old man turned the emerald between his fingers, stroking and squeezing it, nodding with satisfaction as he felt it before holding it to the lamp. He stood and walked to the nearest window. He spread apart two slats of the blinds and admired the depth of the color in the bright natural light. The Colombian stone seemed to contain the concentrated green fire of the jungle of its origin. Finally he sat and took a jeweler's loupe from a pocket in his blue silk gown and set it against one eye.

Viktor Polyak removed a heavy pack of currency from the first envelope and pinned it to the table with his hook. He could discern no reaction in his host. The old gangster acted as if all his guests suffered some deformity. The Commissar licked his thumb and used the thick fingers of his hand to lift the corner of the first bill. He began to count while Big Ear moaned and admired the emerald from different angles.

Before louping the stone, Hak Lee breathed on the gem and polished it on his silken sleeve. The only flaw was a single tiny feather, an imperfection near the upper left corner of the emerald, almost concealed by one of the platinum prongs that secured the stone. He slipped the choker into a pocket and returned to his chair, watching his guest without speaking.

When the second envelope had been counted Hak Lee leaned over and lifted the lid from the platter. Fragrant steam rose in a layer from a plate of dumplings that rested in a dark sauce.

"Ten thousand," said Polyak. He slipped the money back into the second envelope and put it in the satchel with the first. He glanced up with the next envelope in his hand, distracted again by the aroma rising from the platter.

"Keemun dumplings?" offered the Chinese.

Viktor Polyak stared at his host and hesitated. Each man knew the reputation of the other.

The Commissar took out the next packet of cash. He held one well-creased bill up against the light. "Sino-Belgian Bank, Ten Mexican Dollars Local Currency," he read. "*Dix Piastres Payables En Monnaie Locale, Shanghai, le Premier Juillet, 1908.*" He turned over the bill and saw the lion of Belgium printed beside the dragon of China.

Mr. Hak Lee lifted one of the small dumplings with the ivory chopsticks and stirred it about in the sauce before popping it into his mouth.

"Twenty-five thousand dollars," said the Russian, forcing aside his hunger to continue the slow process. As if his empty belly were not bad enough, Polyak's dark mood was aggravated by Katerina's new liaison with her rich yellow lover. How could any Russian, let alone a Bolshevik, forget that Japan had supplied weapons to the Whites and landed 70,000 men in Vladivostok during the civil war?

The Master of the Mountain ate another dumpling as the agent lifted the next envelope.

The Russian squinted at the first banknote and pinched it between his fingers before holding it to the light and recognizing the black eagle of Germany. "The Deutsch-Asiatische Bank Promises to Pay the Bearer Fifty Dollars Local Currency at Its Office in Shanghai."

"Sixty thousand." Viktor Polyak stuffed one more envelope into the satchel. By this time the plate was half empty. Hak Lee belched. His chopsticks reached across and took one more dumpling. He masticated slowly.

At last tempted beyond restraint, the Russian put down the next envelope and leaned over the satchel to snatch a dumpling with his fingers. He put it in his mouth and swallowed almost before chewing.

"That is good." The Commissar nodded and took two more. "Very good." He devoured both with the same ravenous speed.

As the counting resumed, the Chinese began to cough. He put back the dumpling poised between his chopsticks and covered his mouth with one sleeve.

"Ah, ah. Excuse me." Hak Lee rose abruptly and hurried to one corner of the room. He leaned both hands on a high table near the side door and spat and vomited into a blue bowl.

Polyak paid no mind to the display. "Seventy."

"Forgive me, I am not well." The Chinese resumed his seat and wiped his mouth on his sleeve. He noticed the platter was empty. The Russian pig had devoured the rest. It was time for delay.

"I believe that other envelope may have been incorrect," Big Ear observed mildly.

Polyak looked up and narrowed his eyes, a thick pile of currency in his hand. "Which envelope, Lee?" When the gangster did not reply, his hook clattered twice against the table. "I said: which envelope?"

Hak Lee ignored the rudeness. That would be rewarded later. "The last one, I believe." He pointed at the satchel with one fingernail, then reclined with his hands in his sleeves. He watched the slow recounting of two envelopes.

"Seventy was correct." Polyak said querulously. He did not look up as he seized the next envelope. "It was seventy."

His host did not respond but merely refilled the cups. The warm tea would ease the dissolution of the doughy shells of the dumplings.

"Eighty." The Russian paused to gulp down the drink. He never forgot that when he was a boy in St. Petersburg, a glass of tea had been a privilege of the rich. His hook held the satchel open while his hand inserted the next envelope. "Fifteen more, Lee, and we will never see each other again."

"True," sighed his host, hearing a slight commotion in the hall as something seemed to settle against the bottom of the door. He noticed that the narrow line of light under that door had dimmed. Perhaps Serge had disposed of Polyak's bandy-legged coolie.

Soon one or two of the thin strips of tightly-coiled bamboo should be released by the dissolving dumplings. Each fine bamboo strip was no wider than the moon of his little fingernail, but over one foot in length and razor sharp along both edges and pointed at each end. Long enough and sharp enough to pierce and lacerate a man's organs as if a tiny warrior were trapped inside his belly and was fighting to cut his way out. One bamboo pill was sufficient to kill any man. Two or three should dispose of this barbarian. He himself, of course, had known by their shapes which dumplings to select. Even if he chose a bad one, his illness might save him when he spat it up, though hopefully not as the bamboo was uncoiling.

It was impossible, thought Hak Lee, for two men such as us to believe that the other would release either emerald or currency. But only one man could leave with both. How could this savage think to challenge him?

He himself had started life by stealing ducks' eggs and lotus roots from street vendors, then by selling protection alley by alley to small merchants. He brightened as he recalled the morning when he had been pursued by a dangerous rival through a warren of small open shops. The young Hak Lee had seized a straight razor from a street barber and turned around to face the brute and open him from throat to belly like a perch. Now his interests were spread across Shanghai like the nearly-invisible web of a poisonous spider, and he was dealing personally in the treasures of rich long-noses.

He wondered how this Commissar had trained for his trade, how he had learned to mix his own stew of murder, rape and politics. If the man appreciated such original dishes, Big Ear would serve him one. It would be a pleasure to assume the mortal obligation of Count Karlov. Such a service would bind him more closely in the memory of his young friend.

In general, Hak Lee favored a rigid adherence to his word in all transactions. It was less costly in the end and made for more and better business. But there were exceptions to this principle. One was for the demands of friendship, which here required him to clean the rice bowl, as earlier Triad leaders would have expressed it.

"Eighty-five." As he spoke, the Commissar bit his lip and pressed his hand to his belly. A puzzled look came to his face from the strange sensation.

Hak Lee welcomed the first signs of discomfort. This lizard thought he was tough and hard, but nothing was stronger, more versatile than bamboo. Had there been time, he could have bound this villain in his walled garden above a green bamboo shoot, the fastest growing plant on earth. He could have watched each day, while he sipped his tea and nibbled a young lover's sensitive foot as the giant tropical grass grew directly through the man's body.

Soon his guest's stomach and his intestine, the snake of life, would be in worse condition even than his own. Lacerated, torn and bleeding from esophagus to anus.

"Ninety," said the Russian slowly. He sat back and pressed his hand inside the waistband of his thick trousers. His expression had changed to a rictus of pain.

The bamboo pills were doing their work, killing the snake of life.

Coughing deeply, Hak Lee rose and shuffled back to the bowl on the corner table.

Polyak stared after him. He pressed the last pile of currency against the table beneath his hook, but his hand was now clutching his side as if attempting to hold closed an open wound.

The Chinese leaned one hand against the wall and vomited into the bowl, standing to one side so that his guest might observe the discharge of food and blood that dripped from his lower lip and chin. A moment of mortal confusion could be useful.

"They have poisoned me!" cried Hak Lee before his guest could say the same.

As if on cue, Viktor Polyak began to gag and retch. Wincing, he stuffed the last handful of cash roughly into the satchel and struggled to close both clasps with hook and hand.

The Commissar stood.

"*Sobaki!*" he cried, retching violently as if vomiting up the organs of his belly. "Bastards!" Blood bubbled on his lower lip.

Hak Lee leaned against the side door near the blue bowl. He glanced down at the Russian's dry cuffs and boots and knew that the bamboo pills had not quite finished their work. He wiped his mouth and moaned.

"Someone is trying to kill us!" Hak Lee exclaimed as he gripped the bolt to the door behind his back that led to the adjoining room.

Polyak turned and took one halting step towards the entrance door with the satchel hanging from his hook. He paused and rocked from side to side. Bending forward, he put his hand to his mouth, then cried out once like a woman in childbirth as her body opens.

The Master of the Mountain looked down at his guest.

Blood now stained the trousers of the Commissar, at first a trickling narrow streak, then a copious flood that drenched the agent's cuffs and boots.

Viktor Polyak collapsed against the entrance door, not able to scream as his mouth filled with blood. Someone pushed against the door from the outside.

Mr. Hak Lee lifted the black mouthpiece of the hotel telephone. He wiped the instrument in his sleeve. One could not tell who might have used it last. He tapped the cradle twice.

"The concierge," he said calmly. "My guest is ill. Please send up two porters with a luggage trolley to carry him to my motorcar so I may look after him." The cart should spare the hotel's carpets. He slid free the bolt to the adjoining room as someone forced open the entrance door against Polyak's heavy body.

Alexander Karlov entered from the side room. He saw the body of Serge lying in the hall and Polyak curled on his side groaning and clasping his belly. Alexander's sword flashed from his cane.

At that instant a bow-legged Chinese dashed in from the hall and squinted about the room before rushing at Hak Lee. The man carried a bloody knife in one hand. He raised the glistening tip of the weapon when he identified the tall gaunt figure of the gangster.

Instantly the two blades inspired Karlov with the disciplined ferocity of the fencing piste. He parried the knife with a fast spanking blow of his sword. But the attacker stepped past him towards Hak Lee and raised the knife again. Alexander took one step with his right foot, bent his good knee and extended both arms as he lunged.

Karlov's short blade entered the attacker's side, spitting him through the body from left to right.

As the intruder plunged at Hak Lee with the sword in his side and a knife in one hand, the Master of the Mountain swiftly freed his own hands from his sleeves. He embraced the onrushing assailant with both arms, as if welcoming a lover, then instantly fell back without injury and only one long tear in his own gown.

The attacker collapsed on the carpet with Hak Lee's Marseilles knife in his back to the hilt. Alexander freed his own blade with a swift twist of the wrist as the man fell. He looked down at the figure and thought he recognized the bow-legged puller who had been watching the Salle d'Armes from the rickshaw repair shop across the road.

Karlov wiped his blade on the dead man's trousers and slipped it back into his grandfather's cane. His old instructor at the Corps des Pages would have been pleased, Alexander thought, with the forceful finesse of his *finale*, the final straight forward movement of the point. But his Chinese partner glanced at him with the disappointment of a sportsman when another gun brings down his bird. How many more opportunities would he have?

"Drag that Bolshevik into the hall and have the porters take him to my motorcar," the Chinese told Alexander as he lifted the satchel. "Then please go home." Hak Lee seemed animated, young again. "First bring Serge in here and lay him beside this dog. The police will know they killed each other. Fortunately we have friends in the French police." He permitted himself a suggestion of humor. "Very costly friends."

In minutes the matched Chryslers were speeding to the Green Dragon Teahouse. There the two drivers each took one of Polyak's arms across his shoulders and hauled the bleeding man through the public room and into Hak Lee's office. An elderly waiter followed them, bending to wipe up the bloodtrail with a serving towel, his face neutral, as if he were performing the routine of his job. No patron looked up at the passing figures for more than the barest instant.

The Chinese gangster ambled behind his desk. He stroked the top of the small black safe that stood nearby. An octagonal brass knob was bolted to the center of its door beneath a round golden medallion. The images of a lion and a unicorn were embossed at the center of the plate, surrounded by the words "C.H. Griffiths & Co., 43 & 45 Cannon Street, London E.C." Four handles were fixed to the rope and bamboo harness that belted the safe.

"Leave me," Hak Lee said to the two coolies who were spreading concrete in the rectangular pit in the alcove near his desk. "Your work is finished."

The grey concrete was smooth but not yet firm. With only a few small bubbles at the surface, the thick mortar was prepared to receive the safe and grip the steel box as the binding agent of the cement dried and hardened.

Polyak began to twitch and struggle.

"Lay this animal on his back," directed Hak Lee to his burly drivers, pointing to the waiting concrete basin. This time the creature would not escape to kill again. "He should just fit." Hak Lee sat at his desk, coughing gently as he lifted a pinch of Pickwick tobacco from a tin.

The swarm of smaller snakeheads seemed in repose, circling with languor in the bottom of their scum-ringed tank. Perhaps they had devoured a few of their younger companions and were sated for the moment. But the two three-foot adults in the other tank appeared to comprehend the activity of the scene. They grew livelier, flexing and turning in their confinement as if wishing to participate. Could they sense, Hak Lee wondered in idle fascination, that the man whose hand they had enjoyed now shared their quarters, and that his remaining flesh was still warm?

Hak Lee lifted the round tin in both hands. The genial Mr. Pickwick smiled at him eye-to-eye from between his thumb nails. Big Ear lowered his nose into the tin until he began to cough too deeply. Exhausted by the long events at the Astor House, he decided not to provide any chosen morsels to the larger fish. In a better world, there would be one hand for each of them, or possibly a foot. If only he were younger and had more time, he would serve them a few souvenirs.

Yanked to his feet, Viktor Polyak spat and cleared his mouth. He tottered in a small pool of blood as the two drivers held him erect on either side. The sensual scent of sandalwood rose around them from the brazier.

Hak Lee extended his arms and looked Polyak in the eye as he pointed with one forefinger to the Commissar's hook and with the other to the immersed bones of the man's missing hand. The Red returned the stare with recognition, pain and hatred. He raised his chin and spat a few drops of blood that reached the hem of his host's gown.

At last we understand each other, thought Hak Lee as his men dragged the Cheka agent towards the alcove. The larger snakeheads, always underfed like lions before a Roman circus, thrashed in the water with violent agitation as he was taken past their tank. One driver struck the Russian behind the knees and he collapsed.

As Polyak fell forward, he freed his left arm and swung it forcefully at the man who had hit him. The double hook missed his captor but crashed against a corner of the fish tank. A small fissure appeared where the two glass panels met to form one corner of the large container.

The drivers forced the Commissar to sit in the center of the pit. One stomped on the Russian's knees to flatten his legs into the hardening concrete. Behind the struggling men, drops of water leaked down onto the red lacquered table that supported the damaged tank. The two full-grown snakeheads knocked against the glass as their heavy tubular bodies lashed the water.

Realizing his peril, Polyak screamed and fought with new strength. His heavy limbs resembled fragments of a grey stone sculpture whenever he freed one from the concrete. He made a violent exertion and his hook caught one man's thigh. The driver screamed as the two prongs pierced his leg and he himself set a foot into the deep concrete. The Chinese staggered back as he freed himself. His bloody shoe remained in the concrete as he fell backwards against the fish tank. Water sloshed out as the tall tank rocked on its table. The crack extended down the corner of the glass container like a spiderweb.

"Idiot!" exclaimed Hak Lee, though he still watched calmly like a man observing a drama on some distant stage.

The wounded driver belted Polyak across the face. Blood dribbled from the agent's mouth as the two Chinese forced down his head and shoulders. The snakeheads continued to pound against their prison walls. Water ran down onto the floor from the widening cracks and found its way to the depression in the floor where the concrete was setting.

Now the Russian guest of Mr. Hak Lee was lying on his back. He was breathing but almost entirely bathed in concrete. Big Ear pointed at a large tin bucket. One of the drivers scooped a bit more of the thickening mix onto the Commissar. His body twitched. Only Polyak's face and his hand showed above the grey sludge.

"Lower the safe into place. Quickly before the concrete sets."

Each driver grabbed two handles of the harness that bound the small safe. They lifted it from the wooden floor, then staggered a few steps to the edge of the pit.

At that instant the whipping bodies of the large snakeheads struck the glass together. The two damaged glass corner panels fell apart and crashed to the floor. Water cascaded down.

Big Ear tucked up his blue gown and lifted his feet onto the seat of his desk chair. His pointed American boots stuck out past the edge.

The two men dropped the black steel box directly onto the chest and belly of Viktor Polyak. Hak Lee heard the crack of breaking ribs. The concrete rose a bit as the Commissar was pressed lower. A gasp of air was forced from the Russian's body as if a blacksmith had dropped an anvil on his bellows.

"Bastards!" yelled Polyak as water flooded the pit.

Like giant eels fighting for their lives, the two large snakeheads whip-sawed about the floor of the office. First bending double, then straightening with snapping jerky motions, they seemed to spring about the room on the slippery wet floor. One clamped its jaw on the bare ankle of the driver who had lost his shoe. As the long row of teeth set in his flesh, the driver screamed and drew his revolver.

Gunfire and the sharp smell of cordite filled the room. Although struck twice, the bleeding snakehead hung on as the man flailed and struggled towards the door, dragging with him the wounded creature fixed to his leg. His third shot hit the other fish tank, sending a spray of glass and water across his master's desk. Scores of small snakeheads swarmed over the floor.

"Leave this room, Chin, and you leave my service," said the cold surprisingly powerful voice of Hak Lee from his chair. The man hesitated with his back against the door. The words were death. He might survive a vicious fish, but never the Master of the Mountain. He looked down and fired his last three shots into the creature that thrashed beside him. Finally it released him and scuttled about the floor in slow death. Smaller fish gathered and sucked at its wounds as if they were piglets at the teats of a sow.

The other driver had slipped and fallen at the edge of the pit. Polyak seized his wrist and held the man down beside him like a lover on a concrete bed. The second big snakehead and several smaller ones joined them in the watery pit. The bottom of the black safe was set at an uneven angle across the torso of the Commissar. It slipped a bit and settled in place, pinning down the Chinese driver whom Polyak was holding tight against his side. Aroused by the blood in the water, several of the smaller snakeheads were nipping greedily at the man's neck and face.

Also excited by the spectacle, Hak Lee's eyes were on the Commissar. The jaw and nose of the Russian were small islands in the bloody roiling water that had settled into the pit. The Chinese saw his guest struggling to secure air as he formed a snout with his lips and gasped and spat. Big Ear was impressed that even during such a trial, and with his chest crushed, the agent did not release his hold on his own victim, who now seemed permanently caught between the bottom edge of the safe and the hardened concrete.

Mr. Hak Lee watched the second mature snakehead, his favorite, wiggle up beside Polyak and clamp its long toothy jaw across his face as if kissing him. The Commissar was not free to scream as he endured the violent suffocation.

- 44 -

"*Spasibo*, Oleg," said Alexander Karlov to Mr. Hak Lee's new red-bearded bodyguard as the man gently set down Mei-lan Wong at the head of the gangway.

Alexander kissed her hand before Mei-lan walked to a rattan chair in the First Class lounge of the *Burma Star*. Big Ear sat beside her against the aft wall of the cabin. He was even more gaunt and wax-like. Only his black eyes seemed alive, shining like moist marbles, the pupils immense. Mei-lan had told Alexander that her old lover was starving to death, unable to hold nourishment. Opium, once a diversion, had become his only fuel.

Four colored engravings of a campaign in Burma in 1824 hung on the wall behind the two Chinese. Lines of redcoats and sepoys from Bengal and Madras were storming the massive wooden stockades outside Rangoon. The Union Jack was already flying over one corner of the battered fortress. But Alexander's pride was with a different empire.

The *Burma Star* would sail in two hours, calling at Hong Kong and Singapore before stopping in Colombo. There Karlov and Mrs. Hammond would go ashore before the vessel sailed for Goa, Port Suez and Marseilles on her way home to Southampton. During the Great War huge red crosses had been painted on her sides and funnels on the way out, replaced each time by naval camouflage on her way home as fresh regiments from India and Ceylon, Australia and South Africa fed the hungry trenches.

Chung had come as a guest to the sailing party, but the cook wore his crisp white uniform from the Salle d'Armes. He had brought platters of Russian canapés to honor his master's departure. The P & O steward, his fists tight against his hips, glared as he watched the small Chinese push the offerings of the *Star's* chef to the edge of the buffet table and center blinis and pickled mushrooms, red salmon caviar and boneless anchovies around a silver bowl of sour cream. Only the old samovar was missing.

Hervé du Moulin sat smoking on one side of a backgammon table, as if waiting for a gambling opponent while he sipped champagne and idly rolled sixes with the yellowed dice his young patient had given him as a parting present. After a few moments the physician pinched the cigarette from his holder and walked over to introduce himself to Mei-lan with a bow. He flirted easily, no doubt discerning the subtle signs of her profession, thought Karlov, hoping the Frenchman would not antagonize his old Chinese partner.

Lily appeared like a sunburst, hesitating and waving from the doorway, dressed in a cloche hat and tall heels that drew one's eye up the long slit in her cheongsam. Alexander glanced over at Laila, dreading the introduction, but the elderly surgeon spared him by immediately diverting the film star with his own generous attentions. No doubt he would find something they could exchange.

Alexander glanced through a starboard window across the harbor as a frigate flying the Union Jack anchored nearby and piped her horn. He saw the powerful European facade of the Bund, and the dense busyness of the Chinese waterfront. He recalled unloading their two horses from slings into sampans and struggling up the stone embankment before his father led him for the first time through the streets of Shanghai, never looking back to see if his son was following.

Ivan Semyonov smiled across the cabin and lifted a vodka to toast young Karlov, perhaps also thinking of those first days ashore. The bullet loops on his knee-length jacket were empty but the long straight blade of the Caucasus Cossack, his *kinjal*, was secured in his rope belt.

Distracted by the thought of her, Alexander watched Laila walk out on deck to greet Katerina and Hideo as they approached up the gangway. Katia took Hideo's hand as she stepped on board, as if requiring his assistance, although her brother knew that she did not. Tanaka will never change, thought Alexander, so she is pretending that she will. He wondered how much of her character now came from the Cheka, how much of her spirit from the gentler revolutionary attitudes of the Decembrists, and how much of her demeanor was related to a woman's thoughts of relationship, security and the future.

One thing he knew was that his twin was torn about abandoning her child by Viktor Polyak. She despised his paternity but loved her lost boy, knowing that she could not return to Moscow to seek Leon's liberation. Association with her would only make her child's life still harder. Perhaps in time Alexander could find a way to help her.

Hideo Tanaka followed Katia into the lounge, bowing with stiff distance to the Chinese gangster and madam. No doubt he was influenced more by his country's growing hostility to China than by the personal reputations of the two friends of his friend.

Alexander watched through the glass as Laila walked towards the bow by herself instead of reentering the cabin. She wore a pale blue linen frock, French shoes and her pearls. He could not imagine being without her. She had promised to initiate her divorce, but her problems and responsibilities endured in Ceylon and in the south of France.

The ship's bell rang.

"Thirty minutes," called the steward from the door. The departure party must end.

Alexander Karlov wished that the world would stop, that the *Burma Star* could sail as she was, with everyone he loved on board. He limped about the cabin, saying affectionate goodbyes to all who were not sailing with him. He knew he would not see some of them again.

Mr. Hak Lee lifted two envelopes and a silk box from his lap. The square case was scarlet with an embroidered two-headed bear at its center. He handed all three objects to Alexander with long cold fingers.

"Whenever the day comes, my son, please take this green stone as a wedding present. The letter of credit should provide for our plantation in Ceylon," said the Master of the Mountain. His eyes shone and focused as if they would follow Alexander forever. "The other letter you will read when you no longer hear from me."

"Thank you, sir." Karlov helped his partner rise as Mei-lan waited for him near the door.

"Take care of my sister," Alexander said to Hideo Tanaka, though knowing that it was Katia who would be taking care.

"Of course, Alexander-san." Hideo bowed.

Ivan Semyonov wiped an eye after clasping Alexander like a mother bear.

Alexander walked out on deck to follow Mrs. Hammond to the bow. He was comfortable with his cane and doubted that he would ever be able to walk without it. He felt older.

"Count Karlov," Laila had whispered that morning, her warmth beside him, their bodies eased. "You and I are no longer alone." She had placed his hand on her smooth and still flat belly.

"All ashore that are going ashore," cried the steward. The ship's bell rang a final time.

A Note About *China Star*

The author has been fortunate to recognize in the adventures of Alexander Karlov a number of experiences of his own. As a boy first visiting France before the age of ten, I was not interested in the charms of the Louvre or even the Tour d'Argent, let alone the great fashion houses to which my mother occasionally dragged me. But my imagination sparkled when I climbed the walls of the Château d'If searching for the Count of Monte Cristo, and when I floated through the shadowy tunnels of the Paris sewers in a *bateau-vanne*, a treat no longer available in the City of Light.

In later years, I discovered details of Alexander's life when I spent time in Port Saïd and on the train from Alexandria to Cairo, in the Portuguese officer's club in Macao, at the tea planters' clubs in the mountains of what is now Sri Lanka, and in what had been the old French quarter of Shanghai. There, I should point out, the *Cercle Sportif Français* was in fact not completed until 1926, and the Canidrome did not open for dog racing until 1928.

Whenever possible, I have visited each location myself, sought the conversation of old-time residents and read whatever is available of the period. In Shanghai, for example, I owe a debt to Lily Yen, who was a girl at the time of my story and died in 2003 at the age of one hundred, one year after recounting to me what it was like to grow up in the grand style in 1920's Shanghai. At that time in China, she has written, "When girls were born, they were often dumped in the road."

Most of all, I am obligated to the writers and editors of *The North-China Daily News*, the English-language newspaper of Shanghai, which I read on microfilm every day from May, 1918 through February, 1924. Nothing conveys so well the daily life of that port city.

In visiting these scenes and establishing these settings, I have been blessed with spirited friends and generous hosts familiar with the worlds I have sought to recreate. As the founder and chairman of the Maritime Museum of Hong Kong, Anthony Hardy, the friend of my youth, assisted me with details of the old shipping lines and vessels that served the East, and the ports that welcomed them. In 1963, Anthony and I shared, among too many other things, martinis at the Clube Militar in Macao, a celebration we repeated there forty years later with his wife Susan, herself a distinguished scholar of Chinese antiquities who assisted me with details of both this book and *Shanghai Station*.

In Sri Lanka, I was favored with the energetic friendship of Sir Christopher Ondaatje, a member of a distinguished Ceylonese family and the brilliant author of *Woolf in Ceylon, The Man-Eater of Punanai* and *Hemingway in Africa*, among other notable works. Few men combine the depth of Christopher's understanding of both civilization and nature. In Kandy, Hambantota, and Yala National Park, he more than kept his promise to introduce me to the heart of Ceylon and the complexities of its colonial culture. His erudite friends Ismeth Raheem, Lakshman "Lucky" Senatilleke and Dr. Raj de Silva shared their remarkable scholarship with me as I sought to develop a sense of time and place. Travelling in Sri Lanka with Frances Schultz made these adventures still more charming. At their lovely old house in Galle, Jo and Jack Eden, with whose grandfather my own father had served in the House of Commons, helped to make it a visit of cheerful friendship as well as homework.

In Sri Lanka's old royal capital of Kandy, Frances and I had the pleasure of staying on the lake at the still-gracious Hotel Suisse, where my parents had spent Christmas on their honeymoon seventy-three years earlier. In Colombo, Anura Lokuhetty enhanced my visit to the magnificent Galle Face Hotel, one of the great colonial hostelries, where my parents also stayed on their honeymoon in 1931. My own travels seemed to make their romance young again. In Galle, Henri Tatham provided a generous welcome at the splendid Dutch House, an eighteenth-century grand house converted to a small hotel. In the tea country, both the Hill Club and the

Bandarawela Hotel received me graciously and retained a sense of the atmosphere that Alexander and Laila enjoyed. The animals of Sri Lanka, elephant and crocodile, leopard and buffalo and monkeys, often reminded me of my days in Africa.

Following the adventures of Alexander Karlov requires more diverse expertise than this writer possesses, and I have been privileged to draw on friends who are masters of his varied interests and experiences. No individual that I know is better at what he does than Robin Hurt, the "hunter's hunter," recognized as the finest safari leader in Africa today. Once again, Robin reviewed my hunting scenes, and made each one correct and better. The extraordinary range of his expertise reminded me why he had been the youngest licensed hunter in the history of the East African Professional Hunters' Association.

Attending Robin's wedding celebration and sixtieth birthday at his glorious Groot Gamsberg Ranch in the rugged mountains of Namibia in 2005, I met the top South African hunter, Garry Kelly, who invited me to his stunning safari lodge Bonwa Phala, north of Johannesburg. There, after stalking white rhino on foot with Garry's Zulu tracker, Sibusiso, I worked each morning on this book, writing the scenes of conflict between Viktor Polyak and Mr. Hak Lee as nyala and warthogs wandered nearby and lilac-breasted rollers flitted in the thorn trees. On his magnificent unspoiled ranch in the wilds of northern Florida, Pat Corrigan and his courageous dachshund, Cadillac, taught me first-hand the challenges of boar hunting in a landscape of alligators, armadillos and rattlers, before he reviewed the details of Alexander's hunt.

Although I rode a horse myself around the mountain race track in Nuwara Eliya, Sri Lanka, to get a sense of that setting, I needed the patient assistance of America's greatest horse breeder, Preston Madden of Lexington, the master of Hamburg Place (the home of seven Kentucky Derby winners), to enhance my equine scenes and make certain that Count Karlov and Hindoo were racing true to form.

The name "Palliser" in this novel is borrowed from Sir Samuel Baker's favorite hunting companion in Ceylon in the 1840's, F.H. Palliser. Percy Palliser's dog Lucifer is named after one of Baker's hounds at Nuwara Eliya, said by that great explorer of Ceylon and the sources of the Nile to be a "fine specimen of greyhound and deerhound." Robbie Knox is named for Captain Robert Knox, an English sailor who left a remarkable account of his eighteen-year imprisonment in Ceylon in the seventeenth century (including the original image of the elephant execution illustration that begins Chapter 30). My character Adam Kulikovski is named after a distinguished Polish admirer of my mother. I took the name of my Goan trader Reshi Boktoo from a Kashmiri mountain guide and shikar scoundrel who for years dunned me from across the globe for fees to cure and ship the skin of a Himalayan bear I had shot in 1963 with a slug from a 12-gauge shotgun (at the request of villagers who claimed the animal was eating their winter food). I have yet to receive this pelt despite numberless payments sent to Reshi.

The *Tokushima Maru*, anchored in Colombo when Alexander arrived there in Chapter 26, was in fact the first Japanese vessel to pass through the Panama Canal (in 1914). She was torpedoed and sunk by the U.S. submarine *Picuda* in 1944. The Nippon Yusen line that owned her now has a fleet of six hundred vessels. The *Diana Dollar*, seen in Shanghai harbor in Chapter 39, was one of the United States-flag steamships owned by the Scottish-born American, Robert Dollar, who painted huge dollar signs on the funnels of all the ships of the Dollar line, which later became the American President line.

A top gemologist, Hoda Esphahani, a lady with experience at Christie's and Sotheby's, and in Geneva, Antwerp and New York, educated me about emeralds, pearls and auctioneering. The masterful James Niven of Sotheby's verified the details of auction. Donald Zilkha assisted with researching the details of Paris life in the 1920's. Michael Blakenham, the former chairman of the Royal Society for the Preservation of Birds, reviewed my ornithological passages, taking excessive pleasure in his few corrections. Laurence Heilbronn found satisfaction in improving my French. Once again, I used the period music suggestions of the late Bobby Short, who himself played the piano in Shanghai. (Bobby told me that Harry Warren's song "Nagasaki," though not written until 1928, best represented the old dance music of Shanghai.) Stuart Johnson, the lord of New York City's youngest scholars, and himself a man who strolls with Livy and breakfasts with Ovid, sought without success to assist with my classical references. Peter Horn, the sportsman-scholar of Beretta's, the world's oldest gunmaker, confirmed certain details about pistols. Carole Holmes McCarthy honored me with a first edition of that 1939 classic of global bartending, Charles H. Baker, Jr.'s *The Gentleman's Companion* ("Being An Exotic Drinking Book, Or, Around The World With Jigger, Beaker and Flask"), with which I confirmed the ingredients and correct preparation of both an Imperial Cossack Crusta and an Astor House Hotel Special.

Among the patient friends and/or hosts who endured my dawn writing schedule were Gahl Burt on Gibson Island, Sibilla Clark in Lyford Key, Anthony and Susan Hardy in Hong Kong, Robin and Pauline Hurt in Namibia, Kate and Garry Kelly in South Africa, Tarek and Marina Kettaneh in Soto Grande, Jackson Campbell May in Gainesville and Costa Rica, Tom and Diahn McGrath on Lloyd's Island, Christopher Ondaatje at the magnificent guest lodge in the Yala National Park that he gave to Sri Lanka, Connie and Ted Roosevelt in Montana, Frances Schultz in Sri Lanka and St. Bart's, and Savvas Vavilis and his staff at the Morning Star Café. Karen and Everett Cook were supportive friends of the entire campaign.

I owe much to my patient but merciless readers: my demanding son Bartle Breese Bull (whose reporting from Iraq in the *Financial Times, The New York Times, The Wall Street Journal* and *The Washington Post*, and whose forthcoming book on Mesopotamia, make him easily the best writer in the family), Gahl Burt (who endured an out-loud reading of the entire manuscript), Barbara Hackett, Winfield P. Jones, Marina Kettaneh, John Paine, Frances Schultz and Dimitri Sevastopoulo. My son edited out one of my sentences, now permanently lost to literature, by calling it "ponderous and naive." Thanks also to my agents, Eric Simonoff, Mort Janklow and Lynn Nesbit in New York and Ron Bernstein of ICM in Los Angeles, and to my Carroll & Graf editor Will Balliett, whose civilized sensibility is rare in today's publishing world. Once again, that extraordinary Chinese artist, Pan Xing Lei, turned the varied images I gave him into the splendid illustrations that introduce each chapter.

The only regret I carry from writing this book is the cruel tragedy that befell Sri Lanka and its lovely people the day after I left the island on December 25, 2004, after completing my long research visit. The following morning the great tsunami roared across the Indian Ocean at five hundred miles an hour. Seventy-foot waves struck the coast I had just travelled. The second largest recorded earthquake in history, the cataclysm killed 35,000 Sri Lankans in fifteen minutes. The ancient fishing village of Hambantota, where I had stayed as a guest of Sir Christopher Ondaatje, dining on fish curry and breakfasting on *hoppers* and *pol sambol*, was washed away. In the Yala National Park, the magnificent seaside bungalow of my new friend Pradip Jayewardene, where I had lunched and napped a few days previously, vanished, together with its staff, numerous beachgoers and the entire neighboring village. Along the coast, crowded railroad trains were hurled about like toys and many thousands of livestock were drowned. But when the waters receded, not a single wild animal, not one wild boar or jackal, mongoose or elephant, was found to have lost its life.